W9-CTP-305

Whispers from Yesteryears

Book II in the ColourBLIND Series

UZOMA UPONI

WestBow
PRESS
A DIVISION OF THOMAS NELSON

Copyright © 2013 Uzoma Nkechinyere Uponi.

All rights reserved. No part of this book may be used or reproduced by any means, graphic, electronic, or mechanical, including photocopying, recording, taping or by any information storage retrieval system without the written permission of the publisher except in the case of brief quotations embodied in critical articles and reviews.

WestBow Press books may be ordered through booksellers or by contacting:

WestBow Press
A Division of Thomas Nelson
1663 Liberty Drive
Bloomington, IN 47403
www.westbowpress.com
1-(866) 928-1240

Because of the dynamic nature of the Internet, any web addresses or links contained in this book may have changed since publication and may no longer be valid. The views expressed in this work are solely those of the author and do not necessarily reflect the views of the publisher, and the publisher hereby disclaims any responsibility for them.

Scripture taken from the Common English Bible®, CEB® Copyright © 2010, 2011 by Common English Bible.™ Used by permission. All rights reserved worldwide. The "CEB" and "Common English Bible" trademarks are registered in the United States Patent and Trademark Office by Common English Bible. Use of either trademark requires the permission of Common English Bible.

All Scripture quotations in this publications are from The Message. Copyright (c) by Eugene H. Peterson 1993, 1994, 1995, 1996, 2000, 2001, 2002. Used by permission of NavPress Publishing Group.

This is a work of fiction. All of the characters, names, incidents, organizations, and dialogue in this novel are either the products of the author's imagination or are used fictitiously.

Any people depicted in stock imagery provided by Thinkstock are models, and such images are being used for illustrative purposes only.

Certain stock imagery © Thinkstock.

ISBN: 978-1-4497-9553-5 (sc)
ISBN: 978-1-4497-9554-2 (hc)
ISBN: 978-1-4497-9552-8 (e)

Library of Congress Control Number: 2013909090

Printed in the United States of America.

WestBow Press rev. date: 07/09/13

To my husband, Matthew
and to our children — David, M-D, Paul and Michael
answers to prayers, totally beloved

⚮

To my mother – Salome Ekeleme
*The tears you cried many years ago, after you
passed me through a window into the crowded
train that would take me from Umuahia to FGGC
Kazaure, were not in vain. I am what I am today
because of the love you invested in my life*

⚮

And to my Lord – Jesus Christ (especially for my Lord)
*Because from Him... and through Him... and to Him
are all things*

Acknowledgements

There are many to thank for making *Whispers From Yesteryears* a reality — some are identified here, but the majority remain unnamed but never unnoticed or unappreciated.

Special thanks to Ellen & Jonas Darko who showed commitment, support and encouragement throughout the writing and production of the book. They wouldn't let me quit when I was tired, and I am forever grateful.

My deep appreciation also goes to Adesua and Chuks Ezeokafor, Evelyn Wali, Elizabeth Abidogun, Omolara Agoye, Cristabell Simbi, Lourine Osamusali, Queen Okafor, Reverend Gloria Uchefuna, Abigail Osahenye, Mummy Winifred Oyelese, Toyin Odufeso, Clementine Osah, Clara Uponi, Lara Omoniyi, Kathryn Fasegha, Natalie Lusignan, Reverend Yinka Odunayo, Patti Eboagwu, Bunmi Fawehinmi, and Layide Aina.

I am also grateful to Angel Olabanji – a ten-year old girl I've never met, who read ColourBLIND and has been phoning me constantly to ask when my next book will be published.

Thanks also to my brothers and sisters — Godson, Nwabu, Nnenna, Christie, Joe, Ijeoma, Chidinma and Uchechi — who have always been there for me.

Also to all my in-laws, thank you, each and every one!

PART 1

Chapter 1

Abuja

Chuma Zeluwa did not believe in ghosts.

He was a Christian. He believed in God the Father, the Son and the Holy Spirit. He believed in life hereafter. But he did not believe in ghosts, as in once-dead, now-physically-alive type of ghosts—especially when the person had been dead for more than a decade.

That was why the sight of the lady on the podium, playing the keyboard with the worship team, sent shivers down his spine. So he shut his eyes and shook his head. But when he opened his eyes again, she was still there. She hadn't disappeared.

He must have been more tired than he felt. Or maybe his mind was playing tricks on him. *Concentrate*, he urged himself. He closed his eyes, clapped to the rhythm of the song, swayed to the beat. This was time to praise the Lord, time to be happy in his presence, not time to awaken unpleasant memories.

Who is like unto thee, O Lord? Among the gods, who is like thee? Glorious in holiness! Fearful in praises! Doing wonders!

Some songs never fade. Chuma reminisced as he sang with the congregation. His parents sang "Who is like unto thee?" as university students. He sang "Who is like unto thee?" as a young man at the University of Benin, and now, more than a decade later, at the Jubilee Power Conference, he was still singing "Who is like unto thee?" and still being transported into the presence of holiness with awe, driven to his knees in thanksgiving and lost in an overwhelming sense of spiritual refreshment. Some songs did that to you.

There are just too many reasons to be thankful, he thought. For his family. Especially for his family. For his sisters Amaka and Zola. What a turn their lives had taken in the space of two years. Both sisters married within months of each other, to two of his best friends. His parents couldn't be more proud of their daughters or fonder of their new sons-in-law. Since then, his mother hadn't stopped teasing him about finding a wife of his own. "You brought your friends to my house, and I welcomed them," she would say. "In return, they took my daughters away from me. Now I am all alone. You have to go get another daughter for me o!"

Her nagging almost always called up memories he would rather forget, so he firmly shook his head now and refocused on the lyrics of the song. He had learned long ago that instead of dwelling on wrongs he could not correct, lamenting over a past life he could not undo or cringing in the shadows of a sin for which he had been pardoned, he would live in the present and look to the future in faith.

"Who is like unto thee ..." the congregation sang.

Chuma lifted his hands to heaven and sang right along with them.

The auditorium was filled to capacity. The conference attracted delegates from different parts of the country, their local churches easily identifiable from their name tags. There were some like him, who had come by themselves, not part of any delegation. Still, he felt right at home in the congregation. It didn't even feel like he had been overseas for years. As the worship continued, he realized how much he had missed Nigeria. The rowdiness, the heat, the sweat—everything felt just right.

The unease descended again as he glanced at the podium and watched those fingers flying across the keyboard. He sighed and scratched his head. Who could she be? He picked up his notebook, fished out the folded conference brochure he had tucked between the pages and quickly scanned through the programme. Thursday worship service was being led by the choir of the Jos Jubilee Church. That was all the information provided. There was nothing to identify members of the worship team.

He stretched slightly and observed her again. Could two people be so alike? It was the same profile, the same smile, the same fair complexion, just a little taller frame. *I wonder if she has a gap between her two front teeth too.* He angled his head slightly but couldn't quite check this out as the lady bent over the keyboard again. His heart pounded and he closed his eyes. *It is a striking resemblance,* he thought. *Nothing more. A strange, weird resemblance but a resemblance all the same because dead people do not suddenly rise from their graves!* Besides, the girl he had known had no musical ability that he could remember.

But she had a younger sister.

Yes! Relief surged through him, releasing pent-up emotions. That must be it. Why hadn't he thought of that? He recalled his shock at the resemblance between the two sisters when he had visited their house that October afternoon many years ago. The lady on the podium had to be Urenna's sister. He took a deep breath and whistled in relief. He would try to meet her before the end of the service, find out how she was doing. Did their family still live in Calabar? Were her parents okay? Would she even recognize him? Maybe not. By his calculations, that girl had been about 13 or 14 years old when he had called at their house to offer his condolences at the untimely death of her big sister 11 years ago.

What an experience, Chuma marvelled when a 30-minute break was announced. He dabbed at the perspiration trickling down his face and looked toward the front of the auditorium. Some members of the worship band were still hanging around, but the lady he wanted to see was not with them. The young man kneeling by the chair on his right was still caught up in the atmosphere of worship, so he stepped into the back row and joined the crowd heading out of the auditorium. He needed a cold drink.

He and this great army!

A long line had already formed in front of the Coke kiosk. He shrugged and made for the end of the queue, right behind two young men deep in conversation. The camp meeting reminded him of the NIFES conferences he had attended when he was a student at UniBen. The teachings and instructions he had received at those conferences had profoundly impacted his life. He hadn't attended any such conference in a long time.

As he waited, his eyes swept through the crowd. He was not bothered that he did not know anybody at the conference. It had been Amos and Amaka's idea for the three of them to attend the conference, but Amaka had fallen sick at the last minute, and Amos had stayed back to be with her. He had thought about cancelling, but in the end had been persuaded by the prospect of visiting Nigeria's federal capital for the first time ever. A sightseeing tour of Abuja on Saturday was part of the programme, and he planned to be part of it.

His phone began to vibrate in his pocket. He smiled at the caller ID.

"Ol' boy, how now? How's it going?" Amos asked.

"Very good. How are you guys? How is my sister?"

"She's pregnant."

"Ah ha!"

"Ah ha what?"

"I suspected as much. Congrats, man."

"Thanks."

"How is she feeling?"

"Much, much better, thank heavens. At least now we know why she was feeling so miserable. We hadn't planned on having a baby yet, so when she started to get ill it didn't occur to us that she may have become pregnant. She still feels yucky and nauseated, but at least now we know what's up with her."

Chuma laughed. "Has she told Zola?"

"Of course! She called her before we left the clinic."

"And my mother?"

"She doesn't know yet. Amaka has invited your mom and dad over for lunch on Sunday, and the plan is to tell them then."

"I doubt she can wait that long. I've never known my little sister to keep a secret for more than a few hours. She's too exuberant."

"I like exuberance."

"Of course you do. That's why you married her." Chuma laughed. "Anyway, I'll be home on Sunday morning, and I'm inviting myself over for lunch at your place too. I want to see my mother's face when she learns she has another grandchild on the way. You are happy, aren't you?"

"*Weeell*, I had hoped to have my wife to myself for one more year, but ..." Chuma heard the shrug in his voice. "I'll have to get used to sharing her with my baby now. It's all good."

Chuma laughed, drawing interested stares from people around him. He cupped a hand over the phone and lowered his voice. "Ol' boy, you sound jealous of your own child. Don't you know that it is the hand that disturbs the bee that gets stung? *When Mr. Trouble dey sleep and Miss Inyanga go wake am, the thing wey she see na the thing she been find go.*"

"Yeah, yeah ... I guess." The smile in his voice belied Amos's grumpy words. "Look, don't let the cat out of the bag o! Don't tell your parents. Your sister wants to tell them herself."

"No problem. My lips are sealed. Just let her know that I want to be present when she tells them. I want to see their reactions."

His mind settled on the news of Amaka's pregnancy for several minutes after he bade Amos good-bye. He could imagine his mother's joy at this news. Two grandchildren expected in one year. He could also hear the nagging wheels churning in her brain. *Chuma, it s your turn-o ! Chuma, you re not a small boy anymore Chuma, your father was a young man when we had you Chuma, if you get married and have children now you won t still be training them in your old age. Chuma, you can t be single forever! Chuma, anagh agba okoro na nka o ! Chuma Chuma Chuma*

He shrugged. Although he missed home, living overseas had its advantages—there was a limit to how much he could be influenced by his parents.

The queue wasn't moving. Chuma looked to the front, and his heart almost stopped as he spied the keyboard lady again. She had her back to him and was listening to another girl chattering animatedly, but it was her all right—same dress, same stature, and the same sinking feeling in the depths of his stomach. Was this indeed Urenna's sister? The resemblance was uncanny.

The two girls appeared to be deep in conversation. The second girl, slightly shorter but as dark as her friend was fair, was doing all the talking while the keyboard lady listened attentively, nodding intermittently. A camera swung down the other girl's neck and she paused occasionally to share photographs with her friend.

The girls were next in line for the drinks. Chuma braced himself, waiting for them to turn around. They would pass him on their way back to the auditorium. This time he would take a good look, just to see how far the resemblance to Urenna went. Part of him hoped he would find that he was making much ado about nothing, that the girl would not even be Urenna's sister. Still another part of him rose in the excited anticipation that he was on the precipice of a monumental discovery.

Without meaning to he registered the simplicity of her dressing, a long skirt and blouse made from the same African *adire* fabric. The skirt was form-fitting, revealing an overall slender and curved body. Low-heeled sandals made it easy for him to estimate her height to be about 5 feet 7 or 8 inches. Urenna used to have very thick, long and curly hair. The lady he was staring at had her hair wrapped in a headscarf so he couldn't make any comparisons there, but even from behind, the resemblance was uncanny.

She paid for the drinks and waited while the vendor gave her change. Her friend opened the bottles with a bottle opener dangling from a rope nailed to the kiosk. The two ladies then turned and headed straight toward him, still engrossed in conversation. Chuma stood there waiting for the moment she would look up. He wanted to look into her eyes and confirm once and for all that apart from Jesus Christ, no other mortal has ever died and come back to life.

He knew the exact moment her eyes met his. There was a flash of recognition, and she stopped dead in her tracks. Chuma remained standing, paralyzed, every muscle frozen, as the truth exploded through him. This woman was no ghost. She was Urenna in flesh and blood and there was no doubt about it. Pulse racing dangerously, hands clammy with sweat, he suddenly felt disorientated. Blood drummed in his ears. The sun felt hotter and cooler at the same time. His legs suddenly sagged and his entire body felt weak.

"Ure!" he whispered in disbelief, lifting a hand to steady his spinning head. Then he watched as slowly, like a scene in a slow-motion movie, the bottle of Coke slid from her hands and she collapsed in a heap on the ground.

The whirr of panicking voices around her slowly flickered through her subconscious, the sounds getting louder and the words more distinct. Grace forced her eyes open, gradually making out the sky, her hands feeling the dry sands of the campground. She felt a hand on her upper arms and closed her eyes again. A familiar voice was shouting her name.

"Grace! Grace! Can you hear me? Grace! What happened to you?"

Slowly she opened her eyes and blinked several times. Sweat oozed through her pores. She took the hand Ayesha offered as she slowly sat up, embarrassed and anxious to get away from the converging crowd.

"What happened to me?" Her voice shook, so low she almost didn't hear herself.

"It's the sun," Ayesha explained. "This is exactly what happened to my cousin. One afternoon, while she was in Sokoto, she stepped out into the sun and the next thing, she collapsed and had to be rushed to the hospital."

A young camp official came rushing from the auditorium. "What happened, Sister Grace? They say you fainted."

Grace was now standing, trying to regain her balance; she felt better and assured everyone she was fine.

"She's not fine," Ayesha spat her words. "She has not eaten anything since last night. The heat and the empty stomach have weakened her body. She—"

"Ayesha! I'm okay," Grace said. "Really I am. I just need to drink some water." Someone ran for a bottle of *Ragolis*.

Her eyes scanned through the crowd, searching until she found Chuma standing under the huge pillar by the entrance of the auditorium. Their eyes met again and held. She shook her head in denial. It had to be a coincidence, someone who looked exactly like Chuma. He couldn't be here. He should be married and living out his dream in London or America. He wasn't even religious, as far as she knew. What would he be doing at a Christian camp meeting? She shuddered again. Painful memories crowded her mind and she closed her eyes, praying earnestly for help from above.

The camp official put a hand under her right arm. Ayesha held her left hand. They led her toward the auditorium. Their path would come very close to where Chuma stood.

His eyes met hers again and he felt her panic. Did she think he would confront her in the presence of her friends or that he would expose the lie she seemed to be living with these people? *Grace* indeed. Dropping his forehead into his left palm, Chuma gave her one last look and shook his head on his way back into the auditorium.

Chapter 2

Lagos

Three days later Chuma drove his parents to his sister's house, all the while second-guessing his decision to accompany them. Under other circumstances he would have enjoyed spending time with Amos and Amaka, but his unexpected return from Abuja on Friday had aroused his family's curiosity, and he had no desire to be under the microscope of their questioning. All he could think of was how soon he could be on his way to Jos in search of answers.

When the gateman ushered them into the compound, another vehicle was in the driveway, much to his relief. As long as there was a third party present, he would be safe from everybody's well-intentioned questions. He got out of the car and opened the door for his mother. But when he moved to his father's side, he was on the phone and waved them off.

Chuma hugged his sister at the door and high-fived Amos. The other guests were Amos's parents. He went over to greet them, shaking hands with Amos's father and allowing his friend's mother to pull him into a light hug. When his own mother and her in-laws began their happy greetings he turned to his sister.

"Congrats!" he mouthed quietly. "Have you told the in-laws?"

"Nope. I'm even surprised they haven't guessed already. I'm not being very subtle here, am I?" She looked down at her chest and he understood. The words BABY ONBOARD were inscribed on the blue T-shirt she wore over a black skirt.

"You may have to spell it out eventually." He laughed and walked over to open the fridge. "They probably think it's the latest fashion in T-shirts."

"*Mazi* (Mr) Chukwunalu!" he heard his father call to Amos's parents as he entered the living room.

"*Dike nwokem! Ichie deede,*" ("Brave one! I greet you!") Amos's father hailed him, and the two exchanged the traditional Igbo three backhand slap and handshake *(ina ito)*.

"*Omee okachie!*" ("One who acts bravely and signs off with confidence!") Professor Zeluwa replied.

"*Ugo chara acha n'adighi echu echu!*" ("You're the mature eagle that remains ever pure!") responded Mr. Chukwunalu. "Prof, you have been tried and tested, and you have withstood the test of time!"

"*Aka a na-ana dike di ka gi bu itube ya abuba ugo!*" ("The appropriate reward for a man of your valour is to decorate your cap with eagle feathers!") Professor Zeluwa answered. "Your greatness is appreciated!"

The two men laughed heartily.

"Prof-Prof! It looks like our children have planned a surprise family reunion. They didn't tell us you were coming over."

"Providence must be on their side too. You will not believe who I was speaking to on my phone just now."

"Who?"

"*Nnukwu ozo* himself, the strong man—Chief Ojiefi."

"What?" Everyone turned to him. "You were speaking with the chief?"

"Oh yes. He just arrived from Asaba and wanted to come over to our home for a visit. I took the liberty to invite him over here. Amaka, I hope you have enough food for one more guest."

"Of course we do, Papa. If we don't we'll serve him Chuma's portion."

Everyone laughed and conversation buzzed again.

Chief Ojiefi was one of the wealthiest and most influential men in Nigeria. He was also a member of the Zeluwa's extended family following the marriage of his youngest son to Chuma's sister. Despite the social differences between the two families and the tough opposition from the chief's wife, Kenny and Zola had insisted on their feelings for each other, got married and were now living in the United States. That was two years ago. From reports he got from his mother, Chuma knew that the two fathers-in-law had become good friends since then. Once, when he had called from the States, his parents were having dinner with the chief at his Ambassador Hotel. *Wonders shall never cease*, he'd thought.

"Marion, my sister," Mrs. Chukwunalu began as the women followed Amaka toward the kitchen, "how are the young couple doing in America? When is Zola's baby due? Will you be going there for *ömugwö*?" *(ömugwö is an Igbo tradition requiring mothers or older female relatives to take care of younger women for a period after childbirth.)*

Amos pulled out his latest gadget, a digital camcorder Chuma had bought for him from the US, to show the men. They took turns commenting on its speed, performance and the high resolution of its pictures. Amos shot video clips of the two older men at different activities to demonstrate exactly how it worked.

Chuma later found the sports channel on television, and all the men followed his lead. They were absorbed in watching a European league soccer game when Chief Ojiefi's black Jeep rolled into the compound. From where he sat inside the house, Chuma thought the black jeep looked strong, much like the man doubtlessly sitting in the backseat. It had black, tinted windows with a metal trim on the door panels and the heavy tyres were held by silver rims. Expecting a chauffeur, Chuma was surprised to see the chief himself step out of the driver's seat. He wore casual clothing, just jeans and T-shirt. The first time he had met him at his home in Asaba, during his 36th wedding anniversary celebrations, Chuma remembered thinking the chief looked too young to have been married that long. He still thought so.

"My security men are parked in front of your gate. I hope you don't mind," he explained when Amos opened the front door to let him into the house.

"No problem, sir," Amos assured him, bowing in greeting. "What of your driver, sir?"

He laughed. "Not today, Amos. I like to drive myself sometimes."

Chuma joined his father and Mr Chukwunalu at the door in welcoming Chief Ojiefi. The men exchanged the *ina-ito*, hailing him as they shook hands.

"Nnukwu Ozo! Ekelem gi o! I greet you!"

"Ichie!"

"Onwa n'agbara ora 1 of Nigeria!" ("The moon that shines brightly on all Nigerians!")

"A n'eto, O n'eme!"("One whose benevolence increases as he is showered with praises!")

The women came from the kitchen to greet him too. Chuma was impressed at how quickly he soon put everyone at ease, exchanging jokes with his mother and Amaka.

"So what gives, Amaka?" the chief asked. "Why have you called everyone together? What are you celebrating?"

Chuma saw his sister blush and look away in embarrassment. The chief followed her movement and for a second squinted at her T-shirt.

Then he let out a shout. "Well, well, well! Congratulations. Prof, you didn't tell me this was a celebration dinner."

"Celebration?" Professor Zeluwa turned to his daughter. "What are we celebrating? Amaka and her husband only invited us to lunch!"

"Hmm, 'only to lunch' indeed." Amaka pouted. "Chief, thank you for noticing o! I was beginning to think this was all in vain! You won't believe that neither my parents nor my in-laws have noticed that this is a special occasion! They have not heard what I've been trying to tell them since they arrived."

"Tell us what?" Nwamara Chukwunalu put a hand over the "o" of her open mouth as hope warred with disbelief in her heart. "You mean, you mean you're … are you pregnant?"

"Yes, Mama, I'm pregnant. You're both going to be grandmothers!"

Chuma watched as first the mothers and then the fathers burst out in excitement. The two women screamed, hugged each other and drew Amaka into their embrace. The men shook hands with Amos, congratulating him.

"It's about time!" Mazi Chukwunalu told his son. "You can't play *okoro* ("bachelor") forever. It's time to be a man!"

As the congratulations continued, Nwamara Chukwunalu clapped her hands with joy and started the customary song of celebration:

"Ife mamna, we kugide,
Ife ma nma, we kugide
Ife ma nma, we kugide
Woooooo! Woooooo!"

Everyone joined in the singing and the celebratory dance began. Chief Ojiefi placed a chair in the middle of the room, and a laughing Amaka was made to sit on it while they all danced around her. Chuma happily took over video duty from Amos as he was dragged over to dance for his wife.

Each person had to suggest a traditional song of thanksgiving for the occasion. Chuma couldn't think of any, so his mother raised one for him. In the midst of the rejoicing he realised he was glad he'd come after all. The visit was worth it, even if it was only to witness the happiness blazoned on Mrs. Chukwunalu's face. The woman was breathless with excitement. He could not keep count of how many times she was shouting praises to God or how often she hugged Amaka.

"Are we still having lunch?" Mr Chukwunalu finally asked. "Can we be eating and celebrating at the same time? I'm getting quite hungry."

Amaka moved to stand up from the chair but her two mothers wouldn't hear of it.

"You should have called me to cook for you instead of exhausting yourself," her mother-in-law insisted. "The first weeks are the most critical weeks, you know. You should be taking things easy. Amos, my son, how could you have allowed your wife to cook all these meals in her condition?"

"Tell him, Mama." Amaka pouted, trying to summon a frown, but failing miserably.

Amos laughed. "She didn't cook everything, Mama. She had lots of help from the house girl, and from me. We all pitched in."

Chuma stopped himself just in time from declaring that from what he knew of his sister, she probably never lifted a finger to help. The Amaka he knew never liked to cook. Still, two years of marriage could have changed all that.

When the evening ended, Chief Ojiefi thanked the Chukwunalus, hugged Marion good-bye and asked Professor Zeluwa and Chuma to follow him out.

As they walked to his truck, he turned to Chuma. "So how are your sister and my son?"

Chuma knew who he meant. "Great, sir. Really great. Pregnancy really suits Zola. I've never seen her happier with herself. Kenny is not doing badly himself."

"Good. I'll be seeing them in a couple of weeks."

"You're travelling to Chicago."

"Not directly. I have business in Houston, but I will stop by and spend a night or two with them."

"They'll be happy to see you, sir."

"Yeah, likewise. Listen, I have a favour to ask of you."

"I will be honoured, sir."

"Do you have time?"

"How much?"

"Two to three weeks. Prof, you don't mind if I send him to check out a business venture for me, do you? I would have gone myself or sent my sons, but everybody is tied up with one thing or another, and I would like this business sorted out as soon as possible."

"Where do you want to send him?"

"To Jos, Plateau state. I've made an offer to purchase a piece of land in a prime location there. The land comes with some old buildings I don't really want. I need to send someone out there for a building inspection, someone who understands buildings, a professional. Kenny tells me you're the man for the job seeing that you work in construction. I'll pay for your time, of course. But think of it as an extension of your holiday. Jos is Nigeria's tourist city, you know. Have you been there before?"

Jos, Chuma thought. *Going to Jos is all I've been thinking about since Thursday.* "I've been to Jos before," he said.

"You have?" his father asked.

"Sure, many years ago. Didn't we spend one Christmas holiday there?"

"But you were too young then—9 or 10. I doubt you remember anything about it."

"You're right, I don't. But I would love to go again." He nodded to the chief. "I can do this for you, sir."

"Great. I'll call you tomorrow with the logistics—flight, hotel accommodations and vehicle for moving about in Jos. It's all on me."

After Chief Ojiefi departed, Professor Zeluwa turned to his son. "Your godmother still lives in Jos. She will be happy to finally see you. She's been asking after you for a very long time."

Chuma nodded, but he wasn't thinking of his godmother. He was thinking instead of miracles and divine interventions. *Are you trying to tell me something, Lord?* Was the hand of God in this? Or was it just a big coincidence?

Chapter 3

Calabar

Egoyibo Okolie, Ego for short, felt the weight of her 58 years as she bent low to clear the wildflowers around the headstone. A trickle of sweat ran a straight line down her spine, and she shivered in the evening wind. She paused to wipe her face with her outer wrapper before leaning over her hoe once more.

The cemetery was part of the University of Calabar's environment department, located right beside the Malabo campus park, with a major road on either side. The university labourers generally did a good job keeping the site clean. Most times she didn't need to clear any grass or water any plants, but she still came with a hoe and a rake. And with a heart consumed with the same sorrow and guilt that had taken root since that dreadful evening Odili came home from the mortuary and confirmed that the bloated body that had been pulled out from the Itu River after that tragic motor accident was indeed their daughter.

With time, her friends had told her, she would forget. Time would lessen the pain, they said. Time would dull the memories and heal her broken heart. But time had come and time had gone—11 full years this September. Still she mourned. Still she cried. Still her guilty conscience mocked her. Her only hope was that one day she would pass to the other side too. She would find her daughter and beg for forgiveness. Maybe *then* she would find peace. A lump lodged in her throat and tears burned behind her eyes. She brushed them off and sneezed lightly into her outer wrapper, turning to observe the multi-shaped graves and headstones around her.

Over the years she had come to the conclusion that cemeteries did not really exist for the dead. They existed for the living, for people like her who would be lost without a stone upon which she could express her grief. Like most of her generation, Ego had grown up on folk tales about zombies and ghosts of the dead parading burial grounds, searching for human blood to feed on. In the years immediately after the tragedy, she had wished that particular tale was true, that maybe the spirits of the dead would devour her since she didn't deserve to live.

A sad smile firmed the contours of her lips. She knew a lot of people thought she was crazy. And she may well be. Her husband certainly believed it. She marvelled at the emotional strength of that man. His conscience didn't seem to bother him. Not as much as hers did anyway. Maybe she too would one day banish the memories and move on with her life like he had apparently done; but not yet. Those memories were now her constant companion as she continued to mull over how to make amends to the young child she had failed so badly.

Ego sighed and felt a contraction in her chest. She reached for her water bottle and took a few sips before she sat down on her dwarf stool, stretched and crossed her legs at the ankles. Two feuding flies landed on her elbow. She shook them off and sneezed into her wrapper again. Although it was so long ago, she still got emotional whenever she recalled the events that finally ended her daughter's life.

That night, Odili had brought out his *koboko*, summoned the girl into the living room and made her strip down to her underwear. When Ego demanded to know what he planned to do he had ordered her out of the room and locked the door behind her. It was from the other side that she heard the piercing screams that split the silence of the night as Odili flogged their daughter over and over again. With every stroke the girl had screamed for her mother but Ego could not help. She could only shout and plead with Odili to have mercy on the child from behind the locked door. When she finally broke her way into the living room with a club, Odili had turned the whip on her and would have flogged her too if the phone hadn't started to ring at that very moment. The sight of her daughter— her wrists tied to the dining table with a rope, her body covered with lacerations and bloody slashes, and her face filled with sheer terror — were forever etched in Ego's heart.

Afterward Odili had shown no remorse, no regrets. *A stubborn chicken*, he'd informed her, *will learn its lesson in a hot pot of soup.*

"*Ndo, nwam,*" she whispered to the girl who lay six feet in the ground, and coughed quietly to dislodge the phlegm that had lodged in her throat. "So sorry," she repeated.

Her cell phone buzzed. She looked at her watch. Was it one hour already?

"Mama." Anuli's voice came across the phone. "I'm at the filling station. I'll be at the junction in ten minutes."

Sighing heavily, Ego gathered her hoe and rake and the black polythene bag into which she had gathered debris from the site. She re-tied her wrapper, knotted her head-tie and picked up her stool. She wiped her face once more before she began the short trek to the intersection where her second daughter was waiting to take her home.

Chapter 4

Jos

The tangerine light of dawn spread across the ceiling of Grace's bedroom. It surprised her because she was always up long before sunrise. She quickly sat up and reached for her wristwatch. It was six thirty, not as late as she had imagined. Not that she really needed to wake up early today. It was Saturday, after all, and Saturday mornings tended to be a bit more laid back than weekday mornings. Still, she had a business to run and couldn't afford to sleep in, even on Saturdays.

Grace stretched and yawned loudly before she pushed out her window latch to welcome the new day. The gust of air that flowed into her room was cool with a slightly crispy chill, and she remembered that last night, while the town of Jos slept, a heavy rain had fallen. Curiosity sent her to the flowerpot on her window ledge, and she smiled faintly at the tiny buds of colour already peeping out between the folded petals stretching out from the black dirt.

She switched on her bedside lamp and knelt by her bed, grateful for this quiet time before the daily responsibilities of her role as acting manager of Sonshine Holiday Estate would come knocking on her door. With the Easter holidays only weeks away, the estate was almost full, and she needed all the help she could get, divine and otherwise, to be on top of it all.

At seven a.m. Grace stepped into the bathroom and grabbed her toothbrush. She counted to 30 as she brushed her upper left teeth and to another 30 as she brushed the lower left. A fair-complexioned woman mimicked her gestures from the other side of the bathroom mirror. Long, thick, twisted hair fell down her neck and framed a heart-shaped face with wide-set eyes and long lashes. She repeated the routine on the right side, over and over until her teeth shined and her gums felt clean.

The cold shower drove the remnants of sleep from her eyes. Afterward, she pulled on faded jeans and a free-flowing T-shirt. She brushed back the curly tendrils of hair that had escaped the twists and massaged petroleum jelly salve over heart-shaped lips with her fingertip. She pressed them tightly together and thought of the Igbo adage, *if a man fails to lick his lips, the harmattan will do it for him.* This was not the harmattan season, but still …

After slipping on her open-toed sandals, she shut the apartment door and made her way to the recreation centre.

She turned her head from side to side as she walked, savouring the feel of the gentle wind and the fragrance of the fresh flowers in the early morning light. Sonshine Estate was made up of 12 semi-detached two-bedroom houses and a large recreation centre, popularly called the RC. The RC housed the lobby, kitchen, restaurant and gym. A sidewalk connected all the houses in the estate although they were a good 20 meters apart from each other. The estate kept a horticulturist on payroll, and it was no surprise that its carefully cultivated gardens and scenic landscape were popular with holiday-makers.

Faint voices floated to her, and she went to the dining room to see if any of the guests was having an early breakfast, but no one was there. The huge room looked the way it always did—clean and orderly with dining tables covered in fresh linen and a vase of fresh flowers providing each table with its own particular scent. There was only one other place the voices could be coming from, so she headed for the kitchen.

Despite the clatter of cutlery and a small radio streaming the morning news, Grace could not mistake Bola's deep baritone. She was talking to Edith, and as Grace quietly approached the kitchen, she heard their earnest conversation.

"*Chei*, my sister. That man wicked no be small o!" Bola hissed. "Hmm. The sand over his mother's grave never even settle before he put her house up for sale, like say the money wan run. *Na waa-o!*"

Edith shrugged as she arranged a set of cutlery by the covered dishes on a serving tray. "That's why they say dead men have no teeth. If they did, Madam Mairo would have risen from her grave to speak some sense into her son. Gidan Mairo was her life's work."

Bola shook her head sadly and rubbed her hand across her eyes. "You no think say the Mission fit take him go court to stop him from selling that building? Everyone know say Madam Mairo been promise that house to the mission."

Grace was surprised they hadn't noticed her presence. Edith squeezed fresh oranges into a pitcher before responding to her friend. "I don't think they can do that. Idris is the only heir to his mother's estate, and he can do whatever he wants with his inheritance. But you know that this is not the first time we've heard about an offer for the building. Let's just hope that ... oh, good morning, Grace."

"Good morning, Edith, Bola." Grace shook her head, smiling to take the sting from her next words. "Please lower your voices. I could hear everything you were saying from the dining room."

The waitresses smiled and murmured their apologies. Grace knew her gentle rebuke would not offend the ladies. She had known them for a long time, and Bola's loud voice and insistence on speaking Pidgin English was always fodder for much teasing in the kitchen.

The kitchen was ultra-modern. A huge stove sat in the middle of the large room, surrounded by large cupboards and cabinets. Grace appreciated how the ladies meticulously kept everything clean and organised. She inhaled the aroma of scrambled eggs and fresh tea as the waitresses prepared to take out breakfast.

She turned to an older woman cutting fresh vegetables on the huge chopping board on the granite counter. "Morning, Mama Remi. I hope you had no trouble getting home last night. Did you get caught in the rain?"

"Not at all," the assistant cook looked up from her task. "Adamu na better driver. Him no waste time at all! He even pick up his wife from NASCO Centre before taking me home; and we still reach GRA before the rain started."

Grace nodded. "Uncle Tunde and Auntie Bukky are fine?"

"Oh, yes." The woman's head bobbled. "Which reminds me, she say make you call am as soon as possible."

"Who? Auntie Bukky?"

"Yes."

"Did she say why?"

"No, she just say she wan make you call am first thing today."

Auntie Bukky and her husband were the owners of Bukuru Christian Academy, a boarding school an hour's drive from the hotel. Mama Remi had lived with the couple since they hired her as a nanny for their baby more than 20 years ago. The baby was now a graduate student at a university in London while her own daughter, Remi, had dropped out of school to follow after boys and parties, much to her mother's dismay and Auntie Bukky's disapproval.

Grace greeted the chief cook, who was switching the dishwasher on and off with a frown. Whatever was the matter again? Since they purchased the appliance less than ten months ago, it had broken down more times than she cared to recall.

"What's up, Ma Mabel?" she asked.

"I no know o! The thing just pack up this morning without warning. I use am yesterday, no problem, but now I turn and turn the switch and it just dey make this fuzzy noise before it stop. See, water no dey flow inside sef."

"You think that maybe it's from the controller? Here, let me try."

Several minutes later, she gave up. "I'll send for the technician. Hopefully it will be something easy enough so he won't charge us too much."

Grace visited with the kitchen staff for a few more minutes going through the plans for the day. Finally, she filled a plastic bottle with water from the filter and made for the door. "If anyone needs me, call my cell phone. After I call Auntie Bukky, I'll go for a walk."

Once at the reception desk, Grace pulled out the message log and placed the call. She found a pen while the phone connected to Auntie Bukky's number.

"Good morning, Auntie. It's me, Grace."

"Ah, yes. Good morning, my dear. How are things at Sonshine?" The woman's deep voice reflected her matter-of-fact attitude.

"Everything is going well, Auntie." *Minus a broken-down dishwasher*, but she wasn't going to complain about that. If push came to shove, they would manually wash the dishes. It wouldn't be the first time. "There's no problem, Ma."

"That's good. Have you been hearing from Simbi?"

"Oh yes. She calls regularly. She sent me a postcard from Paris."

"I know. When she called me yesterday I told her to concentrate on enjoying her holiday instead of worrying about Sonshine. She put you in charge, and I'm available if you run into any problems. Still, she worries."

Grace smiled, a wave of tenderness sweeping over her as she thought of Auntie Simbi. The woman had a heart of gold, but she did tend to worry a bit.

Grace hastened to defend her employer. "She hasn't been on any holiday since I've known her. Sonshine has been her whole life for many years now. I would find it difficult not to worry if I were in her shoes."

"But, my dear, you probably know as much about running that hotel as she does."

Grace detected a slight irritation in her tone.

"You've been understudying her for years and know the process inside out."

Grace heard the long-suffering sigh from the other end of the phone and smiled to herself.

"Anyway," Auntie Bukky said with a yawn, "she wanted me to remind you about your medications. I told her not to worry about that either because you are not a baby. But now I feel I must ask. How is your health?"

"I'm fine, Ma. Thank you."

"When is your next checkup?"

"I have an appointment this afternoon. I did some tests last month and the doctor wants to go over the results. The last time I saw him he said that as long as I eat a balanced diet and do my exercises I should be fine."

"That's good, but don't overdo things. If you need help anytime, you know I'm just a phone call away."

"Yes, Ma. Thank you, Ma."

"Was this why you fell sick at the Power Conference?"

"Was this why I fell sick at the Power Conference?" Grace repeated slowly.

"That's what I asked. Simbi said you were rushed home early from Jubilee Power Conference because you fainted."

"Umm ..." Grace paused to consider her words. "Yes and no. The doctor said it was mostly because of the heat but that my illness didn't help matters."

Grace wondered who else Auntie Simbi had told about the reason for her returning early from the Jubilee conference. She suspected the whole church knew she had fainted at Abuja and that everyone had a theory about what caused her to faint. She had ignored the speculations, hoping the story would fade away if she didn't feed the rumour mill. It was not as if she even knew what to say.

"Tell me, does Sonshine have a vacancy for a long-term guest?"

"Pardon me?" Grace tried to follow the woman's sudden change of topic.

"My godson is coming to Jos this evening. I haven't seen him in years, since he went abroad for his studies. He lives in America now. He's coming to Jos and I want him to stay at

Sonshine, but I want to be sure you have a vacancy before I suggest it to him."

"How long will he be staying?"

"I can't say for sure. He is coming on a working vacation. His mother said he might be here for a while, two to three weeks."

"Is he travelling alone?"

"Yes. Marion, that's his mother, mentioned that he is still unmarried. I honestly don't know what this world is coming to now. He is older than 30 and still not married. No children either. Can you imagine that? Older than 30!"

Grace could certainly imagine it but made no such comment. Instead, she opened her reservation logbook and checked the entries. "That shouldn't be a problem, Auntie. We have three vacant suites right now."

"Ah, thank God for that."

"What time is he arriving?"

"He's flying Ambassador Air from Lagos and will be here at seven-thirty. Your uncle will pick him from the airport to our home for supper before we come over to Sonshine."

Grace held the pen over the book. "Can you give me his details so I can register him, Auntie?"

"Of course, my dear. His name is Chukwuma. First name is Chukwuma, middle initial A, and last name is Zeluwa."

How Grace managed to remain standing she didn't know. Auntie Bukky's words struck her like a physical blow. It took a huge effort to concentrate on the rest of the conversation with a dry mouth and her heart beating heavily in her chest, but she managed to hold on.

After she hung up, she sat limply on the chair and covered her face with shaking hands. Then *Chuma!* she mouthed disbelievingly, propping her elbows against the registration desk. She'd known from the time their eyes met across the crowd at the conference that she would see him again. She didn't know it would be so soon. A wave of dizziness swept over her, and she pressed a trembling hand to her throat. She sat there for the next five minutes, trying to calm her shivering heart. Then, taking a deep breath, she completed the reservation and went off on her morning walk.

Later that day, Grace sat opposite the doctor, waiting while he read through her file. She took in a deep breath and braced herself for whatever he had to say.

After thumbing through the reports, Dr. Taju Deen took off his glasses and nodded at her. "Everything appears fine, Grace, and that can only mean that you have been following my instructions."

"Yes, sir. I've been doing everything you asked me to do."

He nodded again. "I can see that. You're taking your medications, watching your diet, eating the right foods and exercising regularly."

"Yes, sir."

"Very good. Your blood sugar average reading is 6.3 percent. This is not bad, but with continued exercise and dietary controls you can bring it lower. Your blood pressure is good, your weight is good. I'm impressed."

"Thank you, sir."

"Good. Are you sleeping well?"

"Yes," she nodded.

"What time do you go to bed?"

"Em … it depends on what's happening at Sonshine. Most nights I'm able to retire by ten thirty."

That wasn't entirely true, but she did make the effort and generally had no trouble falling asleep once her head hit the pillow. What the next few days might bring was anybody's guess. Auntie Bukky's early morning bombshell was still heavy on her mind.

"I want you to watch out for fatigue and stress. In your condition they can have dire consequences."

"Yes, I know, sir. I'm trying my best."

"Good. But until your madam comes back, I want you to increase the frequency of your monitoring. Call me if you get any unusual readings."

"Okay, sir."

He went through more instructions and wrote on a prescription pad before he closed her file. "That's all for today. If you continue doing what you're doing, you won't need to see me for another six months. Until then, if you run into any problems, call me."

As Grace left the doctor's office and stepped out into the cool March evening, she slowly let out a huge sigh of relief.

Chapter 5

Jos

"*You did what?*" Grace cried in astonishment.

The waitress flinched at Grace's shocked expression before calmly repeating, "I don assign Unit 7a and 7b to the two families that arrived this afternoon. Is there any problem with that?"

Grace shook her head and tried to pull herself together. "But ... but ... didn't you see the note I left this morning? Auntie Bukky's guest is checking in tonight."

"I been see your note, Grace, and I don assign am to Unit 11b. See for yourself." She opened the register and flipped through the pages. "I no forget. I just think say it go better make we keep the two new families in adjoining suites as them dey travel together. Plus, I sure say Auntie Bukky's guest go appreciate the privacy for 11b."

Her words made sense but did nothing to allay the tightening in Grace's chest. She had accepted the inevitability of meeting Chuma again. Having him in the same community was hard enough, but having him right next door was not something she was prepared for.

Grace took a deep breath. "It's all right, Bola." She nodded. "I thought for a moment you had filled up all the units."

The smile she pasted on her face to reassure the waitress was wobbly. Bola watched her closely.

"How long are the new families booked for?" Grace asked.

"Six nights."

"Well, that's good. We are full this weekend. Auntie Simbi will be happy." Grace reached for her water bottle and took a sip in an attempt to stop her lips from trembling, hoping the waitress would not notice.

Bola continued to study her. "Are you okay, Grace? You don't look like yourself."

She made a play of examining the documents in her hands. "I'm fine, Bola. Shouldn't you be on your way?"

The waitress hesitated but nodded. "Good night, Grace."

Grace smiled, waved her on her way and then sat back in her chair to chew at her pencil and check the time again. She had three hours. Three hours before she faced her past. Three hours to fortify her defences. *To be fore-warned*, they say, *is to be fore-armed*. And wasn't she deluding herself by imagining Chuma's visit to Jos had anything to do with her? He had business in Jos, according to Auntie Bukky.

She opened the lock-box and took out the key to Unit 11b. No harm in confirming that everything was in order.

Like every other suite in Sonshine, the walls in 11b were covered in delicate, plain olive-green paint. Cream-coloured lace curtains hung over the windows, contrasting with the light-brown leather settees in the living room and with the light-green carpets. The curtains were drawn together — their sheerness allowing the setting sun to filter through and cast spider-web patterns across the room. Fresh scents from the flower vase on the centre table — an assortment of African sunflowers, violets, and lilies — swam up to her nostrils. The plaque on the wall was from Proverbs: *Trust in the Lord with all your heart and lean not on your own understanding. In all your ways acknowledge him and he shall direct your path.* Grace closed her eyes momentarily, took a deep breath and let those words resonate in her heart.

Later, she visited with the guests who were still hanging out at the Recreation Centre. Big Jim was a long-term guest. He claimed he was an artist, but Grace didn't think that was entirely true. Every week officers in vehicles bearing the MOPOL (Mobile Police) logo visited him. She suspected he was a secret agent on a special assignment but she had never bothered to confront him. Instead she played along with his artist story. And in all fairness, he was always travelling throughout the plateau basin, collecting different artefacts and sketching picturesque sites in Jos. Maybe he really was an artist.

He looked up from his newspaper as Grace approached the patio table on which he had placed a bottle of wine.

"You look like you need a drink. Care to join me?" Jim remarked when she took the empty chair beside him.

Grace smiled brightly and bent down to pet Rufus, Jim's friendly German shepherd.

"Thanks, Jim, but you know I'm working. I don't drink while I'm working."

He lifted his eyebrows at her. "The way you say that, one would think I had an ulterior motive in offering you a drink."

"I don't think anything of the sort, but you know me, Jim. I'll not drink when I'm working."

"How about when you're not working?"

She smiled. She'd stepped into that one. "I'm always working."

"Oh, come on! That's not true. You need to lighten up, Grace. One glass of wine can't do you any harm."

She laughed but shook her head.

Rufus thumped his tail excitedly on the floor and looked up at her. She patted his head. "What a big dog you are, Rufus. Is your master treating you right? Huh?" She took his head in her hands and dodged as he tried to lick her face. "Because if he's not, you'd better tell me now so we can throw him out of your suite!"

"Throw me out of his suite?" Big Jim laughed. "Ha! That's a good one."

Grace smiled at him. "Exactly. You'd better look after Rufus or else."

He laughed again, watching as she played with the excited dog. Rufus rolled onto his back and lifted his legs up in the air, begging to be tickled. Grace was happy to oblige.

"You must excuse me, Jim, won't you?" Grace stood up finally. "I want to visit with the other guests. We had two families arrive today, and I haven't met them yet."

"You're the boss." He toasted her over the rim of his wine glass. "Go do your thing."

For the next three hours Grace operated on two levels— one, the competent hotel manager, making sure everything ran smoothly for her guests, and the other, a frustrated woman who couldn't stop thinking about Chuma and the implications of his visit.

It was well past ten o'clock when the call came from security that Auntie Bukky was at the gate. In the few seconds it took to return to the reception desk, Grace breathed a prayer for wisdom and strength, checked to ensure she looked okay, took a deep breath and braced for the inevitable.

It was Chuma all right. He stepped out of a station wagon accompanied by the driver, Auntie Bukky, and Uncle Tunde. Not quite the entourage she had imagined. When he strolled to the trunk and lifted his luggage, the driver rushed to take it. There was a slight argument, but eventually the driver prevailed and Chuma let go of the heavier luggage and carried only his briefcase, walking beside his grinning hosts. Grace saw Uncle Tunde slap Chuma's shoulders. He must have said something because the trio burst into loud laughter.

Ignoring the wild panic in her heart and trying to act as normal as possible, Grace stepped out from behind the reception desk, summoned a smile and waited for them in the lobby.

"Auntie." She embraced the older woman.

Auntie Bukky was shorter than Grace, and at least 65 years old. The arms that enfolded Grace were soft and warm. "Grace, my daughter!" Auntie Bukky beamed. "It's good to see you. I hope we haven't totally disrupted your routine by arriving so late."

"Not at all, Auntie," Grace pulled away just far enough to reassure the woman. "It's not even ten thirty, and you did warn me you might be late." She was not ready to end the embrace yet. The longer she held on to the woman, the more time she was buying to cool her tingling nerves.

But Auntie Bukky was eager to make the introductions, and Grace was soon forced to let go and look up into the dark eyes of her past. For one endless moment she locked eyes with her old friend Chuma Zeluwa, a man she had every reason to dislike, a man she still had reason to fear. Quickly calling on an inner strength, she broke the eye contact and turned to curtsy in greeting before Uncle Tunde.

"Sorry to have kept you waiting, my dear," the older man apologised. "But you know your auntie. She had the cook make all kinds of food for Chukwuma. It was as if she was afraid he had been starving since the last time she saw him."

Grace smiled at his faint Yoruba accent when he pronounced *Shukuma*. "It was no problem, sir."

"Of course I had to feed him," Auntie Bukky interjected dryly, reaching for an orange from the fruit basket on the counter. "They don't give them solid food in that America of theirs, only vegetables and fruits—no *eba*, no pounded yam. Honestly, how can anyone survive on vegetables and water?"

Grace glanced at Chuma. His mouth was slightly open and his speculative eyes were fixed on her.

"Yeah, right, Auntie," she offered in a voice shaking with nerves. "If everyone in America lived on vegetables and water we wouldn't be hearing of MacDonald's and Burger King. Fast food restaurants would have gone out of business a long time ago."

In the ensuing laughter she stole another glance at Chuma. He was still staring at her and slowly shaking his head, as though he was in shock, as though he couldn't believe his eyes. But he recovered well enough to lift a well-shaped brow and press his lips into a perfunctory smile. His watchful eyes remained trained on her face, and it was difficult for her to keep breathing normally.

"Well, you won't get any arguments from me there," he finally said. His voice was husky and deeper than she remembered. "I like my pounded yam and *egusi* soup any day."

"Then you are in the right place," Auntie Bukky proclaimed with pleasure. "My sister's hotel has the best Nigerian food in all of Jos—assorted dishes from all over Nigeria. She's away on vacation right now, and Grace here is managing the hotel in her absence. You're in good hands here with our Grace—she'll take care of you."

She linked her arm with Chuma's and proudly turned to Grace. "This is my godson, Chukwuma, the one I told you about this morning."

Trusting the Lord to help her, Grace stretched a hand to him and smiled brightly into his eyes. "Chuma Zeluwa, right?" she angled her head, managing to keep her voice steady. "When Auntie Bukky gave me your name I thought it might just be my friend Chuma from Government College, Benin. One look at you and I knew I was right. You haven't changed at all."

It was his turn to hold her hand and look into her eyes. He smiled politely and looked as though he wanted to say something, but she hurriedly pulled her hand free.

Turning to Auntie Bukky, she quickly launched into her prepared speech. "I remember him from my secondary school. He was in his A Levels when I was in SS2. He was the best student actor in our drama society at school. We all knew him, but of course, being a star, he didn't know most of us. I have been watching all these years to see if he made it to the big screen. Everyone who knew him back then would be disappointed that he didn't," she concluded, suddenly out of breath.

There was a slight pause as Auntie Bukky tried to understand what she was saying. "Oh my goodness! This is wonderful. You two know each other? You were in secondary school together?"

"Yes, Ma."

"That must have been what? Ten years ago?"

"Yes." Grace bobbed her head. "Almost 11 years. It really is a small world, as they say."

Auntie Bukky stared at her in surprise. "I didn't know you attended Government College, Benin. You never said anything. That was one of the best schools in the Midwest for a long time. Chukwuma, do you remember Grace?"

He squinted and turned his gaze to her, and for a few seconds she had to endure his quiet scrutiny. Her fears surged as she waited. He must have seen the apprehension on her face and decided to cut her some slack because his chin finally tilted in acknowledgement. "Yes, I remember her."

She heard a hesitation in his voice and waited for the axe to fall. He had not known her as Grace. "I remember umm ... Grace. She was one of the school nerds, if my memory serves me well, never too far away from her biology textbook. We all expected she would end up in medical school. Did you?"

Grace shook her head, painfully aware of the pairs of eyes closely observing them and totally relieved he hadn't exposed her.

"Well, well, well." Auntie Bukky eyed Grace from above her eyeglasses. "School nerd? Biology textbook? Grace, what is Chukwuma talking about?"

"Nothing!" Grace turned to him. "You're not going to start telling tales out of school now, are you? Your godmother here thinks all I know how to do is to play the keyboard and manage a hotel."

"Both of which you do admirably, my dear. I just never knew you were the academic type. Your girls are both doing very well, mind you, and I have always wondered if they got their brains from you or from their father."

Grace swallowed and caught her breath. "Believe me, Auntie, they got their smarts from their father, not from me."

There, it was out. How long could she have expected to keep her children a secret from him if he would be staying for a month anyway? Everyone who knew her knew about her girls. And he would probably meet them when they came back for the Easter break if he was still around.

"Girls? You have kids?" His voice was sharp. His keen eyes bore straight into her soul.

Grace prayed silently for Auntie Bukky to drop the subject. "I'll tell you all about it later. Why don't we just check you in now and we can all retire? Tomorrow is Sunday and some of us go to church early."

Uncle Tunde came to her rescue. "I agree. We should be on our way."

"But this is amazing," Auntie Bukky enthused. As though she hadn't heard her husband, she anchored her handbag on the reception desk and watched as Grace's hand flew over the computer keyboard. She began to peel the orange in her hand with a small knife.

"Things couldn't have worked out more perfectly." She grinned at Chuma. "I was worried I would be too busy to show you around Jos, but this is fantastic. Grace will definitely take care of you. She might even throw in a personal tour of the city while you two catch up on each other's lives."

Chuma nodded. "I'll look forward to that."

Grace prayed that her composure would hold as she broke into nervous laughter. Auntie Bukky was funny. A personal tour for Chuma? Not if she had any say in the matter.

"Of course I'll be glad to help in any way I can," she said in her most professional voice. "Jos is a beautiful city with lots to do and see. We offer sightseeing tours every Saturday to our guests. We have a standing contract with the Jos City Tourism company, so our guests get special tours. We'll have to arrange something for you." She pressed a few more buttons and clicked the mouse pointer on the print icon.

"But more of that later. Here." She pulled out the paper from the printer and marked an "x" at the beginning of some lines. "You're checked in to Unit 11b for three weeks. Please initial on these two lines and sign down here. Would you like a beverage before you retire?"

"Water will be fine," he muttered.

She watched his long fingers scribble on the dotted lines. His nails were long and neatly cut. He must have seen a manicurist recently, she thought, and hurriedly looked away when he looked up.

"There's bottled water in the fridge in your apartment. You will find the instructions for the Internet and WIFI connections in the welcome letter on the table in your suite." She lifted the handset and punched some numbers on the telephone pad. "I'll get the porter to take your luggage and show you to your suite."

She was conscious of his eyes as she waited for someone to pick up the phone on the other end. Instead of staring back, she focussed on the room, relieved that the simple, refined surroundings smacked of elegance and good taste.

Thankfully, Uncle Tunde engaged Chuma in discussion over their plans for the next day. She couldn't resist staring then, watching as he spoke quietly and easily to his hosts. He must have grown several inches taller since they last met. As a teenager his looks had been handsome and boyish, but now as a man his face had grown more angular, his nose straighter than she remembered and his hair was cut in a modern style that enhanced the natural pattern of tight waves and ridges forming circular patterns around his head. He wore a brown blazer over a black T-shirt and jeans, and she could see he had maintained his athletic physique over the years.

Good for him, she thought, and looked away when he turned her way. A shiver of apprehension tingled down her spine.

The porter came then and picked up his luggage. Chuma didn't linger after that, quickly bidding his hosts a good night before turning to Grace. If he wished her a good night's rest she didn't quite hear it as she was not looking at him.

It was only after she watched him walk down the sidewalk to his apartment that she congratulated herself. This was round one, and by her estimation, she had aced it. He had broken into her world, learned about her children and the world had not come crashing down on her head. Why had she even panicked? She could do this. She really could maintain a polite friendship with him for the duration of his stay at Sonshine Estate. All she needed was to make sure she saw as little of him as possible. The fact that he was here at the behest of their employer's sister would even be a strong enough motive for the hotel staff to attend to him specially. It could be that she had nothing to worry about after all.

Chapter 6

Calabar

"It looks like we have visitors," Egoyibo observed from the passenger seat in Añuli's car. She did not recognise the Peugeot station wagon parked in front of her house. The vehicle bore out-of-state licence plates, and the dirt and dust on the body spoke of a long journey. Her husband's Toyota was not in sight. She frowned. The last thing she needed was strangers in her home while her husband was away. A dull ache settled over her heart, and she closed her eyes to knead her forehead as she completed how to escape seeing them. Why couldn't people phone you before they visited? How could they just show up and expect you to be waiting for them?

She turned to look at Añuli, but her daughter shook her head before she could utter a word.

"No, Mama."

"Añuli, please!"

"Nope." She stubbornly shook her head. "I'm not coming in. It's been a long, long day and all I need now is to get back to my flat, take a cool bath and hit my bed."

"Just until your father comes home, Añuli. Please."

But the girl was resolute. "Mama, look at the time. Tomorrow is Monday and I have to be at work early. Besides,

Papa will soon be home. It's already quarter past seven. Doesn't he eat dinner promptly at seven o'clock?"

"Yes, but today is the first Sunday of the month, and he's gone for the Umuebere Progressive Union meeting. I'm not expecting him back soon."

The familiar sound of the Toyota interrupted their conversation. Ego sighed with relief and unbuckled her seatbelt while Anuli switched off the car engine and stepped out to greet her father. Ego was not prepared to answer her husband's questions about why she didn't come for the village meeting, so she picked up her handbag and walked toward the front door. Greeting the visitors was a preferred option to confronting her husband's disapproval.

"Mama, you're still coming on Thursday, aren't you?" Anuli's voice floated to her. "You know nobody cooks *okazi* soup like you."

Ego stopped to smile wryly at the young girl. "You don't have to bribe me with flattery, Anuli. I've already bought the ingredients. I'll be there."

She waved to her daughter and took a deep breath before stepping into the house to greet their visitors. There were five of them: two older men, two women and a little boy. Ego recognised one of the women and smiled.

"Beatrice! What a surprise! It's been a long, long time! How are you?"

"I'm fine, Ma." The younger girl fell on her knees in curtsy.

Ego took her hand and brought her close for a hug. "It's been a long time o! How come you remembered us today? It's been what?—almost five years now. My husband told me you went back to Nsukka."

"Yes, ma."

"Are you still at Nsukka? Are you working at the university? Or are you back in Calabar?"

The girl cleared her throat before replying. "I still live at Nsukka, ma, but I'm not working at the university anymore."

Ego felt Beatrice's lithe body shudder against hers before she withdrew from her embrace. From the way the girl kept her eyes focussed on the floor tiles and bit on her lower lip, Ego sensed that she was nervous and uptight. She turned to the older folks in her sitting room, obviously family members of the young girl who had been her husband's secretary six years ago.

"These are my parents, ma." Beatrice did the honours. "My father, Mr. Godwin Ogbalu, my mother, Mrs. Elizabeth Ogbalu, and my uncle, Mr. Obinna Ogbalu."

Ego bent her knees and enthusiastically welcomed them to her home. "What brings you this way? Are you all on holiday around here?"

Nobody responded. Instead, they all seemed to glance at the young boy Mrs. Ogbalu was carrying in her arms. He seemed to be about four or five years old. The boy returned Ego's stare with steady eyes and didn't respond when she touched him. He leaned tightly into his grandmother's bosom and turned away. Ego would not be deterred. She smiled and opened her hands, as though to carry him, but the boy covered his face with his hands and mumbled something meant to keep her away.

"Is this your baby?" she turned to Beatrice.

The girl had been pregnant when she quit her job at the university and moved away from Calabar. When rumours of her pregnancy had started to spread round the campus, Ego had worried about her, knowing from experience Odili's hypercritical nature and the societal ridicule that pregnant unmarried girls could be subjected to. The fact that Beatrice's family lived 600 kilometres away had made her pity the girl more. But strangely, Beatrice had warded off every attempt Ego had made to get close, and when Odili came home one day and announced that his secretary had quit her job and moved home to her family, Ego had been relieved.

"Yes, madam, this is my son. His name is George."

"Ah-ha! George." Ego tried again, slowly, testing the name, playfully touching the boy's legs. She reached to pat the boy's cheeks but he slapped her hand away and turned into the other side of his grandmother's bosom. Smiling, Ego reached out to his sides and began to gently tickle him. He twisted this way and that, and although he still clung to his grandmother, she detected the smile he was trying hard to hide. Beatrice's parents and uncle followed her actions. When the boy's laughter burst out, his relatives laughed with him and Ego was glad.

"I hope you haven't been waiting for too long. Has Ulunma offered you some *kola*?" she asked, even though she could see the pitcher of water and the tumblers her house girl had presented the visitors. As far as she could tell, they hadn't touched any of it.

"Yes, she has, but we wanted to wait for your husband to come home before we eat or drink anything. We have come to discuss some serious issues with him, not to eat his food or drink his water," one of the men responded.

"Odili is just parking his car. He will be in shortly."

She saw the two men exchange a glance and felt tension in the living room. Was it her imagination or did Beatrice and her mother exchange a guarded look? Even the little boy's expression seemed to have become cautious at the mention of her husband's name. Ego hoped there was nothing wrong.

The fitful glances between the visitors continued, and by the time Odili stepped into the parlour the atmosphere was so charged you could hear a pin drop on the black and white floor tiles.

His shock at the sight of their visitors was palpable too, at least to Ego. His eyes went straight to Beatrice, and the two looked at each other for what seemed like eternity. When her husband's gaze shifted from his former secretary to her young son, Ego felt a nervous flutter in her stomach.

"What are you doing here?" Odili addressed his question to Beatrice.

For the first time in as long as she could remember, Ego heard a trace of fear in her husband's voice, and she shook her head, hoping to whisk away whatever bad news the visitors might deliver.

"I ..." The girl's voice shook. She cast a nervous glance at her mother and suddenly fell silent.

It was her father's angry voice that finally responded to Odili. "Mr. Man, na you be Odili Okolie?"

Ego watched as her husband turned guarded eyes to the older man. "Yes. Yes, I am Odili Okolie." There was something else in his voice, something she couldn't quite identify.

"Then what nonsense question are you asking my daughter? You know why we are here. Why are you pretending?"

The flutter in the pit of Ego's stomach intensified. *Oh my God, what is happening?* She crossed her fingers on her chest and watched with mounting unease the scene developing before her.

"No, sir, I ... I don't know why you are here."

Ego listened carefully. Her husband's voice was small. Hoarse. Shaky. Fearful. *Guilty?* Another sliver of apprehension slithered down her body.

Odili looked at her but his words were directed at the visitors. "No, I don't know why you are here. But you look like you have travelled a long distance today. Our elders say that no matter the sweetness of a conversation, it should never take the place of food. Why don't you all relax and eat something first? Then we can talk. Ego, please bring them some refreshments."

The second man spoke up. "We don't want your food, Mr. Man. We are here on a mission, and you know what it is. This matter has gone on for too long. It must be resolved today. You have been dodging every attempt to discuss with us over the phone, and this is why we decided to come. We want to settle this today."

She tried to read her husband's mood in the silence that ensued. All she heard was his deep sigh and the loud cracking of his knuckles.

"*Nn'anyi*," she entreated Beatrice's father. "Surely it can't be that bad. My husband is right. You all have travelled on a long journey, and you have never been to our home before. Let us welcome you properly, and then you can discuss your mission with my husband. It is because the teeth have no one to direct them that they go in a zigzag path. Let me bring some *kola*. When you have eaten and refreshed yourselves, you can discuss your issues with a calm spirit and with wisdom."

The old man seemed to consider her words for only one second before he dismissed it. "I respect you, madam, but this is not a social visit. We did not drive hundreds of kilometres from Nsukka to Calabar to eat kola. Your husband knows why we are here, and the sooner he tells us what we want to hear, the sooner we will be on our way."

Ego turned toward Beatrice and her mother. "What about you, madam? Won't you even drink water?" she asked gently but received only a harrumph and a deep frown for her trouble.

"I repeat that I do not know what you want," Odili stated again and sat down. "I do not even know who you are. I'm prepared to be hospitable because of Beatrice here, who used to be my secretary, and I assume you are members of her family. But if you have come to my house to look for trouble, you give me no choice but to ask you to leave immediately. My wife does not need your stress, neither do I."

The visitors rounded on him with open-mouth shock. The older man, Beatrice's father, began to laugh in amusement. "Haba! Mr. Sugar Daddy. You have no shame o! You have no shame at all! A man cannot throw away the stone he used to break palm kernel. Not so? If he does, he will look for it again when his hunger returns."

Ego watched her husband shake his head as though he was annoyed by the old man's words. Her apprehension increased. Why did the man refer to Odili as *Mr. Sugar Daddy*? Why was Odili not outraged and protesting?

"Look, I don't know what you are talking about. I don't understand your proverb. You must either spell it out or leave my house now. But if this is something we need to discuss in private, then maybe I can ask my wife to excuse us. *Ngbo*, Ego?"

The old man threw his head back and roared with angry sarcasm. "It is now you want to remember your wife, *eh kwa*? It is now that you want her to excuse you. No! Let her stay.

This matter affects her also; it even affects your daughter if she's around. It affects your whole family."

What had her husband done again? Ego wondered. She hoped the man was wrong, that whatever it was did not concern her. Since her older daughter's death years ago, she had resolutely kept to herself and avoided associations with her husband's social or public relationships. Had she become like the ostrich? While she buried her head in the sand, was her bottom exposed for the world to see? What had Odili done again?

"Beatrice"—she turned to the younger girl—"what is this about? Did my husband offend you while you worked for him? Does he owe you any money?"

"It's nothing of the sort, Ego." Odili came to her then, reaching for her arm. "Please excuse us for a few minutes. I'll explain later."

"No, I want to know what this is about." She moved away from his reach. "What have you done, Odili? Why are these people angry with you?"

She shifted her gaze again to the strangers in her home, watching Beatrice's mother, then her father, and finally the uncle. Despite their anger, she could see they also seemed uncomfortable, even nervous. Each looked away from the question in her eyes.

"Beatrice?"

"It's because of George, ma," the young girl finally said.

"George? Your son?" Panic began to fill her chest. "What does Odili have to do with your son?"

"Everything, ma."

"Beatrice, stop it!" There was no mistaking the fear in Odili's voice this time.

"*Oga* has everything to do with my George, ma." The girl continued quietly. "Na him give me belly. George na his pikin."

That was all Ego heard before her head began to spin. Heat spread through her body and she felt stabbing pains in her chest. A vigorous twist in her stomach caused her to double over and her vision clouded. She heard Odili shout and saw him come toward her but she managed to wave him aside as she stumbled out of the living room. She barely made it to the bathroom before the contents of her stomach emptied into the washbasin.

Chapter 7

Jos

After their meeting the previous Saturday night, Grace knew Chuma would want to speak with her, but she managed to stay out of his way all of Sunday and Monday. By the time she heard his voice on the phone on Tuesday morning, around eight o'clock, she was not completely surprised.

"You and I need to talk," he started without preamble. "Can you meet me for lunch?"

"How did you get my cellphone number? I don't remember giving it to you."

"Aunty Bukky gave it to me."

She closed her eyes and tried to speak calmly. "I see. I'm sorry I can't go out with you. I'm busy."

"You're not. You're avoiding me."

"Why would I do that?"

"You tell me."

She sighed. "I don't have time for this, Chuma. Just tell me what you want so I can go back to my work."

"You heard me the first time. We need to talk."

"Really? I don't think so. You and I don't have anything to say to each other."

"Sure we do. We have a lot of catching up to do."

"Not you and I. Catching up is what friends do when they meet after a long time. You and I are not friends. You said you never wanted to see me again, remember?"

She heard him let out a deep breath. "Okay, I deserved that. But on Saturday, when Auntie Bukky was talking about your children, you said you would fill me in about your life, didn't you?"

Her children. Her fingers tightened around the cell phone. What could he know about her children? What had Auntie Bukky told him?

"I know you're married and have a family now." His voice was low and husky. A flush of heat spread over her chest and she shuddered. Once beaten, they say, twice shy. She had to be really careful.

"I know you don't owe me any explanation but I do have some things to say to you, and I would like you to hear me out."

Still, she said nothing.

"And what's this 'Grace' business? Is that a pet name?"

She closed her eyes and covered the bottom of the cell phone with her hand so he wouldn't hear her uneven breathing. If she remembered anything about him, it was that he wouldn't rest until he had his say. He would probe until he got to the root of an issue.

"Let's meet for lunch," he went on smoothly. "I have a meeting at the Ambassador Hotel this morning but I'll be done by noon. I can meet you at the hotel lobby at quarter past?"

Grace swallowed, managing to remain calm. For all her determination to steer clear of him, a small part of her yearned to hear what he had to say, to learn what he'd been doing with his life. She knew they had to talk some time, and his suggestion that they meet away from the hotel was definitely better than the curiosity their meeting anywhere at Sonshine Estate would generate.

"Hello, are you still there?"

Grace closed her eyes and for a moment remembered how she used to be enchanted with that voice. Thank goodness she was no longer the foolish teenager she used to be. She was 26 years old, a grown woman in her own rights, and it would take more than a husky voice and an expensive lunch at a prestigious hotel to deceive her.

"Oh, all right, lunch then, but not a long one. I have a heavy workload. All the suites are fully rented, and I have to be around and available to the guests."

"I will try not to keep you long, I promise. And congratulations on your hotel. One only hears about the inefficiencies in the Nigerian system, but we all forget to recognise people like you who against all odds are providing service worthy of commendation by all standards. You should be proud of Sonshine Estate."

She heard the smile in his voice and refused to let down her guard. "I'm sure the owner will be glad to hear that. As you may have heard from your godmother, her younger sister owns and runs the hotel. I'm only helping out in her absence."

"I think you are doing a great job."

She didn't know how to respond to his compliment, so she kept quiet.

"I'll see you at noon," he said finally, and hung up.

Chuma was waiting in the lobby of the Ambassador Hotel when Grace showed up that afternoon. She detected the subtle admiration in his eyes and wondered if she'd made a mistake with her choice of clothes. She stiffened as his eyes travelled over her. She had chosen a flowered dark blue *ankara* ankle-length skirt, camisole and jacket, which she had been told accentuated her slim body. Her twisted kinky hair fell loosely down her shoulders. Her makeup consisted of the slightest shades of powders, mascara and lipstick. High heels and a matching handbag completed her professional look. Hopefully he would remember that she was supposed to be a married woman and not think she was anxious to impress him.

"Hi there," he said, reaching a hand as though to pull her to his side in a hug.

Retrieving her hand, she put some space between them and watched him warily. When he smiled at her she looked away, determined not to be influenced by his charms.

"My apologies. I have to keep reminding myself that you are a married woman now. It's still a lot to take in."

He led her to a door marked "Sahara Diner" toward a table for two at a private corner. She sat on the chair he pulled out opposite him and made a point of checking out the decor. The lunch-hour crowd at the hotel was beginning to build. She observed, as she usually did whenever she visited the hotel, that the business atmosphere of the Ambassador Hotel was a direct contrast to the homey, relaxed ambience Sonshine Estate provided for its guests. Thankfully, their outfit had carved out an exclusive niche for itself in catering to large families on holidays and was not in competition with any of the five-star hotels.

"Very nice," she commented truthfully, her tone as casual as she could muster.

A waiter appeared at their table to take their drink order. She was surprised that he ordered only a Coke. Some exotic wine would have been more down his alley. In turn, she asked for a glass of iced tea.

"I hope you are hungry." He stared at the menu the waiter had left for them and smiled. "I missed breakfast this morning, so I am quite famished. What will you have?"

She hesitated only briefly. "Well, this hotel is famous for its seafood salad. I think I'll have some of that."

He shut the menu and tossed it aside. "I'll have the fish pepper soup and some vegetable salad. I meant what I said the other night, you know. I like Nigerian food."

"Even *fufu*?" She was sceptical.

"Even fufu."

Grace made a face. She couldn't help it, and she was disconcerted when he burst out laughing.

"Why the face? Don't you like to swallow?"

"I don't like fufu." She shook her head. "I like pounded yam and eba but not fufu."

"Ah! You don't know what you're missing. I like them all—garri, eba, fufu. I can eat fufu with correct *egusi* soup any day."

She had to smile at this. "And how often do you get to eat this in the America? Maybe you're just missing Nigerian food. If you lived here and could eat fufu every day, you may not be so enthusiastic."

"I don't think so. Up until two years ago I could only eat Nigerian food at parties and special events. But God smiled on me two years ago when my sister, Zola, got married and came to live in Chicago." He shrugged. "Right now, my wish is her command. I only need to pick up the phone and she delivers whatever I want to my apartment."

Her smile grew wider at his expression, and she felt her defences slightly relaxing. She cautioned herself. She had to be very careful.

After the waiter brought their drinks, she plunged straight into the reason for their meeting. "What do you really want, Chuma? You and I have nothing to say to one another."

"Says the lady who fainted the moment she laid eyes on me at the Jubilee power conference, and then turned tail and ran away before I could say anything to her."

"What?" she countered. "First of all, Chuma, I didn't faint because of you. And secondly, I didn't run away from you. I left the camp because I was sick and needed medical attention."

He continued to hold her gaze, his eyes telling her he didn't believe her. "Well, good for you," he finally conceded. "But you know, you actually beat me to it. I almost fainted when I realised who I was looking at that day. I'm not sure how I made it through the rest of that evening. Or the next day, when I heard you had left the camp."

"You almost fainted when you saw me?"

He nodded slowly. "Yes, and I would have if you hadn't fainted yourself. You see, when you have lived for a decade believing someone you knew was dead, you don't suddenly see her alive without experiencing some shock. I was totally shocked to see you."

Grace was rescued from responding by the arrival of the waiter with their order. Chuma's words confused her. Something wasn't adding up.

As soon as they were alone again she frowned at him. "You thought I was dead? Seriously?" Part of her expected that he was joking, but he wasn't smiling. She exhaled quietly. "Well, as you can see, I'm very much alive."

He considered her words for a moment and to her relief didn't pursue the topic. "And two children. I'll say you've done very well for yourself."

Grace's fingers tightened around the glass. She stared at her iced tea for a few seconds. Why did he keep referring to the children? "Look, Chuma—" she started but then stopped.

"Yes?"

But she only shook her head. "Forget it."

He lifted his hands in surrender. "I know. It's none of my business." He then added deliberately, as though daring her to deny it, "But you know, I can't help thinking that if I hadn't acted so stupidly years ago I may have been the one you married. Your husband is one lucky man."

Stunned into speechlessness, Grace stared at him. She wondered if he'd been drinking before she joined him. Or maybe she wasn't hearing properly because not once in her life had she seriously imagined she would hear those words from his lips.

"Acted stupidly?"

He nodded gravely. "You don't know how much I wish I could turn back the hands of the clock. I would have handled things very differently given the same circumstances."

She shut her eyes to suppress the anger flaring within her. Was this why he had invited her for lunch—to make a token confession and get absolution for how he'd treated her?

"Chuma, don't tell me you called me here to say you regret your actions years ago because I honestly don't want to hear it. I am not the same impressionable girl you knew at Government College. I am a grown woman now and I'm not easily fooled by flattery."

Chuma looked like she'd kicked him in the gut. He winced and started to say something but changed his mind. Instead, he picked up his fork and nodded to her. "Do you want to say the grace with me?"

"No."

"Nevertheless ..." After bowing over his food, he lifted his spoon and blew gently at the hot liquid before sipping some.

Reluctantly she picked up her fork and took a bite of her salad. It tasted good. She looked up to see his eyes bearing down on her, the hint of a smile lurking deep within them. "What do you think?"

"You're right," she conceded. "It tastes good."

He chuckled at her admission. "I won't say I told you so."

As they ate they talked about the food, compared Sonshine Estate with Ambassador Hotel, they even talked about the mild Jos weather, which he said he liked.

She was wiping her mouth when he suddenly asked, "Aren't you even curious about me?"

"Excuse me?" She looked up and was struck by the pleasure he made no attempt to conceal as he held her gaze. She remembered that Chuma had a way of giving someone his whole attention when the person spoke and it could be quite unnerving, like now.

"You don't seem to be interested in knowing what I've been up to in the past decade."

She shrugged. "No, I'm not interested."

"Ah." He bit his lower lip. "I'm glad to see you've not entirely changed. You're still the frank and outspoken girl I used to know."

She looked away, but he was not done. "Have you kept in touch with your friends from Government College?"

"Like who?"

"Your roommate, Pamela Ighodalo."

Grace's eyes widened as she shook her head slowly. "Not really. Why?"

Taking a deep breath, he lifted the glass of water to his lips and looked at her. "It was Pam who gave me your house address."

"My house address?" she blinked at him, not understanding what he meant. "Why did she do that?"

"Well, you told me your dad taught at the University of Calabar, and that you lived on campus. After you left school and didn't come back I called your father's office several times but couldn't get through. That was when I asked Pam and she gave me your home address."

Grace stared at him, not quite buying his story. "I'm not sure I understand. Why did you want to see me? You said we were through and that you never wanted to see me again."

He closed his eyes and took a deep breath. "I know. It was wrong of me to have blamed you the way I did. I'm really sorry."

Grace caught her lower lip between her teeth and shook her head. "Look, Chuma, it doesn't matter. I really don't want to talk about the past. It's over. We've moved on. Let's keep it that way."

After studying her face for endless seconds he continued quietly. "I know you don't want to talk about it, but please hear me out. I just want to let you know how sorry I was, still am, about everything."

A pregnant silence, one that seemed to stretch forever, greeted this apology. He did look sincere enough, but she didn't feel sorry for him.

She felt she had to say something. "You tried to contact me. Why?"

"Because I suddenly came to my senses. After you left my room that day I realised what I was asking you to do was to risk your life for something that was really my fault." She heard the break in his voice before he continued quietly. "The more I thought about it, the more I saw all the options open to us. But when I came to the school to talk to you, Pam told me I was too late."

Her raised eyebrow and the shaking of her head told him she didn't or wouldn't believe him.

"Pam said you took ill when you came back from the clinic," he continued, "and that you insisted on going home to your parents. That was the last any of us ever heard from you again."

That much Grace knew was true. Pam had taken her to the clinic that morning and waited until the nurse called her name before leaving. The next time Pam saw her, she'd been lying on her bed trembling with fear. Her roommate had sat with her for a whole two minutes before telling her to snap out of her guilty feelings and move on with her life. "You must think you are very special," she remembered her friend telling her. "You're not. This happens to every girl. It's part of growing up."

"Have you," she remembered asking quietly, too embarrassed to say the words out. "Have you done this before?"

"Of course I have. How else is a girl supposed to live in these modern times?" Pam had laughed without mirth.

Chuma's quiet voice brought her back to the present. "I waited for you to return to school. After one week I got very worried, so I called your father's office. When I couldn't get through I wrote you a letter but you did not reply. I wrote a second time but I still didn't get a reply. I thought I had the wrong address, but finally, after two weeks, I got a response."

He let out a shaky breath, appearing to struggle with his next words. She saw how his hands gripped the stem of his glass. "One of the letters was sent back to me with the word DECEASED written across your name."

It took her a few seconds to fully absorb the meaning of his words. "What did you just say?" she asked angrily.

"I'll show you." He lifted a hand to plead with her. "Just give me a few minutes, please." He reached for the briefcase by his side, unzipped the flaps and brought out an old flat file, which he placed in front of her. The muscles in his cheeks tightened. "Take a look at this and tell me what it all means because I do not understand."

His voice was barely a whisper. She noticed the slight tremor in his hand. After a moment's hesitation she opened the file. It was a collection of old newspaper clippings. She flipped through and checked out their titles—*Cross River Chronicle, Niger Delta Tide, Malabo Gazette, the Gong of Calabar.* Someone had marked some of the stories with bright yellow highlighter. Grace's eyes went round when she recognized herself in a picture accompanying one of the articles. She could not mistake the black and white pinafore and black beret. She turned to the headlines and tried to see where he was coming from. What did these clippings have to do with her?

Passenger Bus Plunges into Cross River—All Aboard Feared Dead ... Fatal Accident along Calabar-Ikot-Ekpene Road ... Tragedy in the Southeast Cross River death toll rises—now 73 ... Mass burial for accident victims ... Prof's daughter among the dead.

The Cross River Chronicle story caught her interest. It was dated October 15 and headlined "Prof's Daughter Laid to Rest". She lifted trembling hands to her cheeks in horror, unable to believe what she was reading. There was a photograph of her parents and her younger sister sitting by a casket in a church service.

In an inset beneath a portrait of a much younger Grace she read, *"Urenna Okolie, 15, daughter of Professor Okolie of UniCal, died September 26, 2000, when the west-bound luxurious bus she was travelling in skidded off Itu bridge and plunged into the icy waters, killing all 73 passengers. The professor's daughter was returning to school in Benin after visiting her parents."*

Goose bumps flooded over her as she kept scanning through the articles, dazed and confused. It felt weird to see her face staring at her from the obituary page of the *Weekend Star.*

"Oh my God!" She trembled. "I don't understand.... This is impossible. I ... it can't be true ... oh, God ... oh, God ..."

An envelope was attached to the last page of the file. It was addressed to her and she recognised Chuma's bad cacography. True to his account, the words "BACK TO SENDER: ADDRESSEE DECEASED" were written in perfect cursives with a bold black marker over the address and an arrow pointed to Chuma's address on the top left hand of the envelope. She bit her lips. There was only one person she knew with those cursives.

Grace closed the file, her mouth dry, and stared blindly at the collar of Chuma's shirt. She caught her lower lip between her teeth. She had thought she was over it but pain and rejection washed over her again and her eyes grew moist.

He reached across the table and folded her trembling hands in his. "That's why I was shocked when I saw you at Abuja," he continued quietly. "That's why I almost fainted. I thought I was seeing a ghost."

Grace stared at their joined hands as one tear trickled down her cheek.

"Explain it to me, Ure, why did you do it? Why did you decide to drop out of school, fabricate a wild story about your death and quietly disappear?"

She remained silent.

"And while we're still on the subject, there's another piece of the puzzle I still can't figure out, maybe you can help me there too. My third letter to you had been marked "deceased" and sent back to me even before the accident. How was that possible?"

This brought some reaction from her. She reached for the file again to check the dates. The post office stamp on the envelope was dated September 24. The accident had occurred September 26.

"I was totally devastated by the news. I blamed myself. If it hadn't been for me none of this would have happened. You would not have needed to go home at the beginning of the school year. You certainly wouldn't have been in that doomed bus. You would have been at school with your friends and preparing for your exams. I felt so guilty I wanted to die."

"You said you went to Calabar?" She wanted to know why. "Just to confirm the news?"

"Looking back ..." Chuma bit his lips and pinched the bridge of his nose, fighting for control. Grace knew a momentary pity for him.

It took a few seconds for him to find the words, but finally, he looked up again. "Looking back, I think I needed closure.

I'd hoped it was a lie, one big mix-up. I told myself that people didn't just die like that. Not people I knew anyway. It was almost three weeks after the burial that I went to Calabar to see your parents. My sister Zola went with me. You remember her, don't you?"

She nodded. How could she not? He used to talk about his sisters all the time.

"It was the most traumatic experience of my life. Zola told your mom that she was your friend at Government College and that I was her brother. They were still mourning your supposed passing when we arrived, your mother especially. She was so sad that the church kept her under suicide surveillance. She was the one who took us to the university cemetery and showed us where you, or as I know now, some girl she believed was her daughter, had been buried."

Stunned, Grace could only stare at him. His story was too bizarre.

He reached out and grabbed her hand again, desperation written into his expression. "I still need to know what happened, Ure. Why did you suddenly disappear? Who is this Grace whose name you have assumed? Was she the girl in the accident? Does your husband know you are really Urenna Okolie, or is he also part of the plan? Do your parents know you are alive?"

Chapter 8

Jos

Giving up any pretence of trying to sleep, Grace adjusted the pillow behind her and stood up from the bed. The early morning light that filtered through the skies was grey and uncertain, a worthy backdrop for her thoughts. As she stood by the window the heaviness in her heart sank lower, and she blinked back the tears that weighed heavily on her eyelids. Somewhere at the back of her mind was the doctor's warning about the devastating effects stress could have on her health.

I should have known, she thought again, for the hundredth time. *I should have known.*

Chuma's revelation should not have come as a complete shock. Her father had told her plainly the day he had beaten her up, that to him, she was better off dead than alive. All these years she had believed he had been speaking out of anger, but the letter Chuma showed her yesterday suggested that maybe he had really intended to kill her. How was that possible?

She switched on the bedside light and picked up her Bible. Over the years she had learned to find solace and comfort in the Scriptures for her worries. As she let the familiar weight rest in her hands she knew she would find in the book, promises that would console and reassure her spirit for the day. She flipped through the pages, looking for verses she had underlined, verses she had long committed to memory for a time like this.

"Don't be troubled. Trust in God. Trust also in me."

"When you pass through the waters, I will be with you; when through the rivers, they won't sweep over you. When you walk through the fire, you won't be scorched, the flame won't burn you."

"Don't fear, because I am with you; don't be afraid, for I am your God. I will strengthen you, I will surely help you; I will hold you with my righteous strong hand."

Grace closed her eyes in meditation, letting the promises echo in her mind. She knelt by her bed and prayed. *My heart is troubled, Lord. I'm afraid and I do not know what to do. Help me, my father. Protect me. Show me your will. Grant me wisdom and courage to face whatever the future may bring.*

Later, as she buttoned up a short-sleeved red blouse over her faded jeans, Grace felt some restoration of her sense of balance. Her heart was not totally at peace but she had poured it out to her heavenly father, and she had to trust that he would make it all right.

The morning was unusually dark, prompting her to check her watch as she stepped out on her way to the Rec Centre. It was only seven o'clock, but the dawning sun was almost entirely obscured by grey clouds. The wind was chilly. As she walked down the familiar path, Grace crossed her arms and rubbed her palms down her upper arms. Perhaps she should cancel her morning walk with Ayesha, she thought. She flipped open her phone and dialled her friend's number and waited but Ayesha didn't pick it up.

By the time she was done with her rounds the sky had cleared. A reluctant sunlight was gently streaming into the restaurant but the wind still felt cold. She dialled Ayesha's number again. When her friend still didn't answer, Grace decided to risk the uncertain clouds and meet her as planned.

"Ayesha!" She hugged her friend. "Long time no see! How you dey?"

As usual, Ayesha had a camera hung from her neck. "Look who's talking. You're the scarce commodity, *ke*. Person no dey see your break light again o! I called you on Saturday night and left a message but you didn't even return my call. Wetin come happen now?"

"My sister, na long story, no vex," Grace apologised as they set out on the trail. "Ooh, it's so cold. Looks like it might rain. I was calling you to cancel, but when you didn't answer I figured you had already left. Let's head back, I beg."

"Shhh!" Ayesha stopped suddenly and pointed. Grace watched as she turned her camera lens on a huge grasshopper trying its best to blend in with the green leaves. At the flash of the camera it flew off. "I'm making an album of tropical animals for the children at the orphanage. You'd be surprised at how many species I've found so far. See, on my way here, I got this long column of soldier ants. When I turn the zoom lens you can actually see their powerful pinchers. Look!"

Grace recoiled at the photographs, as Ayesha anticipated she would, at which she laughed.

The weather cleared slightly as the two ladies caught up with each other's news. Grace felt like a fraud, for although she truly liked Ayesha and the two were best friends, she had never disclosed to her the details of her past. She had tried her best to move on with her life, seeing no possibility of ever meeting Chuma again. She had never anticipated that he would suddenly show up in Sonshine Estate of all places, and after 11 years! It was too bizarre. And now, try as she could, she didn't know how to broach the subject with her friend.

"You said you wanted to ask me a favour," Grace reminded her. "What's up?"

"Two things. First, I heard that someone has finally made an offer for Gidan Mairo."

Grace shook her head helplessly. "I overheard Bola and Edith talking about it on Saturday. Is it true?"

"Apparently so, because Idris sent word that he will be coming for a property inspection on Saturday. The only other time he's ever done an inspection was when he was taking inventory of the properties he inherited from his mother. It was soon after the inspection that he put the building on the market."

"But why would he keep this a secret? Are you sure there's really an offer?"

"My sister, nobody knows for sure." Ayesha shrugged. "But he's coming for an inspection on Saturday. Matron wants all of us to pitch in to clean up the place; she wants everywhere neat and tidy. I won't be around in the morning, so I'm hoping you will stand in for me."

"Why won't you be around? Are you travelling?"

"No, I'm not travelling, but Madam Lois came in yesterday and she wants me to accompany her to Bishop Zahra's special deliverance night vigil on Friday night. If I go, I can't be at the orphanage before noon on Saturday."

"Oh, Ayesha! Not again!" Grace turned anxious eyes toward her friend.

Ayesha shook her head and looked away. "She has a friend in the bishop's deliverance team who has arranged a special audience for us. Madam Lois knows somebody the bishop prayed for who is now six months pregnant. I might be so lucky."

Grace frowned. Ayesha's words were not enthusiastic. And no wonder, because in the five years that she had been married and trying to have a baby, her anxious mother-in-law, convinced that evil spirits had locked her womb, had taken her to different prayer houses, to several "giant" men and women of God who boasted they could pray the strong prayers that were needed to set her free to conceive and bear children. One failure story after another over the years was enough to make anyone lose hope. Even more worrisome to Grace was that her friend seemed helpless to say no to her mother-in-law.

"Do you think it's wise for you to be following Madam Lois to all these places?"

Ayesha shrugged again. "I don't want her to think I'm ungrateful. She's doing her best for me. Many other mothers-in-law would have kicked their barren daughters-in-law out of the home long ago. She's been nothing but kind and patient with me."

"Ayesha, stop calling yourself barren. You're not. How many doctors have told you now that there's nothing wrong with either you or your husband? All the tests you have done say there's no reason you can't have your own baby in due time."

"But it's been five years, Grace. I've been trying for five years. When will this 'due time' come? Girls who got married long after I did now have two, three children, but I'm still waiting." Ayesha looked away before mumbling under her breath, "I'm not sure whose prayers God answers these days, but he doesn't answer mine."

"Please don't say that."

"And the worst thing is I suspect I'm going into early menopause."

Grace rolled her eyes and shook her head in disbelief. "Why do you say such things about yourself?"

"Because it's true. My period has almost stopped. The thing has always been inconsistent but at least it always came after two or three months. The last time I saw my period was almost four months ago."

"Maybe you're pregnant."

"I wish," Ayesha scoffed. "The last time it was this late I thought I was pregnant but on the day I was planning to go to the clinic to check, the thing came out in full force, complete with cramps, aches and pains." Pain clouded her eyes and she sniffed as she continued. "God just has to do something for me very quickly. I am not Sarah Abraham, Grace. I don't want to have children in my old age."

Grace didn't want to argue with her friend. Otherwise she would have reminded her that the last doctor they had visited had suggested it was partly her anxiety and partly her husband's constant absence from home that might be responsible for the delay in conception. Ayesha's husband worked on an offshore rig, on a 28-days-on/21-days-off shift rotation.

"No, you're not Sarah Abraham, but you're in danger of becoming Naomi Elkanah."

"Huh?"

"Yes. Remember Naomi? She chose to believe the lie of the devil that God had dealt bitterly with her, and decided to call herself "Bitterness", not knowing that God was preparing a spot for her in the lineage of Christ."

Ayesha wiped away silent tears. "That is easy for you to say, Grace. You're not even thirty and you already have two children. I'm hitting thirty-five on my next birthday."

Just then there was a flash of lightning, followed by a loud clap from the darkening skies—a roar of thunder strong enough to force the girls to stop in their track and reassess the sky. A fierce wind whirled around them, threatening to bring down the rain. Grace didn't want to be trapped by a heavy downpour, but there were things she had to tell her friend. So when the wind died down, she took Ayesha's hand.

"The Lord answers our prayers in different ways. The last time we spoke, you said you would look into invitro fertilization. Have you been to the doctor?"

"Yes, but Nelson says we can't afford it. Besides, I've heard many Christians preach against in vitro. Madam Lois won't even hear of it. She's convinced that the children conceived through invitro cannot be normal. It's God that gives children, not doctors."

Another loud clap of thunder reverberated, this one closer than before. The girls looked up as a bolt of lightning flashed across the sky. There was only one thing to do.

"Let's run for it," Grace suggested, sprinting off immediately in the direction they had just come from. By the time they reached the hotel gates, huge raindrops were falling and they were soaking wet and out of breath. Thankfully there were no guests in the dining room.

"Where's everybody?" Ayesha panted.

"Room service, I think." Grace shook the water from her tresses. She hurried into a bathroom and emerged with two towels, handing one to her friend. "I would rather be indoors in this type of weather too."

Thick, dark clouds, strong winds, thunder and lightning all combined into one of the heaviest downpours Grace had seen in Jos that year. The howling wild winds beat down on the RC, threatening damage. Thankfully, the building held on.

Soon the electricity went off. Grace was not worried because a typical rainstorm in Jos wouldn't last longer than two or three hours. She rather liked the stillness and silence that followed the power failure. No humming fridge or air-conditioner, no whining thread mill, and none of those commercials from the television—only the splatter of the rain on the roof and on the trees and on the flowers, and the sound of the flooding waters as they rushed through valleys and crevices in the ground. When she was much younger, rainy days were fun days. She used to enjoy running around in the rain with her sister, each balancing buckets or basins on their heads to gather rain water and getting deliciously drenched in the process.

Someone switched on a small battery-operated radio in the kitchen. Grace offered to turn off all the appliances. She lowered the window louvers to let in more sunlight while Ayesha went into the kitchen to check the progress on their breakfast order.

Grace heard a voice from the gym, a woman's laughter. She approached the gym door guardedly, wondering how she could help the guest return to her apartment in the pouring rain. She did not expect to see Chuma standing by the elliptical trainer and Remi, the assistant cook's daughter, churning the wheels of a spinning bike. Grace must have made a sound because they immediately turned to her and for a few seconds the stillness around her intensified and the world around her faded as she met his eyes.

"What a wet day it's turning out to be," Remi exclaimed brightly, effectively breaking the silence. "Where have you been, Grace? I thought your madam left you in charge of her hotel."

Grace ignored the barb and glanced politely at Chuma. "Hi."

He nodded. "How are you?" he asked quietly, placing emphasis on the age-old greeting. They had not seen since she ran out on him from the restaurant at Ambassador Hotel two days ago.

"I'm fine, thank you." She responded with a polite smile.

"Chucks was just telling me how badly he misses the tropical rains in Nigeria. And I was telling him I could trade all this rain for just a *li'rl* snow. I have never seen snow before. I can't even imagine it." Remi giggled and glanced coyly at Chuma, flicking her long braids and earning a politely amused glance from him.

Grace scowled. So he was *Chucks* now? And what's with the phoney accent?

"Are you coming for breakfast?" Grace asked Chuma.

"Sure," Chuma and Remi answered in unison. She looked pointedly at Remi. The fact that her mother worked in the kitchen didn't automatically earn her a free meal.

Remi eyeballed Grace for a few seconds before she turned to Chuma with a pout. "Aren't you glad I decided to come and visit you this morning? You would have been sitting at the breakfast table all by yourself ... all by your lonely self. You've got to pay for my time now," she added prettily.

Grace's raised eyebrow was lost on the other girl. Watching her flirt with Chuma, Grace concluded, not for the first time, that Remi was a truly beautiful girl. She was as dark complexioned as Grace was fair, not as tall but definitely more rounded. She was also a lot more social and outgoing than Grace could ever hope to be. Still, it was with difficulty that she kept a straight face when Remi tucked in her tummy and swayed her curves in a catwalk in front of a bewildered-looking Chuma. No wonder Mama Remi constantly worried about her daughter.

Ayesha's eyes widened as they filed in. Remi must have given her a hostile look because Grace could almost see her friend's hackles rise as she came toward them.

She stretched out a hand to Chuma. "I don't believe we have met before. My name is Ayesha," she started. "Grace is my friend. You must be Auntie Bukky's godson. We've all heard about you. She mentioned you would be staying at Sonshine Estate."

Grace completed the rest of the introductions, but Ayesha was not done. "Have you guys had breakfast yet? How about you join Grace and me? There's enough room at this table for all of us."

Before Chuma could respond, Remi shook her head and smiled brightly at Ayesha. "Not today, Ayesha. Chucks and I are in the middle of planning for the plateau tour on Saturday. Besides, Auntie Bukky wants me to go over the logistics of the reception party she's giving for him soon, so if you'll both excuse us." Remi's eyes swept over Ayesha triumphantly before she led Chuma toward a table at the far end of the restaurant, leaving the girls to stare after them.

Ayesha finally sat down and loudly exhaled. "That girl is crazy, and that guy is in trouble. I'll bet his godmother doesn't know about this."

Grace made no comment as she sat opposite her friend and poured hot water into a mug. It was none of their business. He was old enough to look after himself, and if he couldn't see through Remi's character, he had only himself to blame. As far as she was concerned, there was a limit to what anyone would allow for the sake of politeness. He would have to set his own boundaries.

Settling back in her chair, Ayesha watched Grace. "You okay?"

"Yes, of course. Why?"

"I'm not sure. You just seem … different all of a sudden."

Grace felt different, but she didn't understand why. Or how to put it into words. "I guess it's really none of our business who Auntie Bukky's godson decides to spend time with during his visit to Jos. Besides, Remi lives in Auntie Bukky's boys' quarters, so they do have some things in common."

Ayesha seemed to consider Grace's response while she took another bite of her sliced bread.

"Tell me," Grace invited, "how is Nelson doing? Will he be home for Easter?"

Ayesha took the hint and their conversation veered off to more comfortable topics. They talked about her husband and the photography studio Ayesha was hoping to open soon. She had found the perfect location, she said, right in front of Jos City Museum, and as soon as Nelson sent the money, she would be making the required deposit.

"Until then, I will focus on completing and delivering the picture project for the orphanage," she told Grace. "I know I shouldn't, but I'm secretly praying that this offer for Gidan Mairo, if indeed it exists, does not go through. I know Idris needs his money but it would be a shame if the orphanage were to shut down, even temporarily. What would happen to the children?"

Grace felt the same way. The sale price Madam Mairo's son had put on the building was so high that everyone had concluded he would never sell. It would take a corporation or a millionaire to buy the estate at that price. Not that it wasn't worth it, because the building was massive, the grounds on which it stood even more so. Years ago, during the Nigerian civil war, the estate had even served as a military garrison.

"So what time should I expect you on Saturday?" she asked Ayesha.

"Two o'clock, maybe three. The prayer vigil is from ten on Friday night to five on Saturday morning. I just need to sleep for a few hours and spend an hour or two with Madam Lois before I come over."

A burst of laughter from the table at the other end of the restaurant interrupted their quiet conversation. Luckily Ayesha was so caught up in her private issues that she only spared them a fleeting glance. Grace wondered what Chuma and Remi were talking about, but her eyes did not flicker from her toast.

"You take care of yourself, Ayesha. I'll be praying for you."

Chapter 9

Calabar

Egoyibo pulled open Añuli's deep freezer, grateful for the blast of cold air that hit her face as she rearranged the frozen food packages to make room for more. It was a hot day and there was no electric power in Añuli's apartment. She had opened all the windows and rolled up the curtains as soon as she arrived at noon, but she was still sweating from the heat.

"Something good is smelling in my flat!" Añuli announced as soon as she came back from work. "Mama, the aroma of your soup can be smelled one mile away. Hmm …" She crinkled her nose appreciatively and went to hug her mother.

Ego was pleased. She opened her pots so Añuli could check out the *okazi* and *ogbono* soups. She had also made a pot of stew and boiled a little rice.

"Wow! I have enough food for one month. Thank you, Mama. You are the best."

"Not one month, Añuli. If NEPA keeps taking the light, bring the food home so we can freeze it for you. At least we have a generator."

"Sure, I will. Can I eat now? I want to taste a little of everything."

"Go and change out of your work clothes first. I will set the table."

Later, after they had eaten, Añuli offered to wash the dishes but her mother waved her off. "You've just come back from work. I'll wash them. You go and rest for a few minutes while I finish up."

Añuli stopped protesting when her phone rang and she went to answer. As soon as she left, Ego took out the dish soap and sponge and set to work. She hummed a tuneless song as she washed, stopping frequently to wipe the silent tears that escaped from her eyes every so often. She did not want Añuli to see her crying. *I will survive*, she told herself quietly as she scrubbed the pot. *If the pain of Urenna's death did not kill me years ago, Odili's affair will not.*

When she was done, Egoyibo swept the floor and wiped the dining table. She could hear Añuli's voice still chatting away on her phone, so she went to stand by the open window to wait for her, taking in the hospital complex, the staff quarters, the student hostels and the Calabar downtown. From where she stood, Egoyibo could easily spot the city's points of interest.

When she heard Añuli's footsteps returning to the parlour she went to the faucet to splash water on her face. She was bent over the sink when the ceiling fan started to rotate and she realised the electricity was back. She waited for a few seconds before she turned on the refrigerator.

Añuli went to the sofa and began to fiddle with the TV remote control. "Thank God for the lights. I don't like it when everywhere is so hot and quiet. Come and sit down, Mama. I bought some Nigerian movies last weekend. I'll put one on so we can watch before you leave."

Ego shook her head sadly and went to sit by her daughter. "Añuli, my dear, we can't watch movies today. I have something to tell you. I'm afraid it's not good news."

Then she recounted the events that took place on Sunday evening.

When she was done, Añuli straightened and gave her a searching look. "You are joking, right?"

Ego wiped her tears with her handkerchief. "I wish I was. I wish I didn't have to tell you this, I wish it was something I could keep from you, but you need to know because it affects your future. You know our custom—now that your father has a son, everything he owns, no—everything *we* own—will go to his son when he dies. Even if I am alive when he dies, I won't be entitled to anything. His son will inherit everything."

Her frustration echoed in every syllable as her voice broke and the tears fell. "That includes the house in the village, the farms, the cars, his bank account—everything we've built over the years. You and I will be left penniless."

The stabbing pain in Ego's chest had returned several times since Sunday night, each time lasting a few more seconds. Every time it happened, she practiced the deep breathing exercises she had learned in preparation for labour years ago. Now she pressed her left breast, willing the pain to stop.

"The hypocrite!" Añuli snapped. "Is he not the same person who warned me that if I ever got pregnant before marriage he would disown me? Is he not the same person who said Urenna was a disgrace to him and drove her away because she got pregnant in secondary school? If it weren't for him, my sister would be alive today. Why the double standard? How come it is right for him to betray you with Beatrice—a girl who is young enough to be his daughter—and it is not right for anyone else?"

Ego slowly shook her head. Thankfully the pain had eased. It was strange to hear Añuli repeating the same words that had been going through her mind since Sunday. She had not even realized how strongly her daughter blamed her father for her sister's tragedy.

"Mama, I don't care about the house in the village. I don't care for his cars or bank accounts. In fact, I don't care for him at all."

Ego watched her daughter vainly try to control her feelings. She knew Añuli's passionate nature could be provoked very quickly. The girl's breathing had quickened and Ego knew she was close to tears.

"And since he already threatened to disown me, I can also disown him now. It works both ways." Añuli choked back on a sob and reached for the tissue box on the side table.

"Shhh, don't talk that way." Ego tried to hug her but Añuli wriggled out and went to the window. "He's still your father despite everything."

"Mama, please don't annoy me, don't add insult to injury." Añuli blew her nose, discarded the tissue, and took a deep breath.

"You know in your heart that I am right. He is still your father. You are a dentist today because he paid for your education. And besides, what can you do? He is not your husband or wife whom you can divorce from your life. His blood runs through your veins."

"Then you're lucky he is only your husband and not a blood relative. You don't have to put up with his insults any longer. Mama, you don't have to continue living with him! He has a new family now—complete with a son. You and I have become outsiders. Respect yourself and get out of that house before they force you out."

Ego had thought the same thing. But what would she do if she left Odili? Moving in with Añuli was out of the question. It would only complicate issues. The poor girl was not even married.

Maybe I should get a job. She had left the labour market years ago to look after her daughters, with a plan to go back once the girls were grown up. *That was when my problem started*, she thought. *If I hadn't become so dependent on Odili I wouldn't be so affected by his unfaithfulness.*

Añuli dragged a hand through her braided hair and began to pace the room, anger and tension visible in every step. She stopped and pleaded with her mother again. "Mama, you can move in here with me. I'm sure we can manage."

Ego slowly shook her head. "It is kind of you to offer, my dear, but I can't do that. You are a young woman. One of these days you will get married. You don't want to be dragging your old mother around with you. You have your own life to lead."

Ego saw the incredulous look shooting across her daughter's face. The young girl shook her head emphatically and cried, "But I'm never getting married, Mama. I will never—ever—willingly give control of my life over to anybody—man or woman. Papa has taken away your freedom, your dignity, your self-esteem and your happiness. Nobody will ever have that kind of power over me."

As their conversation continued, Ego felt the heart palpitations coming on again and began her deep breathing exercise, hoping Añuli would not notice. It was all her fault Añuli had this attitude, she acknowledged, and even now, if she was a good mother, she would be doing more to dissuade her daughter from this particular trend of thought. Instead, she understood and even agreed with her. No man was worth all this pain and suffering. Certainly not Odili.

"People are different, Añuli. Our people say that *akaraka di n'iche n'iche.* Everybody's fingerprints are different. You have a different personality from me. I am not the fighting type. If I was I wouldn't have let your father trample over me all these years. But I don't think any man can do that to you and get away with it. You are my exact opposite."

Añuli plopped on the sofa and sniffed, tears trailing down her cheeks, her feet drumming up a tattoo on the carpeted floor. Ego felt her daughter's pain, and her hand tightened with longing to hug her, but she decided to let the girl work through her emotions by herself.

When her tears ceased, Añuli turned again to her mother. "Seriously, Mama, there's got to be a way out of this misery for you. What are you going to do? You can't continue living in that house."

"I know, Añuli."

"Does he want you to leave?"

"Actually, no. He says he wants me to stay and look after the child for him."

"What?"

"Hold your fire!" Ego chuckled at the fierce anger in Añuli's eyes. "He says he will not marry Beatrice. He gave her two options that night—one, to leave the child with him and he can pay her off, or two, to take the child away with her and he will give her an allowance for his upkeep."

Añuli shook her head and hissed. "Pompous man! He's still giving ultimatums. I hope you didn't agree to raise his bastard for him. He will just set up his mistress in a flat somewhere and continue seeing her behind your back. And when they have another son they will send that one to you to babysit for them also. Ugh." She shuddered. "I don't believe that hypocrite's blood actually flows through my veins. I wish I had been adopted."

"I have sent a message to Umuebere."

"You did?"

"Yes, I called your grandfather last night and reported the matter to him."

"Why did you do that? There's nothing anybody can do now. It's already done."

Ego nodded. "I know, but your grandfather has shown me nothing but kindness since I married his son. He called your father last night, and they spoke for a long time. I didn't stay to listen. But later, he called me and said he is sending your uncles to Calabar to discuss the options with us. They'll be here next weekend."

"They're coming to tell you to accept the child," Añuli commented, matter-of-factly. "After all, he's a boy."

"You're probably right. I know I cannot forbid him from marrying another wife, nor can I insist he keep his child from his home. But just as our culture allows a man to marry a second wife for the sake of having children, it also provides the first wife the choice of walking away from the marriage if she finds the new arrangements unacceptable. I can go back to my family if I choose to."

Añuli waited.

"But that is out of the question for me. I am not a young girl with the hope of getting married again. If I go back, I will only succeed in bringing shame and ridicule to my family."

There was a thoughtful silence as the two women pondered the hopelessness of the situation. "I'm going to try to make a deal with him."

"What kind of deal?"

"I've been thinking that maybe, instead of him paying his mistress off, he should pay me off."

"I'm not sure I understand."

Egoyibo sighed, standing to look out through the window of the tiny flat. "Twenty-eight years of my life, Añuli. I have given that man 28 years of my life. The least he can do in return is to give me a good settlement and I will get out of his life forever."

Through the window, she watched the traffic build up along Gbongobiri Market Road, praying in her heart for help from above. Somewhere out there, there had to be a new home and a new life waiting for her. Somewhere out there, there had to be a job waiting for her. Somewhere out there, there had to be a husband waiting for Añuli.

Ego closed her eyes and let her head fall in a reverent pose. It was at times like this that she wished she hadn't lost her faith after the death of Urenna, because somewhere in heaven she knew there was a God who could lead her out of this confused maze. If only she could find her way back to him.

Chapter 10

Jos

Grace needed fresh flowers for the reception, so when she heard the gardener tending the garden early on Friday morning, she picked up her basket and went out to join him. She loved the heady smell of the earth after the heavy rainfall. It was called petrichor, the gardener had once told her. In her mind, it was one of the most pleasant scents ever, definitely one that could lift her solemn mood that morning.

The rains had awakened the earth all right. Everywhere she turned there was a new flower stretching toward the light. To her untrained eyes everything looked vibrant and gorgeous, and she commented as much to the horticulturist.

But he disagreed. "How you arrange the flowers makes a huge difference to the garden," he told her. "If you want to enjoy the fragrance of the flowers to the fullest, you must design and plant them strategically. Don't just scatter the seeds. You must be intentional. Take for example …"

As he continued to speak her mind drifted off to the potential sale of Gidan Mairo. That would be a tragedy, she thought. Gidan Mairo was a two-fold ministry—a safe house for unwed pregnant teenage girls and an orphanage for motherless babies. Madam Mairo had founded the ministry on her own, operating from her huge family estate, but when the demand for the ministry grew beyond her ability to cope she had turned it over to Heavenly Missions, a missionary society with headquarters in Jos. Immediately after Madam Mairo's death in a motor accident last year her son had put up the buildings for sale despite several appeals from the missionary organization to give them enough time to relocate.

"Woof! Woof!"

Grace heard the yap before she saw the dog.

"Oh no! Here comes trouble!" she ran out to meet Rufus on his lightning-fast race toward her. She couldn't let the dog destroy the flowers and incur the gardener's wrath. The two collided on the sidewalk, and she almost fell to her knees. Laughing, she bent to pat the boisterous German shepherd.

"One of these days," Grace heard the gardener grumble loudly, "one of these days ..."

But the dog had rolled on its back, waiting to be tickled, and she was happy to oblige. "That's right, Rufus. Don't allow anyone to intimidate you, okay? Life is too short to be lived in fear of man. Come, let's take the flowers in and we'll see if Big Jim will let me take you for a walk."

She chained the dog to the metal railings in front of the Recreation Centre and went in to arrange the flowers in the kitchen. Mama Remi and Ma Mabel were already going through the grocery list for Saturday shopping.

"That girl no go kill me, God knows. I will not die because of her," Mama Remi was complaining to her friend.

"Wetin she want again?"

"She want make I buy am rat poison. Can you imagine that?"

Ma Mabel laughed. "What for?"

"Rats, of course. They no dey let person sleep for night. She want drop the poison for them."

"My sister, be careful o! That thing dangerous well well. It fit kill person."

"Why don't you just buy a rat trap? It's just as effective," Grace offered.

"Ah, Grace, that thing no dey work o! We don buy am before. As soon as it catch one rat, all the others learn their lesson and them no go near the trap again. The rats get sense no be small."

Grace laughed. "I need to be at the orphanage tomorrow morning. Please tell Adamu that I will be going with you when you leave for the market. He'll drop me off at Gidan Mairo."

She carried the flower vases to the dining tables and returned to speak to the women in the kitchen. "I'm off for my walk. Please be careful with that rat poison matter. I've read that the manufacturers sometimes add potassium cyanide to the formula to make it more potent."

Mama Remi looked up. "Potassi wetin?"

"Potassium cyanide—a very dangerous chemical used in making poisons, very powerful."

Mama Remi's mouth opened wider, her jaw dropped lower.

"I wouldn't buy it if I were you," Grace added, before swinging the door open and unchaining the dog.

After clearing with Big Jim, she set off on her walk with an excited Rufus. The air was refreshingly cool because of the rainfall. The reflection of the sun on the trees showed traces of the dew that still clung to the leaves. Moths and butterflies, grasshoppers and chirping birds all lent their particular sounds to the beauty of the morning. As they rounded a path she felt

Rufus straining against his leash and stopped to let him do his thing in the bush. This was a day meant to be enjoyed, she told herself, a day to be content and joyful and to praise God for his wonderful creation.

As was usual these days, her thoughts soon drifted to Chuma, whose friendship with Remi had become the talk of her kitchen staff. Remi had become a constant visitor at Sonshine since his arrival. Some nights, she didn't leave the hotel until well after ten p.m. causing the hotel staff to speculate that she was no longer working. When Bola asked her mother, Mama Remi said she was still working with Jos Tourism. "If you ask me, *sha*" Bola muttered when Mama Remi left the kitchen. "Remi just dey work make she get American visa. Other people dey get admission for university for that side, she dey find man wey go carry am go there."

On his part, Chuma seemed to treat his dinner companion with politeness and friendship—the same way he treated everyone at Sonshine. He was a source of intrigue for the hotel staff and they seemed to like him. He had a way of putting people at ease, insisting that they call him Chuma instead of *Oga Chuma* and joking with the staff when appropriate.

Something strange had happened two nights ago, Grace recalled. Chuma was having dinner with Remi and Grace was sitting with the guests from Unit 6 two tables away, joking and playing with the children. She had felt his eyes on her before she looked up. When their eyes met, he had winked at her, and it had taken her a few seconds to recover and turn again to the children.

"Rufus, no!" She lost her balance and almost fell to the ground when the big dog lurched in pursuit of a smaller dog yapping on the other side of the road. Following the small dog was a group of women balancing baskets on their heads on their way to the market. Grace wasn't sure if the dog belonged to any of the women, or if it was a stray. She guessed it was the latter. People didn't take their dogs to the market.

"*Sannu.*" She greeted the women in Hausa.

"*Yauwa,*" they replied. "*I na kwana?*"

I should be glad, Grace thought, holding tightly to Rufus until the women turned around the path. *The more Remi occupies his time, the less the likelihood that he would seek my company, and the easier it would be for me to avoid him. I really should be very, very happy.*

The wind picked up as she turned on to a wooded corner by Tudun Wada Trail. She halted at Rufus's sudden bark and gasped in shock when she saw Chuma jogging toward her. How did he do that? She was just thinking about him and he just materialised, as though summoned by her thoughts. As his equally surprised gaze trapped hers, her skin prickled with apprehension.

She held the dog close to her side and waited for Chuma to pass, but he didn't. Instead, he abruptly stopped and crossed to her side of the trail. Grace watched as he completed the few steps toward where she stood, each long stride making her throat tighten with tension. If she must talk to him, she preferred the security of the hotel where they wouldn't have to be alone, not in this middle of nowhere. Since their lunch date when he had asked pointed questions about her life, all of which she had refused to answer, she had been dreading being alone with him again. But she knew him well enough to be sure he wouldn't rest until he had got the answers he desired.

Chuma stood in front of her now, his tall frame blocking her vision. A tentative smile played on his lips. "Hi!"

His tone was pleasant but that didn't stop the trepidation that beat a quick drum in her chest. His bright gaze was surveying her in a friendly manner, first taking in her twisted hair before dipping to her face and then lower, lingering on her brown T-shirt and faded, blue denim pants and running shoes. She clamped her lips together and looked away.

"It's good to know you're still fond of walking. At least this part of you I still recognise."

"Some things never change." Her voice came out stiff as he fell into step beside her.

"Right," he agreed. "But why are you out by yourself? Do you live around here?"

She smiled briefly and shook her head. He wasn't so smart after all. "I live at the hotel."

"I know you stay there when you're working, but what about when you're not? Is your home close to the hotel?"

Stooping, she stroked Rufus's mane and let the dog leap up for a hug. She needed the diversion. "I live at the hotel," she repeated. Rufus was straining against his leash again. Perhaps it was time to head back.

Chuma watched her for a moment before asking quietly, "Don't you live with your husband?"

She looked up, shook her head and looked away. "I don't have any husband."

He hesitated, and she could feel his intense glare. "You mean ... you are divorced, separated, widowed?"

"Nope," she courageously shook her head firmly. "I am not any of those. I am not married. I have never been married."

Almost as though he couldn't help himself, he reached out a hand to turn her to face him, effectively stopping her walk, the intensity of his shocked eyes burning a hole through her face. "What are you talking about? What about your children?"

"What about them?" she asked evenly, angrily, and jerked her head away.

Rufus picked up the anger in her voice and growled menacingly at Chuma, forcing him to drop his hand.

"Ure, I know it's not my business, but—"

"Then don't go there, Chuma." A fury that surprised her burned in her eyes and simmered there. "Just leave it alone. I mean it. My children are my business. I don't owe you any explanation for them."

They stood there a moment, facing each other in silence. He looked shocked, whether at her words or at her anger, she couldn't tell. She would try to analyse her outburst later, but right now she didn't care. How dare he stand in judgement of her?

She put a reassuring hand on Rufus when he growled at Chuma again. Then, giving vent to her anger, she went on carelessly. "And what game are you playing with Remi?"

"I don't know what you mean." His voice was quiet, his eyes watchful.

"Oh yes you do, Chuma. Stop pretending."

"She and I are just—"

"I hope you're not planning to treat her the same way you treated me," she rushed on. "When you were a student and didn't have any money you offered me 500 naira to get out of your life. Now that you are an *Americana* I wonder how many other girls you have paid off in similar fashion. But be careful with Remi. She's not as naïve as the girl you used and discarded a decade ago. She won't let you get away as easily as I did."

She regretted her scathing words as soon as she heard his quick intake of breath. A mask of hurt and anger darkened his face.

"Of all the lowest, meanest, hateful things you could have ever said to me, Urenna, that was the worst. I know I hurt you badly when I broke up our relationship, but I was young and scared and didn't know what I was doing. I tried to make amends but you had disappeared. Next thing I knew you were dead, or so I assumed. I wish—"

She heard the defeat in his voice as he breathed out slowly and continued in a measured tone. "I wish with all my heart that I could undo the past but I can't. I don't know how many times I have to say it before you believe me, but I am very sorry, okay?"

Without another word, he turned and strolled away in the opposite direction, an angry Rufus barking at him.

A deep ache settled over her heart as she watched him go. If she could take back her words, she would have. But words are like spears, she knew. Once they leave they can never come back.

Even before he got to his apartment, Chuma's heart was beating with excitement. His anger at Grace's rudeness had quickly dissipated as the full implications of her revelations took root in his heart. He kicked off his runners and went straight to the fridge for a drink. Then he sat on the sofa and stared blankly at the television screen. A whole new rush of possibilities slammed around his mind. *Dear Lord, could it be true? Grace was not married, had never even been married.*

What was with the twins then? Auntie Bukky said they were in her school. He'd never paid attention to the school. He wondered how old they would be to be eligible for boarding school. Kids get into secondary school as young as 9 years, sometimes even 8 years if they are exceptionally smart. That would mean that she had become pregnant a year or two after she quit school. He shook his head impatiently. Something wasn't adding up with the story. Grace's life over the past 11 years seemed to read like a mystery novel, with every new chapter revealing a new twist to the original plot.

He took a swipe from the water bottle and tried to think things through. He had to put his priorities in order, and the priority for now was Grace, not her children. If what she'd said was true, if indeed she was not married, had never been married, then ... the possibilities before him sent chills down his spine.

Chills that were good, not bad.

Chapter 11

Jos

It was almost ten o'clock that night when Grace retired to her apartment. She crinkled her nose at the stuffiness and opened her windows to let in fresh air. She slipped off her sandals and made her way into the kitchen where she grabbed a bottle of orange juice from the fridge. Back in the living room she flopped on the couch, feeling exhausted, and ripped open an envelope she knew contained two letters from the twins. Their handwriting had improved since the first term. They missed her, she read, and they were counting down the days to their Easter break. So was she.

A gentle breeze blew softly into her apartment through the open windows, and she watched the patterns on the curtains sway quietly to the rhythm of the wind. *How could I have been so rude? I insulted him. He was only trying to be friendly, but I insulted him. Why did I have to lash out like an angry fishwife?*

For a moment, just for one moment, the muscles of her mouth twitched in amusement at the expression. How on earth did man discover that fishes had wives, anyway? She'd heard the expression for the first time at Government College. The library prefect was always angry and slamming down at everyone. One day the principal called her out at the assembly and described her actions as consistent with that of a fishwife. Grace had snickered at the image the metaphor had conjured in her mind, and for that, her punishment had been to research the meaning and origin of that phrase and to present her findings before the entire school at the next assembly. She had to write the meaning one hundred times without a single mistake or cancellation.

A fishwife is a woman regarded as coarse and shrewishly abusive

She drew her curtains slightly apart to peep out at Unit 11b. Soft light peeked from under the blinds. She wondered what Chuma was up to. Remi had been around earlier, but he hadn't shown up for dinner. The girl had spent the night talking with Big Jim instead.

It was almost eleven o'clock. The hotel staff had retired for the day and she probably should also, but her mind was too active to allow her body to rest. So she grabbed a light shawl over her nightgown and stepped out.

The night was cool and brightly lit by a large yellow moon. The grass beneath her feet was a rich green carpet, thanks to the recent downpours. Grace quietly walked over to the garden chair under the almond tree that demarcated her apartment from Chuma's and tried to soak in the tranquil night and the exotic scents of flowers. She had spent many nights under this tree, nights like this when she needed to think.

For so many years survival for her children had been her highest priority. She had worked hard, prayed hard and God had sent Auntie Simbi to her. The woman had reached out and practically adopted her. Until the twins started school, she had lived with Auntie Simbi, ostensibly as her housekeeper but in reality more like a beloved daughter.

Grace stood up and walked over to the garden again and inhaled the fragrant scent. *My family doesn't want me*, she thought, and that hurt. Chuma's newspaper clippings had raised more questions than they'd answered. Was it possible none of them had gotten her letters? She had written to her father, her mother and her sister. Not once but several times. Not one of them had replied.

The wind was gaining traction with gentle consistency. Grace walked back to sit on the garden bench. She pulled her knees up beneath her chin and rested her feet on the bench. Hugging her shins, she let her head drop onto her knees. The lyrics of a song the choir had sung recently at church floated into her spirit and she hummed, determined to relax in the gentle serenity of the night.

A shadow crossed the light of the moon and remained over her bent form. When she looked up her heart leapt to see the object of her earlier musings standing a few feet away and looking down at her. So lost in thought, she had not heard him approach.

"You scared me." Automatically, she tightened her wrap around her shoulders and got up from the bench.

Chuma smiled in response. "I saw you coming towards my unit and I waited. When you didn't make an appearance I decided to check on you, and here you are."

"You thought I was coming over to your unit?" She frowned. "Why would I do that?"

"I don't know." He shrugged. "Perhaps to visit with an old school friend ... or to apologise for your harsh words this morning."

Grace looked away. She wasn't going to apologise. She probably should but she wasn't going to.

"You're not turning in soon, I hope," he continued. "Stay and chat for a few minutes. For old times' sake, okay? Hmm … I love this fresh air. I love the flower gardens you guys have planted all over this estate. There is a sweet fragrance everywhere I turn, especially on nights like this when the moon is shining and the wind is blowing softly. It's quite a unique setup you have here."

Grace's skin grew warm. She kept her tone casual as she turned to respond to his compliments. "It's always been like this. Auntie Simbi loves flowers and has always kept a horticulturist on staff. Sonshine has won many garden and landscape awards and been the subject of many TV shows and magazine reports."

He was facing the moon, so she could see his face quite clearly. The moonlight seemed trapped in his eyes. When he smiled again, she turned away. Chuma walked to the flowerbed and returned with a small flower. As she watched, he reached for her hand.

"No," she gasped. What was he trying to do? Her eyes filled with fear and she tugged her hand out of his grasp.

He laughed and lifted his hand in surrender. "Whoa! Take it easy, Ure. I'm not about to leap on you."

"I'm sorry," she muttered and stood up again. "I really would like to retire now."

"Please don't go. You have nothing to fear from me. See, I'll return the flower if it offends you." He walked back to the plant and placed the flower back into the bush before walking back to her.

The silence between them stretched.

"Sometimes I'm not sure I recognise the girl I knew in the lady you've become, Ure. You've changed from the carefree girl I remember into a quiet girl who watches over every word she utters. Except when she's angry, of course. You're supposed to be the mother of two children, but all I see in you is innocence, and sometimes I see fear and anger. I'm intrigued by the innocence and can understand the anger, but I can't make out the fear."

Grace stiffened. "I don't know what you're talking about."

"I see a little girl's unspoiled innocence in your eyes. That fresh, innocent flower reminded me of you."

She tilted her head and looked at him, trying to understand. Chuma stared back, and their eyes locked for a few seconds before she looked away. There was something in him that always seemed to make the blood rush over her. It would be so easy to slip back into that type of relationship again, especially now when his eyes were filled with a definite invitation. Rather than accept, she closed her eyes and shook her head slowly to clear the cobweb of confusion in her mind.

"Let's call a truce, Ure." He gave her another smile. "Let's say that you and I don't have any history. Let's pretend we met for the first time here in this hotel."

Grace felt her insides twist as she raised her eyes to his. "That would be impossible to do. You and I go too long a ways back for that."

"But let's say we just met."

"Mmm hmm?"

"Could I interest you in becoming my friend?"

Her eyes darkened with instant refusal. She made to stand up but his hand caught her wrist.

"Come on, Ure. I'll even start calling you Grace if it'll make things easier."

It was with great effort that Grace looked away from him. His smile had brightened his eyes with that warmth that always seemed to totally disarm her. When she pulled her hand he let go. She folded her hands under her shawl. "It would certainly make things less awkward for me if you started to call me Grace like everyone else."

"Grace what, exactly? What's your last name?"

"Anthony."

He looked at her again, but she focused her gaze on the twinkling lights in the distant sky. He regarded her thoughtfully for a few seconds. "Grace Anthony," he repeated. "That's interesting. Who is Mr. Anthony?"

She pursed her lips and continued to watch the moon.

"Can you at least tell me your girls' names?"

"Erinma and Ojiugo."

He seemed to think about the names for a second or two, leaving her to guess if he liked them. Tough luck if he didn't.

"*Erinma*—a beautiful thread; *Ojiugo*—a gift for an eagle. I'm surprised you didn't go with Chi or Ada, names that are popular among the Igbos."

"I didn't want names that were too similar," she explained and kicked herself for bothering to explain. "I wanted each child to have her own identity even though they are identical images of one another."

"I like the names. You won't have the confusion my parents had with my sisters. We had Chiamaka and Chiazolam. At first everyone called them Chii-Chii until it became confusing. Then we got rid of the prefixes and simply called them Zola and Amaka and the problem was solved."

Grace didn't want to hear about his family. It was too personal and she wanted to keep him at arm's length.

He tried again. "It must be exciting to be the mother of identical twins. Many girls I know dream of having twins but I don't personally know any who has ever had any. My sisters are both pregnant. Zola is about four months now and she knows it will be a singleton—a boy. Amaka found out only recently that she's pregnant and she's already hoping they would be twins."

"Is she?"

"Is she what?"

"Having twins."

"Don't know. It's too soon to tell, I think. But we don't have twins in our family so I'm pretty sure it's going to be the one child."

"My mother is a twin," Grace offered before she could stop herself.

"Really?"

"Really." She nodded. "And she used to say she wanted to have twins, which, of course, she didn't. Me, I was more shocked than anything when I was told I was carrying twins. I was totally miserable when only a few months into the pregnancy I was as big as a whale. I never imagined I could lose all that weight."

He looked at her again and nodded. "You delivered them then?"

"What do you mean?" She looked up.

"I thought maybe you adopted them."

"Why? You think I can't have children of my own?"

"No, no, it's not that. You don't look old enough to be a mother. You don't look an inch older or bigger than you did when you were in secondary school."

"I'll take that as a compliment. But really, I don't even care anymore whether I am big or not." She shrugged. "Those girls are the best things that ever happened to me, and if it cost me some extra pounds to have them, then so be it."

"I'm glad for you," he said quietly, and they both lapsed into silence for several seconds.

A gentle breeze blew past them, and she closed her eyes and tried to absorb the fresh air, but it was difficult to stay relaxed. Not with him so close. She felt his gaze long before she heard his anxious voice.

"Ure, I know I promised not to bring this up again, but I really am sorry about the way things ended between us. I have asked God to forgive me and I hope you will forgive me too."

"Don't—don't keep apologising," she finally stammered out. "Nobody is perfect. Everybody has done something wrong, something that is not acceptable to God. If you've never stolen, you've probably lied. If you've never killed anyone you've probably hated someone. But God forgives us all, and we should also forgive ourselves. Our standard of righteousness cannot be higher than God's."

He looked at her for endless seconds and then nodded. They fell into silence again, but it was a companionable silence.

After a while, he spoke again. "So, Ure. I'll ask again. If we didn't have this history between us and we were meeting for the first time, would you have considered being my friend?"

She flashed him an impish grin. "I don't think so. I am a Christian lady, I don't get into meaningless friendships with men."

"What are you talking about? Genuine friendships between two people of any gender can never be meaningless."

"I hear you, but in my opinion, there usually has to be a basis for friendship between a man and a woman. It's either that they are related or that they grew up in the same neighbourhood and have been friends from childhood, or they are involved romantically. None of that is true in our case."

"Ah-ha, but I'm your neighbour. My suite is right next door to yours, and considering how long I've known you, we practically grew up in the same neighbourhood. Doesn't the Bible say we ought to love our neighbours as we love ourselves?"

For the first time since they met at the Jubilee power conference, Grace laughed out loud. He was funny, and she couldn't help it. She was surprised at how liberating it felt to be sharing a joke with him

"Well, that just goes to prove that anybody can interpret the Scriptures to suit their purpose."

"But you are my neighbour, aren't you?"

She laughed again. "If I agree, will you stop talking about the past all the time?"

"Yes."

"And will you stop calling me Ure?"

"Yes."

"Yes...?"

"Yes, Grace."

Grace felt her muscles relax. A truce would be a reprieve. It would give her space and time to think, time to strategize. "All right, but you must promise that you'll never get me into trouble again. I still have scars from our friendship a decade ago."

Chuma let out a deep breath and stretched out a hand. He smiled. "Sounds like a deal to me. Let's shake on it."

Long after she lay down to sleep that night, Grace still felt the imprint of the long fingers that had gripped her hand.

Chapter 12

Jos

Dressed in black denim and a pink cotton blouse, backpack ready and hung over her chair, Grace sat on her chair and frowned at the computer screen. She had already entered all the required fields on the Excel spreadsheet and now busied herself inserting the explanatory notes and comments accompanying each expense item. This was her real job—keeping the hotel's financial books. Although her official title was Assistant Manager, her main assignment was monitoring and accounting for the hotel's incomes and expenditures. Auntie Simbi was not very organised and could get horribly confused with figures and calculations, so Grace paid close attention to the numbers for her.

"I can't believe my eyes!" She winced at Bola's loud exclamation.

Whatever was the matter? Grace hurried to the office door and peeped. Bola was looking out of the RC window with great interest. Luckily there were no guests around to witness the waitress's loud outburst. Grace shook her head in frustration. She had to find a way to make that lady either speak in low tones or confine her remarks to the four walls of the kitchen.

"Wetin?" Edith's voice joined her friend's at the window.

Grace grimaced. Ernie and Bert. Abbott and Costello. What else was new?

"Look! No be Remi I dey see dey talk to Oga Chuma so?"

There was a slight pause when Grace imagined Edith looking out of the window. "Eh, na she. Wetin surprise you? her mama no tell us say she still dey work for Jos Tourism?"

"Oh yes, I know that one. But Mama Remi say she no dey do tour guide again, say she dey work for office. "

"You sef! You no see the connection? Na because Oga Chuma register for the tour na im make Remi dey do tour guide today. I no blame the girl for trying her luck, sha. The *bobo* fine well, well," Edith said.

"But she came to see him last night!"

"So? Today na another day."

"You sure say she even go home yesterday? She been fit sleep with am!"

"*Bola!*"

Bola had the grace to apologise. "Cool down, my sister. Na joke I dey joke."

Their voices carried very clearly through Grace's closed door. If she opened it just a bit she could see the two ladies as they continued their commentary.

"The bus full well well today. I can see the two families in Units 3 and 4. See—"

"I hope say Remi go give attention to all the tourists, no be only to siddon dey look Oga Chuma for eye. The poor man don enter trouble and him no even know."

"Which kind trouble? Na by force? A beg, na love them dey do! Love *nwantinti*."

The two ladies laughed and walked back to the kitchen.

Grace had lost her concentration on the spreadsheet. She clicked on the save icon and shut down the computer. It was time to find Mama Remi and Ma Mabel so she could get a ride to Gidan Mairo, where she would be useful instead of sitting in her office and listening to gossip. After all, Remi was doing her job. Her own task this Saturday morning was to help clean the orphanage for the building inspection.

Chapter 13

Calabar

Ego was startled by the knock on the door. She looked at the time—it was only quarter past eleven. It was probably Ulunma, back from the market and coming to confirm what to cook for lunch.

She opened the door and came face to face with Odili. Before she could slam it shut he pushed her aside and stepped in. This was the first time she would be alone with him since Beatrice's baby bombshell. She had moved into Añuli's old room that night, leaving the house girl to attend to her husband.

"What do you want?" she asked, stepping back.

"We need to talk," Odili replied with an expression that brooked no argument. He was taller than her by more than a foot, which put her at a distinct disadvantage.

She went to stand by the window.

"What's going on here? What are you doing?"

"What does it look like I'm doing?" She turned to pick up a blouse from the floor. She folded and threw it into the open suitcase on the bed.

"You," he sounded incredulous. "You can't leave me."

"Watch me."

"Look here—"

"No, you look here," she snapped. "You have humiliated me for the last time in your life, Odili. I will not stand by and be your doormat any longer. Twenty-eight years of marriage, through triumphs and tragedies, and this is what I get for my loyalty."

"But I told you—"

"I've had enough. This house is not big enough for more than one woman. Let your mistress move in. I'm done with you." Angry tears spilled down her cheeks, but she wiped them with the back of her hand. Turning to the closet, she yanked more clothes off their hangers and threw them into her suitcase. She wasn't planning to be part of the welcome party for his mistress and son.

"Have you considered what people will say?"

"Have *I* considered what people will say?" she spat out, feeling a renewed sense of indignation. "How dare you even talk to me about what people will say? Did you consider what people would say when you had your clandestine affair? Have you considered what people will say when they know you have a concubine and a son out of wedlock? Shame on you, Odili. How dare you talk to me about what people will say?"

"Will you stop shouting and listen to me?"

"No, I will not stop shouting. I do not want to hear anything you say. I do not want to see you, I do not want to talk to you and I want to forget I was ever married to a two-faced hypocrite like you. In fact, you can begin now by getting out of my room."

Huffing, Odili regarded her through narrowed eyes. "*Oya*, if that is how you want it, Egoyibo, I'll give it to you. This is my house. If anybody is getting out of this room it's you."

"What?" She gasped.

"Look," he hesitated, and then continued in a voice full of tension. "All I'm asking is that you calm down so we can discuss this like two rational human beings. Why won't you even listen to what I have to say?"

"Because it's all lies, lies and more lies, and I am tired of listening to them." She took a deep breath. "This is the end of the road for us, Odili. I want out. I want out now!"

"So what do you want me to do with Chike and Mbachu when they arrive and you're not in? After all, you invited them."

"They're not coming until Saturday. If that is all you're worried about, then relax. I'll be here when they arrive. In the meantime, I have located a flat in town and all I need from you is money for two years' rent. Don't say you can't afford it because you and I know you can."

He gave her a look that said she must have a few loose screws in her head. "You can't be serious. You want me to rent a house for you? Here in Calabar?"

"Of course it will be here in Calabar. Where else do you want me to live? My daughter lives here, and I will not be separated from her."

"Then you'd better go and live with her because I am not renting any house for you anywhere."

"Oh yes you are, Odili."

"No, I'm not."

"Yes, you are."

"Let me see you force me."

"Odili, listen to me. If you love your job, if you love your life, if you love your reputation, you will rent that flat for me."

"Or else?"

"You're calling my bluff?"

"You can't do anything."

"I can't do anything, Odili? You think I can't do anything?"

"What can you do?"

Ego smiled without mirth, folded her hands across her chest and shook her head. "Odili, the cock that is drunk has not yet met the hawk that is irate."

"You're a mad woman."

"Odili, if you force me to, I will destroy you. I will expose you, and I will destroy you."

"Ha!" He sneered. "Go and sit down. You cannot kill a wounded fly."

"Odili, me?"

"Yes, Egoyibo, you!"

"Odili!" Angrily, she clapped her hands twice, loudly. "Prepare to lose your job. Do you hear me, Odili?"

"*O di ka ara agbapula gi.* I think you've gone mad."

"You don't know the half of it. Your memory is too short. You have forgotten where I was working before you married me. I still have my connections. My friends in the media will just love the scoop. And what do you think your conservative vice chancellor will do when he hears what I have to tell him?"

"You will not dare!"

"Just try sending me out penniless to the streets and see if you will be holding your prestigious position longer than the next two months. You will be out of work in no time, and you and your concubine will be forced to go live in the village. Who knows, you may even make a good palm-wine tapper."

She heard him expel a heavy breath and knew she had overstepped her boundaries. She didn't care.

"Don't try my patience too far, Ego. There's a limit to the insult I will tolerate from you. How many times do I have to tell you that Beatrice is not coming to live in this house? The boy, yes, because he is my flesh and blood, but not the mother."

Ego shook her head in disbelief—he was already singing a different song. "I'm not sure which part of your arrogance I find more annoying—your audacious presumption that I have nothing better to do with my time than to look after your bastard, or your shameless declaration that the boy is your flesh and blood."

"I cannot deny the boy, Ego. He's my son. The son you could not give me."

"The son I could not give you, Odili?"

"Well? Did you give me a son?"

"Ah!" Egoyibo swung around to the window, feeling the force of his words like a physical blow. She crossed her hands over her head. "Aahh! Women of Africa," she cried, "I weep for you! Ah! Women of Nigeria, you have been deceived! You all hurry and get married in church, thinking that the cords of religion are stronger than the cords of tradition. But our husbands have the last laugh. When they want our love they blackmail us with religion. When they want to marry another wife, they remember their culture. Aahh!"

She turned to her husband. "Odili, you saw how I almost died trying to give you a son. How many miscarriages did I have? And all these years you have been pretending that you were happy with your daughters, but it's been one big lie! You have been exposed, Odili. You lied to me. You lied. You lied." Her voice broke. Sobs and tears of anguish racked her body. She sat on the floor and cried.

"How can you say I lied, Ego? I didn't plan any of this. It just happened."

"Then why didn't you make her have an abortion? That is your preferred solution, isn't it?"

"Because she refused!" He glared at her. "There, I've said it. Are you satisfied now? I told her to have an abortion but she refused. That's why she quit her job and went back to her people."

Fury erupted from deep within her heart, and she charged at him. "How did you tell her? Did you beat her? Did you flog her like you flogged my daughter when she refused to abort her own child? It's as they say—the *udara* ("cherry fruit") doesn't fall far from the tree. Like father, like daughter. Ure didn't plan to get pregnant either. Like you, it just happened. But unlike you, she didn't want to abort her baby. She was afraid and was repentant. She came home to us and what did you do? You took your *koboko* and flogged her, determined to kill the baby, or both of them so she wouldn't bring shame and disgrace on you. But now, guess what?"

"Egoyibo, stop it."

"You are no better. In fact, you are worse. You are an arrogant, unrepentant bastard. When I remember how I stood by and watched you kill my daughter, I want to die. You have blood on your hands, Odili. Don't imagine for one moment that you will escape the wrath of God."

"I did not kill her," he bit out savagely.

"You think not? You are even worse than I thought. A man without conscience is already sold to the devil while he is yet alive."

"Ego, listen to me. I did not kill Urenna."

"Of course you did. Granted, you did not drive the bus off the road, but you killed her before she got into that vehicle.

You killed her with your hatred, you hit her and kicked at her stomach and threw her all over the place. You flogged a pregnant child with your *koboko* until you drew blood, until she was battered and bruised. God was merciful that you did not have a gun, Odili, or you would have shot and killed her on the spot. But what you started, the bus driver finished. At the end you were satisfied. Your punishment had been carried out."

"Ego, listen to me …"

"No," she sobbed, hugging a pillow she found in her hands. "What did my daughter do to you? You did the same thing but you let your mistress live. You let your mistress have her child, but you killed my daughter."

She rushed at him then, sobbing and slapping and kicking. "Why did you kill my daughter? Why did you kill my daughter?"

His body was hard and unyielding, like a rock. Her anger surged and she started to throw things at him, anything that caught her eyes. "You murderer! God will punish you. You will die a shameful death. You will suffer the same way you made my daughter suffer. God will punish you, you wicked man. Sugar daddy? *Yeye* ("useless") old man. Shameless hypocrite!"

"Egoyibo, stop it now." He lifted his hands to ward off her attack. "I repeat, I did not kill your daughter. You're making a mistake. She's not even dead, okay? Listen to me, Urenna was not on that bus. She is not dead! Your daughter is not dead!"

"What?"

"She's not dead. She's alive somewhere with her children."

"What did you say? Have you finally gone mad?"

"I'm not mad. When the accident happened, I went to identify the body in the mortuary, except the bodies were so bloated and decomposed that I made a mistake."

"How do you know you made a mistake?"

"Because she wrote me two years later to say she had delivered twins. She sent pictures of her babies to you and Añuli. I intercepted and shredded the letters because I was still very angry with her and didn't want to cause another scandal by declaring that I had made a mistake and that she was alive. Besides, to me she was already dead."

"Odili, Odili ..." She rushed at him and grabbed him by his shirt, her heart beating so fast she knew she would faint if she didn't hold on to something. Her lips began to shiver and her hands were shaking. "Tell me the truth. Please, I beg you in the name of Jesus, tell me the truth. Is my daughter alive?"

When you have lived with a man for 28 years, you get to know when he's telling the truth and when he's lying. Egoyibo looked deep into her husband's eyes and her whole world suddenly collapsed. She crumbled into unconsciousness.

Chapter 14

Jos

Armed with a mop and a brush, a bucket of water, detergent and disinfectants, Grace knelt on the floor and washed the hallway of the orphanage. She worked alongside the administrative assistant to the orphanage, a Youth Corps volunteer named Joyce. All that morning they dusted cobwebs, swept floors and washed walls, bed sheets, pillowcases, napkins and dirty clothes and hung them out to dry on the clothesline in the backyard.

Idris and his inspector were expected any time that afternoon.

The matron had come by with three other volunteers but Grace had assured them she and Joyce could manage on their own, urging them instead to focus their efforts on the girls' hostel.

By noon they were done cleaning and dusting. They settled the children for siesta at two o'clock, then retired to the admin office to sort through files and organize documents. Their conversation did not stray from the potential sale of Gidan Mairo. Everyone was worried, and rightly so. The ministries of Gidan Mairo's Home for Girls and Gidan Mairo's Orphanage were serving a need in the society. It would be a real tragedy if they would be forced to shut down.

"Maybe we can persuade the new owner to give us more time to look for an alternative accommodation," Joyce said.

"That's what we're all hoping for. But it depends on what the buyer's plans are for the property, don't you think? If he's a businessman trying to make money off his investment, he's not going to be interested unless we can afford the market rates for such a huge rental property."

Joyce threw a stapled sheaf on to the high stack of papers on the table. "Maybe we can appeal to the government for help."

Grace took out several files and started to arrange them by their contents. "Heavenly Missions has already applied to the Minster of Women Affairs for a loan, but there's been no response so far."

They looked up as a silent shadow stopped hesitantly by the doorway. When Grace opened the door a little girl about eight years old stood trembling, her gown wet and dripping. Grace saw the fear in her eyes and moved instantly to her side.

"Jumai, honey, what happened?"

The girl looked at her with eyes that seemed as huge as her nose. "I ... I pee for bed."

The evidence spoke loudly for itself. Grace tried to act normally so she wouldn't add to the poor girl's embarrassment. "I see that. Hmm ... I think you need a change of clothes, don't you?"

The little girl nodded slightly. Her lips were trembling.

"Can I carry you to the bathroom and give you a quick bath first?"

"Yes, please."

It was a delicate job, but she was finally able to strip the little girl of every piece of clothing and carry her into the bathroom. She knew a bit about the girl. Her mother had abandoned her with her father and disappeared two years after she was born. The father had married again but the new wife did not want the girl. She had begun to abuse her and use the girl as her servant. The bruises on her body when her father had brought her to Gidan Mairo's orphanage three weeks ago were only beginning to fade. She had cried for days after her father left, waking up at night with recurrent nightmares. Now she was wetting her bed in the middle of the day.

Grace held the girl in her arms and gently rocked her to and fro. "Tell me what is upsetting you so much," she coaxed.

There were usually four girls in a room to take advantage of the twin bunk beds. Jumai was alone in the room today because the girl who slept on the top bunk had been returned to her family about a week ago and the third girl was sleeping in the sick bay with a fever.

Still, Grace spoke gently, hoping to quiet the little girl's mind.

"She say she go burn me alive," Jumai squeezed out the words between stifled sobs.

"Who's going to burn who alive?"

"My father's wife. She say na because of me she no get her own pikin. So she want kill me."

Grace could not keep the shock from her face. How could anyone get off with threatening such a young child? "Ah, Jumai, are you sure she said that?"

Jumai nodded. "She say I be witch. Say I dey fly for night. She say na me eat the three children when be commot for her belle. She say if I no confess she go burn me alive or she go pour acid for my face."

Grace shook her head in disbelief and hugged the girl close. No wonder the poor child found it difficult to sleep. She was consumed with fear. "It's okay, sweetie. Nobody's going to harm you here. Your daddy knew you would be safe here. That's why he brought you to us. And as long as you're here we'll do everything to protect you. You know all the children here are protected by God, don't you?"

Jumai's nod was not immediate, like she wasn't really sure. Grace prayed silently for the right words to allay the little girl's fears.

"But my father's wife, she say God hate witches. She say God go burn them. She say if I run away, that God will see me, and he go burn me for fire."

Tears rushed into Grace's eyes and she barely managed to stifle it. She did not want the girl to see her crying.

"Jumai, are you a witch?"

"No, Auntie. I no dey fly for night."

"Do you think God knows everything?"

"Yes. My father's wife—she say God know everything, say him dey see everybody every time and nobody fit hide from him."

"And she's right. God does know everything and nobody can hide from him. So if he knows everything he must know you are not a witch, mustn't he?"

This seemed to make sense to the little girl and she nodded slowly.

Grace hugged her gently. "That means you are safe. And you know lying is a sin, don't you?"

"Yes."

"And that God punishes sinners?"

"Yes."

"And that he likes it when people tell the truth?"

"Yes."

"So since God knows you are telling the truth he must also know that your father's wife is telling a lie, don't you think?"

"Yes."

"So who is God going to punish?"

She watched the lights go on in the little girl's eyes. "God no go burn me. He no go kill me."

"No, Jumai, he won't. And it's not just because you are telling the truth. You want to know why else?"

She nodded expectantly.

"It's because he loves you. Can I read you something from the Bible?"

Jumai nodded, and Grace saw the terror begin to fade from her innocent eyes. Grace read from the book of Mark: "The people brought children to Jesus, hoping he might touch them. The disciples shooed them off. But Jesus was irate and let them know it: 'Don't push these children away. Don't ever get between them and me. These children are at the very centre of life in the kingdom. Mark this: Unless you accept God's kingdom in the simplicity of a child, you'll never get in.' Then, gathering the children up in his arms, he laid his hands of blessing on them."

When Jumai started to snore gently on her bed, a thoughtful Grace returned to the admin office. It was because of children like Jumai that Gidan Mairo could not be shut down. What would happen to them? If the home did not exist, where would her father have taken her to escape the wrath of her angry stepmother? Grace wiped her eyes and sighed deeply, racking her brain over what she could possibly do to help save the orphanage.

A red-eyed, tired-looking Ayesha had arrived while Grace was attending to Jumai. Grace looked at her wristwatch. It was already well past four pm. Joyce was signing off for the day.

"How did the night vigil go?" Grace was anxious to know as soon as they were alone.

"It didn't," Ayesha hissed.

"What do you mean?"

"Exactly what I said, but I'll gist you later. I think Idris is already here. I saw his Kia and another car parked at the entrance. I think they have already started to inspect the girls' hostel and will be here before we know it."

"Oh!" Grace's voice was low. "You don't mind if I stay, do you? I'm curious to see who this new owner is. I don't think I have ever seen a real millionaire before."

"By all means, please stay. I'll tell you all about the night vigil after they're gone. You won't believe what happened."

"Good or bad?"

"Neither, but you can be sure I will not be attending any more of those in a long, long while. The thing I take my eyes see last night, no be small thing. We go gist later."

"Okay. At least you survived. Do you want to look around and be sure everything is looking the way you want it before the inspectors arrive?"

"I already have. Thanks for helping out, Grace. The whole place is shining. I'll take over the paperwork. We still have a lot to sort out."

In fewer than 20 minutes they heard voices coming down the corridor and looked up as the matron came into the reception hall, accompanied by two men.

Idris Danladi was no stranger to them, but their collective breaths caught as they turned to stare into the equally shocked eyes of Chuma Zeluwa as he followed Idris into the office.

Stunned, Grace could only stare. She hadn't expected to see Chuma. Not here. Not now. The last she heard and saw, he was on the Jos plateau tour with some of the guests from the hotel. The tour always lasted until six pm and it was not even five yet. She swallowed, and her fingers tightened around the file she was still holding. What business did Chuma have with Idris and the matron? Could he be the anticipated new owner of Gidan Mairo?

Before the matron could say anything, an excited Ayesha reached out and grabbed his hand. "We already met," she reminded him with a smile, "at Sonshine Estate, during the heavy rainstorm."

"Of course I remember." He smiled easily. "Do you work here?"

"Only at weekends. Grace and I are both volunteers here."

"Really? That's cool!"

"Hi," Grace greeted him. She saw the clipboard and pad on his left hand and the camera hanging from his neck. There was a tool bag right beside him.

"Are you the person who wants to buy Gidan Mairo?" she asked before she could stop herself. "Are you going to be the new owner?"

He smiled and shook his head. "Unfortunately, no. I'm only here for the inspection."

"And a very serious and thorough inspection is what he's doing," the matron inserted with a polite smile. "I don't know exactly what I was expecting, but I've never seen anything so detailed. Unfortunately, I have to leave you girls to attend to the gentlemen. A new client is arriving in about 15 minutes. Think you can manage on your own?"

"Of course," Ayesha assured her. "We'll be just fine. Where do you want to start?" she asked Chuma.

Grace watched as he wrote on his clipboard. "In a minute," he said. "Let me first explain what I'm going to do. I'll begin with some questions about the property, and then we will begin from the outside and work our way into the building. I do apologise in advance for any inconvenience I may cause you or any disturbance to the children."

"No worries," Ayesha assured him, "we'll survive. But tell me, does your godmother know you are the one buying Gidan Mairo?"

"I'm not the one buying the property," he repeated patiently. "I have been requested to do the inspection and that is all I'm doing. I'm not the buyer."

"Then you know who it is?"

"Yes, I know, but he doesn't want his identity revealed until the sale is completed."

"And what is he going to do with it? Convert it into a hotel?"

"Believe me, I have no idea."

"But surely—"

"I don't think this is the place or time to ask these questions," Idris interrupted. "Let's concentrate on the inspection. You can ask your questions afterward."

"Oh, I'm sorry, Idris," Ayesha said, and turned again to Chuma. "What was your question again?"

Grace listened as Chuma queried her friend about termites, leaking roofs, cracked walls and floors, air conditioning, electrical services and plumbing. When Ayesha took the men outside to show them the cracks in the wall, Grace pulled on her walking shoes, flung her bag across her shoulder, left a note for Ayesha and took off for Sonshine Estate.

Chapter 15

Jos

Grace pulled her wrapper tight around her shoulders and pressed into the wind as she crossed Murtala Mohammed Way. Less than thirty minutes into her trek to the hotel, the clouds had darkened and strong howling winds had descended on the city, heralding yet another rainstorm. When the drizzle turned into a downpour she dashed into a school building where 50 or 60 people caught in the freaky storm were taking shelter. If she had known there was such a huge storm brewing she would have called for the driver to pick her from Gidan Mairo. There hadn't been a cloud in the sky 30 minutes ago.

A minibus was stuck in a ditch across the road from the school. It stuttered and grunted, blew huge smoke from the exhaust and stopped.

"That one don quench," someone beside her commented.

Grace hoped not. Some of the passengers came down and began to push the bus from the pool of water. She was silently cheering their efforts when she felt her phone vibrate. Bola or Edith checking up on her, she figured. She pulled her phone from the side of her backpack and blinked at the name displayed on her caller id. Why would Chuma be calling her? Was he already done with his home inspection? Had they called it off because of the heavy rain? The vibration stopped after 20 seconds. Maybe he wasn't really calling her. He could have hit her number by mistake. Many of the Smartphones she'd seen recently were really sensitive and could go off at the slightest touch. Ayesha had told her it was called pocket-phoning. Besides, it would have been impossible to talk in her present environment, sandwiched as she was within a crowd that was noisily letting out their frustration at the sudden storm.

As she stood there shivering, the phone in her hand vibrated again and a text message appeared on the screen. It was from Chuma. ARE YOU OKAY? WHERE ARE YOU?

She read it again.

And again.

And again.

She closed and opened her eyes and the words still stared back at her. Was he seriously trying to contact her? What on earth for? The fact that she had agreed to a truce didn't mean they had become fast friends overnight. She ignored the text and snapped her phone shut.

It was raining harder with no signs of letting up. By six-thirty darkness had covered the entire city. The power grid had gone off too. The only illumination for the streets was from cars already stuck in the ensuing traffic jam. She had lived in Jos long enough to know that the chaos that would follow the rain would be worse than the storm itself. She pulled her handbag close and prayed that some sunlight might still come up after the rain, or if not, that the power would be turned on again so people could find their way home.

Wondering how the hotel was faring she took out her phone again and dialled the reception.

"Where you dey?" Bola's anxious voice rang clearly into her ears. "We called the orphanage and Ayesha say you dey trek back. Are you all right?"

"I'll be fine as soon as the rain stops. How are things at the hotel? Have the guests returned from their sightseeing tour?"

"Not yet, but they are okay. We been call Remi and she say them don reach Jos city gate."

"Thank God for that. What of Mama Remi and Ma Mabel, are they back at the hotel?"

"Yes. They came in just before the rain start."

"That's good."

"But Grace, where you dey? Oga Chuma been call dey find you."

"Did he say what he wanted?"

"No, but it be like say him dey worried say you dey stuck somewhere. He say he want come pick you."

Grace was not sure what to make of this. She shook her head and exhaled a deep shiver. "But he can't do that. If he asks again please tell him I'm okay. Once the rain stops I'll be on my way again, and it will take me fewer than 15 minutes to get back to Sonshine."

"But where exactly are you?"

"I'm in front of Barakin Elementary School. There are about 60 or 70 of us taking shelter from the rain here. "

"Okay then. I guess we go see you soon. Driver Adamu dey around too. If you need a ride just call and we go send am to come pick you."

"I will. Thanks, Bola. And please tell everyone not to worry! I'll be fine."

A gush of wind swept in their direction, blowing showers of rain and mud over the crowd. The water drenched Grace

4

and all those standing closest to the front of the building. She edged inside a little more. Her feet were beginning to ache, and she felt dirty sand on her clothes.

Usually she enjoyed the rains, but this one was different. It was totally unexpected and much too heavy considering there had been a similar storm not even a week ago. If this happened in biblical times the Israelite priests would no doubt be asking the Lord right now why he would suddenly send such a violent storm to their land.

"Na waa!" she heard someone cry. "This rain just reminds me of Noah's Ark. I wonder how many people were in the city when the 40-day rain started."

"I hope you're not trying to say the rain won't stop for 40 days," another voice retorted sharply.

"I don't see it stopping anytime soon, do you? We've been here for more than one hour and it's not letting up."

Another voice interjected. "If this was in America they would have predicted this heavy storm, complete with the timing, up to the last minute, so people will take precautions and protect themselves."

"Na waa for Naija," (Nigerian expression of frustration) someone else derided angrily.

"But NTA News provides a weather forecast every day. I listened to the news at noon today and there was a weather report, but there was no mention of anything like this."

Grace listened quietly as the conversations around her took shape. It was going to be a long wait. In moments like this, she mused, it was difficult to see that rain, no matter how heavy or light, was a blessing from above, poured out without measure to everyone, good or bad, just or unjust, and good for the earth.

"That NTA weatherman—Victor Okocha—I thought he studied abroad. They said he learned to tell the weather when he went to school in London."

"My brother, leave the thing when they write for *molue*," (big, uncomfortable public transit bus) "just enter the bus," another man advised in Pidgin English. "Make you no believe everything you hear for radio or TV. No be everybody when go abroad dey go there to study, but all of them dey come back with certificate."

"Some even say them dey go study flower, some say na fish. A beg wetin person dey study fish for? Fish no be to eat am?"

A general laughter ensued. *These are my people,* Grace thought, *this is my level.* If she had completed her education, perhaps she too could have ended up overseas in one university or the other. Like Chuma. Or she may have become a banking executive, working in a fancy office in Jos or other big cities. She may even have made it to medical school and eventually become a doctor. But here she was, with her half-baked education, surrounded by market women and traders, smiling at their crude jokes and feeling like she was getting her just desserts.

"Did you hear about the man who was looking for a job in one *oyibo* country?"

Grace smiled ruefully. She knew what to expect. They would all try to swap jokes now, just to while away the time. That was the way of the Nigerian people. *Suffering and smiling,* they called it. It was the ability to find reason to smile in the face of impossible odds.

"The *bobo* discovered that living overseas is not like living in heaven o! Na real prodigal son, that one. After months of partying and drinking in the *oyibo* land, he don became broke, jobless, homeless and hungry. Another bros from Naija, Ikechi be his name, come tell am say work dey for the *oyibo* zoo. So him apply and he go for the interview. The zookeeper tell am say their gorilla just die and that until they get a new one, they need someone to dress up and act like a gorilla. The dead gorilla used to entertain the crowd and been dey make plenty money for the zoo, so they didn't want the public to know say him don die."

"I don hear this joke before," someone quipped. "Na stupid joke."

"Joke na joke," another person retorted. "Cover your ear if you no wan hear. Make we hear word."

"The job wasn't difficult at all," the storyteller continued. "All he had to do was put on the suit, sit down, eat, sleep and wake up. Who no fit do that kind work? They even promise say they go keep his identity secret. By the time they tell am how much them go pay, the *bobo* quickly agreed to start immediately."

"That one na Igbo man, no argument at all," a voice quipped from behind. The crowd laughed and the storyteller waited for some quiet before continuing.

"When the *bobo* tried on the gorilla costume and looked at the mirror, even he come dey fear the terrible-looking gorilla staring back at him."

The crowd laughed again.

"The zookeeper then put chain 'round his neck and led him into the cage. First he pretended to be sleeping, then he got up and sat down again. When he tire to sit down for ground, he begin waka inside the cage. When he tire for that one, he begin to jump up and down and before you know it, the bros begin to make gorilla noise."

"Na which kind gorilla noise him dey make?" a voice asked. "Like *gorimakpa*?"

"Wetin?"

"Sharrap!"

"Listen!"

"Make we hear word!"

Several people objected to the interruption and urged the storyteller to pick up the tale again.

"Big crowd come gather and begin to watch the gorilla. As he jump up and down they begin clap for am. Some start to throw groundnuts to him. The *bobo* like groundnut well well, and he was already very hungry. So he come dey jump up and down more and more. The more he jump, the more groundnuts they throw him. Very soon, the cinema enter his head and he begin to enjoy himself. So te-h he got carried away. He come see a tree near his cage and him begin to climb am. Ha, the audience don dey shout more and more. And the groundnut rain dey fall heavier and heavier. He grab one branch and start to swing from one side of the cage to the other side. He begin dey do *janglova*. The higher he swing, the more the groundnut rain dey fall, so he continue to swing, higher and higher and higher."

"He will soon meet a real gorilla," someone guessed.

"Or a snake."

"Or a tiger."

"Let the man finish his story, I beg," someone shouted with a loud voice and the noise died down.

The storyteller continued again, only half-succeeding to suppress his own giggles. "He continue swinging higher and higher, up and down until suddenly, the branch break and he was thrown to the ground. At first he think say he fall for his own cage, but when the brother look up, na hungry lion he dey see so. He don fall inside lion's den be that! Fear catch am. Na so the bros begin run, dey shout, 'Help, help! Get me out of here! I no be gorilla o! I be human being o! Na gorilla suit I wear so! *Help!*'"

The crowd burst into laughter again. Grace smiled despite the cold.

"*Tufiakwa!*" someone exclaimed in disgust. "Hm. The thing wey Nigerians no go do for money!"

The storyteller picked it up again after the laughter subsided. "Hold on, hold on. The story never finish. As him dey shout so, pandemonium come break out for the zoo and the people start to run here and there, afraid say the gorilla don become food for the lion. But the lion quickly pounce on the man, hold am very tight and to the bros's surprise he hear a familiar voice saying, "NNAMDI, STOP SCREAMING. IT'S ME, IKECHI. SHARRAP! BE QUIET. YOU WANT MAKE THEM SACK BOTH OF US?"

When the laughter died down, another person quickly started another joke, but Grace tuned him out. She was supposed to be praying for the orphanage, not listening to silly jokes. Knowing what she knew now, she really had no choice but to try and persuade Chuma to tell her who was buying Gidan Mairo so they could make a personal plea for more time for the ministry. What was it Mordecai had told Queen Esther in the Bible? *Who knows? Maybe you were made queen for just such a time as this?* Maybe the Lord had set up this reunion with Chuma to use her to save the orphanage. It was possible. But could she do this without getting emotionally involved with him again?

Luckily the phone was in her hand or she would have missed the vibration announcing an incoming text message. She flicked it open and once more, it was from Chuma. HERE

TO PICK YOU UP —*LAND ROVER ACROSS THE ROAD.*

Grace stared across the road and there indeed was a Land Rover on the other side. Shading her eyes with her hands she peered closely and saw a profile that she recognized instantly as Chuma's. A shiver ran through her and it was not because of the cold wind. How could he have come out in the rain to look for her? How had he even located the elementary school? She blew out an audible sigh, and it trailed in the wind. *God help me*, she prayed and remained where she was.

Five minutes later her phone buzzed again. *COMING TO GET YOU IN 2 MINUTES.*

She knew he meant it and felt a momentary panic. She didn't want him coming out in the rain and wading through puddles of mud to look for her. She looked at her watch and counted to 20, still debating whether or not to call his bluff. Finally she tapped her response, hit send, slid the phone into her handbag and pushed her way through the crowd and into the rain.

When he saw her, he flung open the driver's door and ran across to the passenger side to open the door.

"Thank you," she bit out. "But you shouldn't have bothered. I could have … ughhhhhhh." Her teeth chattered from the cold. She hastily dropped her handbag on the floor and began to rub her palms together to generate warmth.

He spared her the briefest glance before reaching to the back of the car. "What were you trying to do? Give yourself a dose of pneumonia? Why didn't you wait for me at the orphanage? I would have given you a ride to the hotel."

"Sorry. I didn't know you had a car. And I had no idea how long the building inspection would take."

He reached behind the passenger seat and brought out two large towels she recognized from the hotel and draped one around her shoulders. He handed her the second one and then watched intently while she buried her face in it for a few seconds.

He finally answered her question. "We had to stop when the rain started. Why is there so much rain in this city anyway? This is the third time in two weeks that there's been a huge storm. Is it always like this?"

"It's the season," she said simply, and began to wipe the dirt from her body.

Her clothes were wet. She took off her head-tie and grimaced at how wet and dirty it had become. She looked around the luxury car, unsure what to do with the scarf. Before she could ask, he took it from her hands, and opening the driver's door squeezed the water out before shutting the door again. She watched him drop the head-tie on another towel in the backseat. She trembled again.

"What are you doing here anyway?" she muttered through shivering lips. "I thought you went on the Jos plateau tour." She felt more water making its way down from her twists and continued to pat her head, conscious of his watchful eyes.

"And I thought you would be there too," he answered quietly. "Why weren't you?"

"You thought I would be on the tour—because I'm the hotel manager?" She shook her head. "No, I don't do that. Sonshine has a contract with the tour company, but we don't operate the tours ourselves."

There was a slight pause as his gaze locked hers. Only the splatter of the rain on the car could be heard. The heat in the car was already warming her body.

"Well, you promised you would take me around to see Jos," he stated.

"I did not."

"Yes you did. The first night I arrived, when Aunty Bukky realized we knew each other, she practically left me in your care, and you promised me a personal tour."

She looked sharply at him and then relaxed when she realized he was teasing. A reluctant amusement curved her lips. "You can't be serious, Chuma. I made no such promise, and I have no intention of going anywhere with you."

"You did too, and you will. Think of me as a tax collector on this one."

"Meaning?"

"I always collect my debts."

Determined not to respond to his playful tone and definitely not to look into his eyes, she buried her face once more in the towel. Something always happened to her whenever she looked into those eyes, something that made her think of all sorts of crazy things.

"Hey, you're still trembling," he observed. Without asking for permission he took her hands in his and began to rub them together. Her body went stiff and goose bumps multiplied on her arms.

"I'm not making you nervous, am I?"

Her eyes locked on his mouth, at the gentle way his lips moved over his words and the way the air carried the sound and amplified them in the car. A tremor shook her body again and her teeth began to quiver, whether from the cold or from his nearness, she couldn't tell. She pulled away and bit her lower lip.

"Shouldn't we be on our way?" she asked.

"There's no hurry, it's just eight o'clock."

"But what are we waiting for?"

"Let's do the tour tomorrow." His gaze was determined, his voice persuasive. "Will you go with me? Not because I am a guest in your hotel but because I am your long lost and found friend."

"What about Remi?" The words were out before she knew she asked them, much to her embarrassment. Frowning, she tried to summon her normal defences; but anger had deserted her, and in its place was a rising sense of excitement which she was trying desperately to but couldn't quite suppress.

He reached his hand under her chin and gently tipped her face up to meet his gaze. His tentative smile raced through her, warming her more effectively than the heat in the car, more than the towel she still wrapped around her shoulders, sending trails of longing down her spine. When she turned to look out the window again, he let his hand gently slide away from her face, leaving a slight caress.

"What about Remi?" he asked. "What does she have to do with us?"

Grace detected the smile in his voice and was irked. "What us? There is no us."

"Not now there isn't. But there used to be an *us* years ago, Ure, a very big us for that matter. And there's no reason why there can't be an *us* again."

"And how long would it last this time? Until you go back to your life in the States? Until you get tired again and accuse me of trying to tie you down against your will? Or until you get me pregnant again?" She forced the words out before she could convince herself not to say them. "I don't think so, Chuma."

Her words seemed to catch him by surprise and she heard his sudden intake of breath. She swallowed and stared out the window.

"That's what has been bothering you these past weeks, isn't it?" he asked in a low voice, his eyes intent on her face. "You say you have forgiven me, but every time I get near you you behave as if I'm about to pounce on you, and whenever I try to talk to you, you remind me I got you pregnant and abandoned you years ago."

"That's not true."

"All I can say again, until you believe me, is that I am very sorry. I can't do more than that. We were young and I certainly was foolish. I had never been with a girl. When you told me you were pregnant I panicked and reacted badly. But Ure"—his voice broke—"tell me what I can do to make it up to you and I will."

Grace saw the sheen of unshed tears in his eyes and was overcome by the sudden surge of a familiar emotion. The truth was suddenly very clear to her heart. Somehow, sometime in the past two weeks, without her realizing it, he had fallen deep into her heart again. The anger she had been directing at him since he arrived had virtually evaporated, replaced now by feelings she couldn't control. Fool that she was, after the disastrous way their relationship had ended, after all she'd suffered because of him, after all her determination not to give in to his charms again, she had done it again, and inadvertently placed herself in harm's way again. Her hands burned to touch him, to wipe away the tortured look from his eyes and assure him of her forgiveness. But she managed to drag her eyes away and to push her hands against her laps.

"I'm not the person I used to be at Government College, nor are you the girl you used to be," he persisted. "That whole experience changed my life forever. Guilt over the role I played in sending you to a presumed early death 11 years ago sent me into a deep depression which led to a complete mental breakdown. If it was not for my sister, Zola, I don't know how it would all have ended. She threatened to tell my parents if I didn't get counselling. That was the beginning of my search for the meaning of life, which led me to discover the love and forgiveness that can only be found in Christ. I promise you, Ure. I will never deliberately hurt you again. Please believe me and give us another chance."

She stared at him for several seconds before letting her gaze fall. She needed to think but couldn't do it with him staring soulfully into her eyes.

"I think we should head back to the hotel now," she finally mumbled, feeling grateful when he nodded and pushed the gear to drive.

Chapter 16

Calabar

Ego's eyelids gradually flickered open. She blinked until the tiny, multi-coloured stars at the back of her eyes transformed into a gentle glowing sun that seemed unusually long and white. She blinked again and realised she was lying on a soft bed. A strange bed. The white wall opposite nudged at her mind, tugging at a forgotten memory. The sound of distant voices prodded her subconscious, and an unfamiliar tranquillity and peace encircled her heart. She could not remember the last time her mind had known such quietness, so she revelled in it. Perhaps she had died and gone to heaven. Was it possible? She had not been close to the Lord for so many years. Could he have brought her here?

It was the smell that gradually alerted her senses to her surrounding—the smell of medicines and disinfectants and cleaners and alcohol. She saw a plastic wire at the back of her left hand and followed it all the way to a drip chamber. She faintly remembered the last time she had been given a drip—it was after the doctors had cut her open to bring out her firstborn child, Urenna. She frowned. Wasn't there something about Urenna recently? She blinked again and tried to remember. Her breath caught in her chest. She closed her eyes as her heartbeat suddenly began a chaotic rhythm, and memories of her fight with her husband crashed into her heart. *What had Odili said about Urenna?* She whimpered. *That man will kill me before my time if I am not careful.* He knew exactly when and how to turn the dagger he had stuck in her heart years ago and was steadily fast-forwarding her life to certain death. Her earlier feelings of placid contentment disappeared as silent tears coursed down her cheeks. She sniffed.

"Oh, praise the Lord, you're awake." A young girl in starched blue materialised at her side. "How are you feeling, Ma?"

"Where am I? What am I doing here?" Ego managed to croak out. Her words sounded strange to her ears but the girl seemed to understand.

"You're at the Teaching Hospital, madam. Don't you remember? Your husband brought you in this morning."

Ego lifted her eyes to the girl. What was she talking about? She didn't remember how she got here but it couldn't have been that long ago. She had been fighting with Odili only moments ago when he tried to kill her by fabricating that story about Urenna being alive.

"I'll get the doctor," the young girl said again. "Please don't sleep, madam. I'll be right back." She rushed out.

Ego thought she heard her muttering, "Praise God! Praise God!" as she went but she was not sure.

She tried hard to stay awake but her eyes were closing again. She blinked rapidly, willing them to stay open, but she felt so weak and tired. Perhaps it would help if she fixed her eyes on an object, on a bright and shining object like the soft fluorescent light on the ceiling. Summoning all her strength she lifted her eyes and stared steadily into it.

A man in a white overcoat was sitting by her hospital bed. He touched her hand and she relaxed, happy that she hadn't slept before the doctor arrived. Or had he been there all the time? Her memory was all fuzzy; it was a struggle to maintain her focus. Later, she thought, when he was done examining her, she would sleep again. She turned to him, grateful for his presence. Maybe he would tell her exactly why she was in the hospital. She couldn't remember Odili beating her but maybe he had. Her memory about their argument was vague.

But the doctor didn't say anything. He seemed more interested in looking into her eyes than in checking her body. She returned his gaze and was surprised at the gentleness and compassion she saw in him. There was no arrogance or loftiness, no fear. Only kindness, peace, love and all that felt pure all at once. As the seconds ticked by she realized that as she continued to look into his eyes, strength was beginning to surge into her body and spirit. Even stranger was the fact that the longer she looked into his eyes, the less she could hear the tumultuous beating of her own heart and the wild racing of her pulse. In fact, the longer she looked at him the calmer her heart felt within her; so she looked, and looked, until her spirit knew absolute, wonderful, perfect peace.

When he smiled and offered his hand, palm outward to her, she did not hesitate to take it. He lifted her up from the bed. She was already standing at the door with him before she looked back. A familiar figure lay on the bed she had just vacated and a frenzy of activities seemed to be going on in the room.

A doctor was slapping the woman on the bed, poking at her with needles, shouting in her ear to wake up. The poor woman—was she dead? The young nurse was running around in circles, handing equipment to the doctor and joining to urgently call the woman to wake up. Ego could hear the sound of running feet toward the room.

But there was no time to stay and watch. Gentle hands turned her face from the scene and propelled her upward. A gentle breeze fanned her face, and when she looked up, the roof of her hospital room opened to reveal millions of twinkling stars smiling down at her. Her legs took on wings, and before she knew it she was sailing the night sky, her gentle guide firmly by her side.

"Where?" she whispered. "What is happening?"

In answer, he held her closer to his side and they glided faster and higher toward the stars. At first they dipped in and out of the clouds, between snow-white, luxurious balls of cotton that enfolded her in a gentle caress. The soothing wind that lifted them brought waves of peace and serenity, and she closed her eyes to drink in again the peace that surrounded her on every side.

"Oh!"

Just when she thought she had seen it all, they popped out of the clouds into a world filled with thick, lush, green vegetation. She felt compelled to walk on those green fields. She had to feel the verdant grass under her feet and be enveloped in its fluffy softness. How she wished she could lie down on it.

"May I?" She looked at her companion. Her lips did not move but he heard her heart.

He set her down and she felt moisture from the tall blades of soft green grass beneath her feet. The grass swirled around her, right up to her waist. She touched it with the tips of her fingers. It was wet, as though recently touched by rain showers. She looked to her left and then to her right—all around her was the endless verdant fields. She'd never seen such vegetation before. She'd never experienced such beauty. It made her feel happy and peaceful and joyful and completely whole.

She turned at the sound of gentle running water. Across the field somebody who looked exactly like her gentle doctor was watching over a flock of sheep drinking from a flowing stream. Where had the sheep come from? They weren't there a moment ago. Neither was the shepherd. She looked again and realised the shepherd by the river was indeed her gentle doctor. How could he be by her side in one blink and with his sheep in another?

He must have heard her thoughts again, for he looked up suddenly, beckoned her with a smile and she ran to him. In his hand there was a gourd filled with water. The words Revelation 7:17 were inscribed on the gourd. She racked her brain, trying to remember what that verse said, but even when she was stronger in her faith she had never read the book of Revelation.

Tell me, Lord. What does this verse say?

He smiled and offered her the gourd, urging her to drink. She felt more strength and power and courage flow into her body as she drank. *I am the living water*—she heard the words even though his lips didn't move. *He who believes in me shall never thirst again.... Whoever believes in me, as the Scripture has said, streams of living water will flow from within him. Whoever believes in me ... whoever believes in me ... whoever believes in me ...*

The words resounded in her heart. *Lord, I believe in you,* she cried. *I really do.*

In response he took her hand, and they started to mount the clouds again. They sailed past miles and miles of green fields, past indescribably picturesque mountains and streams and valleys, toward the sun.

It has to be the sun, she thought. *I've never seen a light so bright before.*

But they never made it to the sun. Just when she thought they would ascend even higher she found they were descending rapidly through the paths they had already passed. In no time they were back in the vegetation, through the white clouds, through the clear sky and the stars and now she could see the roof of the hospital room from where he had taken her. She realised his intention and held tightly to his hand.

"No, no. No!" she cried. "I don't want to go back there!" Her tears flowed. "Please take me with you, Lord. I want to be with you."

He smiled, and once again she felt his hug even though he didn't touch her as they descended through the roof and into the room. From the door she finally recognised the body on the bed. She saw Añuli sobbing uncontrollably. The young nurse was wiping her eyes as quickly as the tears were pouring and was crying loudly. A man holding a Bible was trying to console them. The doctor was shaking his head in regret, looking defeated and confused. Then she saw the nurse go to the closet and come back with a white sheet and a tray of hospital instruments. The doctor unhooked the drip chamber from her hand, removed the oxygen mask from her nose and picked two pieces of cotton wool and pushed gently into her nostrils. He glanced at his wristwatch, covered her entire body with the sheet and began to write something on the folder by the head of the bed.

But I'm not dead, Lord. Why are they all crying?

She knew the moment he began to withdraw from her. Suddenly she felt his presence leaving, she saw his face fading. *Give me something, Lord,* she cried desperately. *Give me something to remember you by.*

Then his voice came, and it was like thunder, louder than any voice she had ever heard, silencing every other sound. Yet she was not scared. *"You will find me in Revelation 7:17. I am always with you. I will never leave you. Peace I give to you ... take my peace ... my peace ... peace."*

"Amen," she whispered. She wanted to cry. The stench of hospital drugs floated rapidly to her senses, causing her to sneeze softly. The cotton wool in her nostrils was choking her. The sneeze came back into her mouth and panic seized her. They were making a terrible mistake thinking she was dead. She had to let them know. The smell coming from the shroud that covered her body was strong and pungent. What did they pour on that thing? The nausea rose in her again, and this time, praying to God for help, Ego gave a loud sneeze and opened her mouth to let the bile out of her stomach. She tried to reach for the cloth that still covered her face but her hands stayed at her side, unable to lift up. She tried to call to the nurse but even she could not recognise the guttural sound that came from her mouth.

There was silence in the room for a split second before the doctor yanked the cloth from her face. He grabbed her hand. "I've got a pulse!" he shouted to the nurse. "Bring back the oxygen!"

Ego coughed, her throat parched and dry. She wanted to ask for water but everybody in the room had gone into overdrive, running helter-skelter to restore her breathing. Her head was beginning to feel woozy again. Her eyes flickered, and she raised them to her daughter for a few seconds. The poor girl's eyes were filled with tears. Ego wanted to kiss those tears away. Anuli hugged the man with the Bible, and they held hands and watched the flurry of activity with excitement.

She coughed again and the young nurse put a spoon of water to her lips. As she sipped, Ego noticed the pendant the girl was wearing. Her heart gave a lurch at the inscription on the pendant. It looked vaguely familiar.

"What does it say?" she asked the girl.

"What did you say, Ma?" The girl's voice was gentle. There were tears in her eyes.

"Tell me," Ego said again, urgently. "What does it say?"

Frowning, the nurse looked up. "Doctor," she whispered quietly. "Her words are all slurred and disjointed. She's talking, but I can't make out what she's saying."

The doctor turned to look into her eyes. "You gave us all a nasty scare just now, madam. Do you understand what I just said?"

Ego nodded ever so slightly.

"Good. You need to rest. I want you to stay calm. Don't struggle to say anything, okay? Just relax."

"But what does it say?" Ego asked again.

"What? Say that again."

"What—does—it—say?" she asked, as slowly as she could.

"There's no need to get agitated and worked up, madam. Just take things easy for a day or two. The speech will come back gradually."

"Let me try, Doctor," Ańuli said. "Perhaps I can understand what she's trying to say."

He gave up his seat by the bedside and Ańuli took her mother's hand. Ego tried to smile when her daughter knelt by the bed, clutching at her hands and crying for joy.

"I love you, Mama." Ańuli sniffed. "Please don't leave me."

Ego nodded. She lifted a hand to pat her daughter's face and was shocked at how gnarled and disfigured her hand had become. Her wrist turned inward, her thumb bent into her palm and her fingers couldn't keep straight. She must have suffered a stroke, she thought, or a heart attack.

"I yuuv yuu," she said clearly.

Her audience gasped in amazement. The doctor nodded to Añuli and she continued. "Mama, you scared me."

"I twa-tttwa—vuld," Ego whispered.

"What did you say, Mama? Can you speak slowly so I can understand you?"

"I tw-aaa-vull-d," she said again, stretching the words as long as she could.

"Oh, you travelled? Where did you go? Do you remember where you travelled to?"

She nodded slowly.

"That's good, Mama. But you have to sleep now. The doctor says you must rest. You can tell me all about your journey when you wake up."

Ego shook her head slowly, as firmly as her weak neck could move.

"Rrrr-evl-tn 7:17," she whispered.

"What was that?"

"Rrrr-evl-tn 7:17."

"Mama, you need to speak slowly. Don't rush your words so I can follow. You need to speak slowly."

In answer, Ego turned her eyes to the young man hovering by the bedside.

"Bible," she said.

"I heard that." The pastor came to her side. "You want me to read the Bible to you?"

Ego nodded. A collective sigh came from the assembly. She felt beads of perspiration heating up her face. It would be better to rest as the doctor said but she just had to know what that verse said. Añuli dabbed at the sweat from her forehead with a towel.

"What do you want me to read?"

Ego turned to the nurse. "Necklace," she said.

"What?"

She tried to push her chin down to her chest. "N-n-n-eck?"

"Yes, you mean neck?"

She nodded.

Understanding dawned on the nurse. "Oh, you mean my necklace?"

Ego nodded.

The nurse was puzzled. "You want my necklace?"

Ego patiently swayed her head from side to side. If they had to stay here all night they all would, until someone read those verses to her.

"Rrrr-evl-tns," she said again.

"Can I see the necklace?" the pastor asked the nurse.

"Of course." She unhooked it and gave it to him.

He examined it closely. "Ah, I see," he said. "Your necklace says Revelation 7:17. Is that where you want me to read to you, madam?"

Ego relaxed and nodded.

Everybody waited as he thumbed through the pages of his Bible. "Here. It says: the Lamb who is in the midst of the throne will shepherd them. He will lead them to the springs of life-giving water, and God will wipe away every tear from their eyes."

She nodded again, and this time, the tears flowed freely down her cheeks.

"Thank you, Jesus," she whispered.

And everyone heard her very clearly.

PART 2

Chapter 17

Jos

Grace slipped into the manager's office on Sunday morning and shut the door. It wasn't yet six o'clock but the staff were already awake and going about their morning duties. Her stomach growled when she sat in front of the computer and she frowned, realising that in the midst of her confusion last night, she had forgotten to eat dinner.

"I'm just looking for trouble," she mumbled under her breath. She got up and headed to the dining room, returning with a slice of bread and a glass of water.

While the computer completed its start-up ceremony, she propped her head in her hands and began to feel again a ripple of unease as she contemplated what she was about to do. Did her family really believe she was dead? Chuma's newspaper cuttings certainly showed that they initially thought so, to the extent that they had buried someone they must have thought was her. But what about later? What about the letters she had written to them? What about the pictures she had sent them? She never got any of those back. They would have realised their mistake. Her father had threatened to disown her. Had he carried out his threat? Were her mother and sister also part of the plot?

You will know the truth, the Scriptures said, *and the truth will set you free.*

After a night spent alternatively tossing on her bed and staring at the ceiling, she had come to terms with the fact that unless she made peace with her past, she couldn't step into the future. Lack of knowledge, her schoolteacher used to say, is darker than night, and recently her nights seemed to have gotten darker than usual. She bowed her head in a silent prayer for guidance and then clicked the Internet icon and began the search for her sister.

The Google page appeared and she typed "Aṅuli Okolie" in the search bar and dragged the pointer to search the entire Internet. Okolie was not an uncommon name. Neither was Aṅuli, so she expected to see many Aṅuli Okolies on the page. The first entry that caught her eye was the announcement that *Aṅuli Okolie is on Facebook! Join Facebook to connect with Aṅuli Okolie and others you may know …*

She didn't want to join Facebook so she scrolled down. There was a Dr. Charity Aṅuli Okolie of the University of Ife; a Joyce Aṅuli Okolie of Wisconsin, USA; a Susanna Okolie of Greenwich, England; and many others. Her heart sank. None of them looked remotely familiar. If indeed her sister was married and had changed names, she would have to move to Plan B. No—not to search for her father, of whom she was still leery, but for her mother. Egoyibo Okolie, she knew, would be the last person to have anything to do with the Internet. Her recollection of her mother was of a quiet, demure and passive woman, devoted to her family and not particularly curious about what was happening outside her home. But you never know—sometimes even when you don't go putting out information about yourself on the Internet, others do it for you.

She was on the fifth page of the Google search, ready to stop and switch the search to her mother when she saw something that looked like a possibility. It was a newspaper article "Taking Dental Health to Riverine Communities" by Dr. Destiny Añuli Okolie. She clicked on the link and it opened to the article. Clicking further on the highlighted byline linked her to a box that read *Destiny Añuli Okolie, School of Dentistry, Calabar University Teaching Hospital. Contact Dr. Destiny A. Okolie. Add Destiny Añuli Okolie to your network.*

Grace's hand shook as she jotted down the information. This had to be Añuli. The names matched. How many "Añuli Destiny"s could there be at the University of Calabar? And she was a dentist too. Their father had wanted them both to become medical doctors, so that figured. Grace's heart lifted despite her anxiety. Her little sister had made it after all, she thought. Añuli was a medical doctor.

She Googled the teaching hospital's website, and it was surprisingly easy how she could immediately come up with contact numbers and e-mails. She studied the composition of the e-mail addresses. It was easy: firstinitial_surname@cuth.org. She would permutate the different combinations of Añuli's names and see if an e-mail to one of them would go through.

She typed in the subject line: *Looking for Urenna Okolie.* Quickly, before her courage would desert her, she typed out her letter. As soon as she hit the send button, Grace felt a sense of accomplishment. She had done her part. It was now up to the Lord to do the rest, according to his will.

Grace attended the second service at the Jos Jubilee church later that morning. She was not on choir duty, so it was easy to sit in the privacy of a back row seat and try to organise her scattered thoughts. She wished Ayesha was in church. When they spoke this morning, her friend had told her she would be tending to her mother-in-law, who was leaving back to Abuja that morning.

She thought about her own mother. Most people didn't know it, but beneath her submissive and quiet ways, Egoyibo Okolie was stubborn and bold. That night, when her father almost killed her with his *koboko*, it was her mother who had stepped in and helped her escape. Immediately after her mother had broken the door with a club and charged into the parlour, a phone call had come through from the vice chancellor, requesting that her father meet him at the university clubhouse. Grace still shivered whenever she thought about what could have happened to her if the phone hadn't interrupted them. Maybe he had really intended to kill her. Her mother had come to her then, untying the rope with which her father had bound her to the dining table.

"Have you seen my car keys?" he'd asked.

But her mother was sobbing over Grace and didn't answer him.

"Have you seen my keys? I have to meet the vice chancellor at the clubhouse in ten minutes."

"You are a wicked man, Odili. You have nearly killed your daughter, and all you can think about is your meeting with the VC. Go away, Odili, and let me look after my daughter. Just go," Ego had replied.

Finally he had decided to walk to the clubhouse, which was only four blocks away. As soon as he left, her distraught mother had gently led her to her father's car and driven her to a private clinic just outside the university gates. Later, when Grace would think about it, she would marvel, not just because her mother had hidden the keys from her father but because she had dared drive her father's car. Professor Odili never let anyone touch his car.

Grace shook her head to refocus her mind. She didn't want to remember. The past was over and done with. *Forget the former things*, the Bible said. But hadn't she tried to do that? Hadn't she been content with her new life before Chuma rolled in to turn everything upside down? Now even the walls of self-preservation she had carefully erected over her heart over the years were crumbling down with ease. One minute she was avoiding him, and in the next, without any warning, he had found another entrance into her heart. Just like that.

There could not possibly be any point in having these feelings for Chuma, she acknowledged. It was hopeless. Yes, he had intimated last night that he still liked her and wanted to resume their previous relationship, but she would be deceiving herself by expecting that anything serious would come of it. Their disastrous history aside, the things that separated them were much more than the things that could ever unite them.

Grace chewed at her lower lip and shook her head again. *Why, Lord? You know I was perfectly happy the way things were. Why are you allowing this to happen to me?*

Beloved, not one hair of your head will fall to the ground without my knowledge, the gentle response floated into her heart. She swallowed hard and wiped away the errant tears.

Please talk to me, Lord. Are you in this?

I am with you always. I will never leave you nor forsake you.

Please help me believe your promises, she prayed silently. *Help me believe you will cause everything, even this, to work together for my good. Please don't let me stray from your will for my life. Hold me close. Don't let my desires rule over me.*

Remember that I am the Lord. I do not change. I am the same yesterday, today and forevermore.

Dragging herself back to the present, Grace realised the congregation was rising for the worship session. She rose and joined them in singing one of her favourite worship hymns. "When peace, like a river, attendeth my soul; when sorrows, like sea billows, roll; whatever my lot, thou hast taught me to say: it is well, it is well, with my soul."

She clasped her hands tightly to her chest as she sang, moved as always by the lyrics of the beloved hymn. She remained standing as the next song blended with the last. "Great is thy faithfulness, O Lord, my father, There is no shadow of turning with thee, thou changest not, thy compassions they fail not, as thou hast been Thou forever will be."

Grace was amazed at the connection between those words and her conversation with the Lord only a few minutes ago. This was confirmation that she had really been speaking with the Lord. She shivered again. The Lord was so near and she hadn't known it. Hope brightened her eyes. There was comfort in knowing that no matter how confused and heavy her load was, she could draw strength from his abiding presence. God was the author of wisdom, and as long as she kept him at the centre of her heart she could count on him to help sort out the tangled mess of her life and lead her in paths of righteousness.

More music followed, but Grace continued her private dialogue with the Lord. His presence was all around her, and she wanted to hear the words he was speaking to her soul. The heaviness in her heart remained, deep sadness shrouding her heart, but she knew a calm assurance deep within that the Lord would make a way for her.

Grace did not want to linger after the service, but she wanted to order the CD of the sermon for Ayesha. So she smiled at some church members and greeted others as they slowly streamed out from the sanctuary to the foyer.

She heard someone call her name and she turned. It was the leader of the women's fellowship.

"I was hoping to catch you, Grace. Are you coming to the Easter love feast next Saturday?"

Grace shook her head. "I'm sorry, I can't. Both Auntie Simbi and the twins are coming home on Friday. I'll be busy ..."

The foyer was filling up with more people. She hurriedly went to join the queue at the CD counter. The choir leader met her on the way and reminded her to attend the rehearsals for the Easter concert.

It was almost her turn to pay when an extreme hunger pang hit her and she felt weakness sweep through her. Her tongue riveted to the roof of her mouth and sudden panic flooded over her. Her feet wobbled, and she quickly made for the bathroom. Luckily the washbasin was free. She leaned over the sink and reached for the vial of glucose tablets in her handbag, fighting a paralysing weakness. To her dismay, there was only one tablet. She quickly unscrewed the cap, threw the tablet into her mouth and began to chew. She continued to lean over the basin as she gradually regained her strength. Thank God she even had the one tablet, she thought. She had to go home immediately and eat something. She looked up and winced at the pale face that stared back at her from the mirror above the sink. Ripples of sweat were trickling down her face. Berating herself over her negligence, she turned on the tap to splash water over her face. She had just finished when movement in the glass alerted her someone had come behind her. She turned around and encountered Remi's derisive sneer.

"Don't tell me you're pregnant again!" the woman mocked loudly.

Grace shook her and turned away. "What are you talking about?"

"You're pregnant again!" Remi declared.

Grace shook her head again. "What makes you think that? I'm not pregnant."

"Yes, you are. It's written all over you. And you were throwing up in the sink just now."

"I … I wasn't throwing up," Grace replied faintly, conscious of the door opening and another woman coming in. She recognized her as one of Remi's friends and her heart sank.

"Yes, you were. I saw you. You're looking tired. You're vomiting. What other sign should I be looking for?"

"You're crazy."

"Does Auntie Simbi know?" Remi taunted. "Does Auntie Bukky know? Does Chucks know?"

Grace shook her head and made for the door. "I don't have time for you."

"What's happening here? Who's pregnant?" Remi's friend quipped.

Their laughter burned in her ears as she stepped weakly into the foyer.

More people had gathered at the counter, and sounds of their greetings and conversations buzzed loudly in her ears.

After paying for the CD, she scanned the foyer one more time and prepared to exit. She urgently needed to get home.

But Auntie Bukky stood by the exit, in a circle that included Uncle Tunde, Mama Remi and Chuma. They saw her at the same time and she couldn't stop her feet from automatically walking toward them.

"Ah, there you are," Auntie Bukky remarked as she joined them. "Are you all right? You're looking pale."

Grace nodded and bent her knees in curtsy.

"Chukwuma was just telling us you are taking him on the plateau tour this afternoon."

"I am?"

"He says you are." Auntie Bukky looked from Grace to Chuma and back again to Grace's flushed face.

"Of course you are. Did you forget?"

"You asked me. I didn't agree to go."

"You didn't refuse."

"That doesn't mean I agreed."

"But I thought you went on the tour yesterday," Uncle Tunde remarked to Chuma. "Why do you want to do it again?"

"I didn't complete it. I left halfway because I had other engagements in town. But do you remember the first day I came? Aunty Bukky said Grace would show me around Jos. I've been waiting for that personal tour."

"Ah, that's true. I remember. It was on the night we took you over to Sonshine. You promised, Grace."

Grace adamantly shook her head. "I did not, Uncle."

"Yes you did."

"I was there, and I heard you promise that—"

Grace gave up. "Well, even if I did, I can't go today. I have to go back to Sonshine right away."

"Is something wrong at the hotel?" Auntie Bukky wanted to know.

"No, but I didn't tell anybody I would be away all afternoon."

"I'll tell them," Mama Remi offered. "We'll be fine."

"Ugh!" Grace looked around, feeling outnumbered and outwitted. She tried to smile. "Did you all plan this?"

Everyone laughed.

"We'll leave you to sort this out between yourselves," Auntie Bukky concluded. "Grace, my daughter called this morning to confirm that she's coming home for Easter. She'll be travelling down with Simbi on Friday."

"Zuliat is coming home? Auntie, that's wonderful."

"It is. You know what this means, don't you?

"Umm ...?" No, she couldn't remember.

"Chukwuma's reception on Saturday. We now have to extend the invitation to include Zuliat's friends."

"Oh. Okay."

Someone called to Uncle Tunde. "Call me later so we can finalise the details," Auntie Bukky threw over her shoulder as she followed her husband to greet their friend.

Mama Remi spotted a friend and wandered off, and in no time Grace found herself alone with Chuma. He came closer but kept his distance, grinning. Grace looked down at her hands, not certain what to say next. She truly needed to get back to the hotel, but not for the reasons she had given. She needed to eat if she didn't want another attack of hypoglycaemia.

"You're looking exhausted. Are you feeling well?"

His question forced her to refocus, but she only looked away. "I do need to get back to the hotel."

"I'm sorry if we embarrassed you just now. Please allow me to take you back to the hotel."

"Hey, Chucks?" A familiar feminine voice floated to the couple from around the corner.

"Remi," Chuma said. Grace thought his eyes lit up at the sight of the beautiful woman.

With a muffled, "Excuse me for a second," thrown in Grace's direction, he moved toward the voice.

"What a surprise. I thought you said you never go to church."

Remi laughed. "When the right person invites me, I do. How could I possibly say no to you?"

Grace saw her chance to escape and grabbed it. Slipping down the hallway and finding the stairs, she walked out to the parking lot and down the driveway. Church members still milled around, waiting for buses and flagging down taxis. She waved greetings to those she knew but didn't stop to talk to anyone. She had to go home.

Chapter 18

Jos

Instead of waiting for a taxi in front of the church, Grace decided to walk to the next block and to flag down a taxi from there to Sonshine Estate. The hotel was a 20-minute walk, and she ordinarily would have trekked it, but with the roads still wet from Saturday's heavy rain and puddles of gummy dirt covering most of the ground, walking was not an option. And she was getting hungry again.

In a few minutes she branched off Gangare main road into an un-tarred bush path, the so-called Appian Bypass. The steady, rhythmic beat of her shoes as she walked down the road was calming, and for the first time since her encounter with Remi in the bathroom, the tension in her shoulders began to ease. Walking down the path gave her more opportunity to try to make sense of her disconcerting feelings. With every encounter they had since his arrival, she had seen for herself how much Chuma had changed from the arrogant boy she had known in secondary school to a considerate and humble man who treated her and others with respect. He seemed to genuinely care about her. She hadn't given him any reason to think she would ever care for him again. If anything, she had tried her best to show him it was hopelessly over between them. But last night he'd come looking for her in the rain, worried that she might have been stuck on her way home. How was she supposed to resist such kindness? But he'd be gone in a few weeks, she reminded herself, and after that, she could—

Suddenly, the ground beneath her feet seemed to wobble, and a wave of dizziness swept over her. She slowed down to take deep breaths, aghast at the perspiration that was seeping through her face and neck and arms and was beginning to course down a line on her face. She walked for a few more faltering steps before a paralysing weakness overcame her and she began to gasp for breath. She looked around, hoping to see someone or that someone would see her, but there was no movement. Only trees and bush. She heard the distant sound of traffic ahead and knew she couldn't make it to the other side, not unless she could find some way to restore her balance.

Now panicking, she stumbled toward a bench-shaped tree trunk, eased herself down and reached for her cell phone. The buttons faded in and out of focus, but she held on for a few seconds, and willed her fingers to hit the call button. She did not know who she spoke to, or what she said. All that registered was that her body system – inside and out – seemed to be collapsing, and that she couldn't help herself. Closing her eyes, she sent a silent plea heavenward. *Please, Lord, help me!*

"Grace, Grace, is that you? Grace, are you okay? Grace!" Chuma kept repeating. But the voice from the other side had stopped speaking, and all he could hear was faint breathing, and even that was fading. Confusion and panic washed over him. Something was terribly wrong.

"Here, let me talk to her," Uncle Tunde said from behind him. Chuma passed the phone to him and told the driver to slow down.

Tunde listened for a few seconds before shaking his head. "I can't hear anything. Are you sure it was Grace?"

"It's her phone number, and it was her voice, but she sounded strange. She muttered something about Appian Bypass. What could that mean?"

Uncle Tunde's driver spoke up. "I know Appian Bypass, sir. It's not too far from here. But it's a bush road. We can't drive through it."

"Then how on earth did she get there?"

"She must have decided to walk back to the hotel from church. I must have a word with that girl. She's overdoing this exercise thing," Auntie Bukky's irritated voice was laced with concern.

"Maybe she's been attacked," Chuma cried out. "We must find her."

"I can be at the Gangare end of the road in two minutes," the driver said. "I'll drop you at the entrance and I'll drive to the exit. Even if she has crossed the main road, she wouldn't have gone far."

Uncle Tunde agreed. "Chuma and I will go in from the entrance. You can come in from the exit road. Bukky, you will wait in the car. Let's go!"

Panic like he could not remember ever feeling before seized Chuma's heart. He knew all the horrible things that could happen to anyone on the roads in Nigeria. It didn't matter if it was Lagos, Port Harcourt or Jos. Armed robbers lurked in every city, attacking and killing innocent people in broad daylight and getting away with it in the absence of an effective police system.

Oh God, he prayed desperately. *Please, please, please help her, keep her safe.*

Mercy, the fruit hawker, thought the lady sitting propped up by the tree trunk was waiting for someone. Unless her companions were close by, that was a dangerous thing to do. Gone were the days when anybody, especially a woman, could go anywhere at any time without fear of attack by hooligans.

Mercy looked back to check on her own companions. Eliza walked with a limp, and Nasiru had adjusted his steps to match hers. They would all have stayed on the south side of Gangare Road, but there were many others hawking their wares along the road and too few potential buyers, today being Sunday and all. So they had decided to go across the Appian Bypass to North Gangare, hoping for better luck.

Something about the way the lady sat against the tree alerted her senses that something may be wrong. When she got closer, she saw that her head was bowed, and although her cell phone was in her hand, she wasn't gripping or talking into it. Her handbag had fallen to the ground. She was sitting down, yet she almost looked—

"Oh no!" Mercy panicked and rushed to her. Setting her fruit tray on the ground, she dropped on one knee beside the girl and gripped her shoulders.

"*Menene, yarinya?* What is the matter? Are you okay?" Mercy asked in Hausa. When she didn't raise her head Mercy shook her gently and waited. In response, the girl muttered something intelligible and would have fallen on her face if Mercy hadn't stepped forward to cushion her head with her left shoulder.

Mercy's presence seemed to finally register in the girl's subconscious; she opened glassy eyes to stare weakly at her. She tried to speak again but her voice was faint and her lips were trembling. Mercy couldn't hear a word. She wiped at the perspiration swimming down the girl's face with her outer wrapper. As she watched, wondering what to do next, she began to slip into unconsciousness again.

Frantically, Mercy called to her friends for help.

"I think she fainted," Nasiru said as soon as he got to them. "Probably dehydrated from the sun. Let's splash some cold water on her face. She'll wake up immediately."

"Are you sure? See, she's opened her eyes."

"Yes, but she's not fully conscious. We have to wake her up with cold water, and then feed her so she can get some strength back. This was what happened to my niece three years ago. It's just the weather, the heat. Eliza, peel one banana. As soon as I pour the water and she wakes up, Mercy, you put the banana in her mouth."

"But, Nasiru—"

"There's no time. Just watch and see."

True to his words, the lady opened her eyes when he hit her with the cold water. As she started to blink rapidly, they thrust the banana into her mouth and she started to eat, slowly at first, and then more quickly. Before she finished one, Eliza was ready with another, and as Mercy held her in her arms, the young lady quickly downed the second banana.

Before long, her breathing evened and her eyes started to come back to life.

Nasiru doused the sick woman's head-tie with cold water and gave it to Mercy to wrap around her head. Eliza offered her another banana but she shook her head. They all watched anxiously as she closed her eyes and fell back again against Mercy.

"I think she's coming around," Nasiru said. "Let's give her some time."

Almost immediately they heard voices from behind.

"Grace!" the first voice shouted.

"Grace, where are you?" the second voice called out.

The girl opened her eyes.

"Are you Grace?" Mercy asked in a gentle voice.

She nodded weakly.

"Grace! Grace!" The voices were calling urgently.

"Are they your people? Do you want us to tell them where you are?"

Again the girl nodded. When they heard her name again Nasiru answered and led Chuma and Uncle Tunde to their little party.

Chuma came into the clearing first and made straight for her. Grace saw the concern he made no attempt to hide on his face. She realised it must have been his number she had called at the onset of her sickness. Uncle Tunde looked just as worried.

"I'm okay," she answered the unspoken question in his eyes. "Really."

But he did not seem convinced. "You don't look it. What happened to you?"

"I had an attack."

"Hypoglycaemia?"

She nodded. "I'm afraid I haven't been eating well."

"Didn't you have your emergency kit with you?" Uncle Tunde sounded shocked.

"I ate the last glucose bar in church."

"Then why didn't you just go home immediately from church? My goodness, Grace, I thought you were more careful than that. Do you realise what could have happened if these folks hadn't found you here? You may have been here for—"

"I'm sorry, Uncle."

Chuma tried to follow their conversation but he didn't understand what they were talking about. Why would Uncle Tunde be angry because Grace had suffered a bout of hypoglycaemia? Didn't everybody experience fatigue once in a while?

Nasiru was speaking to Uncle Tunde in Hausa. Chuma didn't understand the language, but from the pieces of Pidgin English mixed with the language, he knew Nasiru was explaining how they found Grace in a dead faint and how they had taken care of her. Chuma turned again to Grace and took her hand. His hand was unsteady as he gently squeezed hers.

As the conversation around them buzzed on, he whipped out his cell phone.

"Aunty Bukky, we've found her!"

He still held her hand as they watched Uncle Tunde thank her rescue party. Each of the three fruit hawkers refused the money he offered them but allowed him to buy some fruit from each of their trays. Chuma was not surprised. Among Africans, especially in Nigeria, it was against most traditions to accept monetary reward for emergency acts of kindness done for others. It was commonly believed that when the tables are turned, you would want others to be kind to you too without seeking monetary reward.

Twenty minutes later, Grace sat beside Chuma in the Land Rover, on their way back to Sonshine Estate. Auntie Bukky had invited her to go home with them but when she insisted on getting back to Sonshine so she could check her blood sugar level and take her medication, Chuma had offered to take her back.

Despite the potholes on the wet road, he tried to make the drive as smooth as possible. He glanced her way often and felt his heart lurch at how pale she looked. Her eyes were closed, but he could tell from her pursed lips and the evenness of her breathing that she was not sleeping. He didn't press her to talk, sensing she might still be upset about the reprimand from Auntie Bukky when they came out from Appian Bypass. *How could you have been so careless, Grace?* she'd demanded as she handed her a bottle of ginger ale. *If anything happens to you now, what will become of your children?*

Chuma wished the journey was longer and the road smoother so she could really relax and possibly sleep. Part of the problem with Grace, he figured, was that she was too alone and much too independent. That in itself was unhealthy. She was also stubborn and unwilling to accept any help from anybody, especially him. He had to find a way to break down her defences.

Soon they reached an unfamiliar fork in the road and he had to disturb her. "Grace," he said in a quiet voice to avoid startling her, "where do I turn from here?"

Her eyelids flickered open and she sat up. "Make a left at the next corner. Dilimi Junction is just down the road. Another left will lead you directly to Sonshine Estate."

Within five minutes Chuma stopped at the hotel entrance and waited while the security guards opened the gates. He pulled into the parking lot in front of the Recreation Centre, but when Grace started to open her door, he restrained her, his touch gentle but firm. "Wait, don't go yet."

Arching her brows in surprise, she sat back again.

"How are you feeling?"

"I'm fine; a bit shaken but otherwise okay."

Chuma's eyes pored over her. He could see that she was looking significantly stronger than she did thirty minutes ago. Her eyes were bright and clear, her trembling had subsided significantly and she did in fact look more like herself. He exhaled slowly in relief.

"Do you have these attacks frequently?"

There was a little silence as she appeared to consider his question.

"Not really. This afternoon's was the most intense so far. But it wouldn't have happened if I hadn't been careless."

"Because you skipped a meal?" He shrugged. "Everybody skips a meal every now and then."

Angling her head, Grace seemed to choose her response carefully. "When you have diabetes, you can't take such chances."

His heart sank. "Is that what you have?"

She nodded slowly and looked away. "I was diagnosed less than a year ago. I'm still getting used to it."

She fell silent again and he thought she looked embarrassed. He was at a loss for words to comfort her, so he kept quiet.

"What do you know about diabetes?" she finally asked.

He shook his head and tried to think clearly. "Not much, I'm afraid. An old classmate died recently. I was told he had diabetes. That's all that comes to mind; I've never been exposed to it."

Grace shrugged indifferently. "It is a disease you get when your body fails to properly utilise the sugar in your blood, either because of insufficient insulin production from the pancreas or because the insulin that is produced is not working effectively. Instead of being used for energy, the sugar builds up in the blood."

Listening to her fluently explain in layman's terms a medical condition he suspected to be quite complicated, Chuma shook his head sadly, regretting that she had not pursued her dream of being a doctor. A pang of guilt assailed him again as he considered the part his actions had played in derailing her from this dream. He wished again, for the umpteenth time, that he could turn back the hands of time to undo the wrong he did to her.

"There are different types of diabetes,' she continued. "In my case, my pancreas produces some insulin but my body is unable to regulate it with the sugar. The doctor says I can help my body achieve the desired balance through watching my diet, exercising regularly and through proper medication. When I do all that, I am fine. But I was careless today. I exercised a lot, on an empty stomach. That's why the crisis happened."

"I'm sorry," he whispered.

"I usually carry some emergency supplies, including candies and glucose bars, but I have run out. In their absence, some energy-giving snacks can provide immediate relief."

"Hence the banana," he said as understanding dawned.

"Hence the banana," she nodded. "But that was a temporary measure. As soon as I get into my suite I will check my blood-sugar level, take my medication and eat a proper meal."

"Should you be on your own, though?"

"What do you mean?"

"What if this happens again when you are all by yourself?"

"It won't as long as I'm careful."

He wasn't convinced she was fine, even though she seemed so confident. Her confidence hadn't averted the medical crisis he had witnessed less than one hour ago.

"Look, maybe I should go and bring Ayesha to stay with you. Or even one of the waitresses. You shouldn't be on your own when you're feeling sick."

"Thanks for your concern but I'll be okay. I'll call Ayesha later."

"Don't you have to check in with your doctor?"

"I don't think it's necessary. I know how to get it under control again."

"You're not a doctor, Ure. Call him now."

"Now?"

"Yes. You have his number, don't you?"

"Of course I do, but don't you think I need to check my blood-sugar level and eat something before I call him? That way I can answer his questions."

"Okay. When you do, would you let me know what he says?"

"Why?"

"Because you might need to go to the clinic, and if you do I would like to drive you there myself."

She sat back and closed her eyes again. "Thanks for the offer, Chuma. Don't get me wrong, I truly appreciate it but I can manage on my own. You don't have to worry about me."

"But that's just it. I do worry about you. You are too young to be living your life alone."

"I'm not alone. I have my children."

"Who do not live with you, and even if they did, they're kids. You take care of them, they don't take care of you."

"I have my work, my aunt, Ayesha, and my—"

She stopped when he rolled his eyes upward.

"I don't need your pity, Chuma. My life may not be perfect, but I am happy and thankful for what I have. Do you know how many people are homeless, or sick in hospitals or even dead? I have a roof over my head, money in the bank, children who love me, friends who—"

"And I am not denigrating any of them," Chuma hastened to assure her. "My point is that you don't have to continue living like some independent superwoman, rejecting every offer of help because you are afraid to open your heart to genuine friendship."

"Stop analysing me, Chuma. Leave me alone," she muttered, and reached to open the door again.

"You know that's not possible." His words stopped her. His hands tightened on the steering wheel, and when he turned to her he made no attempt to hide the vulnerability in his eyes. "I could never leave you alone before, Ure. I can't leave you alone now."

"Chuma, I … I don't know what to say."

"Say you believe me when I say I'm sorry for what I did to you years ago, say you forgive me."

"Chuma, I…" Grace hesitated again, shaking her head. She looked out toward the hotel entrance and suddenly smiled. "I think you have a visitor."

He followed her eyes and frowned. Remi was standing at the entrance to the Recreation Centre, arms akimbo, apparently waiting for him to come out of the car. He didn't look perturbed. "What is she doing here?"

"You tell me."

"Ure, I didn't invite her here," he protested. "I only invited her to church."

"Well, someone must have invited her. She doesn't visit Sonshine Estate on Sunday afternoons."

For several seconds Grace's eyes clashed with Remi's. Her hand tightened around the door latch. "Look, I really have to go now. Thanks again for everything."

"Wait." He restrained her from opening the door again. "I'll be done with the inspections before lunch tomorrow. Let me pick you up about twelve. I can take you to see the doctor and we can have lunch together afterward."

"I don't know, Chuma." She hesitated. "I honestly don't think I'll be seeing the doctor tomorrow. I feel fine."

"Then let me buy you lunch. Or we can just hang out. You do owe me one for all my troubles today, you know. Go out with me tomorrow and we'll be square."

Chuma opened the driver's door of the Land Rover and circled the car to open her door. She ignored the hand he offered as she stepped out of the car.

"Tell you what. If the weather is good tomorrow, we can do part of the Jos plateau tour."

"Are you serious?" His eyes were sceptical.

"Yes. Call me as soon as you're done with your inspection and I'll meet you at the Rec Centre."

"You're serious?"

She glanced at the hotel entrance again. Remi was still standing at the door. "Of course I am. You just said I owe you one. I have to settle my bill."

"Ure."

"Not now, Chuma. Your girlfriend is waiting."

⌒*ψ*⌒

With her nerves twisting her stomach, Grace slowly made her way into her apartment, berating herself for making that offer. But it had to happen sooner or later, she reasoned. Chuma was nothing if not persistent when he wanted something. And he wanted to go out with her.

Her reflection in the mirror above the washbasin was not reassuring. She looked harassed and drawn, she thought, and proceeded to check her blood-sugar level. It was still a bit low but nothing a carbohydrate-rich snack couldn't fix. She tore open a pack of crackers and began to peel off the dirty clothes from her body. She would take a shower and change her clothes before going down to the Rec Centre for lunch.

If anything happens to you, what will become of your children? Auntie Bukky had asked. It was a legitimate question. She glanced at their sweet, innocent faces smiling at her from a picture on her wall and a cloud of regret passed through her mind. How could she have been so careless?

Indeed, if anything happened to her, what would become of her children? Nobody knew who she really was. Not Ayesha. Not even Auntie Simbi. Since the day she arrived almost dead at the hospital in Jos, everybody had assumed she had been raped, beaten up and abandoned. She had never denied it. Even to Auntie Simbi. She had only told the woman that her parents had kicked her out of the house because she got pregnant.

She lingered in her room after her shower, not willing to immediately go to the Rec Centre. She didn't want to take the chance of running into Remi and Chuma. She suspected there was nothing serious between them, at least on Chuma's side. But there was no question that Remi had designs on him. As for herself, she smiled in self-deprecation, she was becoming too preoccupied with recollections of his warm touch and compassionate eyes, and that was a very dangerous preoccupation.

She started when her phone rang. It was Auntie Simbi, much to her relief.

"Grace, are you okay?" The anxious voice from the line warmed her heart. "Bukky said you had a crisis."

Chuma's thoughts were chaotic as he watched Grace disappear into the Rec Centre that evening. He couldn't sit still. It was true that he didn't know much about diabetes, but from what he'd heard it could be a dangerous, potentially fatal illness when it is not properly managed. With the lack of proper medical care in Nigeria, even seemingly harmless illnesses become fatal. He had heard too many reports of people dying from headaches and fevers and minor injuries. Fear wrapped around his heart and he fell on his knees by his bedside to pray. When he got up, he reached straight for his laptop—it was time he knew more about diabetes. He needed to know more about his enemy before he could hope to defeat him in battle.

Chapter 19

Jos

When Grace opened her door Monday afternoon she felt excitement curl inside her at the sight of Chuma. He wore a pair of stonewashed blue jeans with a matching light-blue golf shirt. His cap was pulled down so she couldn't read his expression, but she could tell by the flash of his smile that he was pleased to see her.

Grace was dressed in a light-blue T-shirt over black jeans. She had brushed her twists back from her face and fashioned it into a ponytail looped to one side. Her makeup was lightly applied, but she had darkened her lashes and eyebrows. Her pink lipstick faded gently into her fair skin colour. She had finished her casual look with a pair of matching blue sandals.

"You didn't need to come for me. I would have met you in front of the Rec Centre."

"Why?"

"People talk."

"So?" He shrugged slightly.

She picked up her shoulder bag and preceded him out of the door, carefully avoiding the hand he extended. It was enough that her staff knew she was giving him a tour of the plateau, but to let them see him holding her hand as they walked to the car would be like throwing fodder to the gossip mill. She was right, because when she looked at the Rec Centre lobby, Bola and Edith were staring at them through the open restaurant window.

Chuma raised a hand to wave to the two ladies before ushering Grace into the car. His amused glance held hers before he fiddled with the car stereo, turning until the quiet strings of instrumental praise and worship music filled the air conditioned vehicle.

When he chuckled at her embarrassment she looked out the window, hiding her own grin. "So how are you today?"

"I'm okay," she replied, surprised that she really was okay. And that she was looking forward to the tour. Instead of the usual tension, she felt lighthearted and excited. The last time she felt like this was at Government College. "Jos is called the city of peace and tourism for a reason, you know," she told him. "Where do you want us to start?"

"You decide." He turned slightly to her. "I don't care."

"Well, we have the Wildlife Safari Park, the Game Reserve, the Architectural Museum, the National Museum, rock formations, waterfalls, Shere Hills—"

"We're not going to see all that today, are we?"

She laughed at his stricken expression. "I thought you wanted a tour."

"Yes, a real tour, not a drive-through."

"Well, we can't see everything in one day. I think we should do the rock formations and Assop Waterfalls today. There are some spots there that might interest you. We'll have to drive through Sherre Hills and maybe the Game Reserve. We won't need to stop, just a drive-through. The rest of Jos plateau you can see another day."

The sun bathed the road with a sparkling glow as Chuma drove down Akwanga Road. He soon turned off the air conditioner and pressed a button on the dashboard. A gentle breeze filled the car from the sun roof and fanned her cheeks with natural coolness. He glanced at her intermittently while he navigated the narrow winding road.

Grace opened her bag and took out a pair of fashionable sunglasses and stuck them on her nose, and she laughed at the admiration he made no attempt to hide when he looked at her. She looked out the window and tried not to act too excited. When she turned back it was her turn to be impressed. He was donning a pair of the coolest sunglasses she had ever seen. He returned her stare coolly and his lips curved in a sideways smile that drummed blood to her face.

She couldn't suppress her admiration. "You look … you look like a movie star."

"So do you."

She laughed. "Some people are bound to ask us for autographs today then."

"How come?"

"Assop Falls is a popular spot with Nigerian movies and advertisements. On a day like this you can be sure to find tourists picnicking, swimming or just having fun in the sun. Your American accent will seal the impression that we are movie actors."

"We mustn't disappoint them then. How about we introduce you as Julia Roberts's darker-skinned twin? You really look like her."

"Yeah, right."

"I mean it. You may not be as tall, but you are definitely as slender. Your smiles are identical."

She didn't believe him of course, and her glance said as much. She pushed errant curls back from her face and held them in place with her sunglasses.

"Tell me about Gidan Mairo," he invited. "Remi mentioned that on the sale of the building, the orphanage and the girls' home may stop operations. Is this true?"

"It depends on when the sale goes through, and if the new owner will let us rent it for a few more months."

"Us? Are you a part of the ministry too?"

"Yes, I am. I volunteer there every other Saturday. You'll find that most of us—Auntie Bukky, Auntie Simbi, Ayesha, the girls at Sonshine Estate—almost every one of us supports the ministry one way or another. So if you or your client decides to kick us out without considerable notice, you will have many enemies here in Jos."

He looked at her and shook his head. "I'm not the one buying the building. Seriously."

"On the other hand," she persisted, "if you guys let us stay for a few more months, until we have organised alternative accommodations, you will have many champions in this town for whatever you want to use the building for."

She then proceeded to describe in detail the ministry of Gidan Mairo Girls' Home and Gidan Mairo Orphanage. She was relating the story of little Jumai and her stepmother when they came upon the breathtaking view of Riyom Rocks. He followed the signs through a side road that led to an observation point and parked the Land Rover under a tree.

Grace could see he was impressed with the spectacular rock formation. Riyom was a unique stretch of purple-coloured rocks with different shapes laid out symmetrically and picturesquely. The dexterously chiselled rocks were surrounded by luxurious green fields. Chuma stared open-mouthed at a dramatic arrangement that seemed to spiral steeply upward.

Grace stood beside him. "It's beautiful, isn't it? I'm filled with wonder and amazement every time I come here."

"I can see why."

Grace was quiet for a long while, hoping he would experience the feeling of tranquillity and serenity that seemed to reach out to her every time she came to Riyom. The scent of the air was delicate. The topography was open, making it easy to have a view of many rocks at the same time.

"It makes you feel closer to God," he commented.

She gave him a surprised, pleased smile. "You feel it too?"

He nodded.

"That's exactly how I feel whenever I come here. Sometimes I just bring a book and sit under one of those rocks and enjoy some peace with God and with myself."

"I would be too scared to sit under those rocks. How on earth can that tiny rock carry the weight of one that is 10 times its size?"

There were other tourists around. Chuma saw a family of four—man, woman, two children—enjoying a picnic under the shade of one of the huge rocks.

"Can you see that formation over there?" She pointed. "That one that looks like a monkey's head?"

He nodded.

"That's my favourite spot. Do you want to go closer? You have to visit with the rocks to truly experience their majestic splendour. You have to touch them and feel them to appreciate their uniqueness."

Chuma agreed. "Just give me one second to grab my camera."

From Riyom Rocks they drove to Assop Waterfalls. As Grace predicted, there were many people picnicking by the falls. It was a beautiful day, clear and bright.

"Over there." She pointed to a small crowd in a semicircle on their right. They started walking, and somehow it seemed perfectly natural for their hands to find each other.

Neither said a word. Grace had no idea what Chuma was thinking, but she was desperately trying to quell the voices in her head telling her this was a mistake and she should let go of his hand, that she was giving him the wrong impression. But when she looked up, the slow smile that started at his lips and lit a fire in his eyes easily dissolved her resolve.

The crowd stood behind make-shift barricades constructed out of stones and ropes watching a film crew recording a scene between a boy and his dog. The storyline was easy to follow—a young child being maltreated by his stepbrothers finds solace in friendship with his dog. In this scene, he is telling the dog that they had to run away from home together, that they had to find a way into the land of the dead, in search of his dead mother.

Grace and Chuma watched for a while before they wandered off, still holding hands.

"You were right," he remarked. "It is a popular spot."

"I've been here long enough." She shrugged.

The sun was much hotter by now, so Chuma bought a sun hat from a hawker and slapped it on her head. Laughing, she took it off and stuck it on his head instead. He bought another hat for her, and asked the hawker to take a picture of them donning the hats. She pulled him toward another vendor with delicious-looking oranges. She selected five and took out her purse but he reached over and pushed her hand aside.

"Allow me," he insisted. "How much?" he asked the hawker.

"Five hundred naira, sir."

"What?"

"Na so, sir. Better orange dey cost well well these days."

Amused laughter bubbled from within Grace but she stifled it, waiting to see what Chuma would do.

"I'll give you 50 dollars—10 for each orange."

"You go give me 50 dollars for the oranges? A beg, give me 50 dollars, sir."

Grace gasped and burst into laughter again. Chuma turned to her with a frown. He didn't seem to understand what was wrong, but she only laughed harder.

"He meant 50 naira, not 50 dollars," she explained to the orange seller.

"Haba! Fifty naira *ke*? That one no go work o! Make you bring 400."

"We'll pay 200," she offered.

"E no do. Sister, make you consider, a beg. This na special orange, no be anyhow orange. Na imported orange be this. Na from Cotonou them bring am come."

"Two hundred or we will move on," she insisted.

"Sister, consider ..."

"I'm serious. You know oranges are five for 200 naira."

"Sister! Haba! Why you want treat your brother like this now? You no want make I follow you chop? You and your fine bobo dey enjoy life. Make me enjoy too. Make am three-fifty."

"Take," she began to replace the oranges on the tray. "We will buy from someone who sells local oranges. Your imported oranges are too expensive."

"Okay, okay. Why you dey vex now? Na market I dey sell. Bring the two hundred. But no tell anyone say I sell am for that price o! Na because of you I dey gree to sell am so. If na another person …"

Chuma brought out his wallet and leafed through the bills. In a few seconds he was looking hopefully at Grace again. She saw that he had no naira bills, only US dollars. At the end, she paid for the oranges, and both of them were laughing as they continued their tour.

She steered him toward the sound of the falls and carefully led him through a winding trail into a nook between two big rocks. From there they had an unobstructed view of the waterfall, and they stood side by side.

He gave her a sideways hug and kept an arm loosely by her side. "This place is amazing," he whispered.

"You like it?"

"Mmm hmm."

The wind was high enough to blow her hair into her face. She wove it into a single braid and placed the sun hat over it. "It's not just the majesty of the waterfall that I find so beautiful. It's the feeling of oneness and unity with the Creator. Sometimes, when I come here, especially when it's not crowded, I feel like I have stumbled into a divine secret. The twins and I often come here with our lunch during the weekends. I stay in this very alcove and read while they collect wild flowers and chase butterflies. To me, watching the Assop waterfall on a quiet Sunday afternoon is one of life's greatest pleasures."

She should remove herself from his embrace, she thought, but somehow it felt right. As they stood watching, the sunshine shifted, clouded and brightened again. A grey cloud drifted over the sky. When her feet grew tired she urged him toward a smooth rock within the alcove where they could sit comfortably. From there they had another view of the waterfall, no less majestic than from their previous spot.

"I believe I'm in your debt again," he said after a while, turning to her. "I never knew places like this existed in Nigeria. Thank you for bringing me here."

A thrill of excitement shot through her heart at his words and she lifted smiling eyes to him. "It is my pleasure," she murmured. "If there is time before you leave, we can go visit some other natural tourist spot. There is never a shortage of them in Jos."

"Of course," he said after a pause. "You know I will have the time. The question, I believe, is will you have the time to accompany me?"

She didn't want a debate over it. Instead of replying, she bent over the last orange and began to peel off the rind with her bare hand.

"I spent some time last night researching diabetes."

Her body tensed and she stopped peeling the orange for a moment. "And?" Before he could answer, she rose up and walked away from him to stare at the hills beyond the waterfall.

"I don't mean to be nosey, Grace." He spoke slowly. "But after your crisis yesterday, I couldn't help wondering if your life was in danger."

"And if it is?"

"Well, I ... doesn't it bother you?" he asked incredulously.

She wrapped the orange in paper and dropped it in her bag. Then she picked up stones and started to throw them into the swirling waterfall. The silence between them stretched.

He tried again. "I'm here for you, Ure. I'll do whatever I can to help."

"If you read about diabetes," she finally responded, "you would know that type 2 is a chronic disease, which means I will have it for life. There's no cure for it and chances are that it will get worse as I grow older. So yes, my life is in danger, and yes, it does bother me, but I'm trying not to let it rule my life. I'm following doctor's orders and I'm doing well so far."

"Are you on insulin?"

"Right now, no. I don't need insulin. The doctor says that as long as I can control my blood-sugar level, I should be able to live a normal life. There are no guarantees that it won't get worse, but for now I'm okay."

"What about your medication? Are they readily available here?"

"So far, so good. I haven't had any problem getting them. I only run out of test strips for the glucometer once in a while. Auntie Simbi's buying me another metre from England, along with extra testing strips. But there are pharmacy shops here in Jos where I can get them if I need to."

There was silence for a while. She hadn't been aware of him getting up from the rock, but now the warm draught of his breath against the back of her neck warned her that he had come to stand behind her. His arms came around her from behind and he gently turned her to face him.

"These things are readily available in the United States, and they're cheap." he told her. "If there's anything I can do for you, promise you will ask."

Heat flooded her body as he held her, and she closed her eyes. Moments later, she felt the feathery touch of his lips against her eyes and she trembled.

"You know it's happening again, don't you?"

"What?" Her voice was breathless.

"You and me—falling in love again."

She looked up at him and looked away.

"Don't you feel it?" he urged, slightly tightening the pressure on her upper arm.

The emotions that filled her heart rendered her speechless, which was a good thing because it was difficult for her to articulate her feelings at that moment and give him the answer she knew he wanted to hear. But she didn't pull away when he hugged her closer, and she lifted her hand up to his chest. She felt a shudder go through him at her touch and sucked in an uneven breath.

After a while he lifted her hand and placed a kiss in her upturned palm, at the area just below her wrist. Then his hold on her arms slackened, and he gently pushed her away.

"What do you want from me, Chuma?"

He turned and the vulnerable look on his face forced her to pay attention to his carefully chosen words. "This is not easy for me. There are still so many unanswered questions between us—your family situation, your children—but all these seem insignificant compared to the way I feel about you. The way I have always felt about you."

Before she could say anything he turned again and took her left hand in his.

"Ure, saying I'm sorry for driving you away 11 years ago is of no use; I can't undo the past. But trying to make it up to you for the rest of my life is very possible. This time I'll do it right, God help me. If you will have me, Ure, I will carry wine for you. I will go to your parents and ask for their permission to marry you."

Her eyes widened. "You want to marry me?"

His hand shook slightly as he reached out to cradle her cheeks and force her to meet his gaze. "Ure, I have loved you for so long."

She turned away, fear and distress confronting the hurt in his eyes. "I can't marry you, Chuma."

"Why can't you marry me?"

She sighed. "I should think it is obvious. Diabetes is a silent killer. Why would you deliberately encumber your life with a sick woman?"

"I'm not being naïve. I told you I spent all night researching diabetes on the Internet, so I know there are risks associated with it. But I also know that I love you, and without you my life cannot be complete. I would rather have one year with you, sick and all, than another 10 years without you. Besides, Ure, nobody is guaranteed tomorrow. Not me, not you. Our times are in God's hands. I don't know how much time we'll be blessed with, but if you marry me, I'll treasure every day God gives us. Please say you'll marry me."

Tears filled her eyes and her hand tightened against his. But she shook her head. "I'm sorry, Chuma."

"But why? I thought you were beginning to like me a little."

"It's not that. It's just ... it's just ... it's too complicated." She stared at the falling water for a moment and tried to find an excuse. "There are too many things to consider. You live abroad and do not understand the ways of our people anymore. I know that with good management diabetes does not need to be a terminal disease but taboos are still very strong in Nigeria and most families will not accept a chronically-sick woman into their home, especially when the disease is hereditary. Have you even thought about that?"

"I just told you—"

"And the twins. You haven't even met them. I can't make any plans for the future without them."

"Listen, Ure—"

"And there's Auntie Simbi. She's been like a mother to me all these years. I have to talk to her, I can't just agree to—"

He put a gentle finger over her trembling lips. "Just stop and listen to me. My heart froze and died the day I was told you had died in that accident. Since then, I have been like the living dead. Five weeks ago, I saw you at the Jubilee camp and my heart came alive again. I felt like I had been reborn— all because of you. Ure, I need you to make my life whole again. I don't care if you are sick, I don't care if you have 10 children. I will do my best to be the best father to them. I'm not indigent, Ure. I have the means to provide for you and your children."

"But you haven't even met them, Chuma. What if you don't like them? What if they don't like you? I haven't even told you about their father."

"How can I not like your children? It's not possible. I haven't seen them but I already love them. Just … just give me a chance. I don't care who their father is as long as you'll let me be their father in the future. And if you just say the word I will talk to your Auntie Simbi. Is she not Auntie Bukky's sister? I don't imagine that she'll disapprove of me."

"Shhh …"

"I've just found you again. I love you. Give me a chance, please."

It was her turn to press her fingers against his lips and to wait until he was calm again. The defeated look on his face smote her heart. "How about we wait until you meet them?"

"When?" He covered her fingers with his and squeezed them gently.

"The girls will be out of school on Friday for Easter break."

"Auntie Bukky's school?"

"Yes."

"Why don't we go visit them tomorrow? Why wait until Friday?"

"For one, tomorrow is not a visiting day, and second I cannot afford to be out of the hotel tomorrow. Auntie Simbi and Zuliat are coming home on Friday too, so I am going to be busy all of this week getting everything organised for their arrival."

"Okay, I get it. You're busy and we cannot see the twins before Friday."

She nodded. "And don't forget the reception dinner Auntie Bukky is planning for you and Zuliat on Saturday night. Sonshine Estate is hosting that as well."

He raked his hair with hands that were shaking rather badly as he waited for her to finish.

"The twins will be at the party on Saturday so you'll meet them then and maybe you can help me look after them on Sunday."

"And if I am able to cross the hurdle of the kids, will you consider my proposal?"

The hopeful anticipation in his eyes tugged at her heart. His voice was filled with doubt. Wanting only to ease his fears she put her hands around his neck and hugged him tight. "Please understand that I'm not trying to be difficult," she whispered. "It's just that everything seems to be happening too fast. Let's not rush into anything, okay? Instead, let's take a deep breath, calm down, pray and see where the Lord will lead us in this matter. Besides—" she paused. Was this the time to tell him the truth about that abortion he believed she had done 11 years ago?

"Besides what?"

She shook her head, deciding to wait. "Let's talk again after you have met the twins. You may change your mind."

He stared at her as though she had taken leave of her senses. Then he held her close again. "Never," he whispered into her ear before he let her go.

Chapter 20

Calabar

The doctor explained to Añuli that Egoyibo had suffered a stroke a few minutes after the heart attack, which was why her speech was still slow more than a week later. "Your mother had a myocardial and a cerebral infraction. Her heart had stopped pumping and her brain was as good as dead. I can't explain how she survived."

When she was well enough to leave the hospital Añuli took her to her apartment.

"It's the Lord ... who healed me," Ego repeated to everyone who was patient enough to understand her slow speech. De Chike and De Mbachu, the extended family members her father-in-law had sent to mediate in her quarrel with her husband had visited her in the hospital and heard how Jesus visited and took her on a trip to heaven. She told the story to everyone who visited her. Of course they didn't believe her but nobody questioned her for fear of upsetting her and triggering a relapse. Instead, they all thanked God with her that she was able to speak at all.

As far as Añuli could tell, her mother's near-death-experience had left her very religious and fanciful. Since she woke up at the hospital, all she wanted was to have someone read the Bible to her over and over again. Añuli had assumed this responsibility and could now recite Revelation 7:17 by heart just from reading it so often to her mother. She didn't mind doing this, but she began to worry about possible dementia when Egoyibo started to insist that Urenna was alive and not dead.

Añuli consulted with the doctor, who told her to humour her mother and not argue with her. "As much as possible, keep her talking," he advised. "Her best chance to regain her full speech is in the first weeks after the stroke. No matter how fanciful or senseless her words sound to you, encourage her to speak them. It will make her feel better, and she will gain more self-confidence and be less frustrated with her efforts."

It was with a huge relief that Añuli watched her mother drift off to sleep on Tuesday night. She covered her with a light wrapper and briefly brushed her hand against her temple. Ego's skin was slightly warm but not anything to worry about.

Añuli wondered how her father was coping with his new life. Beatrice and her son hadn't yet moved in. It was only a matter of time, she knew, despite her father's protestations that he wouldn't bring his mistress into their home. The more acceptable explanation was that he was afraid such a move would deal a blow to his reputation seeing that his wife has just suffered a bad illness. If he moved too quickly the talk will be that he and his mistress tried to kill his wife so he could marry the mistress. Whatever his reason, Añuli did not really care. As long as her mother was out of his reach, she was content. She wanted nothing at all to do with him.

As she sat on the couch for a much needed rest, she thought about her mother's reaction to her father since her illness. Ego was no longer angry with Odili and Añuli didn't know how to deal with that.

"Pray ..." Ego had urged only yesterday, "for your wicked ... father. Pray that his soul ... will not be lost."

Añuli had tried to hide her irritation. Mention of her father always filled her with anger. He could be lost for eternity for all she cared. But in the interest of encouraging her mother to keep on talking, she'd asked, "Mama, can you forgive what he did to you, how he betrayed you?"

Ego had smiled without hesitation. "Oh yes," she'd nodded slowly. "I can forgive ... because of Jesus."

Her mother sounded genuine in her prayers for her husband. Añuli couldn't understand this.

"You can forgive him all you want, Mama," she said aloud, "but you're never going back to live in that house. You're staying with me now."

Añuli yawned and picked up a novel from the side stool. She'd been struggling to finish the book for almost a month. As she flipped through the pages, her cell phone rang and she looked at the caller ID. Speak of the devil.... She let it ring for a while, debating whether to answer or not, anger flooding her heart.

"What do you want?" she finally barked into the phone.

Harsh breathing from the other end was her immediate answer. "I will forget you spoke to me in that tone. I will forget your rudeness for now and ask to speak to your mother."

"Listen to me, Mr. Sugar-Daddy, do not call this number again. Go and live happily with your mistress and your son, go to your big house in the village, or better still, get lost—forever!"

She slapped the phone shut, fuming. He must think she's a fool that she would want to speak to him after he had caused her mother to suffer so. The phone rang again but she ignored it.

"Time to see what's been happening in the office," she muttered and went to the tiny work station at the corner of her living room. She'd been so busy caring for her mother that she hadn't checked her e-mails recently. Arrangements had been concluded for one of her cousins to come to Calabar as soon as school was out for Easter to help look after her mother. That wouldn't be for another week. Until then Ulunma, her mother's maid, would come and help because Añuli had to return to work on Monday.

"Okay, let's see what's going on." Her patients had been redirected to another dentist in her absence, but she was able to use her remote access authorisation to log into the system and review some of the cases her colleagues were attending to.

"Just the usual stuff," she muttered and scrolled down the spreadsheet—filling cavities, capping chipped teeth, removing decayed wisdom teeth—all in a day's work.

She clicked on her office e-mail and was not really surprised that in two weeks of absence she had received almost 250 e-mails. *You would think these people did not see my out-of-office message,* she grumbled, already regretting that she had given in to the impulse to check her inbox. She scrolled up and down for anything that might be important. There was nothing as far as she could see. Lots of e-mails commiserating with her over her mother's sickness, colleagues who had heard of her mother's near-death experience saying wasn't it a miracle and praise God, general announcements and other e-mails she had been copied on.

An e-mail address that looked different from the official university e-mail accounts caught her attention. The subject line mentioned something about Urenna. She clicked on it and began to read. As she read, her eyes widened with shock. Slowly her hand rose to cover her open mouth, and her heartbeat increased rapidly.

> *Dear Dr. Okolie, I'm afraid you don't know me. My name is Grace Anthony. I am writing to ask if you are in any way related to my friend Urenna Okolie with whom I attended Government College, Benin, and if you can tell me how I can connect with her. I saw her recently in Abuja and she gave me her phone number but I didn't follow through and now I have lost it. I got your information from the Internet and couldn't help noticing the similarity between your names so I thought you might be related. Are you her sister? Can you connect me to her? Thanks for your time. I wait anxiously for your reply.*

Chapter 21

Calabar

At exactly eleven a.m. the next day Añuli sat in the anteroom by the Vice Chancellor's office, waiting for the University Council meeting to end. She had planned to confront her father at their home, but when his secretary mentioned that he was scheduled for lunch with the VC today after the council meeting, she realized there might be a quicker and safer way to get what she wanted from him. For all his arrogance and haughtiness, her father was a sycophant, eager to earn and remain in the VC's good books. He would control his temper in front of the VC.

The door to the council chamber opened at exactly 13 minutes past noon and two Council members came out, shaking hands as they bade each other good-bye and went their different ways. Añuli stood by the window and watched as more council members filed out. They chatted as they walked through the French doors and down the steps.

Eventually her father came through the chamber doors, bent over his wallet, searching for his car keys. He withdrew a set of keys and had almost made it to the French doors before she walked up noiselessly behind him.

"What did you say to my mother that caused her to have a heart attack?" Her voice was harsh.

Whirling around, Odili's face registered shock and then anger at her war-like posture.

"What are you doing here?" he demanded.

"What did you say to her?" Añuli was not intimidated. She looked her father up and down, and his eyes glistened in a way she had never seen before.

"You have no right to question me. I am your father. I am not answerable to you," he replied sharply.

"Oh, but you are," Añuli said with certainty. "My mother is all that I have, and anybody who tries to hurt her, whether verbally or physically, is answerable to me."

"I see. Did she send you here to threaten me?"

She came closer. "Listen to me. If my mother dies and I find out you are responsible, directly or indirectly, I will kill you, I will kill your mistress and I will kill your bastard. I don't care if they lock me up in jail for the rest of my life, but you have my word that you will not get away with it," she swore.

"How dare you. You are actually threatening me?" Odili blinked angrily.

"You told my mother that my sister did not die in that motor accident 11 years ago."

A sneer crossed Odili's face. "Is that a statement or a question?"

Infuriated at his attitude, and seeking to wipe the smirk off his face, Añuli continued loudly, "You told her that Urenna was not in that accident."

Staff from the vice chancellor's office were gathering at the raised voices but Añuli did not care. "You said Ure wrote you a letter and sent photographs of herself and her kids but you didn't tell anyone."

"You're crazy. Grief over your mother's sickness has made you mad! I will not tolerate your insolence. I am your father." Odili advanced menacingly toward her.

"I am not crazy. You are the one who is crazy. How could you do that to your wife of 28 years? Did you think you were being funny? You thought that was a joke?"

"You don't know what you are talking about. This is between your mother and me."

Instead of Añuli's anger diminishing, it flared more at Odili's attempts to shush her up. She trembled, her fists tight and her fingernails digging into the palms of her hands. "For the first time I see you for what you really are. You are heartless. My sister's death left my mother heartbroken and changed her life. She has been in mourning for 11 years. Not only have you betrayed her with your secretary, you are now telling her that her daughter did not really die and that you shredded the evidence. If that is not enough to give her a heart attack, what else would?" she asked disdainfully.

"That's enough! You will not talk to me like that." Odili warned and took a threatening step toward her.

Añuli saw his fists balled. "What will you do? Slap me. Beat me up? Try it and see if I will not slap you back. I will make sure today that you—"

The resounding blow her father gave her sent Añuli spinning to the floor. The door to the VC's boardroom opened and the VC, his secretary and two security men rushed to her as she lay on the floor, moaning in pain and holding her face.

"What is happening here?" The VC took in Añuli's horrified expression and the blood dripping from her mouth. His eyes opened wide with shock. "Professor, did you do this to her? Did you hit Dr. Okolie in my office?"

Odili's face was distorted with fury but he quickly assumed a look of consternation before blustering, "She came in here accusing me of causing her mother's illness and abusing me."

"And so you hit her?"

"I'm her father. She has no right to talk to me the way she did. I don't care how old she is, she will respect me."

Ańuli shook her head and turned to her father. Their eyes met and she stared, trying to see beyond his words. "Tell the truth, Papa." She tasted the blood in her mouth and swallowed. A small crowd had gathered.

Odili's body stiffened again. "Watch your tongue now. Mind how you talk to me."

Very deliberately, Ańuli turned to the vice chancellor and spoke slowly and loudly. "He betrayed my mother with Beatrice, his former secretary. They have a child together."

"Ańuli!"

"It's true. When my mother tried to leave him, he told her that my sister, Urenna, did not die in that accident years ago. He told her she is alive and living somewhere with her children."

"Cheeeeiiii!" the small crowd exclaimed collectively.

"All I wanted to know was if he was serious or not. I wanted to know if he meant what he said so I can decide whether or not to start looking for my sister. That is all I asked him and he slapped me."

"Eiyaaahh!" the crowd exclaimed again.

The VC signalled to his security officers and they started to clear the crowd. He helped Ańuli to her feet. His secretary handed him an ice pack that he crushed and placed on her swelling cheeks. "You need to see a doctor," he said gently.

Ańuli felt the sting of the ice and cried out in pain. "Sir, please ask him for me. Please ask him what he meant. He won't talk to me but he won't lie to you. My mother now believes her daughter is alive. He has raised her hopes. She wants me to go look for her and I don't know what to do," she sobbed.

He patted her hand gently until she stopped crying. He pressed a glass of water into her hand and watched her drink up.

Odili paced up and down the room muttering and scowling darkly.

"So how about it, Professor Okolie?" the VC eventually asked.

"How about what, sir?"

"Is it true you have a child by another woman?"

Añuli looked around. Apart from her father and herself, there were only the VC, his secretary and two security men in the room. She heard her father's heavy breathing, but he offered no response.

"I suspect your silence is enough confirmation," the VC said sadly after a while. "And I daresay that that what you do in your private life is none of my business. But what about your older daughter, Professor? You identified the body in the morgue. You had a funeral service here at the university. You buried her in the university cemetery. What is Dr. Okolie saying now? Have you since got any reason to believe you identified the wrong person and that she might be alive after all?"

"No, sir! Of course not. I ... I really don't know why Añuli or her mother would make up such stories. In my wife's defence she has been sick, and I suspect she has become delusional. But Añuli, I don't know why she should believe such a thing."

"There, you have your answer, my dear," the VC said to Añuli. "It's not true that your sister is alive."

Odili's countenance was guarded. His eyes darted rapidly round the room. Añuli's heart sank. He was lying. It was as clear to her as the sky was blue that her father was lying. She knew him too well not to be able to read his expression. He knew something he wasn't telling her.

"I got an e-mail," she told the VC.

Odili turned and his eyes met hers across the hall.

"No, not from Urenna but from someone who saw her recently, someone who was at Government College with her. She wanted me to give her my sister's contact information."

"Well, I'm sure it's all a mistake. You heard your father. Unfortunately, your sister didn't come out of that accident alive. If she did she would have contacted you all by now."

"But she did, sir. Papa told my mother that she had written to us and that he had destroyed the letters."

"My dear, your mother has been sick. I doubt that she knows what she's talking about. Why don't we all wait until she's much better before we jump to conclusions, eh?"

Añuli's body stiffened and she looked at her father. "He's lying, sir. I know he's lying."

"We need to get you to the hospital, Dr. Okolie. Your face is still swelling. You need to see a doctor. Someone get my driver to take her to the teaching hospital."

"No problem, sir." Odili came forward. "I can take her to the hospital."

"Not you, Professor Okolie." The VC's voice was harsh, and traces of anger lurked beneath his polite tone. "You and I have some unfinished business."

"We do?"

Añuli thought she detected a note of fear in her father's voice.

"You assault a female member of the university staff—and don't tell me she's your daughter—in full view of my office staff, and you don't know about our unfinished business? You can't be serious, Professor Okolie."

Chapter 22

Jos

"Oh my God!" Grace whispered slowly, shocked. "Oh God!"

She read the e-mail again, not quite believing the words. Waves of shock coursed through her veins and heated up her whole body. She shut her eyes and covered her face with her hands, wishing the words on the screen would magically disappear when she opened them again. So it was true after all. She knew Chuma hadn't been lying to her, but still the hard evidence in that e-mail felt like the final nail in her coffin. It was as if she had been standing on the edge of a cliff and someone had just pushed her over.

She covered her face with trembling hands, but the tears ran through her fingers onto the table. She stuck a fist into her mouth to control her feelings, but in a few minutes all the pent-up emotions of the past few weeks exploded in a surge of misery and she doubled over on the floor. Rocking her body to and fro rhythmically, she let out a loud wail and began to cry.

Oh God, was I that easy to forget? Is it so easy to forget your flesh and blood?

When your mother and father forsake you I will be with you. I am your father.

The tears flowed. Spasms rocked her body.

"Oh God, oh God, oh God!" She moaned.

I will never leave you. I will never forsake you.

"Oh God!" She shouted. "Where are you? I call to you but you don't answer me."

I am here, beloved, right beside you.

"I can't feel your presence anymore. Have you also abandoned me? Have you forgotten me, Lord? Have you also ... aborted me?"

She heard the distant sound of running feet and in a few seconds, someone pounded on the door.

"Grace! Grace! Are you okay?" It was Bola.

Edith's voice followed. "Please, Grace, open the door."

She looked up from the floor. Weakness paralysed her limbs. Her body was curved into a foetal position. Tears rained down her face, checked only by hiccups. She wished the waitresses would go away. She wanted to be left alone so she could moan and cry until her heart broke. But she got to her feet and walked on trembling legs to the door. If she didn't, Bola and Edith would continue to knock and shout her name until they woke up the entire estate.

"Whatever is the matter, Grace?" Edith's arms went around her immediately, drawing her into an embrace. Dazed, Grace clung to the older woman. Bola drew out the chair and urged her to sit but she clung desperately to Edith.

"It's okay," Edith said soothingly. She wiped the tears from her eyes. "There, there, it's all right to cry. As long as you are crying to the Lord, keep crying. Release your tears to him, and he will wipe them away forever."

Grace tried to stop the shudders and hiccups that racked her body. Her lips were quivering and her teeth were chattering uncontrollably.

Bola went to the computer and began scrolling up and down the screen with the mouse. After researching for a while, she turned sadly to Edith. "E be like say her friend been die. Them send her e-mail say her friend, Urenna Okolie, don die. Na im make she dey cry so."

At Bola's words, fresh tears filled Grace's eyes. She took a deep breath, released it slowly and sneezed. How true. Her "friend" Urenna Okolie was dead.

The waitresses eventually led her back to her apartment and insisted on helping her into bed. She thought she heard them say they would call Ayesha to come and keep her company, but she wasn't quite sure. Exhausted, she collapsed on the bed and closed her eyes.

The next thing she knew her cell phone was ringing under her pillow and bright sunlight illuminated her bedroom. Her table clock said it was already eight a.m. Had she been asleep for two whole hours? She checked but didn't recognise the caller ID.

"Hello."

"Grace?"

Her heart sank. "Hi, Remi, what can I do for you?"

"You can start by leaving Chucks alone."

"What?" A hiccup escaped her.

"This is a warning. Leave Chucks alone."

"I'm not holding Chuck—I mean—" She sneezed. "Excuse me."

"Don't think I can't see through those innocent girl tricks—your so-called fainting spell on Sunday, tricking him into going out with you on Monday. You've had your fun now, Grace, but it's over. Keep your greedy hands for the father of your bastards. If you try any more tricks like this I will deal with you."

Grace yawned. "Remi, I'm sorry I really have no idea what you are talking about and I'm afraid I have to go. I don't have enough credit on my phone."

"Stop right there."

"What?"

"Don't you dare hang up on me, I'm not quite finished."

Grace yawned again. "Okay, Remi. I'm listening."

"I have only one word for you, Grace: Rufus."

Grace wiped her hand across her eyes. Maybe she wasn't fully awake yet.

"Rufus? Big Jim's dog? What happened to Rufus? Is he okay?"

"Don't say I didn't warn you. Good-bye, Grace."

Before she could say another word, the line went dead.

Grace sighed. That girl was crazy. She reminded her of a viper—beautiful, colourful, robust and deadly. Of all people to be friends with during his short visit to Jos, why did Chuma have to pick Remi?

Ugh! Grace groaned in disgust and dismissed her. When she looked down, her eyes fell on the crumpled paper on which she had printed her sister's e-mail and her eyes began to fill up again. But she didn't want to deal with that either, so she curled back into her bed sheets and started a series of deep-breathing exercises, knowing she needed to control her stress level or risk another diabetic emergency.

When her doorbell rang it took her a few minutes to orient herself again and stumble to the window. It was Chuma, and the time was almost nine o'clock. She must have dozed off again. After a glance at the mirror she hurried to the bathroom to freshen up. Her eyes were red and puffy, her twisted hair was in tangles and she was still in her pyjamas. She picked up her toothbrush and was almost done when the doorbell rang again. She quickly splashed water on her face, shrugged into her housecoat and pulled the door open.

"Bola told me you weren't feeling well," Chuma started as she preceded him into the sitting room. "Did you have another attack? Have you called the doctor? Are you feeling better?"

Instead of responding, she moved toward a chair by the window. She stiffened when he rested his hands lightly on her shoulders to turn her around. Before he could say anything a succession of hiccups escaped her.

"Ure, you've been crying," he exclaimed.

Tears rolled down her cheeks and hit the back of his right hand.

"What is the matter? Did anything happen to the twins?" His quiet voice was doused with alarm, and despite her misery she was touched.

"My children are okay."

Cupping her face with his hands, he angled it toward him and wiped away her tears with his thumbs, searching her troubled eyes. "What is it then? What has happened to upset you?"

A torrent of hiccups was her response. Chuma stared at her for several seconds before purposefully taking her into his arms and hugging her tight. His actions opened the floodgates again and she started crying. He led her to the sofa and made her sit down, then pulled her into his arms again and let her sob against his chest.

What a difference a pair of arms can make, Grace thought in the midst of her sorrow. Edith had held her only a few hours ago but she had not felt the way she did now in Chuma's arms—safe and secure. He held her tight, as though he was trying to pass on some of his strength to her, and even after the tears stopped he continued to hold her.

"Talk to me, Ure."

In response, she lifted the paper in her hand and watched as he read Añuli's e-mail.

Dear Ms. Grace Anthony, thank you for your e-mail. Yes, Urenna Okolie was my sister. Unfortunately, she is deceased. She died in a car accident 11 years ago. You must have seen someone who looked like her

If she thought Chuma's eyes were filled with concern before, she had no words to describe the deep regret she now saw as his gaze held hers. He of all people understood perfectly. His arms tightened around her again.

"I'm so sorry, Ure. You really had no idea."

She shook her head. "It's not that I didn't believe you when you told me. I mean, the newspaper accounts were evidence enough, but I wrote to them years ago. I wrote letters to my father, my mother and to my sister but none of them replied. I thought that when they saw the twins they would forgive me, but—"

He studied the emotions flitting across her face for a moment and once more, very gently, he brushed his fingers across her cheeks and erased her trail of fresh tears. His breath was warm on her face as he kissed her eyelids before tucking her head under his chin and folding her into the shelter of his arms again. She felt cocooned in a blanket of comfort and warmth.

"It's not easy to be told you are dead when you are alive," she mumbled into his shirt.

Chuma patiently waited until her hiccups subsided. "What are you going to do?" he asked.

"I don't know." Her voice was hoarse. "I guess I have to find a way to let them know I am alive. It's bound to change everything."

"Tell me about it." He breathed quietly. "But try to keep an open mind until you hear from them. Don't judge them. I'm sure it was a mistake. The family I saw in Calabar 11 years ago was in deep mourning for their daughter. They were not pretending at all. They truly believed you had passed away."

Held in his arms, Grace closed her eyes, tried to relax. They sat quietly for a few minutes, and all she could hear was the droning of the fridge. Somewhere on the estate a man shouted something in Hausa and a female voice answered. Grace thought it was the gardener and his wife but she could not be sure because even though she was listening intently, the only sound that registered in her mind was the rapid breathing of his heart, and all she could feel were the corresponding ache in her own heart and the shudders racking through the body holding her close.

A tingling excitement began to sweep through her. She was treading on dangerous ground. *God, help me*, she prayed and made to withdraw from him. When she looked up he reached out and framed her face in his strong hands, tilting her head back as though he was going to close his lips over hers. Shivers danced on her spine and she closed her eyes.

Then, quite unexpectedly, he let her go and stood up. When she opened her eyes he was standing and looking out the window. She took a deep breath and dropped her face in her hands. He seemed to be fighting the sensations that had built up between them, fleeing from temptation, as it were.

When he spoke again, his words sounded strained. "I'm sorry, Ure. I shouldn't have done that."

"That's okay," she whispered. "Maybe you should leave now. I'll be fine."

He did not move toward the door as she had hoped. There was silence again. "Have you eaten anything today?"

Her eyes flew to the clock. It was almost ten thirty. No wonder her stomach had been squeaking. "I ..."

He sighed and shook his head. "I'll ask one of the ladies to bring you something."

"Thanks."

She waited for him to go, but still he hesitated.

"You know, Ure, it might help if you told me the story behind your estrangement from your family. If I understand what happened I might be able to advise you better."

"Not today, Chuma."

"Okay, not today. When?"

She shook her head again and looked away. She heard him walk toward her. "Can I at least pray with you before I leave? I can't leave you in this state."

"Sure." She bowed her head and listened as he prayed for God to comfort and be with her.

At the final "amen" she looked up and he told her. "You and I need to have that talk very soon."

She nodded and watched him walk toward the door. It was then she remembered. "Your friend called me this morning."

Hand on the door, he looked back. "What friend? I don't have any friend in Jos."

"Yes, you do—Remi Adenuga."

"Remi called you? What did she want?"

"She wants me to leave you alone."

"What?" His voice was loud with unbelief, confirming her suspicions that Remi's feelings for him were one-sided.

"Ure, you don't really believe I'm going out with that woman, do you?"

Despite her sadness, her lips twitched slightly at the anxiety blazoned on his face. "I believe you, Chuma. But I did warn you to be careful with her. She makes a very bad enemy."

He shook his head and turned at the door. "You're all I care about, Ure. You're the only girl for me. Don't ever doubt that, okay?"

"If you say so."

He left the door and stood in front of her. He lifted her chin and looked deep into her eyes. "I say so."

A quiet pleasure filled her as his words sank into her heart. For endless seconds, they stared at each other. His eyes warmed her all the way from the top of her head to the tip of her toes.

"What are you going to do about her?"

"I don't know."

"Be careful," she said again, and he left.

Checking her blood-sugar level had become so routine now that she shifted into autopilot as she pricked her finger and threaded the blood through the test strips, leaving her mind free to think about the odd turn of events in her life. Never in a million years had she expected that she would get together with Chuma again. She smiled just thinking how much he had changed from the person she remembered. She wondered what would have happened if he hadn't applied the brakes on their physical contact a few minutes ago. God knows she hadn't protested. On the contrary, she had been willing to once again experience the pleasures of his kisses.

Grace read the meter and sent a glance up in gratitude. Despite her emotional distress her blood-sugar level reading was good. She wouldn't take that as a sign to skip a meal, of course, but she was okay for now.

She laid on the sofa and let her mind dwell on Chuma's proposal. It would be dream come true for her if they would marry, but she was not very confident it would happen. He hadn't thought through whether his family would accept her, diabetic and all, and he hadn't met the twins yet.

The twins. Grace closed her eyes and breathed a prayer for help. She really had to tell him the truth about the twins, and soon. She couldn't put it off much longer. No matter the consequences to their relationship, she had to find a way to tell him that she had been too scared to go through with the abortion he had ordered 11 years ago. Even her father's threats and physical abuse hadn't convinced her to go through with it.

In the end Grace decided to take the day off so she wouldn't have to respond to the curious sympathy of her staff. They all thought she had lost somebody, and she knew they would have questions about funeral arrangements and if she would be travelling and what they could do to help and all sorts of things. She couldn't face that today. The pain was too fresh, and she couldn't come up with a counter-story.

After delivering lunch to her later that afternoon, Bola lingered in Grace's living room and updated her on their activities.

"Yes, make you just relax and take am easy today," she agreed when Grace told her she was taking the day off. "No just worry yourself about anything. Everything is going on fine."

"No broken down dishwasher today?"

"No, not even that."

"Unit 6 is checking out today."

"Yes, after lunch."

"No needy guests, no unwanted visitors?"

"None, except for Madam Remi."

"Ah-ah, Bola. How can Remi be an unwanted visitor? Her mother works here. She's a member of the Sonshine family."

"But we know say no be her Mama she dey come visit these days. In fact, she no dey gree come here before Oga Chuma check in. Since then, na every day we dey see her."

Grace didn't want to hear about Remi. She hoped that by not making any comment about her, Bola would get the message and stop.

"But she just dey waste her time," the girl continued. "Everybody know say na you Oga Chuma like."

Grace blushed, and Bola must have noticed her stained complexion because the girl burst into excited laughter. "I knew it. I knew it. I been tell Edith the thing wey I observe but she say make I mind my business. The way Oga Chuma dey take eye follow you everywhere you go, I tell Edith say no be ordinary eye be that. In fact, every time when he see you, na so him body go dey—"

"E don do!" Grace cried, covering her ears with both hands. "Stop it, Bola. A beg, go back to work. Please!"

Bola laughed. "Anyway, e be like Remi don get the message too as she don begin dey switch gear small small. She been come this afternoon, around one, say she dey find Oga Chuma. When she no see him she go find Big Jim for him apartment. But she no fit stay too long with am too because another woman come later to see Big Jim. Be like say na Big Jim dey reign now."

This information stayed on Grace's mind long after Bola went back to work. What was Remi's reference to Rufus earlier? How could Big Jim's dog serve as a warning to her? *Ha, maybe Remi will use juju and turn me into a dog!* She chuckled and pushed the thought aside. She had better things to do with her time than spend a second worrying about Remi and her threats.

She spent the afternoon alternating between sleep and watching television. Her family situation hung helplessly on her mind. She supposed she had to travel to Calabar after all and sort out the confusion, but that would have to wait until Auntie Simbi came back from her vacation. There was no hurry. They'd waited 11 years already. One more week wouldn't hurt anybody.

Grace had just finished mopping her floor when Ayesha knocked on her door. She was surprised because she usually called to make sure Grace had the time to visit with her before showing up. But Grace was happy to see her—they hadn't seen or spoken since Saturday. It was a good thing she wasn't working today after all—they could spend some time catching up.

"Hey, what is the matter?" Grace's smile froze and her heart sank when she opened her door and saw the tears shimmering in Ayesha's eyes. What now? Could a day that had begun so badly for her get even worse?

"Are you okay? Is Nelson all right?"

"Grace," Ayesha whispered, her voice trembling. She stepped into the room and shut the door behind her. "Grace, hold me. Hold me, please. Hold me so I don't faint."

"Okay." Grace nodded and did as she was told. She could feel the tremors going through her friend and searched for words to calm her. Someone or something must have hurt her. Could it be her mother-in-law?

"Take it easy, Ayesha. Take a deep breath in and breathe out slowly, and say a prayer. Whatever it is, the Lord can help."

"You don't understand, Grace," Ayesha muffled through her sobs.

"I don't need to. God understands. He'll help you no matter what."

"No, no, it's not like that. You don't get it."

Grace felt her friend struggling and slackened her embrace. When she looked into Ayesha's eyes again she was baffled to see her friend struggling between tears and laughter.

"Look at me, Grace. Can't you see that I am happy?"

Grace felt some of the weight lift from her heart. "How about you tell me exactly what this is about?"

"I'm ... pregnant."

"What?" Grace whispered in awe.

"I'm pregnant, Grace. I'm pregnant. I'm pregnant. I'm—oh my God, I cannot believe it. I can't believe it. Oh God!" she screamed. Tears welled up in her eyes again and she started to weep.

Grace's heart pounded and her hands tightened around her friend as she led her to the sofa.

"Grace, I'm three months pregnant and I did not know it. All the time I was praying and fretting, angry with God for not answering my prayer, I was already pregnant but I didn't know it." She shook her head and let out her breath. "Oh God, please forgive me."

"How ... how did you find out? How do you know?"

"My sister, it all started on that night when Madam Lois took me to the deliverance service. When it was my turn for prayers, one of the "prayer warriors" put her hand on my head and went into a trance. Then she announced that it had been revealed to her that I had blood on my hands, and that's why I haven't been able to conceive since I got married."

"Blood on your hands?" Grace was shocked. "What did she mean by that?"

"I was confused too. She said that it had been revealed to her that I committed several abortions before I got married, that the blood of the children I had murdered was on my hands, that I had destroyed my womb in the process and that in order for God to forgive and heal me I had to confess openly before the congregation."

"You?"

"Yes, me. At first I was too embarrassed to say anything, but soon I realized the congregation was quiet, waiting for me to confess."

"And?"

"I'd had it, Grace. I had totally had it. I was so angry that I slapped her hands away from my head and told her to look for another person to torment. I called her a satanic agent and told the congregation that everything she said was a lie and that they should all go home to their beds instead of keeping a prayer vigil with a false prophetess. She then got angry and tried to rain curses on me, but I told her she would face eternal damnation if she didn't repent and confess her deception to the congregation. We exchanged a few more charged words before I grabbed my handbag and left. I was so upset that I walked all the way home at two o'clock in the morning."

"Ayesha, you didn't."

"Yes, I did. When I got home Madam Lois was angry with me. Not because I left the meeting but because I walked home. She thought I was taking an unnecessary risk and that anything could have happened to me along the way."

"She was right. That was very risky."

"I know, I know. Anyway, it turned out that she was also angry with the so-called prophetess. According to her, even if what she said was the truth she didn't have to say it in public and ridicule me so openly."

"That's true." Grace nodded.

"Later that morning, Nelson called and I told him what had happened. He was furious. He warned his mother to stop taking me to all these prayer houses or he would forbid her from coming to see me. In fairness to her, she was very apologetic about the whole thing. As God would have it, my husband was so angry that he ordered me to make an appointment with the gynaecologist to explore invitro as an option. He said he would get the money somehow and we will do it if only to ensure that I didn't have to go through such a humiliating experience again."

Bravo for him, Grace applauded silently.

"That's where I'm just coming from, Grace. The doctor gave me a pregnancy test." Ayesha's voice broke on that note, and the tears began to trail down her cheeks again. "She gave me a simple pregnancy test ... and she discovered that I am already pregnant ... thirteen weeks pregnant, Grace, can you believe it? Thirteen whole weeks and I didn't even know it."

The two women looked at each other in wonder and amazement. Grace shook her head and reached for her friend's hand, tears of joy filling her eyes.

"Look at you, Ayesha! Just look at you! Didn't I tell you it was just a matter of time?"

"Yes. Yes, you did, Grace." Ayesha hugged her friend and smiled between her tears.

"Our God is good ..."

"All the time ..."

"Faithful and righteous ..."

"Full of compassion ..."

"Plenteous in mercy, abounding in love ..."

"He will not always chide ..."

"Nor will he keep his anger forever ..."

"He hears our prayers ..."

"He *answers* our prayers ..."

"He makes all things beautiful in his time ..."

"He will never leave us nor forsake us ..."

Grace's cell phone vibrated on the side stool but she paid it no heed. The caller would just have to try again as she didn't have voicemail. Still holding each other, the two girls fell on their knees and began to give thanks for the answered prayer.

It had been an unusual day, Grace reflected as she changed into her nightwear later that evening. It was a bright and clear evening, and from her window she watched the sun set above the western skyline. It was one of those days she should have gone for an evening walk. Her only outing that day had been to the parking lot when she saw Ayesha to her car. Her friend hadn't stayed too long—just long enough to come down from her emotional high—before taking off to her house to call her mother-in-law with her exciting news. Grace had spent the rest of the day listening to worship tapes and memorizing the song the choir would be performing on Easter day.

It was only eight-thirty, too early for her to sleep, so she lay on her bed flipping through the psalms to find something that suited her mood. Ayesha's news warranted nothing but the highest thanksgiving to the Lord.

"Shame on you, Satan! Shame on you!" she muttered.

Her phone rang as she was reading Psalm 139. She smiled before she pressed the green button. "Hi, Chuma."

"How are you feeling now?"

"Good. Very good."

"Really?" He sounded sceptical.

She laughed. "Really, and I mean it."

"How come?"

"Maybe I'm just happy you finally remembered me. I've been expecting your call all day."

He paused, and she could imagine the disbelief on his face. She heard it in his voice. "Em … I'm sorry. I think I have the wrong number. Is this Grace Anthony, a.k.a. Urenna Okolie?"

She giggled and lifted the sheet over her body.

"You mean the one you told this morning that she was the love of your life and then promptly forgot about?"

"Ure—"

"Yes?" She curled her toes, enjoying his confusion.

"Can I come over? Can I come and say good night?"

"Nope."

"But it's not even nine o'clock yet. And you can't talk to me like this over the phone." His voice was so husky that she felt a shudder of longing sweep through her body. "I have to see you. I want you to look at me in the eye when you tell me how you feel about me."

"I didn't say anything about how I feel about you. I just said you didn't call me today."

"Did you want me to call you?"

"Mmm ... hmm."

She heard him sigh. "But you've never really told me how you feel, Ure. I wasn't sure if you would welcome my call."

"Oh no! I'm disappointed with you, Chuma. I thought you were a man of faith."

"I am, I am. But with you I just seem ..."

"Yes?"

"Ure, if you don't stop making fun of me, I'll come over right now and we'll settle this face to face."

"You would have to break down my door if you do. I'm not opening the door for you this hour of the night."

"Ure—"

She laughed. "Just joking. How was your day?"

"Very busy. My client was in town this afternoon and I took him to see Gidan Mairo. There are a few structural problems with the buildings that I wanted him to be aware of if he is going to go ahead with the purchase."

That caught her attention and she sat up. "You mean the person who wants to buy Gidan Mairo was in town? Why didn't you tell me?"

"You were very upset this morning, remember? And he still doesn't want anyone to know his identity. It was a brief visit, and he's gone back to Lagos already."

"Oh!"

"Don't worry. When the time comes I will arrange for you to meet him and to plead your case for Heavenly Missions."

"You promise?"

"I promise."

They lapsed into two or three minutes of friendly silence before he asked, "How did your day go? Are you really feeling better?"

"Mmm … hmm. But it would have felt even better if you had called me."

"You're not going to forgive me, are you?" he asked softly.

"Nope."

"And you'll never forget about it?"

"Never."

"Even if I asked you in person?"

"Mmmm … I'll have to think about that one. You might have to kneel down and really beg, you know. I'm not easy to please."

And on and on their conversation continued. She could tell he was amazed at her audacity. Even *she* was amazed at her boldness. But she knew the freedom she was feeling was partly an overflow of her joy over Ayesha's news, and partly because she could hide behind the cover of the telephone to say things she would never have found the courage to say to him face to face. Maybe it was better like this, she reasoned. Her heart had been bursting to lend expression to her feelings for several days now. She could break the ice this way and give him an indication of her feelings without feeling tongue-tied and awkward in his presence.

"I had a word with your friend today."

"My friend? Ayesha?"

"No, your friend Remi."

"You've got it mixed up, Chuma. Remi is your girlfriend, not mine. Ayesha is my friend."

"Nope, Remi's not my girlfriend. Never has been, never will be." His low voice went even lower. "There's only one woman in this world for me. Always has been, always will be."

His husky voice was oh-so-appealing. His words stoked the fire in her heart and it spread all the way to the soles of her feet.

She clenched her hands and closed her eyes. "So what did the two of you talk about?"

"It was very brief. I told her I was ready to be her friend because that is what God expects from me, and that she should forget any romantic plans she had for our friendship."

"And she said?"

"She told me I was full of it. Said she had been polite to me because my godmother had asked her to. She called me some really uncomplimentary names, but I think we both got the message."

"Why then did she call to warn me if she didn't care?"

"I don't know. I didn't ask her about that. All I wanted was to set the record straight with her. You and I have had more than our fair share of problems with our relationship. I don't want anybody causing any more problems for us."

Grace lay on her bed after they had said good night, unable to sleep. What game was Remi playing? Something didn't quite add up. Why call her up and warn her about Chuma only to deny it later. Why had she threatened her with Rufus? Chuma had nothing to do with the dog.

She got out of bed and crossed to the window. She parted the curtain slightly and stared across the moonlit hotel grounds toward Unit 5. A faint memory nagged at her thoughts, something Bola had said in the afternoon and she tried to think it through. Okay, so Remi had gone to visit with Big Jim when she couldn't see Chuma. What was the big deal? Probably nothing, but Grace wondered if she should pay a visit to Big Jim herself, just to assure herself that everything was all right. And hadn't Remi insinuated that something bad would happen to Rufus that would serve as a warning to her?

Her mind made up, she shrugged into a skirt and blouse and headed out. It was just past 10 pm.

"Hi, Jim," she called as she rapped on the door. "Are you in?"

It took a few minutes before he opened the door slightly to ask what she wanted. His frowning stare reminded her that Bola had said he had a female guest. She felt embarrassed. Perhaps the woman was still around.

"I'm really sorry to intrude like this." She sneaked her right foot between the door opening and the frame. "Umm, I slept all day and am wide awake now. I can't sleep anymore and I'm bored. I wanted to ask if Rufus could come out for a run round the estate with me."

He looked at her for several incredulous seconds before shaking his head in disgust. "Go get yourself a boyfriend, Grace. You don't need a dog for company at night."

He turned and shut the door, causing her to scream in pain when it struck her. She fell on the floor, clutching her right foot in exaggerated agony.

"What the—" He opened the door and reached to help her up but she shouted again.

"What is it, Jim?" A woman's anxious voice called from the living room. He switched on the balcony lights and opened the door wider to see how hurt she was. Grace was bent over, holding her right foot, hoping her gasps were convincing enough. He took her hand as she limped into the living room. Grace glanced at the woman hovering over her and wondered if she was his wife. Not likely. He wouldn't be hiding her in his apartment if she was legit.

"My goodness, Grace! What were you thinking, slipping your foot in the door like that? Now see what you've done?"

"What I've done? Jim, you slammed the door on my foot."

"How was I to know you would—"

"It's okay. What's done is done. I'll get some ice blocks," the woman offered, earning a grateful look from Grace.

"All he had to do was let me take Rufus for a run and there would have been no need for all this," Grace whined dramatically. "It's his fault."

"Oh, was that all you wanted? Jim, why didn't you let Rufus go to her? You mean all this fuss is because of Rufus?"

Grace smiled triumphantly at him. "Exactly. It is much ado about nothing, at the expense of my foot. Ouch! Take it easy! That hurt."

"Be still. It's just the ice block. Get a smaller towel, Rita."

"I think I'll get Rufus for her!" The woman winked at Grace. "The poor dog has been cooped in here all afternoon. He'll be glad for some exercise. Come here, Rufus!"

By the time Jim realised that the ladies had teamed up against him, Rita had already opened the back door to let the dog into the living room.

Rufus didn't appear.

"Come here, boy," they heard her call as she disappeared into the hallway.

Grace stared at Big Jim, an impish smile playing on her lips. He scowled.

"What are you grinning at? If I didn't know better I would swear you were pretending and that you were not hurt at all."

She giggled. "Are you sure you know better?"

He squinted at her for a moment, looking torn between laughter and anger. "What? You weren't hurt? You were pretending?"

"I didn't say so."

"Jim!" They heard Rita call anxiously. "Jim, come here quickly! Something is wrong with Rufus. He's coughing up blood."

Big Jim bolted for the door, Grace close to his heels.

Chapter 23

Jos

The phone woke Grace up on Friday morning. Ayesha was at the other end of the line with an update on her happy state. "When I told Madam Lois, she screamed and cried and laughed. She's so happy for me, Grace. She's moving in with me in two weeks. She says she wants to take care of me throughout this pregnancy."

"I'm not surprised, Ayesha. She's a good woman. She's very committed to you and to Nelson."

They soon said their good-byes and Grace rose from her bed and hurried to the bathroom to get ready for the day. After she brushed her teeth she called Big Jim for an update on Rufus. Last night, the vet doctor had started the dog on activated charcoal and a heavy dose of vitamin K.

"Any news?"

"The doctor thinks he may have picked up some poison. The test results came back this morning and luckily there are no signs of blood clots. He said Rufus is lucky that we brought him early."

"Poison?" Grace repeated.

"That's what he said. You're not dropping rat poison on Sonshine Estate grounds, are you?"

"No, Jim. We don't have rats in Sonshine."

"Well, even if you were it wouldn't matter. Rufus is a disciplined dog. He doesn't eat anything that's not on his plate."

Grace had a sneaking suspicion about what had happened to Rufus but she couldn't voice it. She had to think it through and be able to prove it. Remi couldn't have gone to this extreme to drive her warning through, could she? Nobody could be so devious. She shuddered. She hoped she hadn't heard Remi properly yesterday, because if she had, her own life could be in danger too.

"Umm, Grace, I'm picking Rufus up later today from the vet. Can you keep him for me tomorrow? I need to be in Abuja in the morning and Rita has already left to her base."

"Jim, are you sure that's okay?"

"I checked with the vet and he advised that I don't travel with him yet. Otherwise I would take him with me. I need you to keep him until I return tomorrow evening."

"Couldn't you keep him at the vet's?"

"Don't you want to help?"

"You know I do, but with the poison and all I'm a bit scared that something might go wrong."

"Well, the vet thinks he's over the worst now. He says as long as he gets adequate rest, he should be okay. Besides, the clinic is not open on Saturdays and I don't want to leave him by himself in my suite, especially since I still don't know how he contacted the poison."

Grace worried her bottom lip with her teeth. "The girls will be back today. Does it matter?"

"As long as they don't get him too excited, he should be fine."

"Well, if you're sure ..."

"I am, Grace. Thanks."

"You're welcome," she said, feeling guilty. She had no business accepting thanks for anything when it was possible the poor dog had almost died because of her.

～

The drive to and from Bukuru Christian Academy later that day was pleasant. The afternoon sun was warm, and the cloudless sky was bathed in an azure glow. It was one of those few days Jos City had seen recently, when there was no threat of rain in the sky and the wind was very mild.

"Ahh!" Erinma snuggled close to her mother and sighed in contentment. "No school for two full weeks. I cannot believe it—no waking up at six, no classes, no homework, no punishments and no prefects threatening my life."

Grace hugged her daughter back. "It can't have been all that bad. Auntie Bukky said you girls are having fun at school."

"Yeah, right. If you call living in a military barrack fun, then we had lots of fun, right, Ojiugo?"

Her sister was looking out of the window, enjoying the feel of the wind in her hair. "Me, I had fun, *sha*. I'm going to miss my school-mother."

"It's only for two weeks, Ojiugo. I'm not going to miss anybody. I just want to go home, ride my bike and play with the kids at the orphanage." She hugged her mother again. "I missed you, Mom."

"I missed you too, and I'm hoping you will have a fun Easter break."

"Why, what do you have planned?"

"Nothing unusual. But you remember Big Mommy travelled, right?"

"Yes, she sent us postcards from Paris. But that was weeks ago."

"Five weeks ago, actually. And you know what? She's coming back today." Grace glanced at her watch. "She might even be on her way from Abuja airport as we speak. Auntie Bukky and the driver went to pick them up."

"All right!" They screamed.

"That's not all."

Two identical faces turned eagerly to her.

"Do you remember Zuliat?"

They frowned, squinting and trying to remember. Grace smiled. A rush of love swept through her and she turned to include her second twin into the circle of their embrace. The sight of their young faces tugged lovingly at her heart. She had missed their smiles and laughter and liveliness. This was the blessing the Lord had planned for her, the joy she would never have experienced if she had listened to everybody who had advised her to get an abortion when they were conceived.

"I remember Auntie Zee-Zee. She's Auntie Bukky's daughter, the one who lives in America."

Erinma's voice jolted her to the present.

"Not in America. She's been in the UK for the past two years, getting her master's degree. She's coming back with Big Mommy today."

"What's a master's degree?" Ojiugo was the more thoughtful twin.

"Oh, I know. This is when you get really old and you have to keep reading until your hair turns white, right?"

"Erinma, where on earth did you hear that?"

They continued to chat for several more minutes, watching the Plateau hills come in view as they drove toward the city gates. Sitting between the girls in the backseat of the cab, Grace studied each one in thoughtful silence. Their resemblance to her, as far as she could see, boiled down only to their fair complexion and their long, thick black hair. She shook her head again. They might yet look like her in the future, but today they didn't.

"Why are you staring at me like that, Mom?"

"How am I staring at you?"

"Funny-like, as though you haven't seen me for a long time."

"Of course she hasn't seen you for a long time, silly," Ojiugo intervened. "We've been away at school, remember?"

"Oh yeah? She saw us one month ago, on visiting day."

"Your sister is right. One month is a long time. I have missed you girls, and so many things have happened since you've been away."

"What happened, Mom?" Erinma pleaded. "What happened while we were away?"

She tried to answer their questions, still studying them. They didn't look exactly like Chuma either. Or did they? Well, maybe there was a slight resemblance in the wide slant of the eyes and in the curve of the lips. If she had asked herself this question a year ago, she would have responded with an emphatic no. But now that she had been in his company for more than a month she could see some resemblance.

"How would you girls like to travel for a week or two during the long vacation?" she asked when the cab stopped in front of their apartment. The two girls jumped out and took out their luggage from the boot while Grace settled the fare.

"You mean like go outside of Jos?"

"Yes."

"Outside of Abuja?"

"Yes."

"To where?" Ojiugo wanted to know.

"I'm thinking we can visit Calabar in July. Have you read or heard about the Obudu Cattle Ranch?"

Two identical heads moved from side to side.

"Well, it's close to Calabar. We can tour Obudu Cattle Ranch and the natural reserves in Cross River State. I've only been to the Ranch once but I remember that it's really lovely, surrounded by green mountains. It used to be a sanctuary for rare birds."

"I'm in." Erinma nodded. "Anywhere is better than staying in Jos during the long vacation."

"Do you remember my telling you that I spent a lot of time in Calabar when I was growing up?"

They nodded. "Is it a nice place?"

Grace opened the door to let the girls into the apartment. "I think so. It used to be called the Canaan City. There are beaches and resorts and beautiful rocks. That is where they have the famous *ekpe* carnival."

"Wow, is that a real carnival?" Erinma asked.

"Of course it is a real carnival. People come from all over Nigeria to participate. Añuli and I used to go to the festival every year."

She told the children all she could remember about the festival, which had been a main feature of her childhood. The festival lasted for a whole month with different activities, from traditional dances to wrestling matches and beauty contests. On the last day of the festival big masquerades and dance troupes joined the parade for a grand finale.

"You said our grandparents live in Calabar," Ojiugo said.

Grace knew what was coming next and she hid her smile. They won't have to wonder about their father for too long.

"Yes, and my younger sister—your aunt, Añuli."

"I remember her because I like her name. Is she as happy as her name? Ańulichukwuka—'the joy of the Lord is the best'. If I had a name like that, I will never be sad," Erinma dimpled happily at her mother.

Grace laughed and opened the fridge. She poured cold water into two plastic cups and handed one to each child.

Erinma was an active and inquisitive child. "Hooray! We get to finally meet our grandparents! I can't wait!"

"But what if they don't like us? What if they laugh at us?" Ojiugo held back, raising anxious eyes to her mother.

Grace's hand stopped midair as she poured a drink for herself. "What do you mean? Why wouldn't they like you? Why would they laugh at you?"

"You know, because they are Igbos. My school-mother told me Igbos don't like Hausas."

"That's not true, Ojiugo. The two tribes fought a civil war many years ago but that is all in the past. We are all one country now, part of one Nigeria."

"But, Mom, one day in school, Mama Matron was quarrelling with the chief cook and they said bad things to each other. Why are they still saying such things to each other if everybody is one Nigeria?"

Grace tried to figure out what Ojiugo was talking about. "Mama Matron is Hausa, isn't she?"

"Yes, and chief cook is Igbo."

"And they quarrelled?"

"Oh, yes. That day, I went to the kitchen to get some water and I heard them arguing. Then after a while, Mama Matron started to sing, '*nyamiri yamutu yakari, nyamiri yakari yamutu, nyamiri ta munu ta banza*', and the chief cook was so angry she didn't cook that night."

"Yes," Erinma agreed. "And we all had to eat bread and drink Bournvita for dinner."

"Really? I didn't hear about this." Grace frowned.

"Oh yeah, it was huge. And we were all scared. But the next week, the *Bongwom Jos* came for morning assembly and told us that we are all one Nigeria and that we should not call our fellow students bad names or insult their tribes."

"So are they friends now?"

"Who?"

"Mama Matron and the chief cook."

"I don't know. The chief cook has left the school."

This was news to Grace. Auntie Bukky hadn't mentioned it before. Maybe it wasn't as serious as the girls were making it. Or maybe it was just a misunderstanding.

"So," Grace tried to refocus the conversation, turning to Ojiugo with concern, "you think my family won't like you. Is that because you consider yourselves to be Hausa?"

"No. I know we are Igbos, but sometimes it's confusing. We understand and speak Hausa more than we speak Igbo, and most of our friends are Hausas."

"Yes, and many times we think we are really Hausas even though we know we are not," Erinma added.

"And does it feel any different to come from one tribe or another?"

Ojiugo thought for a while before she shrugged. "I guess not. In my mind, I am just me. I don't think you can feel anything different because you speak one language or another. You are just you and what you are inside has nothing to do with the language you speak. I don't even think in any language."

Grace nodded. Getting up from her chair, she took an apple from her fruit basket and cut it into slices. Then, setting the plate before them, she explained, "The reason you speak more Hausa than Igbo is because Hausa is spoken in Jos. But that doesn't make you a Hausa girl. No amount of speaking English will turn Nigerians into British people. You know that, don't you? It's just another language."

"My teacher says me and Ojiugo are trilingual," Erinma informed her mother.

"And she's right. You speak Igbo, Hausa and English. You are smart kids!"

Before they left their apartment, Ojiugo brought up the subject again. "Mom, do you know we've never even seen their photographs? Why don't you have photographs of your family? We don't even know what they look like."

Grace sighed and patted her daughter's head. "I think a visit home is long overdue. We'll do it during your long vacation."

Grace didn't want to feel she had made a mistake in keeping her children away from her family for so long, but the more they questioned her the more she realised that maybe she should have taken them home earlier. Still, what option had she had?

Later, as they walked toward the Recreation Centre, their hands tucked tightly into hers, Ojiugo looked up again.

"Mom, are we going to see our daddy in Calabar? Is that where he lives?"

Grace tried to sound casual. She shook her head lightly. "I've told you before, Ojiugo, your daddy lives in America."

Chapter 24

Calabar

"Mama, are you sure you want to go through with this? You don't have to see him if you don't want to."

Ego turned from the window at the bitterness in her daughter's voice. The young girl had too much anger for one so young. How had they fallen so low? Theirs used to be a close-knit family, but those days were long gone now. Instead, they had become the poster for a totally dysfunctional family, with one daughter dead, the second daughter emotionally damaged, an illegitimate child by the side and parents on the brink of separation. There was an Igbo adage: *Echi di ime, onye ma ihe o g'amu*? (Tomorrow is pregnant, who can tell what it will bring forth?)

"It's all right, Añuli," she quietly replied. Her speech was still slow, but it was fluent. "Your father requested this meeting. I didn't ask to see him, but I will like to hear what he has to say. Is this why you came back early from work?" she asked gently. "Are you afraid he's going to harm me?"

"I just don't trust that man around you," Añuli snapped. "He's the reason you are in this condition now. At least when I'm here he will think twice about bullying you into believing his lies, or into doing his bidding. He knows that even though he beats me, I'm not afraid of him. You have come a long way, Mama, and I won't have him causing a relapse if I can help it."

Ego sighed and shook her head. "You still don't understand, Añuli. Your father cannot harm me anymore. The very hairs on my head are numbered by the Lord and no one can touch or harm one strand unless my Lord permits it. The Bible says that no weapon that is formed against me will prosper. If the Lord lets him touch me, it's because he wants it to be so and it is for my own good. God has a purpose for everything."

"Mama," Añuli spat out harshly, "I beg, just stop it there. Sometimes you carry this Christianity thing too far. What do you mean by saying if God allows you to be hurt it is for your own good? That doesn't even make any sense. You have to protect yourself and fight for your rights. God is not going to come down from heaven and fight for you the battle he has equipped you with hands and feet and a brain to fight. He does not expect you to just lie passively and say, 'May his will be done'. No, Mama, as far as I am concerned, people who have that kind of attitude are just being lazy."

Ego turned again to quietly watch her daughter. The young girl was so tense with anger that her voice shook and her breathing was quick and shallow. She hadn't meant her words to sound the way Añuli had interpreted them, but she didn't want to get into an argument with her. It was better to let Añuli voice her anger as much as possible. Better still to pray for the healing hand of the Lord to reach and heal the emotional hurts. From all that had happened in the past decade to their family, and from what she had seen in the few days she'd been living with her, it was obvious the poor girl's emotions were totally battered.

"Very well, Añuli. Let's see your father together. He said he would be here at five o'clock. We still have two hours until he comes. Would you be so kind as to read a psalm to me while we wait?"

Chapter 25

Jos

Three hours after the twins arrived home from school, a late lunch had been eaten, suitcases had been unpacked and Grace had heard an earful about the tricks the twins had played on their school-mothers who could never tell them apart and on the school prefects who could never be certain which twin was guilty of what offence. They made no protest when Grace asked them to clean up and change from their school uniforms. While they changed, she called Big Jim to check on Rufus.

"We're back, Grace. And he's looking stronger already."

She let out a shaky breath and waved a hand upward in thanksgiving.

"Poor Rufus."

"I guess I have to thank you for whatever caused you to come knocking on my door last night. It could have been worse if you hadn't faked your injury last night."

"How do you know I faked it? Didn't you shut your door on my foot?"

"Not nearly as hard as you made it look. Even Rita noticed that your limp disappeared as soon as we discovered Rufus's emergency, and while we were together at the clinic last night, you didn't limp even once."

"It's called adrenaline, Jim. That dog is very dear to my heart."

"No be only adrenaline, *Andre Agassi nko*?" He laughed. "You wouldn't know anything about the poison, now would you, Grace?"

"What?"

"I'm still puzzled that Rufus ate poison. You've seen for yourself how disciplined he is. He doesn't eat carelessly."

"You don't think it was an accident?"

"It could well be, but I'm going to investigate it. I have to get to the bottom of this. Otherwise, how can I make sure it doesn't happen again?"

Grace hadn't had time to explore her own suspicion. She didn't want to share her thoughts with Jim either, so she let him talk and offered no help. When he let the subject drop, she breathed easier.

"I'll bring him over in the morning. As long as he takes his vitamin K and drinks lots of water, the vet says he'll be as good as new before we know it."

As they waited for the driver to take them to visit Auntie Simbi, the girls watched TV while Grace paged through their photo albums. But they soon came to sit by her.

"I remember that one." Grace pointed at a photograph. The two girls were dressed in the costume they had worn for the JSS presentation of *Odale's Choice*. "You girls acted the same part."

"Yep, but the audience didn't know it. The part of Odale was too much for one of us to memorise, so we split it into two and nobody realized there were two of us."

"Until the very end, when we came out to take the final bow. They were all surprised to see two Odales on the stage."

There were other photographs—of school-mothers, friends and teachers. With a guarded smile, she reached for the album on the table and showed them the picture of herself and Chuma at Assop Waterfalls.

"Oh wow, Mom. You look very happy in this photo. Who's that with you?"

"Oh." She chose her words carefully. "That is Mr. Chukwuma Zeluwa. He's a guest here at Sonshine. We visited Assop waterfalls together on Sunday. He's Auntie Bukky's godson. I'm sure you'll meet him very soon."

Her cell phone rang at that moment and she flipped it open. She listened for a while before she shut it and turned to the girls. "Well, you're about to meet Mr. Zeluwa after all. He is driving down to Big Mommy's house and has graciously offered to give us a ride."

"Yeah!" The girls exchanged an excited glance, shoved back their chairs, snatched up their shoulder bags and rushed outside.

By the time Grace caught up with them they were already introducing themselves to Chuma. Without giving him time to examine them closely, the eager girls climbed into the back of the Land Rover and waited for their mother to climb into the front passenger seat.

Chuma turned and smiled as he set the car in motion. "So these are the famous Sonshine twins. I'm pleased to finally meet you."

The girls smiled brightly at him and chorused a suitable response.

"I've heard so much about you two that I feel I know you both very well."

"Who told you about us?" Erinma asked.

"Who told me? Why, old Rufus, of course. He's told me everything about the two of you."

"Rufus?" They screeched in disbelief. "You mean Rufus the dog? Big Jim's dog?"

"The one and only."

"But that's impossible. Dogs can't talk," Erinma countered.

"Says who?"

"Says everybody. Right, Ojiugo?"

Her sister nodded.

"Well, animals talk to me all the time and I talk to them too."

"That's not true. Human beings cannot talk to animals," Ojiugo insisted.

"They do if they are Dr. Dolittle."

"Dr. Dolittle, the animal doctor?"

"Not just an animal doctor but the animal doctor who can speak animalese."

The girls' thrilled laughter rang out in the car. Grace smiled. It was hard to be sad whenever those two were around. They reminded her of a poetry verse she had learned in school many years ago: "All you need in the world is love and laughter ... love in one hand and laughter in the other."

"So who's the older twin?"

"Me," the two voices said at once.

"I was born first, so I am older," Ojiugo said.

"That's because I sent you into the world to check and be sure everything was all right before I would come out," Erinma argued.

"Rubbish! That is a myth. It makes no sense at all."

"Sure it does. You should be thankful we are not Yorubas because in their culture the second twin is considered older than the first. You would have been calling me "Auntie Erinma" and running errands for me by now," Erinma laughed at her sister.

"That doesn't even make any sense," Ojiugo insisted.

"Because you don't like something doesn't mean it doesn't make sense."

"Girls!" Grace raised her voice and the two instantly grew quiet. After a few seconds they started to giggle.

Chuma turned to look at Grace. "Did I miss something?"

Grace smiled and shook her head. She knew what was coming. The giggling lasted only a few seconds before the girls burst out in open laughter.

"They have this argument every time someone asks them who is older," Grace explained.

"Well, you must admit it is a good argument, one in which everybody is correct and nobody is wrong."

They all laughed at that, and the rest of the drive to Jos GRA was accomplished in easy companionship.

Movement outside the window alerted Big Jim that someone was at the door. Rufus whined and thumped his tail weakly while he went to the door. To Jim, it felt strange that the dog would lie on the floor while a stranger stood outside. His Rufus would have been on his feet immediately barking at the stranger. He vowed again that he would not rest until he found the source of his dog's poisoning. He had to prevent a recurrence.

He went to the door, smiling slightly because the last time this scene had played out, Grace had been on the other side. It was one of the hotel staff this time, one of the older women. He didn't know her name, but he recognised her instantly as a cook.

"Yes, what can I do for you?" He cocked an eyebrow and waited.

"Can I come in, please?" She wore a long gown that covered her from neck to toe. Her head-tie framed her face and fell down her shoulders. He noticed the tears that brimmed in her eyes but she spoke firmly. "I'm sorry—"

"Excuse me?"

"It's about your dog."

"What about Rufus?"

"I think I know how he contracted the poison. I'm really sorry."

Big Jim stared at the old woman. She didn't sound or look crazy. On the contrary, she looked like she knew exactly what she was talking about.

"Can I come in now? I don't want anybody to see me here."

"Please," he said, ushering her into his suite and firmly shutting the door.

Chapter 26

Calabar

When Odili rapped on Añuli's door, she opened it with a scowl and turned back into the living room without a backward glance. It was a tiny room, made even more so by his tall and heavy physique. He found the hook behind the door and hung his jacket before advancing toward his wife, briefcase in hand, tension in every step.

"You're looking well, Ego. Better than I expected."

"So are you, Odili. Won't you sit down?"

He glanced at Añuli, who was already sitting on the dining chair, as though he wanted to say something, but the hatred flashing from his daughter's eyes stopped him. As the women watched, he sat on the upholstered chair, brought out an envelope and took a deep breath.

Ego turned toward her daughter. "Añuli, please get your father some water to drink," she started to say but hastily raised an apologetic hand in surrender. She didn't want to hear Añuli's retort with that heavy scowl.

"That's okay," Odili said. "It's not necessary. I just have a few things to say to both of you, and then I'll be leaving."

Whatever it is, Ego thought, *it must be serious*. He looked as nervous as he had on the day his mistress and her parents had confronted him.

He took off his eyeglasses and rubbed his palms against his eyes and forehead, and then drew out a handkerchief and wiped beads of perspiration from his nose. He cleared his throat. "Our people say that a man who is trampled to death by an elephant is a man who is both blind and deaf. The fish that can see that the water is getting shallower cannot be stranded in a stream."

For a moment he hesitated and slowly shook his head, seeming to debate with himself whether to continue his tale or back out.

Ego waited patiently. Añuli hissed.

Odili continued. "I am neither blind nor deaf nor foolish enough to be trampled by the elephant. Nor am I stupid enough to stay in a pond when the water is drying out."

"Speak plainly, Odili. What do these proverbs mean?" his wife prompted.

He turned away from her and looked at a painting on the wall. "It's about your daughter Urenna."

The two women sat straighter, each watching him warily and listening with keen interest. He glanced from one to the other and cleared his throat again.

"What about Ure?" Ego prompted.

"Well, as you know, when she came home with the news that she was pregnant, I was very, very disappointed. Here was a girl who was doing very well in school, a truly gifted child, a girl for whom the sky was the limit. I had put everything I had physically and emotionally into ensuring that she would go to medical school and become a doctor. You know I was prepared to do anything I could to support her."

He sighed and wiped his face again with his hankie. His family greeted his words with silence.

"For many days after she dropped her bombshell, I did not know what to do. It wasn't just that she was pregnant that infuriated me. It was more her stubborn refusal to do what other girls her age do with an unwanted pregnancy."

"You mean her refusal to abort the baby," Ego clarified.

"Well, yes. And if I remember correctly, Ego, you also were in favour of her terminating the pregnancy. You spoke to her, I spoke to her but she stubbornly refused. She said she wanted to quit school to have the baby, leave the baby with us and then go complete her education, as though that was what we sent her to school to do."

Ego nodded sadly. "So you determined to beat the baby out of her, regardless of whether she lived or died in the process. All you were concerned about was your feelings of disappointment and not wanting to tarnish your image in the university community."

"I didn't mean to kill her, if that is what you are implying. That was never my intention. I just wanted to put an end to the pregnancy, teach her a lesson she would never forget in a hurry and return her to her destiny."

Ego sighed. "I don't think we are doing ourselves any favours by rehashing this story. What's done is done. What did you really come here for, Odili?"

"Just hear me out, okay? This is very important."

She frowned but waited patiently for him to continue.

"When I came back from meeting with the VC that night she was gone. You had taken her to the clinic and I was sure she was either getting the procedure done or having a miscarriage. I did not believe any foetus could survive the thrashing I gave her. But she ran away from the hospital that night. The next morning the luxurious bus plunged into the Itu River, and you know the rest of the story."

Ego hung her head and closed her eyes, pain and regret etched firmly on her face. He didn't have to remind her. "So I ask you again, Odili, what is this all about? I don't know where you're going with this history lesson."

"What I am about to say now might shock you. Or it might not since I already mentioned it to you on the day you collapsed. I don't know how much of our conversation that day you still remember. I have kept the secret to myself all these years. But as the proverbial fish in the water, the sea is drying up and I have to swim to the deeper waters to be safe. If I do not tell you this now, you will hear it from another source and I will be compounding my wickedness in your eyes."

Ego felt the sudden rush of heat and the tightening of her chest she had not felt since that night she had woken up in the hospital. She took in a deep breath and exhaled slowly, the way the doctor had taught her.

"Anuli, go and sit by your mother. This concerns you too."

His daughter hissed at him. "Just confess whatever sin you feel you have to get off your chest and get back to your mistress."

Ego closed her eyes. "Anuli, please, you're not making things easy with that attitude. Do as your father says. Come and sit by me." She shifted gently, creating a space on the sofa beside her. "Come."

Anuli still hesitated before approaching the sofa. Egoyibo smiled and gave her a sideways embrace when she sat by her.

Odili's voice was dry as he swallowed and continued. "About two years after Urenna left us I got this letter from someone who described herself as my daughter."

"What?" The two ladies gasped.

"Let me see that." Añuli ran to grab the paper from her father's hand but he held it away from her.

"Wait, I'm not done yet. Let me finish what I'm saying."

He waited until Añuli sat before he continued. "When I did not respond to this letter, she wrote again, this time to you, Egoyibo."

The woman clutched at her heart, the pressure in her bosom increasing exponentially. "She wrote me? Where is my letter?"

"I read it, tore it up and burned it. She was dead to us and it was better that way. I didn't want the scandal that would invariably erupt if and when it would turn out she was alive and not dead as we had believed at the time of the accident. I don't even know why I held on to this letter. Maybe it was because of the photographs."

Ego's breath came in quick beats, and her chest tightened.

"She has written more letters over the years—some to you, some to me, some to her sister. I didn't always read them, but I tore them all up and burnt them."

"You're an evil man," Añuli stated in quiet disgust. "What was wrong with admitting that we had made a mistake and that my sister was alive?"

"Continue calling me names and you'll soon see stars exploding in your head this evening. I think the slap I gave you on the other day was not enough."

"It is true then? She's alive? My daughter is alive?"

"I don't know. I haven't seen another letter in almost seven years. You read this letter and you can go and look for her if you want to."

"So why now, after all these years, have you decided to tell us?" Ańuli's voice quivered and tears gathered in her eyes.

"When you said the other day that someone had seen her somewhere, I knew the truth will come out sooner than later. But before then I want to admit what I know, and you can make up your mind what to believe."

Odili dropped the envelope in the middle of the table and shut his briefcase. Then he turned and grabbed his jacket from the door, hurrying out of the apartment as though his tail was on fire.

As soon as he left, Ańuli reached for the envelope. Her hands shook as she examined it. It was so old that she couldn't make out the postal stamp, but she recognised her sister's handwriting as she unfolded the letter. A photograph fell out, and Ego caught it before Ańuli could stop her. They both stared in shock at the picture of Urenna's face smiling at them from between two identical babies who were propped up by fluffy pillows.

Ańuli felt her breathing coming faster as the shock of her father's revelation filled her again. "Oh my God!" she slowly whispered. "It is true after all. Urenna is alive. She is not dead. Mama, you were right."

She turned to her mother but her excitement turned into panic as she saw Ego's eyes begin to turn. As she called out in alarm, the older woman slumped unconscious to the floor.

Chapter 27

Jos

Auntie Simbi lived in Jos Government Reserved Area, two streets away from her sister, on a quiet street where the houses looked like cottages with huge yards and boys' quarters and thick flower hedges. This part of town used to be called the British Quarters because the British officials resided there during the colonial era. Now it is known as GRA and occupied mostly by government ministers and a few rich, private citizens.

As Chuma turned on to the main street, the streetlights suddenly went off.

"NEPA!" one of the twins wailed. "Never Expect Power Always."

"My teacher says they always leave the lights on during the day and take it as soon as darkness sets in," the second twin explained.

"Yes. You'd think it would be the other way round," her sister agreed.

Almost immediately the sound of generators began to rumble through the neighbourhood as first one house and then another switched on their sets. Scattered lights sprang up sporadically. Grace scowled. What a way to welcome Auntie Simbi back from her European vacation.

The lights were still off when Chuma turned the car through an open gate, drove round a circular flower hedge and stopped before the front door.

Uncle Tunde's Pathfinder and the hotel's station wagon were already parked in front of the garage, and Grace saw Auntie Simbi's gateman walking toward the generator house. The twins were out of the car in a flash, rushing into the house to greet their Big Mommy. As Grace opened the door, Chuma's hand prevented her from rushing after them. He smiled.

"Congratulations on your kids, Ure. They are almost as adorable as their mother."

"Thank you," she said quietly, and for a moment their gaze met, held and she shyly returned his smile.

He shook his head after a while. "They look familiar somehow, as if I've seen them before. Or maybe they remind me of someone. I'm not sure who but if I think hard, I'm sure I will remember."

Her heart seemed to plunge right into her stomach but she managed to shrug. "Those girls are not easy to forget, believe me. If you have met them before, you will remember."

"I don't know why I thought they were younger. I didn't think they were this big." He sounded more like he was talking to himself, trying to figure out a puzzle.

She didn't offer to help or to correct him. When she saw she had lost him to his thoughts, she slipped out of the car and went in to join the crowd that had gathered to welcome her benefactor and adopted mother.

It turned out to be a big crowd in the living room—Auntie Simbi, Uncle Tunde and Auntie Bukky, Zuliat, Ma Remi, the two drivers and the twins. Remi was not there, thank goodness. It would have been a bit awkward.

"I think NEPA missed you." Uncle Tunde told his sister-in-law as he hurried back into the house from helping the *mai-guard* power on the generator. Chuma came in shortly after. "As soon as you stepped into the house they took their light."

"No *wahala*. The only agenda I have this evening is to sleep, so I don't mind if there is no electricity," Auntie Simbi replied. "Besides, nobody can make me sad today. I'm very glad to be home."

"I will send my driver with a gallon of petrol for your generator later," Uncle Tunde promised. "What you have there can't run for more than two hours."

"This is one of the strangest things about our dear country," Zuliat commented. "Why can't the government just do something about providing electricity to its citizens? As long as I can remember, the National Electric Power Authority has been totally ineffective but the government doesn't seem to care. It's a real shame."

"Ahhh!" everybody sighed.

"Don't just start about NEPA or we won't be leaving here soon," her mother advised.

"It's because you're a "been-to" that you notice it. Those of us who have never stepped outside the shores of this country are used to living without electricity. We don't complain anymore," Uncle Tunde added.

"Sometimes I think we're all part of the problem, Dad. As long as we don't complain, our infrastructural problems will not be solved," Zuliat insisted. "Do you know how much money our country gets in oil revenues alone? Yet we can't afford to supply electricity to our citizens. Can you imagine what a steady power supply can do for our economy? We can never step into industrialisation without a steady power supply."

This led to a general discussion of Nigeria's social ills. Grace watched and noticed how everybody had an opinion on what was wrong with Nigeria and the solution to its myriad problems.

Everybody, that is, except Chuma. Every time she looked at him he was watching the twins. She was proud of how the girls, sitting on either side of their Big Mommy, listened quietly at the grown-up conversation around them, not interrupting at all.

Then suddenly, "Did you forget our birthday?" Ojiugo asked.

Auntie Simbi shook her head. "Of course not. I shopped for you in France and brought everything with me."

"I remembered too, and I have presents for you as well." Zuliat smiled at the girls.

"Oh, Auntie Zee-Zee." Ojiugo was surprised. "You remembered our birthday? That is so cool!"

Zuliat bent to hug the girl. "Of course I remembered. I remember every year because it is very close to my birthday. You are March 31, right?"

Two identical heads bobbled up and down.

"And I am April 1, which is the very next day. See, I cannot forget."

The two girls smiled delightedly and looked at each other. Grace could see they were feeling special.

"And you"—Zuliat turned to Grace—"you look just fabulous. You don't look old enough to be the mother of two 10-year-old girls. I totally envy you."

Her eyes flew to where Chuma stood beside Uncle Tunde. Their eyes met, and she knew from the way he squinted that he had made the connection. He closed his eyes and she saw him shudder. His voice, when he spoke again, addressing the twins, sounded strained.

"That means you were born in 2002, right?"

"Yes," Ojiugo replied. "We were born March 31, 2002."

Zuliat didn't appear to notice anything amiss. "Aren't they adorable? So identical that even Auntie Simbi still cannot tell them apart, and they've been living with her since they were only a few months old. Grace was only 16 when she had them, barely out of secondary school. You're so lucky, Grace. When they grow up, those kids will be more like your sisters than your children. I keep imagining it. By the time you're 36 they will be 20 years old and ready to get married. You may even be a grandmother by the time you're—"

"That's enough, Zuliat," her mother's deep voice cut in. "You're embarrassing the poor girl."

"Oh? Why is she embarrassed?" Zuliat asked in her forthright manner. "These kids are gorgeous. She should be proud of them."

"Zuliat!" Her mother's voice was stern this time.

Zuliat finally stopped, looking embarrassed at the way everyone was staring at her. "I'm sorry, Grace. I didn't mean to embarrass you."

Grace spoke brightly to reassure the girl. "No worries, Zee. I'm not embarrassed. But the grass is not always greener on the other side, you know. Sometimes I wish I had gotten an education instead."

The generator suddenly went dead, plunging the house into darkness again. Uncle Tunde produced a torch, and Mama Remi went around turning off the light switches.

"I think the *mai-guard* is having trouble with the generator," Uncle Tunde remarked. "Chukwuma, come with me. Let's go see what we can do to help before it gets pitch black."

The men left, and in a few minutes they heard the noisy grinding of the generator, and then the lights came on again, much brighter than before. Mama Remi went around again switching on the lights, the fans, and the air conditioner.

The household staff had cooked a welcome dinner for their mistress, and soon the table was loaded with assorted foods.

"Where is that godson of mine?" Auntie Bukky asked just before they ate.

"He didn't come back in. He said he needed to make a call to his mother, and to get some fresh air," Uncle Tunde informed them.

"I'll go get him," Zuliat offered and went out.

"I'm afraid we can't join you for dinner," Grace told her employer. "It's almost nine-thirty, and I have to go and dismiss the staff for the day. Plus we already ate before we came."

"That's okay, but you have to wait for the driver to pack some food for his family. Tell everyone I'll come around in the morning."

"Not too early, I hope." Grace smiled. "You have to give us enough time to roll out the red carpet before you land."

"Red carpet indeed!" Auntie Simbi retorted. "Purple carpet *nko*?" Everyone laughed.

There was no avoiding Chuma as she stepped out of the house with the twins. He was standing beside Zuliat by the Pathfinder, and the two seemed engrossed in quiet conversation. He did not say a word to her but managed to look up to smile at the twins when they said, "Goodnight, Dr. Dolittle."

"I'll see you at the dinner party tomorrow," Grace told Zuliat before ushering her brood into the station wagon where the driver was already waiting for them.

Later that night Grace stood by the girls' room and listened to their quiet breathing before turning off the lights and heading to her own room. She hadn't heard from Chuma yet. His finding out the truth about his relationship with the twins couldn't have come at a worse time. She would be very busy with the dinner party tomorrow and wouldn't have the opportunity to talk to him. They might not be able to talk until Sunday evening.

What about the twins? she asked herself. She wouldn't hurry to tell them Chuma was their father. Not yet. It would be better to first see his reaction to the news. *That will help me decide when and what to tell them.*

She spent a few minutes wondering how she would break the news to her daughters. She didn't need to go into the details about what led to her estrangement from Chuma, but without those details, could they forgive her?

Falling on her knees beside her bed, Grace prayed for wisdom.

Chapter 28

Jos

The next day Chuma woke to children's voices. He looked at the bedside clock. It was already past nine. He pulled back the curtains for a better view.

Ure's children were in front of her apartment, throwing a ball at Rufus and screaming in delight as the dog chased them around.

He turned back into his room and shut the curtains before they could catch him spying on their fun.

In his hand was all the evidence he needed to cement his conviction that the twins were his children, that they were the product of his brief indiscretion 11 years ago. They were the babies he had given Urenna 500 naira to abort. Tears of regret clouded his eyes. *Lord, I don't know if I can bear this any longer. I was just a young boy. I was 19. I didn't know what I was doing.*

He flipped open his cell phone and read again the e-mail he had received from his mother late last night. *Attached is the scan of Amaka's birthday photograph you requested. What do you want it for? Let's talk soon.*

He clicked on a button and stared at the photograph again. There was no mistaking the resemblance between the twins and his younger sister at that same age. Amaka was standing behind a giant birthday cake with 10 candles and smiling into the camera. That picture had been in their living room forever, mounted on the wall, over the television set. He had never paid any attention to it but it must have registered in his subconscious because the sight of the twins yesterday had nudged at his memory, and as soon as he learned their age he knew where he had seen them before—in the face of his own sister.

Chuma sat on his bed and wrapped his arms around his body in a desperate attempt to maintain balance and control over his emotions. No wonder the Lord warned against sexual immorality. The consequences could be tragic, the impact on others far-reaching.

It was only that one time, just once, Chuma thought. *How could our lives have been so monumentally changed by one brief, mindless, careless action?*

Because of that night 11 years ago, he had experienced a lifelong guilt and a depression that almost destroyed his life. Because of that one night, Urenna's life had been totally destroyed. She had dropped out of school, forgone her dreams, become estranged from her family, lost her youth, lived in shame, changed her name and identity, borne two children and raised them by herself.

How did she do it, Lord? How could a 15-year-old girl have gone through all this and still survived?

The words came to him. **Grace. It is by the grace of God that we are not consumed.**

His mind drifted to her family. Why did they insist she was dead when in fact she was alive and had informed them about her whereabouts long ago? The answer was of no importance right now. They had obviously not been there for her. Neither had he, so he had no right to judge them. The only person who had shown her kindness had been a stranger. Auntie Simbi had given her a home, provided for her, adopted and loved her.

God, please forgive me. Chuma fell on his knees by his bed and wept.

There was nothing he could do now to make amends. She was well settled and independent. She didn't need him. She could even refuse him access to the kids. If they were in the US, he could argue and win the right to be part of his children's lives, but not in Nigeria. According to tradition, any child born to an unmarried girl belongs to her family. Even if she later marries the father of her child, her father and extended family members have primary rights over the child and can refuse to give the child over to the biological father.

Tradition aside, Chuma knew the last thing he would do would be to make any demands where the children were concerned. He had lost 10 years of their lives. That was painful enough, but that was his fault, not hers. He flinched, remembering the callous way he had thrown money at her when she told him about the pregnancy, ordered her to go get an abortion and told her it was over between them. He had been so scared and confused that he had even accused her of deliberately trying to thwart his dreams. It was a wonder that she had even spared him a greeting these past weeks.

God forgive me, he cried again, groaning and shuddering. *You know I will do anything, anything at all to undo the past. There's no way I can make up to Ure for all that she lost because of my selfishness and self-centredness. I know I don't deserve it, but please give her the grace to forgive me. Please give me a second chance. And Lord, I thank you for the strength and resolve you gave her to go through with the pregnancy. You gave her reason not to kill the babies, my babies, Lord. I thank you.*

He was still on his knees when the doorbell rang and he glanced at his watch. It was almost ten thirty. He flung his robe across his shoulders and made his way to the living room. On the other side of the door two identical faces and a dog stared hopefully at him.

"Sorry to wake you up, Dr. Dolittle." One of the girls giggled, not looking sorry at all. "We had no idea you were still sleeping or we wouldn't have rang your bell."

"Of course I'm awake. Why did you think I was still sleeping?"

The second twin looked at his robe and he understood.

"I haven't yet showered, that's all. You know we old folks don't have the same amount of energy you kids have. We're lazy on Saturday mornings, taking life easy so we don't break our old bones."

Their laughter was music to his ears.

"You're not old," one twin countered.

"You're funny. Please say you can come and play with us."

"Yes, you have to. Big Jim says we have to be gentle with Rufus because he has been sick. We want to hear you speak animalese with Rufus before we take him back."

He bent down to pat the dog. "What happened to Rufus? He looks tired."

The girls looked at each other. "Why don't you ask him? He'll tell you in animalese."

"Why, did you all doubt that I can speak animalese?"

One of the girls, he was not sure which, angled her head and regarded him for a moment. "You speak like someone from abroad."

"Yes," her sister said, "you speak like an *oyibo*. Do you live in London?"

His heart tightened. His girls were beautiful, articulate and smart. What more could a man ask for?

"No, I live in America. I live in a big city called Chicago. Have you ever been to America?"

"No, we haven't."

"But our daddy lives there, and one day he's going to come and take us all to live with him in America."

"Shhh! Erinma." Her sister nudged at her urgently, speaking in rapid-fire Hausa.

"Wow, wow, wow, what was that?" Chuma asked.

"Nothing," the two girls chorused sweetly.

Rufus barked. "You see, Rufus wants to play too," one girl said. "Can you come now?"

"Please! Please, Dr. Dolittle," they pleaded.

How could he refuse?

"Ok. Dr. Dolittle needs five minutes to brush his teeth and change into his play clothes. You think you can wait that long?"

The two girls nodded in excitement. The dog barked.

The dishwasher broke down again that morning. When Grace called the technician, he told her he wouldn't be able to get to the hotel before two o'clock, so she rolled up her sleeves and joined the staff in washing and drying the dishes. From the kitchen windows she had a partial view of her apartment and occasionally caught a glimpse of her daughters running around with Rufus.

"Poor Rufus." Bola followed her gaze and shook her head. "Dog na dog, sha. Anyhow you train am, he go still chop rubbish. Upon all the training wey Big Jim don train am the dog still go find poison chop. I say dog na dog."

"Many poisons are odourless and tasteless. If they weren't, nobody would confuse them with food," Grace explained to her. "Even human beings can be deceived into unknowingly eating poison."

They heard a crash as dishes fell from Mama Remi's hands and scattered on the floor. The woman's gaze locked with Grace's for a few seconds before she bent to clean up the mess. Grace looked around, relieved the other staff didn't seem to have noticed Mama Remi's nervousness. Edith helped to pick up the broken glasses and sweep the floor clean. Grace allowed the scene to pass, but she made a mental note to corner the woman later for an interview about how Rufus may have ingested the rat poison she had bought last week for her home.

When other children joined in the game, the girls chained the dog to the burglary proof grill on their apartment window and made a bed of old cartons for him so he would have a rest from the play.

Grace's thoughts were still on Chuma. Was he angry with her for keeping the girls a secret from him? Was he thinking he was too young to be saddled with the responsibility of taking all of them in? Was his marriage proposal still open?

Auntie Simbi's arrival at noon was a welcome distraction for the hotel staff. Their employer brought with her a large carrier bag and gave presents to everyone—scarves and T-shirts, sunglasses, nightgowns, earrings, skirts and blouses, wristwatches and handbags. She had an album with pictures of her holidays and the staff gathered around to admire them, fascinated with all the beautiful places and sceneries.

Grace was relieved when the twins came and dragged the woman to their apartment to see the photographs they had brought from school. Their interruption was necessary so the kitchen staff could start getting ready for the reception party starting at seven that evening.

She went along with the children and Auntie Simbi. There was a suitcase and a big plastic carrier bag by their apartment door. Auntie Simbi had brought presents for them. As soon as they opened the door the twins opened the suitcase to reveal jeans and tops, undies, hair decorations, sandals, handbags, story books, puzzles, CDs and DVDs. They launched at their presents with alacrity, their school photographs quickly forgotten.

"I tried to get a little of everything for you girls."

"Oh, I love everything. Thank you, Big Mommy," said one twin, standing to hug her.

"I love everything too. Thank you, Big Mommy," said the other twin.

Auntie Simbi laughed and hugged them back. "I'm happy that two terms in boarding school have not changed my girls. However, this is not your birthday present."

"Where is it, Big Mommy? Where is our birthday present?"

The girls left the suitcase and dove into the carrier bag. There were two boxes in it.

"Oh, oh, oh! be careful girls, that's not for you. That is for your mother."

"It's a computer," Erinma said.

"No," Ojiugo shook her head. "It's a laptop."

"You got our mom a laptop?"

"You bought me a laptop?" Grace exclaimed joyfully. "Oh, Auntie!"

The older woman nodded at her astonishment.

"Thank you, Ma. Thank you, thank you so much!" Grace knelt at the woman's feet and thanked her over and over again. "I've wanted my own laptop for so long."

What would her life have been like without the generosity and love that this woman had shown her since the day she met her at Gidan Mairo? No one in her life had portrayed Christ's love to her more strongly than Auntie Simbi had. She had accepted her when her own family abandoned her, given her a home when she was homeless and given her a life she never dreamed was possible. She remembered the e-mail from her sister again and her eyes welled up. She ran into the bathroom to wipe away the tears before her children would notice and ask why she was crying. In their worldview, the laptop should make her happy, not sad.

"Mom, Mom, look! Big Mommy bought you this blood glucose meter," Erinma was reading from a box when she came out of the bathroom. "What is a blood glucose meter, Mom?"

"They are for measuring the sugar level in my blood."

"What?" Erinma's face showed her disgust. "You have sugar in your blood?"

Grace laughed.

"Mom, Mom," Ojiugo pulled at her. "Big Mommy bought us a PlayStation for our birthday but it's in her house!" They turned to her enthusiastically. "Can we go to GRA today, Mom? Can we go to Big Mommy's house, please?"

"Please, Mom. You even said we don't need to attend the dinner party if we don't want to."

"That is true," she smiled at Erinma, tweaking her nose. "but last night, Zee-Zee said she would reserve special seats for you two. She will be hurt if you don't go to her party."

"But we don't even have any clothes to wear."

"Of course you do. Big Mommy brought you a suitcase full of clothes."

"Patience, my dears," Auntie Simbi intervened with a tolerant smile. "Learn to be patient. The PlayStation is not running away. It's yours and will always be there for you. You can play with it any time you want, but you won't have another opportunity to attend Zuliat's party."

"Oh, all right," they glumly agreed. But their mood didn't stay down for long. "So Mom, can we help you set up your laptop?"

"No, you cannot!"

"Please!"

"I said no! No means no! I will set it up myself."

Auntie Simbi laughed at their disappointed faces. "Tell you what? I am on my way to the orphanage to visit the children. How about you girls come with me? I will bring you back in time for the party."

"Yeah!" they shouted, already making for the door.

"Hey!" their mother called after them. "Who's going to clean up this mess?"

Erinma turned. "What mess? Those are our new clothes."

"Nice try," Grace replied dryly. "You know the rules, don't you?"

"Yeah, Mom." Ojiugo frowned. "If they are not hanging, they should be neatly folded away."

The adults laughed as the girls set about tidying up. Grace's eyes fell on the laptop again and she shook her head again, overwhelmed by gratitude. "Auntie, thanks again for everything. May God bless and reward you abundantly for all you have done and continue to do for us."

"You know it is my pleasure, my dear. You and the girls have been a blessing to me too."

Grace curtsied and bowed her head. "You're too kind."

The woman reached a hand to lift Grace's chin and look into her eyes. "After church tomorrow, you must come to GRA with the girls. While they are introducing themselves to their PlayStation you will bring me up to speed with what has been happening at Sonshine Estate since I have been away. It looks like it was more stressful than you'd told me."

"The hotel was no stress, Auntie."

"I'm glad to hear that. But I know you, and you're looking worried about something. Are you fully recovered from your health crisis, dear?"

"Of course, Auntie, I would have told you if I wasn't feeling well."

"Okay. Let's talk tomorrow. Whatever it is, God is in control. Always remember that."

Grace nodded.

"All done, Mom. Can we go now?"

She turned slowly to face her girls. "There's a young girl at the orphanage that I would like you to make extra time for when you get there. I visited her last week and I told her you would be coming to play with her. Her name is Jumai ..."

After painting her nails, Remi switched on the table fan on high and splayed her hands in front of it. This was the quickest way she knew to dry them. She was not sure what dress to wear for the party. Too bad it was being held at Sonshine Estate. She had done her best to convince Auntie Bukky to move the party to a better location, like Hill Station Hotel, but the woman said it would be too expensive. Remi made a face and shook her head in irritation. Why were rich people so stingy? The woman was the proprietor of a sought-after private school. All she had to do was increase fees any time she was broke and her coffers would be full again. But she wouldn't, of course, because she was a Christian.

And that godson of hers, he was really kidding himself if he thought a few well-chosen words would get him off her hook. He had looked at her with interest from the first day, and no doubt the two of them would have been an item now if it hadn't been for that two-faced, gold-digging Grace, who had ingratiated herself into his affections the same way she had wormed her way into Auntie Simbi's favours years ago. Remi had never cared for the silly girl and would have gone on ignoring her if she hadn't interfered in her life. Chuma was hers. She didn't care what he did outside of Jos, but as long as he was in Jos, he was hers. It was as simple as that.

She glanced at her wristwatch; it was already five o'clock. She had to hurry with her beauty regimen if she was to make it to Sonshine Estates on time.

She tried on a midnight-blue strapless dress. It was a beautiful dress, revealing just the right amount of cleavage. Her mother wouldn't approve, of course. What else was new? The crowd at the party was likely to be filled with boring Christians anyway. They would look down their righteous noses and condemn her instantly. What did she care? She might wear it, just to spite them.

She heard banging on her door and quickly shrugged out of the dress.

"Hold on!" she called impatiently at whomever was at her door. She tied a wrapper across her chest. Where was the gateman?

In front of her door, apparently.

But he was not alone. Three police officers wielding batons stood behind him, along with Big Jim. Before she could get her wits together, one of the men kicked at the door and she fell back. Luckily she fell against the sofa and was able to hold on to her wrapper as the men stormed into the house.

"Madam, we are here to arrest you."

"Arrest me? Why? What have I done? What crime have I committed?

"You poisoned Oga Jim's police dog."

"Me? I didn't poison any dog o!"

Big Jim spoke up. "Yes, you did. When you came to visit me on Thursday, you asked if you could use the toilet. My dog's plate is along the corridor to the toilet. That was when you slipped something into his food. If I hadn't discovered it, quite by accident later that night, he would have died."

Remi laughed. "Haba, Big Jim. How can you say that? Don't you trust me?"

"I don't."

"*Wallahi tallahi!* Jim, I swear to you I didn't poison your dog. There must be some other explanation."

"I'm listening."

She shrugged. "How would I know? He could have picked it up from anywhere. Dogs eat poop, don't they?"

"Rufus doesn't."

"Well, I don't know how he ate whatever he ate or from where. And why are you harassing me, Jim? What about that girl, Grace? Isn't she the one who's always taking your dog for walks? He may have picked it up when they were out walking."

"Except that she didn't go for a walk with him Thursday morning."

"Still, she must know something about it."

"Like what?"

"Ah ha!" she exclaimed after a few seconds. "Why didn't I think of this before? Last Saturday, when my mother came back from the market, she bought rat poison. When I asked her what she wanted to do with it, she told me Grace wanted to drop it for the rats they have at Sonshine. Yes, that must be it. Rufus could have picked up the poison she had scattered for the rats. See?"

Big Jim shook his head. "Remi, do you realise that you have just implicated yourself in this crime? First of all, why would your mother bring stuff home that belongs to the hotel? If she bought the rat poison for Grace, why didn't she just keep it there for Grace? Why bring it home?"

"I ... I don't know."

"Secondly, how did you know it was rat poison? I didn't say anything about rat poison."

"I ... I ... heard it from ..."

"Give it up, Remi. Get dressed and follow these officers to the station."

But she wasn't going down without a fight. "I will not. Never! Tell your men to leave me alone o! Hmm, Jim, for your information, the Commissioner of Police is a personal friend. He will not stand by and see you molest me. *Mai Guard*, go call my aunty for me. Call Auntie Bukky. Phone am now now. Tell am say some area boys want molest me. Tell her make she come quick, quick."

"Sharrap!" one of the officers barked at her. "Na who you dey call area boy?"

"Oga, I want sound this woman mouth o!" the second officer looked at Jim.

"Go ahead!" Jim nodded. "I can't wait for the police commissioner to call me and accuse me of molesting his girlfriend."

Remi couldn't dodge the blow that knocked her to the ground and displayed fireworks in her head.

"That was the warning shot," Jim said. "If you don't get dressed now, my men will handcuff you as you are and take you to the station. Is that what you want?"

"Please, Jim," she pleaded from bloodied lips.

"Why did you do it, Remi? Why did you try to kill my dog?"

"I didn't mean to kill him. I'm very sorry, Jim."

"Not as sorry as you will be when I'm done with you. Rufus is not just my dog, you know. He's my friend. That may not mean anything to you but it means a lot to me."

"Jim, please."

"And for your information, the Commissioner of Police may be your personal friend but the Inspector General of police is my brother-in-law. I accompanied these men out of the kindness of my heart and out of respect for your mother, to ensure they don't beat you up. If you don't cooperate I'll leave you at their mercy. Now, are you going to dress up and follow them to the police station, or should we wait for directions from your personal friend, the Commissioner of Police?"

The technician left at five that evening. Once the dishwasher was droning again, Grace went back to her apartment to rest before the evening party. Plus she needed to change out of the jeans and T-shirt she had been wearing all day into something more befitting of her position as the hotel manager. She would take a quick shower and rest for 30 minutes before going back to the Recreation Centre.

That was her plan, but everything changed when she opened her door and saw the box on the dining table, her new laptop waiting to be opened and connected. Next thing she knew, she was unwrapping the laptop from its plastic cover and reading the set-up manuals. Only God would bless Auntie Simbi for her. The woman hadn't bought just any laptop for her. This had a 17-inch flat-screen monitor and must have cost hundreds of pounds. She started to sort out the connection wires.

Good thing the hotel had WIFI connection. She typed in the password and in a few minutes her laptop was online. She clicked on Google and browsed through news and sports websites, then she checked her e-mail. Nobody sent her e-mails—Ayesha occasionally and sometimes the choir pastor at church. Most other e-mails were Spams and flyers from shops and businesses. She noticed she had two e-mails from Dr. Ańuli Okolie of the Calabar University Teaching Hospital. There was a new e-mail, apart from the one she'd read three days ago.

She clicked on the new e-mail, and what she read next rendered her speechless.

Her mother had suffered a heart attack.

She took some calming breaths and closed her eyes for a few seconds. *Oh God!* she whispered.

Pray!

She started at the voice and turned around in search of the speaker. She didn't see anybody. The television screen was blank. Nor was there a peep from the radio. Apart from the humming of the fridge, everywhere was quiet.

Heart pounding, she turned back to the message on the computer and forced herself to read it again, slowly this time.

Her mother was *"in a coma at Calabar University Teaching Hospital and the doctors are afraid she may not make it,"* her sister had written. She expelled a heavy breath and lifted her hand in a helpless gesture.

Pray! The voice was urgent.

She looked around again but knew in her heart that she would not see anybody. Goose bumps broke out on her arms, and she could not tell if it was because of the news about her mother or because of the presence of the Lord.

Help, Lord! She shivered.

Call upon me in the day of trouble; I will deliver you and you shall glorify me.

Swallowing hard, she closed her eyes and took in a deep breath, trying to suppress the fear that suddenly gripped her heart, and exhaled through her mouth. There was no question what she had to do. She turned back to the e-mail.

"Have you been able to locate your friend, my sister, Urenna? You see, we all believed she was dead. It was the news that she is really alive that caused my mother's heart to fail."

Grace closed her eyes, took a deep breath.

The eternal God is your refuge, and underneath are the everlasting arms, she heard in her spirit, and quietly breathed out again.

"If you have any news about my sister, please call me urgently. I don't know if my mother will wake up again. She has been mourning my sister's death for 11 years now. If Urenna is alive it is my hope that my mother will see her before she passes. Please help me in any way you can, Ms. Anthony. Let me know if you have any news at all about your friend and my sister, Urenna, as soon as possible. You can always reach me through this phone number—"

She took a deep breath again and exhaled, all the while acknowledging that the eternal God—the God who has no beginning and no end—was indeed her refuge. Jesus, the alpha and the omega, the beginning and the end, the one who is, who was and who is to come—was her refuge. He was the one she had run to for safety and shelter years ago and still the one she could turn to again for hope and assurance.

She ran to her bedroom, drew the curtains, grabbed her Bible and knelt by her bed. She clasped her shaking hands, bowed her head and began to pray to God to heal her mother. The words flowed from her deepest soul, a cry for God's healing and mercy, a plea for forgiveness and cleansing through the blood of Jesus Christ, a binding of the plans of the devil who comes to steal, to kill and to destroy. She resisted the devil in every way she knew. Names and faces of her family members cascaded before her mind's eye, and she interceded for all of them, pleading for forgiveness and salvation. Scores of scenes of her father's cruelty and her mother's helplessness rushed into her mind, and she cried for forgiveness on their behalf as well.

Grace prayed. Grace cried. She bound. She cast out. She prayed again.

Her phone rang several times in the next two hours but she didn't pick it up. Guests started to arrive for Zuliat and Chuma's party, the sound of their cars and their laughing voices sometimes carrying through to her apartment. But Grace kept praying. And praying. And praying.

Chapter 29

Calabar

The vibration of her cell phone woke Añuli from a fitful sleep on Sunday morning. She got up from the couch in the hospital room and looked at her mother, searching for any sign that she was merely sleeping and could wake up any moment. But Añuli was a doctor, and she could see from the monotony of her breathing that her mother was still unconscious, totally unresponsive to her environment.

"Hello," she whispered. "Añuli Okolie on the line. Who's this please?"

For a moment, she did not hear anything from the other side of the phone. She looked at her wristwatch. Who could be calling her at five-forty-five a.m.? It wasn't her father. It wasn't the pastor either.

"Hello," she said again, patiently. "Can I help you?"

"Em, hello, this is Grace Anthony. You sent me an e-mail yesterday about your mother. I just wanted to find out, is she still in the hospital? Has she woken from the coma?"

"Oh, Grace? Ms. Anthony?" Añuli's voice brightened immediately. "You were the one asking after my sister, Urenna?"

"Yes."

"Have you found her? Do you know where she is?" she whispered urgently.

There was a slight hesitation before Grace answered. "Yes, I know where she is."

"Oh!" Ańuli felt goose bumps shoot out from every cell in her body. She glanced at her mother again and went to the door. Even though the woman was unconscious, she felt the need to talk out of earshot. She went into the hallway and shut the door.

"Please, can you help me reach her?" she whispered urgently.

"Yes, yes. I can reach her."

"Can you tell her, ... can you tell her to come to Calabar immediately? My mother"—she sniffed—"my mother is dying and—" she bit her lips. "My mother is dying and I don't know what to do. Please tell her to come home immediately. If by some miracle my mother wakes up, she can at least see her before she dies."

"Shhh, don't talk like that. Don't give up hope yet."

"I'm sorry but she doesn't look good," Ańuli whispered, close to tears but trying her best to face the truth. "I'm a doctor, you know, a dentist. It's been two days now since she collapsed, and she's still not responding to her environment in any way."

"But you do have hope that she will wake up, don't you?"

"Honestly, Ms. Anthony, I don't know."

"Yes, you do," Grace said desperately. "Why else would you send for your sister? Is it not in the hope that the two of them can see each other?"

Ańuli swallowed. "She was just recovering from a major heart attack, Ms. Anthony, compounded by a stroke. My mother literally died about three weeks ago. The doctors had given up hope, declared her dead, but she woke up. This is a more severe attack. The doctor said not to hold on to much hope."

"But you can't let that stop you. With God all things are possible. You have to keep on hoping and praying and believing."

Añuli hesitated before she replied. "I'm sorry, but honestly, I'm not much into religion."

"Oh." Grace sounded disappointed.

"It's not that I don't believe in God," Añuli hurried to assure her. "I do, but—"

"You don't have to apologise or feel bad because of your beliefs. It's who you are. I am a Christian myself. I believe in the power of God to save, to bless, to heal and to deliver. And since I read your e-mail I have been praying for God to wake your mother from her deep sleep. Can I pray with you?"

"Sure. But can you contact Urenna for me? Can she come immediately?"

"I've already informed her. She said she will be in Calabar today."

Añuli's gasped, not sure if she heard right. "Today?"

"Yes, today."

Oh, thank you so much. Please give her my phone number. Tell her to call me as soon as possible."

"I will," Grace assured her. "But I really would like to pray with you for your mother."

"Of course. By all means, let's pray for her."

"Do you believe that God is able to heal her?"

"I believe God is sovereign. He can do anything he wants to."

"I know. But for your mother, do you believe he wants to heal her?"

Añuli's silence spoke volumes. Grace waited.

Añuli broke out suddenly, tears in her voice. "I don't know what to believe. I'm sorry, I know that's not what you want to hear, but I have to be honest with you, Ms. Anthony. Otherwise I'll be deceiving myself."

"Please call me Grace."

"Thanks. I know what I'm looking at here, Grace. I have read her case notes, I'm checking her vital signs frequently and it will take a miracle for her to wake up from this coma."

The two girls were silent for a while but it was a thoughtful silence. Añuli wondered what the other girl was thinking.

"Then we have to pray for a miracle," Grace remarked.

"Oh, okay, whatever." Añuli sniffed. "Do you want to pray now?"

"Yes, if you don't mind. I know what you said about not believing, but she's your mother and I would like to have some connection with her as I pray. Are you at the hospital?"

"Yes."

"Can you put your hand on her as I pray out loud?"

"Hold on, let me go back to the room. I stepped out into the hallway to talk to you."

When she got there Añuli whispered, "Okay, I'm touching her hand now."

"Dear Lord, I believe that all things are possible with you. The Bible says that in the beginning everywhere was void and empty and hopeless until your spirit brooded upon it and brought everything to life. I pray that your spirit will brood over your daughter, Mrs. Okolie, this moment, and wake her from this deep sleep. Nothing is bigger than you, Lord. So would you touch her, and heal her, so that your name will be praised and your children will be blessed. According to your love, according to your mercy and according to your power and your grace that is at work in your daughter, Mrs. Okolie, Lord, I ask for divine healing. I ask this in Jesus' name, amen."

"Amen," Añuli responded and opened her eyes slowly to look at her mother.

No change. What had she expected?

"Don't be discouraged, okay?" Grace said as though she knew what Añuli was thinking. "You may not see any change in her now, but God has heard our prayer and will answer us."

"You really think he'll heal her?"

"I know he will answer our prayer."

"And if she doesn't wake up? What then?"

"Then I know that God willed it for a reason and I will try to discover what the reason is."

Añuli paused for a few seconds, trying to control her frustration. "You see, that's what I don't understand about this Christianity business," she bit out. "Why won't God just answer you? Why make you sweat and worry and pray all these prayers if in the end he will do what he wants to do anyway? It doesn't make any sense to me."

"Añuli, I believe God causes all things that happen to me to work together for my good. Even when I don't see it, even when I don't understand, if I keep faithful, I will see in the end that he orchestrated everything for my good, even the seemingly unanswered prayers."

"Isn't that rather an escapist view? If God is God, let him answer the prayers of his children."

"He does, Añuli. Believe me, he does."

There was a slight pause as Añuli tried to control her emotions. She squeezed her nose between her thumb and index finger, effectively stifling a threatening sneeze. "I'm sorry, Ms. Anthony. I know you mean well. I didn't mean to dampen your beliefs—"

"You didn't."

"But I don't like to pretend."

"It's good to be honest. I don't have all the answers. Nobody has. I have questions too. But I want to grow whatever measure of faith I have. It is in exercising faith that you have more faith."

She continued quietly. "If you believe at all, even a little, apply that faith in your life and see what God will do with it."

"Okay. Thank you. But please can you tell my sister to call me soon? It's not only my mother who has missed her. I have also missed her, and if my mother doesn't make it, she'll be all that I have."

"What about your father?"

"Oh, yes, my father. He's around too but she's my sister, you know, my only sister."

"No problem, I understand. I'll give her your number. I'll give you my phone number too. Please call me if your mother's condition changes. I'm praying for you all."

Her mother was still dead to the world when Añuli got off the phone. She watched her for a while and slowly shook her head. Urenna was alive and she may see her today. Tears gathered. How ironic that the best news her mother had ever gotten would land her in a deadly coma. There was an Igbo adage: "May my desires not lead to my death." So apt.

She wished she could believe God would heal her mother, that she had the same assurance of the power of God that woman had just demonstrated over the phone. But what good would it do her? Even after that strong prayer, her mother was still comatose.

She placed a hand on her mother's forehead and gently brushed away a thin film of perspiration. An IV bag was connected, delivering medication into her body at a steady flow. Her mother's Bible lay on the bedside table. An old sticker on it read "With God all things are possible." It reminded her of what Ms. Anthony had just said, that she was praying for a miracle. That woman sounded decidedly religious. Maybe Urenna had turned religious too. Not that it mattered one bit. Even if over the years her sister had turned into a missionary, or become a drug user or spent time in prison or was sick and in a wheelchair, it wouldn't matter at all. Not to her, and definitely not to their mother. She had been dead to them, and now she was alive. What more could they ask for?

But why would the God her mother had served so faithfully since her near-death experience allow this to happen to her again? Anuli silently asked. What glory was in it for her God if he was watching her helplessly slipping into a vegetative state? She remembered the words of a psalm she had read to her mother recently. "The cords of death surrounded me. The floods of ungodliness made me afraid. The snares of death came on me. In my distress I called on Yahweh, and cried to my God. He heard my voice out of his temple. My cry came into his ears ..."

Were those words only for the psalmist? Was that testimony only for the prophets of old? Was God selective about whose prayers he listened to? Why was he not healing her mother? Could he even see her? Was there even such a thing as a personal God?

The answer was obvious to her. There was really no God, at least not the way he has been described by Christians. God was a concept and served as a crutch that human beings hold on to in times of trouble. Including her, for hadn't she been praying although deep within her, she knew she didn't believe? None of it was real. *It's just everybody's imagination*, Añuli concluded, *something that makes us all feel good with ourselves, a logical explanation for things beyond our comprehension.*

She looked at the woman on the bed again. It was almost six o'clock. The nurses would be coming for their first shift change any minute now.

"Urenna is alive, Mama." She whispered into her mother's ears. "Can you hear me? Urenna is alive and she's coming to see you. You have to wake up, Mama. You have to wake up and see Ure and her children, Mama. You have to wake up."

She talked earnestly and long to the woman, but there was no response. She opened the Bible and read the psalms again to her mother, just like she had done since she moved in with her, only to stop in despair halfway. Her mother didn't look like she planned to wake up just yet.

"How about it, God?" Añuli finally muttered, exasperated. "How about you and I make a deal? You wake my mother up from this coma so she can see Urenna and her children before she dies, and I will believe in you. Ms. Anthony said we should pray for a miracle. This is my miracle prayer. If you do this I will know that you are indeed God and that you are not indifferent to the prayers of your servants who call on you day and night. How about it, Jesus? Show me that God exists. Show me that you are God."

She had hardly completed her sentence than she heard her mother take a deep breath, exhale audibly and move her head on the pillow.

Chapter 30

Jos GRA

"I have a favour to ask you," Grace said as she stood at Auntie Simbi's doorsteps later that morning. Her employer always attended the eleven o'clock service at the church, so Grace knew she wasn't disturbing her. It was not nine o'clock yet and she had called earlier to request an audience.

"It sounds serious."

Grace nodded and exhaled. "My mother is in a coma at the Calabar University Teaching hospital."

"Your mother?" Her hand went to her chest.

Grace nodded again. "Yes. She had a heart attack and the doctors think she may not make it."

"God forbid!"

"Amen. I have been praying all night and believe the Lord wants me to go to her."

"With the twins?"

"Yes, with the twins."

Auntie Simbi shook her head in sympathy. "I'm so sorry to hear this, my dear. Come in and sit down and tell me all about it. Don't stand at the door as if you're a stranger."

Grace winced and closed her eyes in embarrassment. She had not realised she had been standing at the door. "Thank you, Auntie. I'm behaving just like Erinma now. It's a good thing she's not here to remind me."

She followed Auntie Simbi into the kitchen.

"Tell me what happened. I thought your parents had disowned you. How did they contact you?"

"They didn't. I did."

"You did?"

She nodded. "While you were away, I decided to Google my sister and I found her e-mail address. I sent her an e-mail asking about her 'sister'. I wanted to know if they still remembered me. I posed as an old schoolmate of her sister's. She replied and told me her sister had died 11 years ago in a vehicle accident."

"Huh?" Auntie Simbi opened her mouth.

"Yeah, that's what she said. I can show you the e-mail. I have it with me."

"They believe you are dead? What about the letters you've been writing them all these years? The post office never returned any of them."

"I don't know the details yet. Maybe when I get there I will find out what happened. Maybe they never got them."

For the next 10 minutes Grace recounted to her employer the details of her search, culminating in the e-mail she'd received yesterday. "She wants me to come home immediately so my mother can see me before she dies."

Auntie Simbi was shocked. Her eyes grew wide as she listened and kept shaking her head in denial. Later, while she thought over the news, Grace busied herself filling the tea cups with hot water and placing tea bags in them.

"Did you print the e-mails? I would like to see them."

Grace hurried to her bag and extracted an envelope.

"It's not that I don't trust your judgment, my dear," Auntie Simbi assured her. "It's just that, in Nigeria these days it is very common for scammers to find new ways to scam people out of money with bogus claims about family accidents and sicknesses and even kidnappings. When I was in Europe, we visited a Nigerian family who just got a call from someone in Nigeria saying she should send money home immediately because her younger sister had been in an accident and the doctors were refusing to perform emergency surgery on her until they paid five million naira."

"Oh no!"

Auntie Simbi hissed. "Hmm. You can't imagine how desperate our people have become. They have devised all kinds of evil ways to steal money from others. Thank God I was there when she got the call. I suggested she should call other family members to verify the story before sending any money to anybody. When she called one of her aunts, it was the same younger sister who picked up the phone."

"Oh no!"

"Are you sure you're not being conned, my dear?"

"She's not asking for any money, Auntie, and when I spoke with her early this morning, she was at the hospital."

"Still, I would be more confident if we can send someone to the hospital to check for us before you go anywhere. I don't want anything to happen to you or to those precious girls."

For the first time, tears sprang into Grace's eyes and she tried to squash them. Auntie Simbi meant well, but she was wrong. And she was wasting time.

"I've prayed about this Auntie. I need to go. The bus leaves at eleven o'clock."

"You know I won't stop you. But it will be irresponsible of me let you go back to the people who tried to kill you years ago without first making enquiries. I don't know anybody in Calabar, but I'm sure my sister can help. She knows a lot of people. Pass me my phone, dear."

"Auntie, the bus leaves at eleven o'clock." Grace tried to mask her impatience with a smile. She hadn't expected this amount of resistance.

"Ah, let it leave," Auntie Simbi waved off her anxiety. "You can't hurry God. If it is the Lord's will that you will meet your mother alive, you will get there in time. The Lord is never late; he's always on time. Did you remember to bring the Sonshine books for me?"

"All the files are in the car."

"Good. Why don't you bring them in while I make a few calls? Write your father and mother's names for me on this paper."

Grace gave her the information and went to the car. When she got back Auntie Simbi was not back in the living room. Grace heard her voice from the bedroom upstairs speaking on the phone. Despite her impatience, she was grateful. This was not the first time Auntie Simbi was demonstrating a practical commitment to looking after her.

While she waited, she called Bola to wake up the twins so they could bathe and change. She prayed silently for her mother again before bending over the hotel books to review the reports she had brought to hand over to her employer.

It was almost nine thirty by the time she heard Auntie Simbi's heavy steps descending the staircase.

"They say it is true o!" The woman threw her arms into the air. "Your mother is in the hospital for real. She was admitted there Friday night. You have to go immediately."

Grace nodded.

"Bukky gave me the address of the Commissioner of Police. The man has agreed that you and the twins can stay in his house while you visit your mother in the hospital. Rest assured, God is working out everything, my dear. Listen, I don't want anything to happen to you. It was your father and mother who beat you up very badly the other time. If not for God, I would not allow you to go back to them. But as you say, we don't know the whole story. You have to be very careful when you get there."

Grace bent her knees to the ground, curtsying deeply.

Auntie Simbi lifted her by the hand and prayed for her. "I pray that your mother will not die. I pray that she will live to see the wonderful blessings the Lord has been preparing for her all these years—her daughter and her wonderful grandchildren. I pray that you all will bring joy and comfort and healing to her."

"Amen."

"When you go home now, you are going to open many old wounds. It's not going to be easy for you. I understand that they even have a grave where they said they buried your father's first daughter, meaning you, right in the university cemetery."

Grace started at this. Chuma had told her about the grave too.

"Hmm." Auntie Simbi turned and looked her in the eye. "It's not going to be easy at all. I wish I could go with you, but there will be no one to run the hotel if the two of us are absent."

"I'll be all right, Ma."

The woman's face was worried. "Remember that I am only a phone call away."

"Yes, Ma."

"But your God is only a breath away. Please be very, very prayerful."

"I will, Ma. Thank you."

"Watch and pray. Keep a low profile. Don't attract any attention to yourself. There'll be enough talk as it is."

"I will, Ma."

She hugged her once more. "Okay, let's quickly go through these reports before you leave. Did you already buy the bus ticket?"

"No, Ma."

"Good. It's too late anyway. I will buy flight tickets for you and the twins. The driver will take you to the airport to catch the evening flight to Calabar."

Surprised and speechless, Grace could only stare at Auntie Simbi with misty eyes and a grateful heart.

Chapter 31

Jos

Chuma heard the knock at his door just before ten o'clock. After a restless night spent wondering why Urenna didn't show up for the party and trying to figure out how to bridge the gap that had sprung up between them again, he hadn't eaten, hadn't shaved, hadn't showered, hadn't done anything except call Chief Ojiefi to give him his final appraisal of Gidan Mairo and his estimation of the work that was needed to bring it up to standard. The building was solid though somewhat dilapidated, but the land that came with it was huge, more than three acres, and his recommendation to the chief was to go ahead with the purchase.

He was looking through the closet in search of a shirt when he heard a faint knock on the front door. It was one of Urenna's daughters, not the two of them, and from the fitful glances she cast over her shoulder he realised she didn't want to be seen. She pushed the door open and ran past him into the living room. Still, he stepped out to look around and be sure she was alone before joining her.

"Well, now," Chuma said gently to the girl who looked back at him through Amaka's eyes, "which of the twins are you?"

She folded her lips, looked nervously at him and shook her head. "I'm not telling."

"I see." He angled his head and pretended to frown. "You know what the forefathers used to do to identical twins to tell them apart?"

She shook her head.

"They gave them different marks on their faces."

Two hands flew to cover her cheeks and her eyes darted swiftly toward the door. Chuma almost laughed. "You're not going to hurt me, are you?"

"No, of course I'm not going to hurt you," he hastened to reassure her. "I'm never going to hurt you. But what are you doing here?"

"Promise you won't tell my mother," she pleaded. "She says we must never talk to strangers and if she knows I came here by myself she'll not be happy."

"So why are you here by yourself?"

"Ojiugo said we shouldn't come but I wanted to. She went in to take her bath, so I came. I won't be a minute, I promise."

"Hmm." He smiled and analysed her words aloud. "Ojiugo wouldn't come so you came—that means you are Erinma?"

"Yes, I'm Erinma. You're clever."

"Thanks."

"I came to say good-bye to you and to ask you for a favour."

"To say good-bye? Why?" Panic wiped the smirk off his face. "Where are you going? You only arrived on Friday. Where are you off to?"

The little girl shrugged. "I don't know. My mother has gone to Big Mommy's house. She called us and said we should get ready to travel this morning. We think that maybe you'll be gone before we come back to Jos."

He took a deep breath and tried to keep his calm. "Okay. What do you want me to do for you?"

She looked down and he saw the piece of paper she was torturing in her hands. Her voice shook in her nervousness but she bravely went on. "This is me and Ojiugo's address," she explained. "When you go back to America, can you look for our daddy for us? Please. When you see him, tell him that we're not mad at him for leaving us. Tell him we have forgiven him. Give him our address and tell him to write us. Ojiugo and I want him to come and take us to America with him."

Chuma closed his eyes and swallowed hard. He pinched his nose and shook his head to steady the emotions surging through his heart. The urge to hurl the child into his arms and tell her the truth was almost irresistible.

"You want to leave your mother here all by herself?"

"No, we can go to America during the long holidays and we'll come back to Jos and stay with her after that. You see, we don't think our mother would—"

Her sister's voice calling her name cut into her sentence, and quickly, before Chuma could say anything, she thrust the piece of paper on the centre table and darted out of his apartment. He watched from the window as the two girls began arguing. He had an idea the dispute was about Erinma's visit to his suite, but he couldn't understand what they were saying. They were speaking Hausa.

He lowered his head onto his hands and exhaled. For the first time in a very long while, Chuma experienced a frisson of panic. The tremors started from his heart, spreading all the way to his fingers and toes. His heart beat quickened. *I can't go through this again, Lord*, he prayed. *I can't be separated from them again.* He had to stop her. He couldn't allow her to leave without a fight. He had to find a way to make her see that they all belonged together.

Chuma rushed to the bathroom to brush his teeth and shower and then took his wallet and cell phone and strode to Unit 12.

One of the twins, Ojiugo, he thought, opened the door. But behind her stood her twin, and they were both dressed in identical clothes and staring back at him with identical innocent expressions. He had to smile in admiration at their ploy.

"I should have put a mark on someone's face this morning," he murmured and the girls started to giggle. They wore blue jeans and cotton shirts with their sweaters tied loosely around their waists. The suitcases behind the door completed the picture of travellers with a long journey ahead of them, and his heart gave another lurch.

"Is your mother back?"

They shook their heads.

"Did you say she's with your Big Mommy?"

They nodded.

Chuma sighed. "Okay. One of you girls really hurt my feelings today."

"Oh!"

"Yes." He nodded. "She was planning to leave today without saying good-bye. Is that how to treat a friend?"

The girls glanced at one another and slowly shook their heads.

"So what are you going to do about it?"

"We're sorry," they chorused.

"Show me?"

"How?" one of them asked.

He did not hesitate in opening his arms and inviting them into a group hug. He held both girls to his heart and savoured the feel of their arms around his neck before letting them go.

"Now that's better," he pronounced, and the girls relaxed. "That's the proper way to say good-bye to a friend."

They heard footsteps coming toward their apartment, and soon Bola opened the front door. She stepped in and didn't look surprised when she saw Chuma with the children.

"Oga Chuma, good morning." She greeted him before turning to the girls. "Una Mama been phone. She say she go soon return. She say make una eat before she reach here."

The girls picked up their shoulder bags. One of them, Chuma suspected it was Erinma, came over and pulled at his hand. "Come with us. You haven't eaten breakfast either."

"I'm sorry," he said quietly. "I need to go out now. I have an appointment in town."

"Will we see you before we leave?"

"You will see me," he replied confidently.

"Yeah!" The girls gave each other a high five and took off toward the Rec Centre.

He motioned to Bola as she tried to follow them. "Do me a favour, Bola."

The woman turned.

"I need to talk to Grace. Do you know where I can find her?"

"She been call from Auntie Simbi's house. E be like say she want travel this morning. But she no tell me where she dey go."

"I'm going to look for her at Auntie Simbi's. If she comes back before I get there, can you find a way to delay her until I come back?"

"Why?" Bola eyed him with a suppressed smile.

"I have to see her before she leaves."

"Why?"

"What do you mean why?"

"Why you want see am before she travel?"

He sighed. "She's trying to run away from me—that's why. I can't let her do that."

"Why? A bi you want marry am?" Merriment was dancing in her eyes.

He smiled and chuckled quietly. "You ask too many questions, Bola. Mind your business."

Her smile broke through as she beamed at him. "I talk am. I talk am but nobody want to believe me."

Chuma shook his head and started for the parking lot. "If you can just make sure she doesn't leave until I have had a chance to talk to her, I'll owe you big time, okay?"

"Praise the Lord!" the woman smiled broadly, then he heard her singing in excitement, "Love nwantinti, love nwantinti, ije mu na love n'ofoduru nwantinti, ije mu na love n'ofoduru nwantinti." (*An Igbo song about the mystery of love*)!

Calabar

Aṅuli watched the doctor shine a light in her mother's eyes and make some notes in her case file. He checked her blood pressure and pulse, listened to her heartbeat and stuck a thermometer into her mouth. Then he wrote some more notes and signalled for her to follow him out of the ward.

"How is she doing?" she asked anxiously.

"Better than I expected. Her reflexes are good. She's beginning to emerge from the coma. She can wake up any time. When she does, it might be for a very short time before she drifts off again. Don't let this bother you. It is not uncommon as she tries to regain consciousness."

Añuli nodded, trying to understand the implications of what he was saying.

"As her wake cycle begins to last longer, she will start to have more movement, and then speech. Just let her take it easy. Don't expect too much at once. It takes time to recover from a coma."

"But, Doctor, how could she have slipped into a coma when there was no traumatic injury to her brain? The CT scan returned negative for trauma."

"Unconsciousness is not only caused by trauma. In her case, I would guess it was triggered by a hypertensive crisis. We cannot rule out other metabolic or endocrine causes. But the good news is that she'll make it, and—"

She'll make it ... she'll make it ... she'll make it ...

Relief surged through her. She took in a deep breath and exhaled loudly. *God!* she cried silently. *God!* Was it only this morning that Ms. Anthony had prayed for her mother? Was it only this morning that she had challenged the Lord to wake her mother from her coma? Was this his response to her challenge? Was it possible that he had kept his side of the bargain? Or was this a mere coincidence?

"You have to be positive around her. Speak normally to her; don't say anything negative or show that you are worried about her in any way. Now that she is emerging from her unconsciousness, she is aware of what is going on around her. Even if she doesn't say anything, she may be hearing what you say and possibly read your expressions also."

"How long do you think she'll stay in the hospital?"

"I can't tell. Two weeks at the minimum would be my guess. We'll keep her here for as long as it takes."

When she came back to the room, Añuli stood and gazed lovingly at the woman struggling for her life on the bed. She was a fighter, her mother sure was. Añuli struggled with tears and sniffed as her nose began to run.

"Mama, can you hear that? I'm crying. But these are tears of happiness. I'm so proud of you. The doctor says you will recover. He doesn't know how well you will recover but God told me." She smiled and touched her mother's forehead. "God said you will recover fully. He wants you to recover fully so you can see Urenna and her twins. Did I tell you they are on their way to see you?"

Egoyibo's chest rose higher as she inhaled and began to sleep more deeply. Añuli reached for the Bible by the side, turned to Revelation 7:17, and read the words out to her mother: "For the Lamb at the center of the throne will be their shepherd; he will lead them to springs of living water. And God will wipe away every tear from their eyes."

Jos

It was all settled. The driver would come for them at two thirty to take them to the airport. Ambassador Air had two flights to Calabar that evening—a direct flight at four fifteen and another one with a stopover in Lagos, departing at six fifteen. Grace was relieved. Even if she had left with the eleven o'clock "luxurious" bus from Jos, they wouldn't have arrived in Aba before midnight, at which time the taxis would have stopped running for the day. They would have had to spend the night there and continued the three-hour journey from Aba to Calabar on Monday morning. It would have been much too stressful for the twins, who had never gone on such a long journey before.

Travelling by air, on the other hand, posed its own challenges. She had never been on an aeroplane before and she wasn't really looking forward to it. She remembered the air crash several years ago in which more than 100 passengers, mostly schoolchildren going home for the holidays, had died. But she also knew plane crashes were rare and that more people die travelling by road than by air. *Besides*, she reminded herself, *there are dangers everywhere; it is only the presence of God that guarantees safety.*

Grace looked at her watch. If she left now, she could still catch the second service in church. She considered the idea for a moment and decided against it. She should rather use this gift of time to prepare for the trip. She would also use the opportunity to pray for her mother and to mentally prepare herself for the consequences of being seen alive by her family after 11 years.

Añuli hadn't phoned her yet. That was good. That meant their mother was still alive. And where was their father in all this? she wondered. Her sister never referred to him at all. Perhaps he travelled out of the country. She remembered once, when they were still young, the university had sponsored him to a United Nations programme in Kenya, where he had worked for six months.

"Please turn off the air conditioner," she requested the driver as soon as they drove by a road maintenance work along Solomon Lar Way, on their way back to Sonshine Estate. She wound down the glass of the station wagon and leaned back on her seat, revelling in the fresh air that flowed in. Her mind and body were exhausted from lack of sleep from the night before, so she closed her eyes and tried to snooze.

"That na Oga ke!" the driver exclaimed, turning to look at the other side of the road.

"Who?"

"Oga Chuma. I see his car pass us just now, on the other side."

Grace turned to look back but they had turned round a corner and she couldn't see the Land Rover. "He's really late if he's going to church," she remarked.

"He even try if na church he dey go so. I been think say he go rest today because of the party last night."

"Adamu," she teased. "I don't think eleven o'clock is too early to be awake on a Sunday morning, party or no party."

The driver grinned and shrugged. "My sister, wetin you wan make I talk now?"

Grace had no sooner finished packing that afternoon when she heard the twins return to the suite. Unlike the bubbly girls who had left less than 30 minutes earlier for the Recreation Centre, they looked scared and subdued. If it wasn't that she saw the tears in their eyes and knew they were upset, Grace would have laughed at the way both girls folded their arms across their heads, as though a huge calamity had befallen them.

She got up from the couch and went to them, biting her lips to stifle the impending smile. They were so cute. "Girls, whatever is the matter?"

She was surprised that they were shivering.

"There's been an accident," Erinma blurted out.

"An accident? Where?"

"On the road to GRA, near Solomon Lar junction."

"How do you know? Who told you?"

"Auntie Bola."

Grace was confused. "Was it bad? Was it someone she knows?"

"They said he's dead."

"Who?"

"Uncle Chuma."

"Dr. Dolittle."

"What?" Grace glared at the girls. "If this is a joke, you two, I will smack you both. Have I not told you that you don't joke with serious issues like death?"

"It's not a joke, Mommy."

"We're not making it up."

"Of course you are," she shouted at Ojiugo. "I saw Chuma on my way back from Auntie Simbi's house. There wasn't even any traffic on the way. How could he have died in a motor accident?"

She stopped when she saw tears fill their eyes again. They were serious about this.

"It's true, Mommy," Ojiugo repeated tearfully.

Grace began to tremble. Her chest felt tight. God wouldn't do this to her, would he? He wouldn't allow this to happen to her.

"Where's Bola? I have to see Bola."

Her hand fumbled with the doorknob until she finally turned it. She made herself walk down the pathway to the Rec Centre where she spotted Musa, Trevor, Bola, Edith and other staff in the dining room, looking as shocked as the twins.

Edith had her two hands on her head, tears flowing down her cheeks.

Grace ran to them. "What am I hearing, Bola? Is it true? Who told you?"

Bola took a deep breath and shook her head. "He was just here. E never even reach two hours ago when I see am dey talk to the twins. He tell me say he dey go find you for Auntie Simbi's house. He been want talk to you before you travel commot."

Grace shook her head. It still wasn't getting through. She looked up into the stricken faces of the other hotel staff and some guests flocking around the room. Was her face as pale?

"But who told you?" Her voice was desperate.

"Ayesha called," Edith replied. "She said she saw his Land Rover near Solomon Lar junction, just after the construction, on the way to GRA. It was totally destroyed. She said he couldn't have come out of it alive."

"Ayesha called you? Why didn't she call me?"

"She said she tried but your phone was off."

"Did she see his body?"

"I don't know. She just said he couldn't have made it out alive. Then I called Auntie Bukky's house and she wasn't there. Mama Remi was crying. She said all of them—Auntie Bukky, Uncle Tunde and Miss Zuliat—have all gone to the hospital."

She felt a hand creep into hers. "Is it true, Mommy?" Erinma asked. "Is he really dead? Do you believe it now?"

Grace had a sick feeling in her stomach. "I don't know, Erinma, I don't know what to believe."

She couldn't believe it. Wouldn't believe it. Because if it was true, then she had made the worst mistake of her life. Worse than getting pregnant. Worse than hiding away in Jos all these years. Having Chuma so close and not telling him about his children, having the children so close to their father and not telling them about Chuma, that would be the worst mistake of her life, and if the story she was hearing was true, she would never be able to live with herself again.

Ojiugo was the first to break down. She covered her face with her hands and sobbed. Grace moved close to stand beside her, arms going around the little girl, but she did not cry. She was too numb.

She motioned to Bola. "Let me talk to Ayesha."

The waitress dialled Ayesha's number and gave Grace the phone.

"What am I hearing, Ayesha?"

"Grace, my sister," Ayesha sobbed loudly. "I honestly don't know whether he's still alive, or if he's dead but that car is a total write-off. The people at the scene said he had stopped at a traffic light and a trailer smashed into him from behind. You know he's an *Americana*—he doesn't know that in Nigeria you don't stop at a traffic light unless you're sure there's no car behind you. It's such a pity, a terrible, terrible tragedy."

"Do you know what hospital they have taken him to?"

"I'm not sure but it might be the teaching hospital. It's closer to the accident scene than ECWA hospital. I've been calling Zuliat but she's not picking up her phone. Let me try again. If I find out I'll call you."

"Okay. Thanks."

"Just take it easy." Ayesha's voice was sympathetic. "And pray. You and I know that with God all things are possible."

She gave the phone back to Bola. "Please dial madam's line."

Auntie Simbi picked it up at the first ring.

"Auntie, is it true about Chuma?"

"Is what true?"

"I hear he was in a car accident a couple of hours ago."

"Really? I haven't heard this. Bukky would have told me."

Grace sighed. "I just spoke to Ayesha. She saw his car on the road. Auntie Bukky and her family have gone to the hospital."

"Which hospital?"

"I don't know but I'll find out." Her voice was breaking and she stopped it just in time. She couldn't give up hope. Maybe it wasn't his car that Ayesha had seen. "If you hear anything, ma, please call me."

"If he's been in an accident, start with ECWA Hospital. I hope someone had the sense to take him there and not to the teaching hospital."

Fighting back tears, she reached for her girls' hands. "Come with me, girls."

Adamu saw them approach the station wagon and ran to open the door. She told the driver to take her to the ECWA Hospital. It made sense that he would be taken to that Christian hospital. The university teaching hospital was not the place you would take someone in an emergency. You could hardly find a doctor on site even for non-emergency cases at the teaching hospital. ECWA hospital, on the other hand, was owned by the Evangelical Church of West Africa and was more reliable because most of the doctors were missionaries.

Grace was in a daze. They drove past downtown Jos before she knew where she was. The streets, the houses, the street hawkers all looked familiar, yet she felt as if she'd never seen them before. The girls were just as silent in the middle seat of the station wagon, and suddenly she felt too far from them.

She glanced back and found them fighting back tears. She didn't know what to say to them.

The driver spotted Uncle Tunde's Pathfinder in front of the hospital and parked beside it. There was nobody in the Pathfinder, not even the driver.

In full shock now and not knowing what else to do, Grace stepped out of the car. The girls made as though to follow but she shook her head. "You stay here. Let me find out what's happening and I'll come get you. Adamu," she said to the driver, "please stay with them."

As she went to the accident & emergency desk, she noticed that everyone was going about their business normally. ECWA hospital wasn't such a large outfit that there would be a death in the hospital and people would be going on as if nothing had happened? Hadn't they heard about the accident? Wasn't Chuma's body in a room somewhere? Or was it already in the mortuary? Didn't anybody care? Or maybe, she breathed, maybe he's not dead. Maybe it wasn't his car that Ayesha saw at Solomon Lar Way. Maybe it was a mistake.

Her legs and feet didn't feel like her own, but she moved forward mechanically. *God, you have always helped me,* she breathed. *Be with me even now. Give me strength.* She felt herself begin to tremble as she approached the reception desk and only barely heard the sounds around her.

"I'm looking for someone who was brought in here earlier today, car accident along Solomon Lar/GRA Junction."

"Oh dear." The sympathetic nurse looked at her. "What's the name?"

"Chukwuma. Chukwuma Anthony Zeluwa."

She looked through her notes and looked up again. Grace thought she saw pity in her eyes. "Are you a relative?"

Interesting question. What could she say? "I'm Mrs. Anthony."

The nurse looked at her again. Grace wiped the tears with her scarf and waited.

"Very well. Room 255 on the right. Just follow that corridor to the end, and then turn right and climb the stairs on your left. The room numbers are on the doors."

Her heart lifted slightly. At least she didn't point her to the mortuary. He must still be alive.

"Please," she asked desperately. "How is he? Do you know anything?"

The nurse shook her head and sighed. "Just thank your God he's alive. It could have been a lot worse."

Grace dashed on shaky legs toward the room. What did she mean by that? Was he crippled or paralysed? Did he have a head injury? *Whatever it is Lord, however he is, I don't care. Just keep him for me. If I have to spend the rest of my life looking after him, I will. If I have to feed him and bathe him and push him in a wheelchair for the rest of my life I will do it, Lord. Only let him live, Lord. Please!*

She thought she heard voices from the room before she knocked and turned the knob.

Even if she lived to be a 100 years or more, Grace would remember the sight that greeted her when she stepped into Chuma's hospital room. He was lying on the bed, propped up on the pillow, white bandage covering part of his left leg, and he was flipping through the pages of a magazine! She staggered with relief and could have collapsed if she hadn't heard Zuliat's voice from somewhere in the room.

"Hi, Grace!"

She stopped and closed her eyes, and then leaned back against the closed door. This was a dream, right? Her dream.

Weren't her staff at Sonshine weeping and wailing even now because Chuma was dead? When she opened her eyes, he was staring at her and his arms were opening to her. This was no dream. This was no figment of her imagination. Chuma was not dead. He was bruised but he was not dead, and he was looking at her with such tender love that she knew without a shadow of doubt that this man was her man, the one the Lord had made and kept especially for her.

A crazy half-laugh, half-sob rose out of her throat, and she tried to stifle it, holding up her fingers against her lips. A second or two passed and her legs shook as she ran across the room to his bedside and folded her arms around his neck. His arms closed around her and for a moment they just held each other as tightly as they could while she gave vent to her emotions.

Spasms ripped through her body, and her tears spilled onto his shirt. When he tried to lift her head from his chest, she held on tight.

"You scared me. They said you were dead," she finally whispered.

"I'm sorry, babe. As you can see, I'm very much alive. It was a bad accident. Someone bumped into me from behind at a junction and knocked me off the road. It could have been worse, I'm told, but the seat belt and the airbags kept me from falling out. I hardly have anything to show for it except a few bruises on my leg."

Grace held him tight again before lifting up her head to gaze into his beloved face. She traced his features with her fingertips and cupped his face in her trembling palms, no longer concerned about hiding what he could see blazoned on her face. "I love you, Chuma," she whispered. "I've always loved you. I'll always love you."

He smiled, and she had never seen anything more beautiful. "I love you, Ure, I've always loved you. I'll always love you."

"The girls are your children, you know. I never had that abortion. I couldn't do it."

"I know, Ure. You don't know how happy I am that you didn't."

"I will marry you today if you will still have me," Grace said.

"Is that a proposal?"

Grace considered it for a second, smiled and angled her head. "I'm not sure now." She still held his face in her hands. "It's probably more a statement of intent. How else will you make an honest woman of me? I've been waiting for 11 years."

They heard movement in the room and remembered they were not alone. A chuckling Zuliat cleared her throat and rose to her feet. "I think this is the point at which I have to quietly disappear and give you guys some privacy."

Grace felt the blood rushing to her face but remained in the circle of Chuma's arms.

Zuliat glanced at her cell phone. "I got a picture just now, of the two of you. So beautiful," she gushed. "One day, I'll show it to the twins. Grace, where are they?"

"In the car with Adamu. We parked beside your father's car."

Zuliat hastened to the door with a wide grin and twinkling eyes. "Just think, I captured the exact moment their mother proposed to their father. This is so exciting!" She shook her head again and ran out of the room.

Grace laughed and turned eagerly back to Chuma. She moved back so he could sit up higher on the bed but willingly went back into his arms when he pulled her close.

He traced the sides of her neck, her lips, her cheeks, her eyes, and her forehead with his fingertips and she did the same - feeling the outline of his jaw and breathing in the fragrance of his cologne. Delicious shivers flushed through her when he tilted her head and looked deep into her eyes. Time seemed to stand still as they looked at each other, smiled at each other. When he brought his lips to hers she almost cried out with the ecstasy of it all. Their kiss was long and slow as they savoured each other the way they had both dreamed of for more than a decade.

"I thought I had lost you."

"Never. You always had me. There's been nobody but you. Only you. It's like you marked me yours when I was fifteen years old. Even when I tried to change my identity, I chose to be called Grace Anthony. Why do you think that was?"

He smiled. "I wondered about that. Forgive my naivety but I really thought it was a coincidence that your husband's name was my middle name. After the way I treated you, I dared not hope that you would ever forgive me. I never imagined we will be together again."

As if she couldn't help herself, she drew his head down to hers and kissed him again. "I think that in my subconscious, I always considered myself married to you and I hoped you would come for me. I love you, Chuma. I never stopped loving you. Even after 11 years it's just as if it was only yesterday that we were at Government College together. All the years in between seem to have vanished."

He hugged her tighter and kissed her again. "The Bible says God can restore all the years we have lost. We sinned when we did not know his word, but he has kept us by his grace, forgiven us and now he wants to restore all that we have lost."

"And add so much more." There was a new seriousness in her eyes, and when he lowered his head to kiss her again, she put her fingers on his lips. "We need to call the hotel and let everyone know you are okay. The news of your supposed death"—she winced—"is spreading like wildfire down there. Can I use your phone?"

He kissed the fingers on his lips. "Where are my girls? I need to see them first."

"They are in the car outside, crying their hearts out that their dear Dr. Dolittle is dead. But you heard Zuliat—she'll take care of them."

Remembering the state she had been in when she came into his room, he could just imagine how the girls must be feeling.

"Do they know about me?"

"Not yet." She closed her eyes as her emotions threatened to get the better of her again. "When I thought you were dead, I almost died, thinking how I had robbed them the opportunity to meet the father they have always wondered about. I don't think I would ever have forgiven myself.

"Also, my mother is ill in hospital. We are travelling to Calabar today to see her. I was planning to tell you about the twins when we come back."

"Let me come with you. You don't know what is waiting for you over there."

The concern in his eyes warmed her heart. "How I wish you could come with me. Now that I have found you I don't ever want to be apart from you again. But you're in no state to travel, Chuma. I doubt the doctor will let you go home today for fear of unforeseen complications."

He lifted a sceptical eyebrow. "How do you know?"

"It's common practice here. Everybody knows that after an accident, the victims are kept in the hospital as long as possible for observation in case of internal bleeding."

Once more, she saw his eyes cloud with apprehension.

"Ure, you don't know what you'll be stepping into when you get to Calabar. I don't want to lose you again."

"You won't. Is it not the same God who has done this miracle today? Is he not the one who has been keeping me all these years by his divine power? Don't worry. He will take care of me."

He held her close again, then prayed. "It's been a long journey, Lord, but your word, your love and your grace have prevailed. There are no words to describe our gratitude, nothing we can give to you that compares with what you have done for us. You've led us through the wilderness, through the valleys, through the waters and even through fire. None of these have consumed us, Lord. Thank you."

Listening to Chuma, hearing the sincerity in his voice, feeling the shudders that passed through his body as he prayed, Grace held him tighter still, and whispered "Amen" when he was done.

Tears glistened in his eyes. "Please go bring in my children. I have to see my girls."

"Are we going to tell them now?"

He thought only for a second before slowly shaking his head. "I want them to know now, today. I don't want a single second to pass without their knowing I am their father. But, babe, you have so many things going on now that I don't mind waiting a day or two."

"I like that."

"What? That I don't mind waiting a day or two?"

"No. I like the way you call me babe so naturally. I have to think of a special name that I can call you too."

He laughed.

She frowned.

"What?"

"We may be too late. Zuliat may have told the girls already."

"She wouldn't. She knows it's not her place to do so."

"I think they'll be excited. They already like you."

"I love them."

She twined her arms around his neck again and relished the feel of his hands enfolding her. The Lord had really turned around their captivity. The words he had prayed were so true: they had been tried and tested in many ways and had come out standing strong. Their children were a bonus, a fitting crowning of their love.

"In the meantime, when they see the picture Zuliat took of us, or when they see you holding hands with their Dr. Dolittle, what shall we tell them?"

"That we're in love?"

"I like that," Chuma said, and smiled.

PART III

Chapter 32

Calabar

The time had finally come. In just a few minutes Urenna would see the sister she hadn't seen in more than 11 years. She still remembered the last time they were together. They didn't really play together a lot that long vacation. Poor Añuli, Urenna's moodiness had ruined the entire two months of holiday. At first she had been grumpy because she was missing Chuma, but later, when she suspected she might have become pregnant, she had become totally miserable. Añuli had been glad when the holidays were over. She had gone back to Federal Government College, Calabar, to tackle her final year of junior secondary school. Urenna, on the other hand, had gone back to Government College, Benin, to tell Chuma that she was pregnant.

She glanced at her watch as they waited their turn to disembark the plane. It was already ten o'clock. They had taken the later flight from Jos because Chuma had insisted on spending as much time with her as possible in the hospital room, with the result that they had missed the four o'clock flight. He wanted them to wait until Monday so they could travel together, but she didn't want to have any regrets as far as her mother was concerned. God had helped her reunite with

Chuma. If his plan was for her to reunite with her mother before her death, she wanted to be there.

"Not too long now." She smiled at her girls. They were yawning and she could see they were sleepy. The plane ride was a first for them as well, so they were still absorbing the experience. She knew the torrent of questions would start as soon as they left the aircraft.

She adjusted the twisted handle of Erinma's backpack and picked up a comic book one of them had forgotten on her seat. When it was their turn to leave she motioned to the girls to go ahead of her.

She had claimed their luggage, and they were each rolling their suitcases toward the exit sign when she heard her name and spun around. Her eyes followed the sound and she inhaled sharply as she stared into the eyes of the sister she remembered so clearly. The twins watched, fascinated, as the two sisters hesitated for a split second before they sprinted toward each other and collided in a tight hug. Erinma barely managed to get out of the way of the suitcase her mother threw aside in her haste to hug her sister.

"Ańulika!"

"Urenna!"

Ańuli was fighting back tears. "Let me look at you." She withdrew after a moment to check out her big sister. "Is this really you or am I dreaming." She closed her eyes, opened them again gazed at Ure for a while and took a deep breath. "You've not changed at all!"

"Neither have you. You look exactly the way you did when I saw you last. You haven't changed in 11 years."

Urenna closed her eyes to quell the tears that were rapidly filling her eyes. Only, it wasn't tears of sadness. They were tears of joy. She looked at her sister and saw that there was no censure in her eyes, no recrimination, only a genuine joy at their reunion, and she thanked God. For the second time that day, the Lord had reunited her with a loved one. It no longer mattered that Añuli had not replied to the letter she had written her years ago. Their unbridled joy and happiness that they were able to meet again this side of eternity was more important.

"You can't say I haven't changed. Not after giving birth to two children."

It was then Añuli turned to the two girls who were staring as though they were watching a movie.

"Hi," one of the girls said, waving uncertainly at her aunt.

"Hi," the second one said, mimicking her sister's wave.

Añuli looked from one to the other and shook her head. "They … they're identical. They're beautiful…. They're so …" Her voice broke and tears started to flow. "So identical, so beautiful."

It was too much for her. Instead of hugging the girls, Añuli sat on the metal seat at the arrival lounge of the Calabar Airport and started to bawl. She stuck her fist into her open mouth to stifle the sound but the tears came out even more and she wept loudly. Urenna went to sit beside her and tried to comfort her, but Añuli kept crying. Passersby stared at them as she held her sister tight and murmured words of comfort into her ears.

Finally she cleaned her eyes and hugged her nieces close. "I'm sorry for embarrassing you like this," she apologised. Her eyelids were puffy, and she sneezed into a handkerchief. "I hope you don't think your aunt is crazy—wailing like this in public."

"It's not only you," Erinma generously excused her. "Our mom is crying too. And we don't think she's crazy."

Despite their tears, Urenna and Anuli smiled at each other. Anuli hugged the girls again.

"It's because you haven't seen each other for a long time," Erinma continued her magnanimity.

"Yes, it's like in the Bible, when Joseph met his brother Benjamin again after a long, long time," Ojiugo agreed.

Anuli thanked them.

"Mom," Erinma tugged at her mother's blouse. "There's a man holding a sign with your name on it."

Urenna looked up and indeed, there was a man in an orange uniform walking around with a sign that said GRACE ANTHONY.

Anuli followed their gaze and saw Urenna waving to the man. "Are you … Grace? The Grace Anthony?" she asked slowly.

Urenna nodded. "It's a long story."

Fresh tears began pouring down Anuli's face and she shook her head again.

The men were from Ambassador Hotel and had been sent to pick her from the airport to the hotel. Chuma had told her he would arrange accommodation for them even though Auntie Simbi had wanted them to stay at the Police Commissioner's house. It had been easy to convince her employer that she would rather stay on her own than in some stranger's home. But she had still written down the commissioner's contact details in her address book, "in case of emergency."

Urenna turned again to her sister. "I wasn't sure if you had accommodation for us. We made arrangements to stay at the Ambassador Hotel. Please say you will come and stay with us."

"I thought you would stay in my flat," she said. "I am staying at the hospital with Mama."

"Every day?"

The younger girl nodded. "Day and night, every hour."

"You must be exhausted. You absolutely must come with us to the hotel tonight. You need to rest. Now that I'm here, we can take turns looking after her. I'll do my part to help."

She intercepted a disappointing glance between her two daughters. They probably didn't consider spending their time in Calabar beside their grandmother's hospital bed such a good idea.

"What?" she asked Ojiugo. "Why the face?"

"You said we could go to Obudu Cattle Ranch."

"But I also told you that your grandmother is very ill. First, we all have to pray for her and look after her until she recovers. Then we can go to Obudu. Do you understand?"

"Yes, Mommy."

When that was settled, Ańuli nodded to her sister. "All right, I'll go with you to the hotel. I brought my car. I'll drive behind you."

"No way. Not at this time of the night," Urenna replied. "You're coming in the hotel van with us."

Urenna spoke to the driver, and it was soon sorted out. The hotel driver had a security officer with him who would drive behind them in her sister's car.

As they followed the driver to the van, Urenna quietly asked Ańuli, "You have not mentioned Papa at all. Is there something I should know before I see him?"

An unmistakeable sneer of disgust flashed across Ańuli's face, and her lips tightened with anger before she muttered, "Only that I hope God will punish him for all the trouble he has put our family through."

Chapter 33

The call came early the next morning, at about four a.m. Egoyibo's nurse phoned Anuli to say she should hurry down to the hospital because her mother was awake and asking for her. Luckily, Urenna had anticipated that they might have to go out any time and had arranged with the hotel for a driver to be on standby. The twins did not like being woken so early, but when their mother told them they might never have another chance to see their grandmother, they took their sweaters and followed the adults to the elevators.

Urenna had often wondered how she would feel when she saw either of her parents again, but after Anuli filled her in on all the family news of the past 11 years, she couldn't wait to see her mother again to assure her that she was all right.

Still, when they got to the hospital, she held back. "I don't want her to have a shock and relapse again," she told Anuli, and waited with the girls at the reception while her sister rushed to their mother's room.

Urenna texted a message to Chuma, asking for prayers for her mother, and then she closed her eyes and stilled her anxious heart by praying in the spirit. The twins promptly fell asleep on the sofa.

Thirty minutes passed before she saw Añuli coming back with a nurse. Añuli was beaming, but it was the nurse who spoke to her.

"Añuli has explained that your mother hasn't seen you for many years. I don't know that it's a good idea to introduce you to her at this time. I have sent for the doctor, and he will be here soon. I want him to decide and possibly be there when she sees you so he can handle any fallout."

Urenna didn't mind waiting and urged her sister to go back to their mother. Añuli hugged her. "She's going to be all right," she whispered. "She's even talking, slowly but clearly. The doctor had warned she may have a speech problem but it's not too different from how she was before she collapsed. Please continue to pray."

The doctor came about seven thirty. It was agreed that Urenna would go in first, and the twins would follow after a while. "Your mother has a tendency to flip into unconsciousness very quickly," he said as she followed him to the private ward. "We don't want to shock her system more than necessary. Just give me some time with her first. I'll send for you when we're ready."

Urenna knew her first meeting with her mother would be emotional. Nevertheless, she was not prepared for what she saw 15 minutes later. Perhaps she had been deceived by the fact that Añuli hadn't changed over the years into thinking her mother would be the same. Now she looked and barely recognized the frail-looking old woman hooked up to wires on the hospital bed. By her calculation, her mother was not even 60, but she looked at least 10 years older. And sick.

Very sick. Her mother had always been a slim woman, but the woman whose hand Ańuli was holding and into whose ears her sister was speaking had thin, bony features. Tears shimmered in her eyes as she continued to quietly observe her mother, waiting to be acknowledged. Finally the doctor nodded and she moved forward on shaking legs.

Egoyibo seemed to sense her presence. She turned and time stood still as mother and daughter stared at each other.

"Mama," Urenna said in a choked whisper.

Egoyibo saw the face, heard the voice and closed her eyes. She had to be dreaming. Her head felt fuzzy and she blinked several times. Her eyes found the young girl's again as she came closer and knelt by her bedside. Tears coursed down her cheeks.

"Mama, it's me, Urenna. I've come home to you."

The moment Egoyibo heard those words she felt the room start to spin. Of course it was Urenna. Hadn't Odili said the girl she had been mourning was really alive and well somewhere? But where did she suddenly spring from? Egoyibo reached a thin hand towards her and the girl covered it with hers. "Am I … is this a dream?"

"No, Mama," Urenna replied, keeping her voice calm and steady. "It's really me, Urenna. Ańuli found me and told me you were sick. I came as quickly as I could."

Egoyibo looked straight into the young woman's heart and knew the Lord had shown her infinite mercy in bringing her daughter home. Like he had done for Mary and Martha when their brother died, he had heard her cry. He had shown pity on her and raised her daughter from the dead. Ego had been bitter all these years, even against the Lord. But he had overlooked her sins and answered a prayer she had not even prayed. The scriptures claim that God is able to do exceedingly abundantly more than we can ever think or ask or even imagine. That was so true. She hadn't thought or asked or ever imagined that her daughter was alive. But the Lord knew. He had found her. He had brought her home. And now the girl she had spent the past decade mourning was kneeling beside her hospital bed.

Egoyibo clung to the hand that held hers and asked, because she remembered clearly something else that Odili had said, "Your children?"

"Yes, I had twins, Mama, two little girls. I brought them with me. They're just outside."

A tear escaped Ego's face and trickled down to her mouth. Urenna wiped it gently away. There was so much to talk about, but one thing was most important. "I'm sorry."

Urenna nodded, her own eyes swimming. Ego felt she understood what she meant. "For ... give," she said again, slowly.

Urenna swallowed and nodded.

"Did you suf-fer much?" She knew she had to speak slowly in order to be understood.

She thought Urenna struggled to answer that one. The poor girl must have really suffered.

"God was with me. He took care of everything."

Her answer lifted Ego's spirit. "You know Jes-us?"

"Yes, Mama. Jesus is my Lord, and my personal saviour."

"Good. Tell your sis-ter ... she's bitter ... too an-gry ... hates Odili ... but ... everyone needs ... forgive-ness ... Anuli should for-give your fa- ... ther."

"Anuli will be fine, Mama. Don't worry about her."

Ego beamed with joy. Añuli passed a small towel to Urenna and she wiped the tears that flowed down her mother's cheeks. "Yes … big sister is … home."

"Yes," Urenna agreed, smiling at her mother. "Big sister is here and she will take care of Añuli."

Egoyibo sighed and looked at her again. "You … you must for-give … your wicked fath-er. If you d-don't forgive … you … fall sick … like me. And he will be fine … and str … ong, but you will be sick … like me."

Urenna hugged her lightly, as much as the gadgets holding her would allow. "You don't have anything to worry about, Mama," she whispered. "I do not hate my father."

Ego sniffed again. "Thank you, Jesus."

"Husband … *nko*?" she asked after a while.

Grace smiled brightly. "Not yet but soon. In fact, very, very soon, and you have to be around to see it. So you have to get well soon."

Ego smiled and took another deep breath. "Thank you, Je … sus."

"Do you feel like seeing your granddaughters now or do you want to take a nap?" the doctor asked.

"Now!" Ego replied vehemently. Everyone laughed.

"I thought you would say so," he replied. "I will let you see them very briefly, and then you must get some rest. If you're thinking of going home to be with your family you have to get well first. Resting as much as possible will get you there even faster."

"I … promise. Please bring them …"

At the doctor's nod Añuli ran out to fetch Erinma and Ojiugo.

"Madam, I think you've been tricking us all these weeks into believing you are sick!" the doctor teased her. "Why didn't you simply tell us to bring Urenna for you? That would have saved us this hospital bed and medicines for people who are really sick. See, she's been here only a few minutes and your strength is already coming back."

Ego lifted her eyes to him and then turned to stare at Urenna again. "Doctor ... you don't ... understand," she told him quietly.

Chapter 34

Egoyibo was alone in a room for two patients. That morning, the twins set up camp on the empty bed while their mother and aunt sat on the visitors' chairs and continued to catch up on each other's lives. When Ego dozed off just after nine o'clock, they all stepped out briefly to get some breakfast.

Apart from that brief interlude, they stayed with their mother all day. The doctor had encouraged them, especially Urenna and the twins, to stay around her. If she was to wake up and ask for them, they were to be there so she wouldn't think she had been dreaming

"Can we go to the swing?" one of the twins asked in the afternoon.

Urenna saw a tyre swing hanging from the branches of an umbrella tree that stood about 200 yards from the hospital room.

"It's just somewhere for hospital visitors to sit and relax while waiting to see their relations," Anuli explained. "There are benches there too, and a cement slab in the shade of the tree where we can all sit. Let's all go so we can get some fresh air. The nurse can see us from here and she can call us when Mama wakes up."

Urenna revelled in the coolness provided by the shade of the tree and the gentle wind that fanned them as she and Añuli continued their never-ending conversation.

"So you still don't believe in God after this miracle he has done for us?" she asked Añuli.

"Actually, I do."

"You do?" Urenna lifted a sceptical eyebrow.

"Yes," Añuli confirmed. "Really, I do. You see, when I thought Mama was dying, I made a deal with God. I promised that if he would so much as wake her up enough to see you again, even for a few minutes, that I will believe in him. I didn't imagine he would heal her completely, I just wanted her to see you before she passed away."

Anxiety belied the excitement in Urenna's eyes. "So what do you think now?"

The younger girl shrugged. "I don't know."

"What don't you know?"

"There's a difference between believing in God and committing your life to Christ, right?"

Urenna nodded slowly. "Yes. The Bible says even the devil believes in God. That is, he believes God exists, but he has not committed his life to God. In fact, he hates the Lord."

"Okay. I get that. But what does it mean to commit your life to Christ?"

"It's just what it says—that you are committing your life to him. It means recognising and admitting that you are a sinner in need of forgiveness from God, believing that Jesus is who he claims to be—the Son of God, the only one who can save you and reconcile you to God, and then, by faith, accepting his finished work for our salvation and inviting him to guide and direct your life. It's that simple."

Añuli shook her head. "I have heard all these before and I think I understand, but I have seen many people who say they have committed their lives to God but their lives are very far from godly."

"Right. But have you also seen others that are so true to their commitment that their lives exude love, joy, peace and godliness?"

Añuli was silent.

"Añuli, the fact that some people are not living godly lives shouldn't keep you from giving your *own* life to Christ. When we face eternity we don't want to say that we didn't do the right thing because others were doing the wrong thing."

Añuli nodded.

Urenna saw that she was paying attention, so she continued. "I know that there are people who say they are committed to Christ and yet live a self-directed life where Jesus is kept outside the life, and decisions and actions are solely directed by self. But for those who are truly committed to Christ, Jesus himself is enthroned in all aspects as the person daily yields to the influence and direction of the Holy Spirit."

"I understand what you mean," the younger girl said after a while. She shook her head. "But I'm not ready to commit myself to Christ, Ure. I'm sorry. It's not a step I'm ready to take yet."

Urenna patted her sister's hand. "That's okay. Don't feel pressured. Do it when you're ready and convinced. In the meantime, feel free to ask me anything you don't understand about it and I'll do my best to explain."

"Okay." Añuli sounded relieved. "Start by telling me how you got involved in this born-again thing?"

Urenna took a deep breath. It was a long story. "The night Papa beat me up and Mama dropped me off at the clinic, there was a woman who was visiting her sick mother at the clinic. She was a retired nurse and was leaving for Kano the next day. She was very angry when she saw me bruised and bleeding from Papa's beatings. She wanted to call the police but I begged her not to. I explained that I was pregnant and didn't want to have an abortion. When the nurses checked that night, the pregnancy was still intact and everyone said how lucky I was. The woman told me about a Christian agency in Jos that catered to unwed teenagers who didn't want to be forced to have abortions. She said she was leaving for Kano the next day and that if I wanted she could drop me off in Jos. At midnight, I stole out of the hospital and joined her where she'd parked her car. I didn't know who she was, and maybe I wasn't thinking right, but I was in fear of Papa and what he would do if he ever saw me again.

"She drove all night and all of the next day. As we approached Jos I got very sick and this woman probably thought I would die. Instead of going straight to the agency she took me to ECWA Hospital in Jos, off-loaded me in front of the emergency ward and disappeared.

"But I didn't die, thank God. I was in the hospital for almost three weeks. I was so sick that I do not remember anything about the first week, plus I did not have any information on me to give anybody a clue about who I was. It was at ECWA hospital that they called me Grace. They said I had lived only because of God's grace. When I got well enough I told them I wanted to go to the pregnancy care centre and they moved me to Gidan Mairo. I kept the name they gave me because I liked it. I added a surname to it, and since then everybody has known me as Grace Anthony. At the time, I was afraid that if Papa found me, he would come and finish what he had started, so I kept my background a secret from everyone.

"It was at Gidan Mairo that I heard about the love and forgiveness that can be found in Christ. It is a Christian facility that offers an alternative to abortion for young girls. It also offers placement and adoption services for children. By its nature, that outfit was established as a witness to the love of God. But although they taught us about Christ, they weren't hounding us to become Christians. We were all encouraged to ask questions and to seek the truth for ourselves. It was in this ministry that I came to understand that God loved me and wanted to direct all my ways and I committed my life to him."

Ańuli remained quiet as she pondered her sister's story. Urenna prayed silently for her, realising this was a monumental point in the younger girl's life. She hadn't believed because of the poor Christian testimony around her. In her distress over her mother's ailment, she had challenged the Lord and he had not only woken the woman from unconsciousness, he was healing her rapidly, beyond everyone's imagination.

Urenna knew a bit about her sister now to hazard a guess at how her mind worked. Ańuli was smart enough to know that there was a difference between believing in God and committing her life to Christ but her smartness could very well be the reason she couldn't surrender her life to God. She needed all her *i*s dotted and all her *t*s crossed before she could say a final yes. But that was not the spirit of Christianity. In many instances, Christianity posed more questions than it answered. Urenna knew she had to find a way to help the younger girl understand that salvation was a work of faith, not reason, and that nobody can ever understand all the whys and wherefores of God's actions until they meet him in eternity.

"Papa hasn't even asked after Mama since she collapsed last Friday," Ańuli suddenly said.

"Are you sure he knows?"

"Yes, I'm sure. Many of his friends, even the VC, have called to find out how she's doing but I haven't heard a word from him."

"That's not surprising, I guess, from what you've told me. But, Añuli"—Urenna tried to refocus their conversation—"what does this have to do with giving your life to Christ?"

"I don't want to give my life to Christ because I cannot forgive Papa for all he's done to ruin our lives. I know that once I say yes to Christ, the first thing he'll want me to do is to forgive Papa, but I can't. I don't want to. I really, really hate that man. Even if he were to crawl on his knees and beg me, I don't think I'll ever forgive him."

"Never?"

"Never."

"You're serious?"

"Absolutely. Every time I remember him, I pray that God will punish him."

"Your own father?"

"Yes, my own father. You see, Ure, you're doing it already. You're judging me and making me feel guilty about my feelings. I can't pretend for the sake of anything that I like that man when I totally despise him."

"And therein is the point about Christianity. It's not based on our feelings, because our feelings are not always right. It is based on faith in the word of God and in submitting our will to his."

"Maybe if God will openly punish sinners more often, more people will commit to following him," Añuli pronounced. "He's all about love and forgiveness, and not everyone deserves that."

"Anulichukwuka Okolie!" Urenna laughed gently. "I thank God that you are not God o! There would have been no hope for anyone on this earth. Imagine how many sinners you would have banished to perdition by now. Papa only beat me with his *koboko* when I disappointed him. If you were God, I most certainly would have been burned to ashes 11 years ago. No second chances with you."

They laughed and Anuli glanced at her wristwatch. It was almost five o'clock. They had been sitting outside for almost two hours. Tired of the swing, the twins had drawn circles and rectangles and triangles on the ground and were playing one-leg hopscotch.

Urenna watched as Erinma balanced on one leg to pick up the marker and turned to her sister. "Don't they remind you of when we were growing up?"

"Mm hmm." Anuli nodded. "We used to play that game all the time. It used to be called swell."

Urenna nodded. "I wonder where that name came from. All over the world it is called hopscotch."

"We also used to play tente. Do you remember tente?" Anuli asked her sister.

They laughed and continued to watch the twins until a nurse approached them to say, "Dr. Okolie, there are two men here to visit your mother. They say they are your relations."

Anuli got up and dusted down her pants. "My relations? I'm not expecting anyone."

"The doctor doesn't want your mother to be disturbed, so I can't let them in. But they are insisting that they have come a long way and will not leave unless they have seen her. I need you to come and explain to them. They are at reception."

"I'll be there shortly," Anuli said.

"I'll come with you," Urenna said. "I need some water from the filter."

"Me too," each of the girls declared and skipped ahead of the adults back into the building.

As soon as she saw the familiar dashiki tops they were wearing, Aṅuli knew it was her uncles. They must have heard that her mother had collapsed again.

"*Nma-nma*, De Chikezie," she greeted them, happy to see them. "Greetings, De Mbachu."

"*Eh heee, ada anyi*,"("same to you, our daughter") they responded to her greetings. "We heard about your mother. How is she doing?"

"She woke up this morning o! Hmm, please join us to give thanks to God."

"Praise to the gods! *Amadioha*, thank you!" De Chikezie exclaimed.

"You mean praise to Jesus!" Aṅuli retorted with a smile.

"They're all the same," De Mbachu observed. "He just goes by different names."

"That's not true." Aṅuli shook her head emphatically. "Jesus Christ of the Bible is not the same as the gods that our elders pour libation to every day. Our people pray to *Alusi*, *Amadioha*, *Anyanwu*, dead spirits and idols. Those things don't even exist."

"How do you know? You are only a young girl. How can you judge the wisdom of elders and old men who lived and died before you were even conceived?"

Aṅuli shook her head and kept quiet. She had no answer, and her uncles laughed in amusement at her confusion.

Urenna and the twins were standing by the open fridge down the hallway, drinking water from metal cups. Urenna raised her finger to her lips, signalling to Añuli not to reveal their identity.

"But, seriously, what is happening to Egoyibo?" one of her uncles asked. "This is the second time that she has fallen into unconsciousness. I hope she's not killing herself because Odili has taken another wife. She will injure herself for nothing. There is nothing shameful about your husband taking another wife. It is acceptable in our culture."

"But Mbachu," De Chikezie interjected. "Let's not fool ourselves. The way Odili is going about the whole thing is wrong. A new wife is not something you spring upon any woman. It's not fair. They have feelings too. He could have discussed this with her and they could have jointly gone to get a new wife if he must marry again. To go and impregnate a woman and then marry her without your wife's consent is looking for trouble."

"I know, but we have to be realistic. What is done is done. She cannot reverse it, so she should accept it with dignity, relax and move on. The way she's going on now, she will die before her time and the new woman will step in and reap the fruits of her labour."

"*Tufiakwa!* God forbid!" Añuli fiercely objected. "Look, my uncles, I was there when she collapsed, and it wasn't because of his new wife."

"What happened then? Tell us."

Taking a deep breath, Añuli decided to throw caution to the wind. It was only right that her uncles should know the kind of brother they had. "You know my mother moved in with me after she was discharged from the hospital, right? Well, on Friday, Papa came to see her to tell her that—"

"Añulika!" Urenna whispered fiercely, "don't!"

The men turned, noticing her for the first time. De Chikezie squinted at her in annoyance. "Who are you?"

Urenna turned her back and motioned to the twins to leave the room.

"No. Let them stay!" Ańuli insisted. "Come here, girls!"

The girls looked questioningly at their mother, who was shaking her head from side to side at their aunt. As they hesitated, Ańuli walked over and grabbed each one by the hand and led them to where the two men sat on the long-backed chairs.

"Just so you know how my father has been treating my mother all these years," she said. "Look at these girls. Can you guess who they are?"

De Mbachu looked at De Chikezie and both men shook their heads slowly in perplexity. "What are you talking about, Ańulika? Who are they? I can see they are twins."

"Identical twins," the second uncle added with a smile.

"Don't tell me they are Odili's offspring too."

"Yes, they are," Ańuli replied firmly. "They are his offspring all right, only this time, not from his mistress."

"Ańuli, stop it, okay?" Urenna interrupted, finally walking to stand before her uncles. "De Chikezie, De Mbachu, *nma nma nu,*" she greeted.

"And you are?" De Chikezie asked again.

Turning, Urenna spoke to her daughters in Hausa and they immediately ran outside to play.

Then she turned to her uncles. "Don't you remember me? I am Urenna Okolie, Odili Okolie's first daughter."

Thirty minutes later the two men had still not recovered from the shock. De Chikezie was furious. He sat drumming his feet and grinding his teeth. His words were disjointed and his eyes glazed.

De Mbachu paced around with his arms wrapped around his body as though he was cold. "And you say Odili knew she was alive?" he asked for the hundredth time.

Añuli nodded gravely.

"And he did not tell anyone, not even your mother. I cannot believe it."

"It was the evidence of the pictures and the letter Urenna had written more than eight years ago that caused her heart to fail. She couldn't have known all these years and continued mourning. You have seen how thin she's grown over the years. She goes to that graveside at least four times every year to keep it clean and talk to the daughter she believed was buried there. Papa wouldn't have mentioned it if Ure hadn't sent me an e-mail and I went to ask him if he knew whether she was alive."

Urenna did not add a lot to the conversation, only answered questions when they were directed at her. She understood their anger, but still, she wished the conversation would not dwell so much on how wicked her father was. After all, she had contributed to the whole mess by getting pregnant in the first place. But her father had obviously behaved badly, and it was difficult to defend him.

"*Ajo e mee na!*" De Chikezie hissed. "*Ife ojoo e mee na!* Odili has committed an abomination!"

"*Tufiakwa!* This is capital sacrilege." De Mbachu shook his head in disbelief.

"Our elders say that when you throw a stone at the Almighty God, it lands right on top of your head. How can Odili play God and expect not to be exposed?"

"*Chei! Ala aruooo*?" De Chikezie hissed again. "Odili has desecrated the land, shamed the family. The wrath of the gods will be unleashed!"

"This is unheard of! This is unprecedented wickedness," De Mbachu agreed.

"So now you know what my mother has been dealing with all these years," Anuli pointed out again. "It's not because of the new wife that she is sick. That woman can have him for all we care."

The two men prepared to leave, but not until they had walked over to Urenna to carefully shake her hand. Each man gripped her hand and lingered to express his apology at the wrong that had been done to her by their brother.

Urenna deduced from the way they were memorizing her face that they wanted to be sure that she was really flesh and bones and not some photo trick.

Chapter 35

Urenna made her daughters wait at the airport lounge with their aunt while she went to the baggage claim area to meet Chuma. He had been discharged from the hospital on Tuesday but had spent an extra day in Jos finalising his business and giving the bruised leg an extra day to heal. He had arranged a meeting between Auntie Bukky and Auntie Simbi with Chief Ojiefi, and the latter had agreed that Gidan Mairo could continue to operate for free for another nine months. The chief wanted to build a hospital on the land and would be commencing work in a year.

It was a miracle, Urenna thought. Not only did Heavenly Missions have nine months to plan, they had nine *rent-free* months. It was so like the Lord to add *jara* ("extra") to his blessings.

She saw Chuma walking toward her and was troubled at the slight limp still evident in his stride. It was the look in the eyes that met hers that drew her from where she stood into his embrace. His arms went around her as they held each other for countless seconds. Presently, he tilted her face up and looked into her eyes. He must have liked what he saw there because he hugged her tighter and took a deep breath.

"I thought I dreamed you up."

Tears of happiness were not far away. She buried her face in his shirt. "The only way it will be a dream is if I am in it with you," she whispered.

As they studied each other again, she knew he wanted to kiss her. She wanted him to kiss her too but they both knew they couldn't get that personal in a public place. This was still Nigeria, and this country's definition of acceptable decency and decorum included keeping personal demonstrations of affections private. Nothing more than a hug or an embrace was acceptable.

"I love you," he whispered into her ear.

She lifted her face to look into his eyes again. Then she locked her hands behind his neck and memorised the tender look on his face.

"Tell me again." She smiled at him. "I want to hear it again."

"I love you, Urenna."

"I love you, Chuma."

He kept a hand across her shoulders while they waited for his luggage and she filled him in on the news about her family. He knew almost everything already as they had spoken on the phone and texted each other regularly in the past week.

"What time is your father expecting us?" he asked.

"I told him we'll be there at four. It shouldn't be a long visit. Thirty minutes, one hour at the most."

"Well, it's only eleven thirty now, plenty of time to visit with your mother and sister and to spend some time with my children."

"They can't wait to see you. It was a good thing I told them only this morning you were coming. They haven't stopped talking in excitement since then. I think we're all going to be competing for your attention from now on."

"Ure, there's no competition for my attention where you're concerned. You have my full attention any day." His words caused a delicious shiver down her spine. "The truth is, I'm the intruder here, not you. I'm the one who's gonna be fighting for everyone's forgiveness and acceptance."

He kept his hand on her shoulder even when they went to meet Anuli and the twins. The girls hurled themselves at him, asking if he had recovered from the accident, if he had bought another car, and if he was still travelling back to the United States.

Anuli recognised Chuma instantly, and when the twins stopped their chattering and were talking to their mother she looked at him. "You're the one who came to see us after Ure was falsely declared dead. I remember you."

Chuma started with shaking hands but finally drew her into a quick hug. No need to stand on formality if they were soon to be related. "Yes, it was me."

Anuli nodded and looked into his eyes. "You've loved her all these years."

"Yes, I have. Even when I thought she was dead I couldn't bring myself to stop loving her. My family has almost given up hope of my ever getting into a serious relationship with anyone. I didn't even try. I couldn't. Then the Lord had mercy on me and brought Ure back into my life. I still can't believe it."

Anuli nodded again. "I take it you're also a Christian?"

"Yes, I am. God used the circumstances surrounding Ure's supposed death to bring me to draw me to himself. It's like the Bible says, that he causes all things that come our way to work together for our good. This has really turned out well for us."

"And the twins?"

He nodded. "Yes, they are mine, but we haven't told them yet."

Ańuli looked at him for a moment, and it was difficult to understand what was on her mind. Chuma held her close one more time before letting her go.

As they went to the car, Ańuli hung back to talk to her sister. "I'm really happy for you, Ure. You have to be one of the luckiest people I have ever met. The day he came to the house after the burial, I thought he was going to die too. But now the two of you have met again, fallen in love all over again, you have two wonderful children and if I am reading the signs right, you'll be getting married soon."

"It is the Lord's doing, Ańuli. The psalmist said God's workings are altogether marvellous. The Lord has blessed us beyond measure. This time, though, we are going to do things the right way. We want to start by making peace with Papa."

"What?" Ańuli stopped in her track. "Is this why you are going there today—to make peace? After all he's done to you? What nonsense are you talking about? What makes you think he wants to have anything to do with you?"

Chuma and the twins turned enquiringly at the angry exclamation.

Ańuli shook her head in exasperation. "It's nothing," she mumbled and hurried out to the car.

Egoyibo had improved significantly since she woke up on Monday morning. Her speech had improved, her heart had stabilised, her medication had been reduced and everybody commented on the perpetual smile she wore. She hadn't added much weight but her cheeks were gradually filling out. Urenna and her grandchildren filled her days and nights.

Even Ańuli seemed to be more relaxed. She smiled more and talked more, as if a heavy burden had been lifted off her shoulder. Only yesterday she mentioned that she might start looking for work in another city soon. With all that had happened in Calabar she wanted to start life afresh. Egoyibo thought it was an excellent idea.

Like Ańuli, Egoyibo recognised Chuma the instant she saw him walk into her hospital room with one hand across Urenna's shoulders and the other holding one of the girls. The second girl was wheeling his travelling bag. Egoyibo's heart swelled with joy. When Urenna had said she was going to the airport to meet a friend, Ego had not suspected it was to bring the young man she was going to marry to visit with her.

"Mama, this is Chukwuma Zeluwa. Chuma, my mother."

"We've met before." Ego forestalled him with a slow smile. "Many, many years ago."

Chuma smiled brightly at her. "I'm glad you remembered, Madam."

"You came ... with another student to see the grave. I ... I thought you were ... going to die too."

Chuma winked at Urenna but addressed his words to her mother. "I thank the Lord for his mercies. How are you feeling, Madam?"

"Fine ... I feel fine! ... like ... a newborn baby."

"Why, Grandma?" one of the twins interjected. "Why do you feel like a newborn baby?"

"Because God has healed me ... from my ... sickness ... I feel as if I have a ... new heart, a new head, new hands and ... legs."

"Oh!" the twin exclaimed, "that is so cool!"

Chuma opened his briefcase and brought out a card addressed to Egoyibo. It was a get-well message from Auntie Simbi.

"You want to ... marry my daughter." Ego nodded after she watched him for a while.

Before he could respond, he felt a tug in his hand and looked down into the awe-struck eyes of Erinma. "You want to marry our mother?"

"What?" Ojiugo had heard it too. "You want to marry our mother?"

Chuma looked at Urenna and thought only for a second before responding. "Why don't we talk about it privately for a moment? Is there somewhere we can go to discuss this?"

"There's a private park over there, or at least something like it," Urenna suggested.

"Will you excuse us, Madam? I need to talk to the twins for a minute. Then I'll be glad to answer your question."

The girls squealed excitedly and pulled him all the way to the park, their mother following.

"Tell us, please, do you want to marry our mother?"

"Which twin are you?" he countered.

"Don't you recognise me? Look at my face. I'm Ojiugo."

He laughed. "I thought you were Erinma."

"No, I'm Erinma," her sister said.

"Are you really going to marry our mother?"

"If she will have me, I will."

"Are you in love with her?"

He smiled and held out a hand to Urenna. "Yes, I love her."

Ojiugo turned to her mother. "Mommy, do you love him?"

She held tight to the hand he had offered and smiled brightly. "Yes, I do. I love him very much."

"And if you marry him, will we go to live with him in America?"

The adults stared at each other. They hadn't discussed where they would live after they got married.

"We will live with him wherever he lives," Urenna told her children.

"But—" Ojiugo started and stopped. The two girls exchanged a frown.

Urenna bent to her daughter. "But what? Honey, what's the matter? I thought you girls liked Chuma too."

"We do," Erinma confirmed. "It's just that—"

"Will you take us to live with you in America?" Ojiugo asked Chuma.

"That's my plan. Don't you want to come to America?"

"But what about our daddy?" Ojiugo whispered in astonishment. "What about our real daddy? We want to live with our real daddy."

"Yes! And if he sees us with you, he will not be happy. He will not know that we love him too," Erinma cried.

Chuma looked at Urenna for endless seconds. Then they pulled the children into their arms, each holding a twin.

Urenna's eyes moved from one girl to the other and pressed her finger to her lips. "Shhh! Listen now, girls. I am going to tell you about your daddy," she began.

"It's not that we don't like you, Uncle Chuma," Ojiugo's voice came from somewhere in his jacket.

"Because we do. We really, really do," Erinma agreed from her mother's shoulder. "But we love our daddy too."

"Stop crying now and listen to me," Urenna said firmly. "I want to tell you about your real daddy."

While the girls fought with their hiccups, Chuma quietly wiped the tears from his eyes.

"Girls," she swallowed, "Chuma is your daddy, your real daddy. You don't have any other daddy."

There was a shocked silence at her words. The girls looked first at her and then at Chuma, not quite believing what they had heard.

"What did you say, mommy?" Ojiugo whispered.

"I'm sorry I didn't tell you before now. We have been apart for many years, before you girls were even born. And since we met again, we've been trying to work on our relationship first, to make sure we loved each other enough to get married. I didn't want to upset you."

"You've known all the while that you are our daddy? You were going to leave us again?" Ojiugo withdrew from him in shocked disappointment.

"I'm sorry, Ojiugo."

"He didn't know," Urenna intervened. "When we met, he thought I was married to another man."

Urenna saw Chuma's hand shake slightly and knew that, like her, he was nervously waiting for the girls to pass their verdict.

The two girls shook their heads in disbelief.

"I'm sorry I left you girls alone all these years." His voice was husky with emotion. "I didn't know about you. Believe me, if I had known, nothing could have kept me from coming for you. But you mustn't blame your mother. We had a fight before I left and I said very mean things to her. She thought I wouldn't want to know about you."

Urenna tried again. "Look, girls, it was all a misunderstanding. It happened a long time ago. But the Lord has cleared everything and brought us together again. He wants us to be a family."

Tears glistened in his eyes as Chuma spoke again. "Your mother and I love each other very much. I have loved the two of you from the day I met you, even when I didn't know I was your daddy, and I will love you forever. Please say you will let me marry your mother and be a real father to you now that we're together again?"

Urenna let out a huge sigh of relief as the girls threw themselves into their father's arms and embraced him.

Chapter 36

The trip back to her old house filled Urenna with nostalgia. As Chuma drove through the university staff quarters, she remembered how she and Añuli used to walk through Malabo Park on their way to and from elementary school. In those days, during the rainy season, all the trees and plants that lined the university streets would be in full bloom, looking very colourful.

"Nneka Ndukwe used to live at Benue River Close," she commented as they saw the street sign. "Where is she now?"

"I believe she's in Lagos," Añuli informed her. "She graduated from Microbiology here in UniCal and then got a job with Federal Ministry of Health. Her parents still live in their old house."

They drove past the home of another friend. Añuli informed her that Elizabeth Isong had not gone on to university, that she had married right after secondary school and was now the mother of four children.

She remembered and asked about many others as they drove on and Añuli filled her in on their whereabouts. It seemed that everyone had gone on to postsecondary institutions and were all working either in the university or for some other government establishment.

Urenna was glad for Añuli's company, no matter how sullen her sister looked. She was thankful that their mother had insisted she accompany them even though the younger girl was openly contemptuous of the reason for their visit.

At exactly four o'clock that evening, the party knocked at the door of their old house. Añuli recognised Beatrice as she opened the door to let the visitors in. She sucked in a sharp breath at the sight of their father's mistress and let out a loud hiss. If looks could kill, the girl would have been incinerated by the fiery hatred flashing from Añuli's eyes.

Urenna squeezed her sister's hand with a smile and drew her into the house.

The living room looked almost the same as she remembered it. Their parents' black and white wedding photo still graced the centre of the living room on the wall, high above the 24-inch television set. A piano stood at the opposite wall bearing the weight of two enlarged pictures, one of their father in his convocation gown, the second of their family.

Urenna stood in front of the family photo and thought how happy the four of them had been. In that photograph their father was young and athletic-looking. He was smiling brightly at the camera, with his wife beside him and their two daughters flanking them.

Another photo on the wall caught her attention. It was one they had taken with their extended family members during a Christmas holiday family reunion at Umuebere. She recognized her grandfather seated between his three wives, surrounded by his numerous children and grandchildren. The old man had fathered 16 children in all, all of whom were married and had borne their own children. In the photograph, her parents, uncles and aunts wore a family uniform made from a flowery veritable wax fabric. The grandchildren wore a different uniform. There were at least 60 people in that photograph. Peering closely, she recognised her parents, her sister and herself.

The sound of voices from the backyard interrupted her thoughts. Añuli went to the window and drew aside the curtain. "Urenna, look, our uncles are still around."

The two gentlemen were relaxing at the backyard. Each was wearing a white singlet and tied a wrapper around his waist. They looked up from their game of draughts, surprised to see them.

De Chike came to the window. "What are you doing here? Odili didn't tell us you were coming today."

Almost immediately they heard a door slam and heavy footsteps coming closer to the living room. Chuma crossed to where Urenna stood and took her hand as they waited for her father to show up.

He has not changed much, were Urenna's initial thoughts. Her mother had aged dramatically but her father was looking good.

"Good afternoon, sir." Chuma bowed slightly.

"Papa." Urenna curtsied.

Añuli looked at him and hissed.

"What are you doing here?" Odili sneered at his younger daughter.

"I see your concubine has moved in. Or was that your house-girl? She certainly looked like one."

"Añuli!" Urenna intervened urgently. "This is not what this visit is about. Just let it be, okay?"

It was as if a reminder of the purpose of the visit only made her angrier. She got up abruptly. "I think you guys are crazy. I'll stay with the uncles. Call me when you're ready to go," she spat out and briskly left the room.

An uncomfortable silence followed her exit. When Urenna looked up, her father was studying her with narrowed eyes. "So, what can I do for you two? You said you had something to ask me."

Urenna gasped. "Papa, it's me, Urenna. Don't you recognise me?"

"Of course I recognise you."

"It's been 11 years, Papa. Aren't you happy to see me?"

"Are you happy to see me?" he asked gruffly.

"Oh yes, I am, Papa. I am very happy to see you."

"Sure you are," he scoffed

Urenna didn't know what to say after that, taken aback by the hostility on his face. After an awkward silence, she turned to Chuma and he came to her rescue.

"Good evening, sir." He cleared his throat. "My name is Chukwuma Zeluwa. My father is a professor at the University of Lagos.

"Mmm hmm?" Odili turned to him.

"Ure and I were together at Government College, Benin, many years ago."

"Yes?"

"I came to apologise to you, sir. I was the one who got her pregnant."

"I see." Odili looked away, clearly not interested.

If Chuma was shocked at the older man's attitude, he did not show it. "I can only imagine how disappointed you must have been and how her pregnancy must have brought pain and heartache to your family, sir. We came today to tell you that we are sorry about everything."

"And what do you hope to achieve by saying you are sorry? How does that solve anything?"

"It doesn't, sir. It does not give you back the daughter you had before the pregnancy. But so much has happened since then, sir, and we would like to plead with everyone to let bygones be bygones, to forgive one another, so we can all move forward into the future without bitterness and acrimony."

As Odili considered his words Urenna peered at him, looking for any sign of softening in his attitude. There was none. The frown was firmly in place.

"You two don't have to apologise to me," he finally said. "What is done is done. It cannot be undone. You did what you had to do and I did what I had to do."

He got up, and it was clear the conversation was over.

"Before you go, sir," Chuma's voice stopped him. "We have another request to make of you."

Chuma quickly opened his bag and brought out a bottle of wine.

Odili looked at the wine in Chuma's hand and lifted a quizzical eyebrow.

"I want to marry your daughter, sir. We love each other. We have a set of twins from that pregnancy, and we would like to get married and provide a home for them. We would like your blessing on our union."

Odili sat down again and remained quiet. It was as if he didn't want to get into the conversation. "And what do you do? How am I sure you can take care of her?"

Urenna was not fooled at all into thinking he was concerned about her welfare. He was only asking because their custom required a father to ask this of any prospective son-in-law.

"I work with a private construction firm in Chicago. I own my own home and I earn enough money, sir. It will be no hardship for me to take care of Ure and our two girls, sir."

Odili scratched his rough beard and continued to look at the wall behind Chuma. Urenna thought his interest flickered when Chuma mentioned Chicago and experienced a twinge of disappointment.

"You live in Chicago, *eh kwa*? The Chicago in the United States of America or the Chicago in Lagos?"

Chuma frowned. He had never heard of a Chicago in Lagos.

"The Chicago in the US, sir. Chicago, Illinois. But my parents live in Lagos. I have two sisters, both married. One lives with her husband in the States and the other lives in Lagos."

"I see. If you live in the United States, what are you doing here?"

Chuma looked at Urenna and smiled faintly. Odili was showing some interest. "I'm on holiday, sir. I came to spend time with my parents but I had to go to Jos to oversee a house purchase for Chief Ojiefi. It was in Jos that Urenna and I met again and renewed our friendship."

"Which … emm … which Chief Ojiefi? The one who owns Ambassador Hotels and Ambassador Airlines?"

"Yes, sir."

"Mmm hmm." He nodded. He thought for a moment and suddenly cleared his throat. "Are you an Igbo man?"

"Yes, sir."

"Then you know that a man does not go by himself to inform his prospective father-in-law that he wants to marry his daughter. If you are serious, you will come back with your father, and the elders of your family. They will bring the wine, and they'll bring the kola-nut. Only then will I listen to you and give you a response."

"Yes, sir. It's just that we—"

Odili raised his hand, effectively silencing him. "You should also know that in our tradition, children born to a girl out of wedlock belong to the girl's family."

Urenna and Chuma listened.

"Those children belong to our family. They are Okolies. Even if we give you Urenna in marriage, you will be required to provide a reasonable consideration before we let you take our children away."

Urenna flew to her feet. "What are you saying, Papa?"

Odili looked at her and looked away.

"What did you say?" she repeated.

"It's not what I said, Ure. It's what our custom demands."

"*Chinekem eeeeeee!*" Urenna shrieked, her hand on her head. She felt as though she would faint. "You want to take my children from me?" Her voice was trembling with shock.

"*Chinekem eeeee!*" she cried again, louder.

Chuma got up and put a hand over her mouth. "Stop it now, okay. Stop it. Nobody is taking the children away from us. It will not happen."

Footsteps rushed into the living room, and when she looked again she saw her two uncles, Añuli, Beatrice and her son standing in the doorway.

Añuli ran to her. "What happened?" she asked. "What did he do to you?"

"Papa said ... he said." Urenna breathed in, staring at her sister with unbelieving eyes. "He said Chuma has to pay if he wants to take the twins with him when we marry. He said ... he said the twins belong to him since I had them before marriage."

After the initial shock, everyone started to talk at once—Añuli shouting insults at her father, the two uncles expressing their disgust, Chuma holding her close.

Urenna felt her body sag against him and disappointment wash over her body. How could anyone be this cruel?

"He is an evil man—didn't I tell you? This is the type of wickedness he's been showing Mama all these years. Just deliberately throwing obstacles in her way and watching her squirm and suffer. That is his specialty. Did I not warn you guys when you said you wanted to make peace with him? Thunder will strike him dead! You guys leave now and don't ever come back to this devil of a human being. He's not worth—"

For the second time in as many weeks, Añuli felt the back of her father's hand on her cheek and fell to the ground.

Pandemonium broke out. His brothers waded in and held Odili to stop him from further pounding his younger daughter. Urenna and Chuma went down to help Añuli to her feet and to keep her from fighting back. Beatrice scooped up her son and quickly exited the room. As the commotion continued, Chuma led the two girls to the car and stayed until Añuli calmed down.

"I told you so," she muttered between tears.

Urenna nodded. "Yes, you did. I didn't believe you then."

Chuma went back into the house and stood at the entrance, listening to the uncles reproaching Odili. Not having met them before now, Chuma did not know who was who. But he watched as they spoke one after the other.

"A man who goes to reap where he has not sown is a thief!" one of them shouted at Odili.

"What you have done to our family is an abomination, Odili. Papa has been told and he has sent for you. When are you going to answer him?"

"Is this how you can prove your manhood—by beating up the female members of your own family?"

"This young girl you have wronged for many years still gives you the honour of asking for your blessing on her marriage—"

"And what do you do? You want them to pay you for their own children!"

"Children you tried to kill before they were born."

"Children you have never even seen."

"What are you two talking about? It's our tradition," Odili insisted.

"Now that it suits you, you remember our tradition."

"Do you know what else is our tradition? We believe in honesty, kindness and truth. Any man who violates these must make amends or *Amadioha* will strike him dead."

"You have desecrated our family, Odili. You have violated our tradition and brought shame on us."

"And you want to compound it by asking for money from this poor girl and her suitor. What next will you ask for—a bride price? This is abomination upon abomination! Capital abomination! Do you want the gods to punish you, Odili?"

"You have no rights over that girl, none whatsoever! You have no rights over her children."

"Odili, I pity you. When the gods are finished with you, you'll not only be required to make sacrifices for cleansing, you will be required to apologise to your daughter and her children."

"An open apology."

"In front of the whole village."

"In front of all the gods."

"You know what that means, don't you?"

"*Chei! Ajo emeee*! Hmm!"

The men saw Chuma standing at the door and turned to address him.

"Our in-law, take your wife, take your children and go in peace," said one.

"Oh yes," the other agreed. "Take your wife and go. This man does not represent the Okolie family. Our father does. And we speak in his name when we give our daughter, Urenna Okolie, and her daughters to you in marriage. Take them and go in peace."

"We are an honest family," the first one stated. "We do not reap where we have not sown, else we anger the gods and their wrath will fall upon us."

"But if you want to carry wine for her," his brother agreed, "we will gladly perform the ceremonies. Just give us a date, and then come with your parents and family elders, and it shall be done."

"Yes. And consider fulfilling the traditional marriage rites in the village. The old man—our father, Ure's grandfather—will like that. He will be glad for the opportunity to apologise for the great wrong that Odili has inflicted on everybody."

"May the gods be with you! May Amadioha protect you!"

"Go in peace! *Gaa n'udo*!"

Chuma nodded his thanks and quietly shut the door.

Epilogue

Jos

Urenna woke up early on the morning of July 7, 2012, with the calm assurance that in fewer than six hours, her greatest dream would come true and her joy would be complete. This was her wedding day.

She opened her eyes and caught a glimpse of the rising sun through an opening in her window covers. The bright eastern sun seemed to be bursting with promise of rest from a decade of emotional baggage.

She stretched and looked around the room, ruminating over all that had occurred in the three months since she had agreed to become Chuma's wife. Trying to keep everything in perspective made her feel giddy. So much had happened. For one, Chuma's mother, Marion, had welcomed her into her family and into her life with wide-open arms. Marion had also become good friends with Ego, who, now fully recovered from her illness, was gradually regaining her weight and her smile.

The corners of her mouth lifted as she recalled the first meeting between her mother and Auntie Simbi. Although the women had been speaking over the phone for several months, it wasn't until last weekend, when Ego arrived in Jos for the wedding ceremony that they had met face to face. When Urenna introduced them, her mother had fallen on her knees before Auntie Simbi, thanking her over and over with words and tears, kissing her feet.

"You are an angel from God," she'd cried with tears in her eyes. "I cannot thank you enough for everything you did for my daughter. Thank you, my sister. May the Lord reward you richly. May the Lord increase you on every side. What you did wasn't only for Urenna. You did it also for me. Thank you."

Urenna got up and knelt by her bed. She opened her Bible to Hebrew 4:9–10 and read, "There remains, therefore, a Sabbath-rest for the people of God; for anyone who enters God's rest also rests from their works, just as God did from his."

There could be no better day to remember God's promises about rest, she mused. It was time she rested from her works too, time she stopped labouring alone. *What a good God you are*, she breathed with gratitude, repeating the verses until she'd memorised them.

As she knelt by her bed, the newspaper clipping on her night table caught her eyes. "Alive from the Dead" was the headline of the two-paragraph story on the third page. It was about her, of course, but it was buried among more important news stories. Her story had broken out when there was a spate of religious violence in northern Nigeria which saw the burning down of churches and mosques and resulted in the death of many. That had proved much more newsworthy than the story of a mistaken identity which occurred many years ago. The media had tried, but since they couldn't get an interview with any member of her family, they had lost interest in her story.

The only dent in her happiness was still her father's unwillingness to make peace with her. She was no longer pushing for it. The ball was now firmly in his court. If he ever decided to change, she would welcome him. For now she had no emotions to spare on begging for reconciliation.

Urenna gave thanks again for a hitch-free traditional marriage. It had been very low key. Chuma, his father and two uncles had brought the wine to Umuebere. Her grandfather had sent for Odili, but when he didn't respond, the old man had accepted the wine on behalf of the Okolie family and given Urenna's hand to Chuma in marriage.

Quiet time over, Urenna rose from her knees and went to her closet. There wasn't much left to pack—only the suitcase for the wedding gown. Everything else had been either given away or packed and sent to a transport company for final shipping to Chuma's home in Lagos.

She could hear the hotel staff setting up the big canopy in the garden. The wedding organiser had already arrived with tables and chairs and she could hear him directing his workers on how to arrange the seats. The initial plan had been to have the small, private wedding in the Recreation Centre, but the dining room was too small, even for the few guests they were expecting. Drawing on her experience as a wedding planner, Zola, Chuma's sister, who had flown in from the US two weeks before the wedding, had suggested minor rearrangements to sections of Sonshine Estate gardens and helped the gardener carve out a wide open space in the middle of the garden for the ceremony. The big canopy, complete with a floral arch at the entrance, would provide a measure of privacy for the event and a shade from the July sun for the wedding guests.

The twins had responded to the flurry of activities regarding their extended families differently. While Erinma had excitedly accepted everyone with open arms, Ojiugo was more restrained. Urenna remembered their reaction the first time they met Amaka. A happy Erinma had allowed her aunt to fold her in a tight hug. Ojiugo, on the other hand, had stared long at her before reaching for her mother's hand.

"Erinma looks like you," she had stated.

Laughing, Amaka had replied, "And who do you look like?"

"I don't know." Ojiugo had side-stepped the question before adding, "I look like my mommy."

But she had resisted for only a few minutes before joining her twin in trotting after Amaka. She was by far their favourite aunt, and the resemblance between the three was so strong that many people thought Amaka was their mother.

Urenna picked up a copy of the wedding programme and read through her vows again. The pastor had let them make changes to the traditional words and she'd already memorised her lines. Thinking of the pastor reminded her that she had promised to pray for him. Bishop Osuji had been called to his brother's hospital bedside only yesterday. Luckily, his son was in town and would step in for his father to perform the wedding. Urenna remembered the younger Osuji very well and was glad he was available for the wedding. He had served as an assistant youth pastor while in Bible school in Jos and was now the youth pastor of another church in Lagos.

She took extra time in the shower that morning. The ceremony would start at noon and last for one hour, and the lunch and reception would immediately follow. Then she and Chuma would catch the six o'clock flight to Lagos. Much as she loved her family, she couldn't wait to be alone with Chuma at the hotel suite that Chief Ojiefi had offered them for the next two weeks. A sweet shiver ran down her spine as she thought about their honeymoon. They had agreed to wait for this day before physically coming together again. It had been difficult, especially after the traditional wedding, but they'd waited for the church ceremony, determined to keep God first in everything about their marriage.

The four sisters-in-law had planned to meet in her room to dress her up for the wedding. By the time they knocked on her door, the twins in tow, she was ready.

The canopy was full, the guests seated and the soft music the pianist created as he ran his fingers over the keyboard blended with the quiet buzz of conversation as everyone waited for the ceremony to begin.

Chuma and Pastor Dozie Osuji stood near the front.

Chuma leaned toward the pastor. "Thanks again for stepping in to do this at the last moment. I really appreciate it."

The pastor looked up from the program flyer with a wide grin. "No, the pleasure is mine. I've known Urenna for a very long time and it is my pleasure to celebrate her wedding. Besides"—he winked conspiratorially—"I don't always get called to perform weddings, so I'm secretly glad my father got called away."

Chuma nodded. No wonder Urenna had only good things to say about the young man. He was friendly and easy to get along with. He was also younger than Chuma had expected.

Chuma turned his attention to the guests. Although they had planned on a small wedding, just family and close friends, he quickly surmised they would still have about 90 to 100 guests at the ceremony.

He smiled at his mother-in-law and his parents, who were sitting behind the row of chairs designated for the bridal train. Behind them were Aunty Simbi, Aunty Bukky and Zuliat. Chief Ojiefi's entourage included his wife and daughter-in-law. Amos was leaning into his camcorder, recording everything. On the other side of the podium Kenny sat with Zola, his hand flung across his wife's shoulder, holding her close. She was more than six months pregnant now, with a pronounced "baby bump" to show for it. When his eyes met hers, Zola smiled and gave him two thumbs up.

There were representatives from Gidan Mairo and staff of Sonshine Estate in the crowd. Ayesha and her mother-in-law were there. Big Jim too. Idris waved to him when their eyes met and he waved back. He nodded a greeting to Urenna's uncles who had travelled from Umuebere to witness the ceremony. There were others he had met at Jos Jubilee Church. It wasn't a huge crowd, but they were enough.

The Jubilee Church worship team was set up at the side of the stage to provide live music for the ceremony.

When Amaka came in and whispered to the pianist, he nodded to the pastor, began to play the processional hymn, and a hush fell over the small crowd.

Chuma's heart pounded with pride as his daughters stepped into the canopy. Each of them wore the floor-length white dress Zola had brought from the United States and carried a basket of confetti. They were too young to be bridesmaids and too old to be flower girls. Not that it mattered. To their father, they looked like angels. As they stepped to the rhythm of the music toward the podium their eyes shone with excitement and joy. Like the mini-celebrities they had become among their families and friends, they stopped occasionally to wave to the guests.

Chuma felt a lump in his throat as he watched them. Everything about them was beautiful. What could he have ever done to deserve this blessing from God? In fewer than six months he had gone from being alone, wondering if he would ever get married, to a father with a ready-made family. His friends and family were all aware that today's ceremony wasn't just a wedding between him and Urenna; it was also the joining together of the four of them as a family before God.

When they came up to where he stood, each of the girls stopped to hug and kiss him before heading to their designated spot at opposite ends of the podium. The guests clapped.

The lump in his throat grew, but Chuma swallowed and shifted his attention to the entrance of the canopy. He didn't want to miss a step of his bride as she walked down the aisle to him.

In no time at all, the pianist ran his fingers across the keyboard, changing to the tune of Uto Verdi's Bridal March, and the wedding guests stood to their feet. Everyone watched and took photos with cameras and smartphones as Urenna entered on the arms of Uncle Tunde.

While they all stared at her, Urenna looked only at her groom. When their eyes met, Chuma took in a deep breath and exhaled slowly, shaking his head in wonderment. He blinked to quash the dampness gathering behind his eyes and smiled at her. She was so beautiful that he felt for a moment that he was dreaming. Only God could have given him such a perfect gift. *Thank you, thank you, thank you, Lord.*

When they reached Chuma, Pastor Dozie cleared his throat, nodded to Uncle Tunde and asked, "Who gives this woman to be married?"

As the bridesmaid, Añuli's job was to take care of Urenna throughout the ceremony. She followed from a short distance as her sister and Uncle Tunde walked to the front of the crowd, watching the train of the luxurious floor-length gown to make sure it didn't get stuck anywhere along the uneven ground.

Añuli's gaze drifted around the standing congregation. Dozens of pairs of eyes locked on Urenna's face as she walked toward her groom. She had expected nothing less, because Urenna was a very beautiful bride. Her long hair was piled on her head in gleaming tendrils and coils, her wide-set eyes were shining and her satin dress shaped itself closely over her upper body, showing the rounded swell of her breasts and the tuck of her waist.

Some of the female guests sniffed into their handkerchiefs. She heard more than one fidgety male clear his throat. Añuli saw her mother wiping at her eyes and managed to hold back her own tears. It hurt a bit that they had found Urenna only to lose her again, but they were thankful for the time they'd spent with her before the wedding. The fact that she was alive was enough compensation for their loss. Besides, after more than a decade of misunderstanding, nobody could begrudge the couple their desire to get married as quickly as possible. The wonder of it all was that they had waited for up to three months to finally tie the knot, but they wanted to give the twins time to complete the school year so they too could be part of the ceremony.

When the pastor turned to Chuma and asked, "Do you have the ring?" Erinma stepped forward and presented the ring to her father. Añuli took the bouquet from her sister and stood behind her as the pastor led them through their vows.

The wedding was beautiful, Anuli thought; the ceremony was like something from a storybook. Her throat tightened as she watched Chuma make promises to her sister. This was the type of love she wanted. Explosive. Palpable. Real. She shrugged off the thought. Men like Chuma were too few. Urenna was lucky. In any case, even if she were to find someone like Chuma, he probably wouldn't want her. Her mother was worried that her attitude could chase men away from her. *You're too wound up, too angry with your father. Let it go. You need to lighten up. Open yourself to love and forgiveness so you can be loved in return.*

"Okay, Urenna, it's your turn," Anuli heard the pastor say. "Do you also have a ring for Chukwuma?"

"Yes, I do."

Urenna turned to Ojiugo, who walked confidently to her mother and presented the open ring box.

Anuli took a deep breath to clear her mind and then focused on Urenna as she publicly declared her love for Chuma.

"And so, by the power vested in me, I now pronounce you husband and wife," the pastor declared. He waited for the crowd to stop clapping before he smiled and inclined his head toward Chuma. "You may kiss the bride."

The crowd seemed to hold their collective breath, watching with smiles as Chuma stepped closer to Urenna and lifted her veil. He didn't kiss her immediately, seeming content to just gaze into her eyes. Urenna smiled tremulously, and a lone tear escaped from her eyes. Then, leaning even closer, Chuma tilted her chin with his right hand and gently kissed the tear away before kissing her on the lips. Anuli glanced at the twins and laughed out loud at the comical look of disgust that passed between them. The guests applauded loudly.

The pastor waited for the applause to quieten, then continued.

"Ladies and gentlemen, boys and girls, I present to you Mr. and Mrs. Chukwuma Zeluwa."

This time the crowd was on its feet. Añuli's eyes sought and found her mother dabbing feverishly at the tears flowing down her face. She scanned the rest of the guests. Every single person was smiling or crying or both.

On cue, the band led the crowd in singing the popular song "O Seun Jesu." Chuma was the first to start the dancing and soon everyone joined. Añuli stood behind Urenna as she swayed to the beat, making sure her gown was safe from the guests who had risen from their seats to dance with the couple.

Añuli thought she heard her name and turned but there was no one behind her. Just the podium. And the pastor. He was standing behind a table decorated in the wedding colours and was flipping through the marriage register, preparing for the signing ceremony.

As she made to look away Pastor Dozie turned his head, and his eyes connected with hers. She caught her breath, and just like that, the noise of the music faded and the crowd disappeared from view. She could not help the way her eyes fixed on the young pastor, or the way her throat seemed to clutch tight. He stood looking at her—tall, dark, handsome and somewhat intimidating in his dark suit. This was crazy. Where had she been throughout the ceremony? Had she really been sitting only a few yards from this man for the past hour and not noticed him?

"Congrats also to the beautiful bridesmaid!" The pressure of Auntie Simbi's hand on hers broke the moment, forcing her to focus once more on her duty to her sister. "You look very beautiful, my dear."

Anuli smiled her thanks and gathered the train of the wedding gown. Urenna and Chuma were moving to their designated seats, and she felt her heart skip a beat as she carefully arranged the long gown behind her sister, who now sat beside her new husband.

Chuma and Urenna were at the hotel counter checking in as husband and wife for the first time when Chuma slipped an arm around her and drew her into a sideways hug. She closed her eyes and leaned into his touch, still enthralled by the wonder of their love and the reality of their marriage.

"Today has been perfect," she breathed. "I couldn't have wished for a happier day. There were moments when I thought I was dreaming the whole ceremony, but I am wide awake and you are still here."

The attendant was typing on his computer, finalising their registration.

"It's not a dream, honey, and the day is not yet over," her husband whispered in her ear, sending shivers of anticipation racing through her veins. "We can look forward to more blessings before the end of the day."

Her cheeks felt warm but her heart and soul were at peace.

"Here you go, sir, the keys to the honeymoon suite," the attendant handed two cards to Chuma. "Congratulations, sir, madam. I wish you joy and happiness. I hope you'll enjoy your stay with us. Don't hesitate to call the front desk if you need anything."

Chuma took his wife's hand and led her toward the elevator—and into the beginning of a new life. His grip on her hand tightened as they approached their room. As soon as the door shut he framed her face with his hands and brought his lips to meet hers. Urenna settled into the security of his embrace, knowing she was right where she belonged.

THE END

Another Inspirational African Fiction by **Uzoma Uponi**

ColourBLIND
2011 – Finalist, Commonwealth Writers
Prize for First Novels (Africa)

If you would like to contact the author, either
to purchase any of her books, or to share your
thoughts and comments on her writing, please send
an email to <u>colourblindnovels@yahoo.com</u>

CPSIA information can be obtained at www.ICGtesting.com
Printed in the USA
LVOW06s0531060813

346384LV00002BD/2/P